"Thoughtful and effective."   —*Kirkus Reviews*

"Rich with alien atmospherics and seething with issues of gender and prejudice, Zahra's dark journey into revolution offers some sensitive signposts to understanding."
                                                —*Publishers Weekly*

More praise for
LOUISE MARLEY . . .

"A fine new writer. I recommend her."   —Anne McCaffrey

"Her characters are quite engaging. She obviously knows something about music and does an excellent job of showing how the musical talents of the Gifted combine with their psychic powers. Many readers, particularly those who love Pern and Darkover, will appreciate visiting Nevya."
                            —*The New York Review of Science Fiction*

"The subject . . . is full of beautiful ideas and the feeling for place is real, specific, substantial."   —Geoff Ryman

"Lively storytelling and engaging characters."   —*Locus*

"While shivering under the weight of our own wintry beast, pick up Louise Marley's books and warm yourself at the fire of Sira's extraordinary heart. You'll be glad you did."
                                                —Elizabeth M. Atwood

"Louise Marley's knowledge of music and story make for a stunning combination of talent."   —Greg Bear

Ace Books by Louise Marley

SING THE LIGHT
SING THE WARMTH
RECEIVE THE GIFT
THE TERRORISTS OF IRUSTAN
THE GLASS HARMONICA
THE MAQUISARDE
THE CHILD GODDESS

More praise for
THE MAQUISARDE

"A complex tale of one woman's struggle against a corrupt regime . . . [A] fast-paced, thought-provoking novel."
—*Library Journal*

"Marley has a way of infusing tragic characters with a sense of purpose and emergent hope, and her portrait of Ebriel is that of a woman in motion, transitioning from shock to grief, from trauma-induced rage to hatred and then beyond. Her change from a sheltered young mother to a focused antigovernment operative is handled with a delicacy that eschews the depressing one-note realism of many survivor stories. Instead, *The Maquisarde* offers a palette of emotions and reactions, including unexpected moments of brightness and splashes of romantic sensibility."
—*Locus*

"Once again, Marley deals with themes of justice and enfranchisement; once again, she does so by revealing the details of her characters' everyday lives, by rejecting unthinking, automatic violence. She insists on hope and lighting candles that burn as unevenly, as tenuously as the lives of her 'starchildren.'"
—*The Seattle Times*

"A literate, musically informed story . . . Marley's writing is lyrical and persuasive."
—*Publishers Weekly*

"Marley reinvents the World War II French resistance movement in a future world divided, haves from have-nots, by the Line of Partition, which totally blockades traffic, trade, and even medical aid . . . Marley never lets polemic overwhelm plot in this passionate story."
—*Booklist*

"Louise Marley has an uncanny ability to make the reader feel that the events in *The Maquisarde* are really unfolding . . . Readers will admire [the heroine's] grit, determination, and courage, but mostly appreciate Ms. Marley's ability to paint a picture of a world turned much colder and nastier than Dickens's worst nightmare."
—*Midwest Book Review*

"Swift, suspenseful, and visceral . . . [A] well-written romantic adventure."
—*VOYA*

continued . . .

THE
MAQUISARDE

LOUISE MARLEY

ACE BOOKS, NEW YORK

This is a work of fiction. Names, characters, places, and incidents either are the product of the author's imagination or are used fictitiously, and any resemblance to actual persons, living or dead, business establishments, events, or locales is entirely coincidental.

THE MAQUISARDE

An Ace Book / published by arrangement with the author

PRINTING HISTORY
Ace hardcover edition / December 2002
Ace mass market edition / May 2004

ISBN: 0-441-01107-1

ACE®
Ace Books are published by The Berkley Publishing Group, a division of Penguin Group (USA) Inc., 375 Hudson Street, New York, New York 10014. ACE and the "A" design are trademarks belonging to Penguin Group (USA) Inc.

PRINTED IN THE UNITED STATES OF AMERICA

10 9 8 7 6 5 4 3 2 1

For Rachael
China's gift to America

Acknowledgments

Many thanks are due to helicopter pilots Jim Lee, an expert in both rotary- and fixed-wing aircraft, and First Lieutenant Matthew Rowland of the United States Army; to Phyllis Hollenbeck, M.D., Dean Crosgrove, P.A.C., and Nancy Crosgrove, R.N., for medical advice; to John Clapp and Catherine Whitehead, for help with French; to Air Force Captain Richard M. "Jake" Marley, Ret., for information on military protocol; to the fine Seattle flutist Paul Taub, for advice on that instrument; to Zack Marley for help with science and technology issues; to June Campbell as first reader; and to my colleagues Brian Bek, Jeralee Chapman, Elisabeth De Vos, Niven Marquis, Dave Newton, Melissa Lee Shaw, and Catherine Whitehead, for their tireless criticism, advice, taste, and guidance.

The *maquis* (ma-KEE) is a thorny shrub that clings fiercely to the rocky ground of the island of Corsica. Since the twentieth century, bands of rebels have adopted its name—calling themselves the maquis—to symbolize the tenacity with which they resist domination.

The bitter cold pierced Ming Xiu's quilted coat and trousers. Jagged Himalayan peaks glittered blindingly above her head. Winter slicked the road with ice, and brown spears of frozen grass caught at her boots. She shivered as she walked through the foothills of Gansu Province with her baby, just twelve hours old, snuggled close to her chest. She had been weeping almost steadily since the birth, and her tears chilled on her cheeks as she trudged along.

Her mother- and father-in-law had taken one look at her child and turned their faces away. Her husband, his face drawn with disappointment, helped her to rise from her childbed and dress. It was he who bundled the child, his first-born, into the blanket of yak wool.

Ming Xiu had carded the wool for the blanket, and spun the yarn with her own hands. She had woven the blanket in the long winter evenings, working in the light of an oil lamp, the wool spilling over her growing belly as the birth drew near. She felt how soft it was, how warm, as her husband laid the child in her arms. He led her to the door of their little house and opened it. She did not look back as she walked away.

Ming Xiu knew her husband and his parents were right. There was not enough food, enough space, enough money for more than one child. She had survived her own infancy only because her father feared the police. The police were gone now, vanished with the government that once united the scattered provinces. The only law for Ming Xiu was that laid down by her husband's family. They wanted a son, to work in the business, to carry on their name, to care for them in their old age.

Ming Xiu's baby stirred against her bosom. Her tears fell on the child's downy head, and she wiped them away with a trembling hand.

When the odd sound reached her ears, a buzzing as of a hundred hummingbirds' wings, she glanced up into the gray sky, and behind her down the deserted road. She saw only sparse juniper trees, their branches silver-gray with ice. Perhaps some little animal had run past, she thought. Or some hardy bird had flown by. She wished she could fly away, too, but where could she go? How would she feed her child? There was little food to spare in Gansu Province.

She plodded on, feet aching with cold, body sore from her hours of labor. She was supposed to go far enough that the little body, when it was over, would not be found by one of her own village. She had begged her husband to take the baby to an orphanage, but he refused. She would have gone alone, but she didn't know where one might be. She had never been outside her village.

The sound came again, like a singing in her ears, an aberration of her confused and suffering mind. It didn't matter. She didn't even lift her head.

She came to a large flat boulder beside the road, sheltered by a little copse of dragon spruce. She cleared rime from the rock with her hand, as if to make her child more comfortable. She kissed the sleeping baby and wrapped the blanket securely around her. Soon the warm little body would be as cold as the gray stone, as her own heart. She laid her child down gently, hoping not to wake her. She kissed her one last time, and then turned back the way she had come. She heard the buzzing twice more, but in her pain she ignored it.

Ming Xiu walked for perhaps ten minutes in the direction of her home before her steps slowed and then stopped. She stood without moving for five more long minutes, the cold of *the road burning through her boots. The pain in her chest spread until she could bear it no more. With a throat-tearing cry, she whirled. On her frozen, clumsy feet she ran back toward the boulder where she had left her baby.*

She didn't care. She would beg, or she would die, she and her child together. She preferred death to living with the knowledge that she had abandoned her daughter to perish in the cold. She stumbled along the road, searching for the little stand of dragon spruce, the flat rock.

There it was! There, beyond that curve, the trees, and the gray boulder . . .

But the little bundle, the soft wool blanket with her baby inside, was gone.

She ran to put her hand on the stone. It was still slightly warm. She cast her eyes around her, frantically, but she saw nothing, and no one. The baby was gone. She was gone, and her mother had never even given her a name.

1

Ebriel Serique hurried, swabbing her flute, uncoupling its black and silver sections to fit them into the embossed leather flute case. Rehearsal had run overtime. She slid the case into her shoulder bag and dropped a handful of score discs on top. She gave her colleagues a hasty wave. *"A demain."*

They nodded to her as they put away their violins, oboes, cellos, horns. The stringmaster, flipping switches, called out, "Ebriel! Are you alone tonight? Come to dinner with me!"

She smiled, shaking her head.

He left his machine to intercept her as she sidled between the chairs. *"S'il vous plait,* Ebriel," he murmured. "Just you and me. A little wine, a summer evening . . ."

Ebriel laughed as she pushed him away with one finger. *"Zut!* I think not!"

The second flute chuckled, and she cast him a sidelong look. He shrugged. "It is the dimple!" he said. "The beautiful Ebriel—what do you expect?"

Ebriel tossed her head. "With this one? Just this!" Laughter bubbled around her as she hastened toward the door.

She was still not free. "Oh, Ebriel, wait," the director called. "I need to speak with you."

"Oui, madame." Ebriel turned back, sighing, and made her way between the standreaders to the desk where the director sat behind slumping stacks of paper and piles of disc scores. She waved a disc. "A new piece for you. Just flute and stringmaster, very exciting, very *nouveau.*"

Ebriel reached for the disc to read the legend. "Is it good?"

"Very good indeed. And there should be a lot of press. The composer asked for you especially after your Ravel, and your agent says you're available."

Ebriel handed the disc back. *"Madame,* may we discuss it tomorrow? Paul and Renée are supposed to call when they get off the train."

"Oui, oui, tomorrow," the director said. "But you are interested?"

"I think so," Ebriel said, hoisting her bag again. "If Michau says I am free. Tomorrow, then, *bien*?" She backed away. The director waved a hand, her mind already turning to something else. Ebriel hurried to the door before someone else could detain her.

In two days, the orchestra of La Villette would give their last concert of the season, and then the students and teachers and staff would be free for the summer holiday. Ebriel had taught for six hours today, and rehearsed for another two. It had been a good day, but a long one. Her *embouchure* was tired, her neck ached, and she was hungry.

Beneath the footbridge, the green water of the canal mirrored the white buildings behind her, the pastel clouds of evening, the auburn flare of her hair. The linen of her dress flowed about her legs as she hurried, the new fabric smooth against her bare legs. She never wore reworked material. She reached the dock just as the barge was ready to cast off, and flashed her wrist at the scanner. She was the last passenger. Laughing, breathless, she collapsed into a seat and dropped her brocade bag to the deck. Near the railing a man in the olive-green blouse and trousers of InCo Forces talked into his lipmike, his head on one side. His earplant glinted as he turned to give Ebriel an appreciative glance.

In the seat next to her a young mother leaned back with her eyes closed. Her child, a girl of about five, held a mini in her hand, giggling at an animated program. Ebriel felt a pang of longing for Renée that swelled into a quiver of nerves under her breastbone. She pressed her hand over it, trying to breathe away the anxious feeling. She looked away from the mother and child to the lights of Paris, a wash of white that drowned the early evening stars. Only the Fleck habitat glimmered in the sky, far to the south. Star Hotel One, relic of a weary Earth's reach for space. There were to have been six, ringing the Earth, but the other five had never been built. The consortia that planned them disintegrated after the Crash.

Ebriel disembarked on the Rue de la Grange and walked up the wide boulevard to their own Rue Georgette, one of the ancient and charming lanes that twisted away from the broader street like loose threads from a cord.

Their apartment building towered above the Rue Georgette. Skywalks connected the upper floors with similar towers around it, and the thick cylinders of Fleck fuel cells packed the roofs. Paul, a physician with the 19th arrondissement, and Ebriel, a prominent artist, were entitled to such a building. Beyond it sprawled a dingy neighborhood of cramped tenements and Social Services clinics. Ebriel averted her gaze from these, preferring the clean glass and concrete of her own home. When she turned her wrist to the panel at the entrance, the doors slid open. A doorman greeted her, and handed her the little bag of her groceries that had been delivered from the *épicier,* eggs, cheese, an expensive *pot du chocolat* in a little foil cup. The elevator carried her to the top floor, where she and Paul and their daughter, Renée, lived in six airy rooms of pastel tile and clear glass. The panel in the entryway was flashing its amber advisory light.

"Merde!" Ebriel exclaimed. She had missed their call, despite her rush. At least the network was functioning. The week before, the microsat feed had been out for ten hours.

The panel's light turned to green, a query. "Panel, kitchen," she said with a sigh. "Two minutes." She went to drop her shoulder bag beside the piano in the music room. Renée's baby face smiled and laughed from a hologlobe in a wall niche, and Ebriel blew a kiss at her daughter's image. She carried the grocery bag into the kitchen. The panel above the table flashed blue, ready, and Paul's gray eyes sparkled out at her.

"Bon soir, chérie," he said. "So sorry we missed you. I hope rehearsal went well. We couldn't wait for you to get home, because the boat has to leave at four. But we will talk to you when we arrive, all right? Here is Renée—she loved the glidetrain!"

He lifted their daughter up to his knee. Renée was six, auburn-haired, hazel-eyed, round-cheeked like Ebriel. *"Maman!"* she piped. "On the train, they have ice cream! I had strawberry!" Ebriel smiled, but the pang of anxiety trembled again in her solar plexus. Renée waved her chubby hand. *"Bon soir, maman!* We miss you!" Paul whispered in her ear, and she kissed her hand to the camera, dimpling. *"Je t'aime, maman!"*

"Moi aussi," Paul said. *"Je t'aime.* Sleep well. We will call tomorrow from the island."

Their two faces disappeared from the panel, replaced briefly by the InCo logo, the globe with the InCo polities shining silver against a field of black. The panel's light flashed green again.

"Panel, no answer," Ebriel said, but she stood for a moment staring at the empty screen, a chill settling in her abdomen, a heavy spot of cold. She shivered and tore her eyes from the blank telepanel, admonishing herself, *"Zut.* Silly."

By the time she woke, Paul and Renée would be climbing off the boat and onto the dock below Paul's parents' villa, would walk up the hot sandy path to the house. Soon, after the concert, Ebriel would be there, too, and the three of them would spend the rest of the holiday together, strolling on the beach, splashing in the warm Mediterranean waters, and she would have forgotten this feeling of foreboding.

She put a bottle of Montrachet under the vacuum screw. With a glass of wine in her hand, she wandered out to the balcony to lean against the curling iron balustrade. The filigreed tip of the old Eiffel Tower rose into the lavender sky. Below, street lamps made still rivers of yellow light. Night improved the view, shadows softening the broken paving of the side streets. Even the courtyard of St. Louis Hospital looked intact, its disintegrating walls blurred by the dusk. She sipped, letting the good wine soothe her.

The headlights of a few cell cars passed below, tiny jewels

flashing from the gathering darkness. A single rare airplane circled the city as it departed from the nearly abandoned Charles de Gaulle. She watched it fly off to the south, no doubt carrying some InCo official. She finished her wine and went inside to toss a salad and whip eggs.

She sat with her meal at the little table. "Panel, Newnet." And after a pause, dutifully, "English." Paul insisted they listen to the news in the official language of the International Cooperative Alliance. They also spoke English with Renée, every other day. Ebriel was prone to forget, causing Paul to chide her for slipping into the easier French.

"Red Omega is suspected once again of violating the Line of Partition," a Newnet reporter was saying. "The Commander General of Security Corps issued a statement from Geneva this morning, saying that InCo will prosecute any and all agencies found to be distributing illegal materials in the latent countries, and that . . ."

Ebriel listened with half an ear as she ate her omelet.

A stillphoto of a lean man with bright brown eyes replaced the reporter's face. "Ethan Fleck, founder of Fleckcell, sent his own spaceplane to repair the comm satellite that brought down the nets last week. Premier Takanagi, with the leaders of the North American and European polities, offered Dr. Fleck the thanks of all InCo citizens and invited him to attend the conference to be held next month in Todokai." No one on the planet had seen Ethan Fleck in years, though every citizen knew his name. After the Crash, his solar fuel cell had prevented disaster. The end of the oil age had made him a modern hero.

Ebriel put her dishes in the sink and set the little *pot du chocolat* on a plate. She sat down again. It was odd to be alone, no Renée to coax into drinking her milk, no casual talk with Paul about the hospital or the upcoming concert. She dipped her spoon into the foil cup with a tiny pang of guilt over the indulgence. Chocolate was hard to come by.

A news icon flashed on the panel. The quiver of unease in her abdomen clenched into a spasm. She froze, the spoon still in her mouth. A voice said, "There will be no response. Terrorism will not be tolerated. Noninterference is at the heart of InCo policy."

Commander General George Glass of Security Corps, InCo Forces' intelligence and security arm, stood beside an enormous desk decorated with the black and silver globe. Behind him, a bank of panels flashed a dozen different scenes. The camera zoomed on one, not a video, but a stillphoto of a sleek yacht with brilliant white sails and a white bird in perpetual flight across its sky-blue hull. The words *"L'Oiseau blanc"* flowed beneath the bird in Gallic script.

Ebriel knew that yacht. She had taken her wedding trip on *L'Oiseau blanc*. She sailed on her every summer to the island of Menorca, where her in-laws kept their summer home. Her family, her husband, her in-laws—and her only child—were on that boat at this moment. Slowly, she took the spoon from her mouth and set it on the table with great care, as if it might shatter. Her eyes burned from staring, unblinking, at the panel. The attention lights beside the screen began a mad flashing, blue and white and red. She didn't move. She hardly breathed.

Glass's features dissolved into those of a reporter. "Late this afternoon," the reporter said, "terrorists attacked a private yacht of InCo registry. The craft sailed from Marseilles, bound for Menorca. Video from the spybugs is being examined now, and we have unconfirmed information that the craft was intercepted south of the Line of Partition. Early reports—"

The reporter's image deliquesced midsentence. Ebriel's stomach turned as Glass's face reappeared. The general's dark hair looked oily and slick, as if it had been painted on his head. A black moustache hid his upper lip, but his lower lip and his nose were fleshy, and his eyes were small. "This is a private vessel," he said, directly into the camera. "It was taken outside Inco waters. We deplore this act of terrorism, but we neither discuss nor negotiate with noncitizens." He glanced to the side and then back at the camera. "We have the spybug video."

InCo citizens were accustomed to the odd perspective of the pictures caught by the little flying cameras deployed around the Alliance's borders. The pictures blurred and cleared, blurred and cleared, with a nauseating irregular rhythm. *L'Oiseau blanc,* rocking on twilight Mediterranean waters, looked tiny, as if seen through the wrong end of a telescope.

The video showed a swarm of men in dark clothes boarding her from a squat motorboat. The picture was too small to make out their faces, or the face of the blond man who gesticulated at them from the deck, but Ebriel recognized her father-in-law's tall figure, foreshortened by the camera.

She gripped the table with both hands. The picture swerved, blurred, and cleared to show a man brandishing his gun at her father-in-law, and Luc Serique raising one arm. The picture blanked, and when it appeared again, the spybug was on the other side of the yacht, showing the motorboat bobbing at the stern, and *L'Oiseau blanc* floating peacefully on the azure water. There was no sign of Paul, or of Renée, but Ebriel knew they were there. Somehow, all evening, she had known. She gasped for breath. The picture disappeared, replaced once again by Glass's thick features.

"This private craft crossed the Line of Partition." He pointed to a map with a familiar red line dividing the waters of the European polities from those of the African continent. "The Serique vessel was several kilometers over the Line and may have been carrying illegal medicines into the latent countries. InCo has no jurisdiction past the quarantine boundary. Security Corps will not intervene. To do so would be to negate sixteen years of progress. Premier Takanagi will issue a statement from Todokai in support of our decision."

He was lying. Ebriel knew he was lying.

He raised a hand. The scene cut to the reporter, with the spybug's video, enlarged and color-enhanced, replaying behind him. "Analysts," he was saying, "are calling this latest incident a test of policy, a challenge by the protest movement. Premier Takanagi has confirmed that . . ."

Ebriel stood up, knocking over her chair, and raced to the bathroom just in time to be thoroughly, utterly sick.

By midnight Ebriel's own face was on Newnet, a publicity shot used by La Villette, one with her hair draped artfully over one shoulder, her lips and cheeks glowing with cosmetics. Michau had given up trying to reach her through the panel and had come directly to her apartment. He held her trembling hand as she called the police, Paul's hospital, and the local InCo representative, who was not at home and had not returned her calls. She spoke several times to her father, who was duplicating her efforts from his own home. Her mother was already in a taxi, on her way to Rue Georgette.

Ebriel called every official number she could find, from the 19th arrondissement's police station to the Paris branch of InCo Forces. A police officer spoke to her, but couldn't help her. At the InCo Forces office, a recorded face smiled pleasantly and announced that all calls would be answered at the opening of the business day tomorrow. Ebriel wept, and swore, and called again and again, the office of the Paris representative to the International Cooperative Alliance, her attorney, her priest, even the offices of *La Présidente*. The answers were always the same. Nothing. Tomorrow. No one. No.

Twelve hours after the yacht was seized, Ebriel, though she threw herself tirelessly against the wall of InCo's policy, had been unable to scale the battlement of Glass's resolve. White and sick with fear, supported by her parents and her agent, she made her plea on Newnet.

"They have my daughter," she said hoarsely, in English. Stress made her accent deteriorate, the consonants nasal, the vowels pinched. "My InCo representative refuses to talk to me. Why should they take this yacht? We are civilians! My husband, a doctor . . . *ma fille*—my daughter—she is only six . . ." Her father, shaking, too, supported her with his arm. "*L'Oiseau blanc* would never have crossed the Line of Partition. Something is wrong, I know this. My father-in-law has sailed those waters all his life! They would not carry anything illegal. Please—I am begging General Glass to talk to me, to check the spybug records—anything. Anyone who can help—please!"

And then the Newnet cameras turned away, having exhausted the prurience of the situation, the pitiful frightened mother, the captured yacht, the beautiful flame-haired child. The netcasters went in search of fresh melodrama, leaving Ebriel and her parents and Michau alone.

2

InCo put Newnet under a gag order. Only the underground nets broadcast a report that ransom for *L'Oiseau blanc* was set at two million InCo dollars. Ebriel's father, a banker, called an associate in neutral Oceania and asked her to put out the word that the family would raise the money. His associate expressed sympathy and concern, but said that her bank in New Zealand could not afford to antagonize InCo.

Ebriel called musicians in every polity, searching for someone with ties to the underground. One man, a percussionist from the Netherlands, claimed to know someone who knew someone, but the links were hard to follow, and time was short. O-Net, out of New Zealand, ran a story that the terrorists had set ultimata, but no one seemed to be able to trace the source. A deadline was given in hours, but there were no instructions, and no details. Ebriel called the percussionist over and over, desperate.

General Frank Dimarco, opposition candidate for the leadership of Security Corps, spoke extensively about the failure of the embargo and the futility of the quarantine. He hinted at some sort of cover-up. After the first day, Newnet dropped his speeches. Only the underground nets and O-Net carried them.

La Villette cancelled the orchestra's performance out of sympathy with their principal flutist. The French president called Ebriel at last, but spoke to Michau. Ebriel had neither slept nor eaten in twenty-eight hours, and one of Paul's colleagues from St. Louis Hospital finally sedated her. It didn't matter. Like the Oceania bank, *Madame la Présidente* had no power to oppose General Glass.

Ebriel woke from the dreamless narcotic slumber to a nightmare of waiting.

The doctor offered her another sedative. She refused. She set Michau to trying to reach her InCo representative, and she struggled to contact the underground nets. They were not circles she was accustomed to, and every link ended in a dead end. She nagged Newnet, and on the second day they interviewed her once more, on the street outside her building. She looked into the camera and swiftly stated the hostage takers' demand, the refusal of Glass to answer her calls. The Newnet people recorded everything, but though Ebriel and her parents watched for the report, it was never broadcast.

Ebriel divided her panel, half to watch for news, half to broadcast a general message into the net. "Please, someone help me," she said, over and over, in French, then in English, then again in French. "Someone who can reach these people, who can tell them. I will do anything, we will get the money, we will—"

At some point during her plea, her net access cut off.

The panel blanked, leaving only the InCo globe and the words "Service interrupted. Please wait." Ebriel put her head on the table and wept. Her mother collapsed moments later, and Ebriel's father had to take her to the hospital. Michau stood helplessly, patting Ebriel's shoulders, struggling not to cry himself.

On the third day, Ebriel's father, haggard and unshaven, returned to the apartment. The horror of his news was written clearly in his bloodshot eyes, his trembling hands. The doctor was at his elbow, a dose of sedative already in his hand.

"Papa?" Ebriel whimpered, knowing, not wanting to know, weak with dread.

He put out his hands to her, but she pulled back.

"Papa?" she cried.

"Oh, *chérie,*" he said. "I am so sorry, my darling child. I . . . They . . ."

"Not—not both?" she wailed. "Paul? Renée? Oh, *nom de Dieu,* not all?"

Michau swore. Ebriel turned to him, but she couldn't see his face. She couldn't see anything. The floor beneath her tilted, her legs turned to water. The doctor, Paul's friend, stepped forward to catch her as she fell.

And now, at last, a Newnet camera was there, to shine its cold light on Ebriel's pale face, her disordered hair. The doctor rolled up her sleeve and pressed an ampoule against the inside of her elbow. The sedative dispersed swiftly into her bloodstream, depressing her nervous system, slowing her heartbeat, blurring the agony of her mind. She fell headlong into a merciful darkness.

Ebriel was mostly unconscious for the better part of three days. When she finally woke, refusing further medication, she opened her eyes to an alien world. The warmth and comfort and beauty of the one she had known had vanished. Her mother had suffered a minor stroke. Michau, exhausted, had gone to his own home to rest. Ebriel's father, hollow-eyed and miserable, dashed between the hospital and her apartment, growing more fatigued by the hour. The panel lights flashed constantly, but Ebriel only huddled in her music room, suffering. After those last pictures, the story disappeared from Newnet as if it had never been.

Ebriel asked her father again and again what had happened, what had been said.

He didn't know anything. No one responded to their pleas. The deadline passed without a word. The underground nets broadcast wild theories, conspiracies, hints of collusion, accusations of InCo misdeeds. All anyone knew was that, in the end, *L'Oiseau blanc* came floating back into InCo waters, stripped and dead. The bodies of the hostages lay on the deck beneath the now-filthy white sails. Claiming concerns about biochemical contamination, Security Corps burned the yacht and cremated the bodies.

One long sleepless night, Ebriel asked her father how they had done it.

"Oh, *chérie*," her father said brokenly. "It is a blessing not to know."

Commander General Glass issued a written statement to be read by Newnet announcers, saying that *L'Oiseau blanc* had been associated with Red Omega, and that responsibility for her fate rested with that organization. It was a great tragedy, of course, but it was one no InCo citizen—or enemy—should forget.

Protests arose in all the InCo polities. Demonstrators shouted and waved placards in front of Security Corps offices in Rome, Paris, Washington, and London. Churches held candlelight vigils. Student marches sprang up in the polities of France and Japan and the Koreas. In Geneva, at InCo's World Headquarters at the Palais des Nations, a small car exploded in the Rue de Paix, and a passerby lost his hand. Newnet covered none of the protests, instead claiming that Glass's approval rating had jumped eight percent. O-Net, from the neutral polities, devoted a two-hour broadcast to listing the acts of terrorism that had marred InCo's sixteen-year history. Ebriel followed all these reports, torturing herself with details and imaginings, agonizing over what Paul might have suffered, how frightened Renée must have been. The ache in her breast turned to fire whenever George Glass appeared on her panel.

She was alone on the day, a week later, that a man arrived in a government cell car to deliver the ashes of her husband and child. He came up in the elevator without warning, having been granted access to the building without her permission. In his arms he carried two gray metal containers, ovoid, featureless, sealed. They were unmarked except for the cold legend "Human Remains" engraved on their lids. He spoke a few words to Ebriel, respectful, but neutral, and set the urns on the tiled floor of her apartment.

She didn't answer him. She carried the containers into her music room and put them on the floor and then knelt beside them to stroke their cool curving surfaces. She didn't know which was which. She searched with her palms, her fingers, for any trace of the energy, the beauty, the vitality that had been Paul, had been Renée. She bowed above them, dry-eyed, for a long time.

When she straightened at last, she had said farewell to the part of her life that had been full of color and hope. She closed away that section of herself, like putting a portrait into a locked closet. She was glad. It was easier. And it left room for a hate so large her body could barely contain it. Hate energized her, gave her the strength to move.

She seized her brocade shoulder bag, pouring out the score discs, letting them scatter across the floor. She threw in a change of clothes and a small purse, without bothering to count the money in it. She rifled every drawer in the apartment for the sharpest knife she could find, testing their blades, leaving the drawers open and jumbled. She settled on a small, pointed paring knife, dropping it into the bag as she sucked away the thin line of red blood it left on her thumb. Casting about for what else to take, she picked up a flat wallet of stillphotos of Renée and Paul. She dropped that in, too. The urns she fit into a polyfiber valise.

At the door she looked back once at her home. Already it seemed empty and cold, a place for strangers. *"Au revoir,"* she murmured. *"C'est finis."*

She shouldered her bag and went out, pulling the valise behind her.

A hot and sunny July had settled over Paris. The glidetrains were full of travelers making their way to the countryside, to the airport, to the sea. At the Gare de Lyon, Ebriel passed her wrist over a scanner and touched the screen to order her passage to Geneva. She found the platform where the Grand Vitesse train waited. In its shining side, she saw a reflection, a redheaded woman that reminded her of someone. Automatically, she glanced over her shoulder to see who it was. There was no one close. She glanced back at the reflection, and with a little shock, she recognized her own pale face, her hollow eyes. The dimple was gone from her right cheek. She looked exactly as she felt.

The panel at the door gave her a seat number, halfway down the car by a window. She found it and sat down, sliding

the valise under her legs, keeping her shoulder bag in her lap.
The train filled quickly. A group of university students in caf-
tans and reworked denims or long tunics like her own poured
into the car, arguing over the seats, laughing, rising and falling
like an unruly flock of birds as they exchanged places. Their
chatter drowned the instructions from the car's panels as the
train lifted and slid out of the station. Ebriel leaned her cheek
against the cushioned headrest, gazing out at the scenery,
though in truth it flowed by so swiftly she could barely make
out details. She snugged the valise tighter beneath her knees
and closed her eyes.

Fifteen minutes outside of Paris the autoserve chimed, and
a moment later the cart rolled down the center aisle with little
cartons of tea and coffee, plates of fruit and pastry. The students delayed it, examining everything, making choices, changing their minds. When the cart stopped beside Ebriel she
gazed at it as if she had never seen one before. She couldn't
remember when she had last eaten—a little soup, perhaps,
yesterday? She wasn't hungry. The cart flashed a green query
light, and one of the students, a young man with long hair,
leaned across it. *"Madame?"* he asked Ebriel. "Did you want
something from the cart?"

Ebriel stared at the boy as if she couldn't understand his
words. He tried again in English. "Ma'am? Some tea, some
fruit?" She shook her head, unable to articulate a response in
either language. A week ago, she had been teaching students
just such as this boy, drilling them, coaxing them, bullying
them, laughing with them. But she no longer lived in the same
world with such people. Music, classes, rehearsals, concerts—
they belonged to another life, a different existence.

Ebriel turned her head to the window again, vaguely aware
that the boy had sent the autoserve on its way.

The glidetrain was swift and smooth on its magnetic track.
At the Swiss border, it stopped for five minutes for the passenger registry to be transferred. The frosted peaks of the Alps
and the Jura rose invitingly around the station, blue mountain
lakes glittering on their white flanks. The scene blurred again
as the train resumed its journey, leaping forward like a thor-
oughbred. Two and a half hours after leaving Paris, the buildings of Geneva sprang up, the old ones brown and beige and

cream, the new ones silver and white. The train slowed.

The same young man who had offered to help Ebriel with the autoserve tried to lift her valise for her. She snatched it away from him, fiercely, awkwardly. He stepped back abruptly, mumbling an apology, his downy cheeks flushing as he looked around at his companions. Briefly, she regretted embarrassing him, but he was already forgotten as she stepped down from the car. There was no room for anything in her mind but her goal. Her hate. It drove her forward when otherwise she would surely have collapsed.

She set her valise on its wheels and hurried away from the train and through the station. She flagged a pedicab on the street. As she spoke her destination, the first words she had said aloud since the day before, her voice cracked. "The Palais. *S'il vous plait.*"

The Palais des Nations in Geneva had been built to house the world's first attempt at a global union, the League of Nations. When that fell apart, the Palais became the European home of the second try, the United Nations. That, in its turn, dissolved after the Crash, when the collapse of the world stock markets and the subsequent interruption of international trade had broken the uneasy compacts between countries. Now the Palais headquartered the International Cooperative Alliance, the coalition of the American polities, the European polities, and Japan and the Koreas, called Todokai.

As a girl, on tour with her *Académie,* Ebriel had played a concert in Ariana Park, on the Avenue de la Paix. She remembered the ranks of flags on their slender standards, the gray stone of the plaza, the intricate rings of the Armillary Sphere, the white facade of the Palais. What surprised her now, as she climbed out of the pedicab, were the dozens of Security Corpsmen posted around the building. They stood, legs apart, hands crossed behind their backs, mirror-shaded eyes forward. Their olive uniforms were perfect, pant legs blousing above polished black boots, shirtfronts creased from shoulder to belt, right ears and lower lips glittering with silver. Caps and pockets bore the black and white globe of InCo. At each hip hung a little Glock 98, and blocks of caseless ammunition studded their belts.

Ebriel stood at the edge of the park, her valise in her hand, her bag pulling at her shoulder. Past the line of soldiers lay the entrance to the Palais, the immense lobby, and the office of Commander General Glass. Her enemy.

Tentatively, she stepped forward. Instantly, two of the soldiers closed ranks, hands hovering over their pistols. Ebriel took another step, and the taller one spoke.

"*Madame,* no entrance allowed today."

"*Pourquoi?*" she rasped. She stared past him, intent on her goal.

"General Glass and Premier Takanagi are meeting," the other soldier said in a lighter voice. Ebriel saw by the flat line of the throat, the slight curve of the uniform blouse, that the second soldier was a woman. Her mouth below the mirrored sunshades was thin-lipped and hard.

"*Oui,*" Ebriel said, her voice a little stronger. "I want go to InCo's offices."

The first soldier shook his head. Sunlight flashed in his glasses. "No one goes in."

Ebriel looked at the woman soldier. "Please let me pass," she breathed.

The soldier's face was impassive. "Dangerous times, *madame,*" she said flatly. "Go home. See the General on Newnet."

Ebriel lifted her wrist to show her implant. "I am a citizen," she said. "I have the right."

The woman soldier shook her head. "Go home," she said. "No one goes in today."

"Tomorrow?" Ebriel asked, looking into the mirrored sunshades. Her own face looked back, distorted by the convex surface, nose unnaturally large, auburn hair bristling.

"Come back and see," the woman said.

The other soldier spoke with a touch of gentleness. "You should call the offices, *Madame,*" he said. "Call first to ask. Don't come out here in the heat."

Ebriel's eyes flicked from left to right. She saw that it was true. No one was coming through the line of guards. The broad stone plaza, the wide steps, were empty, though the grassy park was full of people. To the side of the building, a number of cell trucks waited, also guarded. The woman soldier stepped toward Ebriel, a hand on her holstered weapon.

Ebriel stepped back slowly, reluctantly. She gave the great doors of the Palais one final, regretful glance, and then forced herself to turn. Dragging her valise, she moved away across the grass of Ariana Park. In the distance, the famous fountain caught her eye as it shot joyously into the clear air, brilliant in the sunshine.

3

Ebriel struggled along the Avenue de la Paix, shouldering her way through throngs of people. She turned down a street at random, then another. There were more cars here than in Paris, and military trucks and vans. They whizzed past, making her dizzy, forcing the pedicabs and bicycles into the gutters. Gold and scarlet rays from the setting sun shot through a cluster of silver and white towers, dazzling her.

The great hotels frightened her with their glittering lobbies and watchful guards. She dragged herself on until she found a tiny decaying hotel clinging to the back corner of a much newer property. The Auberge du Saconnex looked as stubborn and damaged as Ebriel herself. She plodded up the steps and pushed through the door into a faded foyer. A few bored-looking people lounged around a telepanel, and a single, sleepy clerk sat behind the reception desk. Even the air felt old and used. Its mustiness stung Ebriel's eyes.

She held her wrist over the scanner and let the clerk choose a room, enter the charge, hand her a card with the number on it. As she stepped back from the desk, the clerk said, "*Bienvenue,* Madame Serique."

Ebriel peered at him through a cloud of fatigue and

wordlessly snatched the room card. If the clerk noticed her odd behavior, he didn't show it. Or he didn't care.

She waited for the elevator, leaning against the wall, staring at the fake marble of the floor. Some impulse made her lift her head suddenly. She caught a glimpse of a tall figure in gray just disappearing down the nearest corridor. A ghost, she thought, and an irrational giggle rose in her throat. The elevator's doors hissed open, and two people stepped out. Ebríel bit her lip, stifling the laugh. They would think her insane. She dragged her valise into the elevator and spoke the number of her room. The elevator carried her up to her floor.

The room was small and dark, with crumbling hangings disguising its windowless walls. A handful of dusty artificial flowers drooped from a cracked vase. A telepanel was parked on a peeling laminate bureau opposite the narrow bed.

Ebriel lay down, but when she put her head back on the thin pillow, the room spun. Groggily, she assessed her need for food. She slid to the floor and sat bracing her back against the bed to speak to the panel. Nothing happened. She spoke again, trying different combinations of words, but it didn't respond. Finally she got to her knees and touched the screen. A menu appeared, and she ordered a sandwich and a pot of tea. She tried other parts of the panel, searching for one of the underground nets, but only Newnet came up.

Afraid she would fall asleep before the food arrived, she tried to focus on the news. An animated voice spoke in English about the increased standard of living in Todokai. Pictures of gleaming new high-rise apartments on the shores of Haeju-man Bay and Kobe flashed on the panel, alternating with bright-looking children in orderly classrooms. Room service arrived just as the report ended and a new one began. General Glass and Premier Takanagi were shaking hands in Glass's office. Ebriel recognized the banks of screens, the InCo flag on its standard beside the ebony desk. She watched over her shoulder as she went to open the door.

She ate without tasting, watching the video scan the crowded assembly hall, the high observation bays where uniformed or dark-suited people looked out over the marble lobby. The exterior shots were all stills, Ariana Park empty, the plaza deserted. There was no mention of heightened security, no shots of the lines of Security Corpsmen ringing the building.

Ebriel drank the tea, then stripped off her tunic and sandals and fell into the indifferent bed with an exhaustion that was entirely physical. The reworked sheets were rough against her naked body, but she was asleep before they could bother her.

The next morning, she returned to Ariana Park, carrying her shoulder bag and pulling her valise behind her. Nothing had changed from the day before. No one was being allowed in. Every side of the sprawling complex was guarded.

Ebriel sat on the grass near the old Armillary Sphere, her valise beside her, her shoulder bag in her lap. She tried to think, to revise her plan, but her mind felt sluggish and dim. An idea would form, begin to take shape, then flit away before she could grasp it. It was like trying to catch butterflies with her hands.

Languages swirled around her, French and English, Italian and German and Japanese and Dutch. Sometime in the mid-afternoon a French couple came to examine the sphere and then sit crosslegged nearby. They spread a cloth on the short grass and laid out a picnic. Their Parisian accents were soothingly familiar. Too familiar. Ebriel prepared to rise, to get away from them.

As she got to her knees, she heard the woman say, "There is nothing going on! Why will they not let us in?"

And the man answered, "Because of the protests, *chérie*. The bomb was just over there, by the museum entrance."

"But how long are they going to keep everyone out? And why is such information not on Newnet?" The woman's voice was plaintive. Ebriel pushed her hair back to look at her. She was dark and petite, the man with her smiling as he shrugged and spread his hands.

"Newnet reports what InCo lets them report. Never mind, *chérie*. There are plenty of things to see in Geneva. We will have our picnic and then go down to the lake, see the fountain."

Ebriel stood, gathered her things, and moved away to stand near the periphery of the plaza, staring past the long circle of soldiers. The object of her journey hid behind layers of security. He could easily outlast her. How long could she stay at the Auberge du Saconnex? Her credit could run out before the security around the Palais was relaxed. By then, who would remember that a beautiful little Parisian girl was dead? And understand who was to blame?

To her left, the sphere's brass ribs glittered in the sun. To her right, a half-dozen military trucks waited in a long line. Behind them, almost in the Rue de la Paix, a boxy white van was parked. It had a transmission array on its roof, and the radiating star symbol of Newnet painted on its side. Ebriel squinted through the sunshine to see the camera crew, two men and a woman, leaning against the shaded side of their van.

She picked up her bags and moved in their direction. The sunshades of the nearest guards flashed as they caught her approach.

She assessed the soldiers' positions, measuring the width of the cobblestone surface on which they stood, the distance from the grassy berm where she now hesitated. She eyed the Newnet crew and moved slightly to the right to be certain she was in their line of sight. She stepped as far forward as she dared without provoking a reaction from the soldiers, and then she knelt to open the polyfiber valise. She took out the two gray urns, the relics of her life, and set them before her on the altar of grass. She broke the hermetic seals, loosened and removed the lids. Then she dug in her bag for the paring knife.

The little blade shone silver in the sun, glinting in her hand. She held it out before her and turned her face to the Newnet crew, waiting for their attention.

This moment was familiar to Ebriel Serique. It was just like waiting for a conductor to lift his baton, or for the stage curtain to rise. She was poised, instrument in place, concentration absolute. She stared at the Newnet people, her audience, and willed them to notice her.

One of the soldiers saw the knife first. She heard his exclamation. His left arm came up, pointing, as his right hand freed his little Glock from its holster. His lips moved as he spoke into his lipmike, his head tilted as he received orders through his earplant. Behind Ebriel, several tourists cried out and took hasty awkward steps away from the threat of the Corpsman's gun.

The little commotion caught the attention of the Newnet crew. All three straightened and stepped out of the shade. Their long camera boom bent toward Ebriel, and then toward the soldier, even as the cameraman hastened across the grass to a better vantage point.

Ebriel knew she had to hurry if she was to accomplish both parts of her performance. Security Corps could bring down the curtain at any moment. She reversed the knife, holding it over her left wrist, making it clear she threatened no one but herself. Then, hard and fast, she sliced her skin where the memory rod, her badge of citizenship, was buried.

She had been seventeen, fully grown, when the identification devices had been issued, when all those fortunate enough to be born on the right side of the Line of Partition lined up at public clinics or made appointments at private ones to be permanently registered. Renée had received hers at birth, and already, at six, the tiny cylinder had disappeared into her tender flesh. Ebriel, fully grown when her rod was implanted, could still see the scar where it had been inserted beneath her skin. She dug at it now with the point of the knife.

Blood spurted, spattering her tunic. She made a vicious small circle with the point of the paring knife, and the memory rod, with the surrounding tissue, flew out into the grass and was lost among the green spears. It took no more than three seconds.

The first Security Corpsman had received an order and was striding off the plaza and across to her berm. The Newnet camera was already there. Another camera was there, too, a smaller one with no designation, braced on the shoulder of a man in a black caftan. She had no idea who he might be, but she turned her face so both cameras could see her, throwing her hair back over her shoulder to make certain they had a clear shot, that anyone who saw would know who she was. Then she took the first urn in her hands and stood up in one quick motion. She saw herself, with her performer's instinct. She knew she made a theatrical figure, her red hair long and wild, her cream-colored tunic splattered now with her own blood.

She cried, in English, "Tell General Glass!" and she turned the first urn over.

Gray and white ashes spilled onto the grass of Ariana Park. Little clouds of them drifted up to catch on her tunic, to fall over her hands. Swiftly, she reached for the second urn.

The soldier had reached her now, and he grasped her arm. She shouted, hoarsely, *"Non!"* and jerked away. The urn, cold and slick between her hands, flew into the air, turning, catching the light as it revolved, spilling its contents.

A corona of ash enveloped Ebriel. The soldier swore and jumped back from the cloud of it, but Ebriel opened her arms, glad of the ashes that fell on her face, caught on her eyelashes, drifted over her hair. A thick flake fell on her lips and she opened them, taking it into her mouth as she would a communion wafer. When she bent to pick up the fallen urn, she saw fragments of silver-white bone scattered on the grass around her feet.

She straightened again, the urn in her hands. She held it high above her head and screamed at the two cameras. "This is what came back to me!" she cried. "This is all General Glass has left me of my family! Do you see? Do you not see?"

Around her Corpsmen stood talking furiously into their lip-mikes, cupping their ears as they listened to their orders. None of them came close to her. Not one would step on the ashes.

Ebriel's arms began to tremble, and she lowered the urn. The tide of adrenaline receded, leaving her weak. Tiny dark dervishes whirled before her eyes.

She sank again to her knees, placing the empty urn gently on the grass. Her hair fell before her face, and she put her hands to it, setting fresh drifts of fine ash floating in the sunshine. She became aware of voices, murmuring as if at a funeral. The little crowd, tourists, Corpsmen, the Newnet crew, the cameraman in the black caftan, left a perfect empty circle around her.

Exhausted now, spent, she simply stared at her open hands. The camera boom swung, catching the whole scene. The smaller camera, held by the man in the caftan, was fixed on her, waiting. But she had nothing more for them. The show was over.

Hard hands under Ebriel's arms dragged her to her feet. She saw the uniform, the captain's bars, and next to him a woman, also an officer. They wore rubber gloves. They lifted her between them and hustled her down the berm and up onto the plaza. Their fingers pinched her skin, and her feet barely touched the ground. Her hair caught on someone's sleeve, and pulled. She saw her blood dripping on the trouser leg of the soldier on her left, and she felt a foolish urge to apologize, then to laugh. They lifted her, hauled her away as if she were a drunk, a vagrant, or worse, a noncitizen. And so she was. Her implant was gone, and with it, her identity.

For a moment she thought she saw, half-hidden by the sphere, the same tall figure in gray that she had seen in the hotel the night before, but the figure vanished behind the trunk of an oak tree. She tried to twist her head, to follow it, but the officers were dragging her up onto the plaza. The great doors loomed before her. The hot sunlight gave way to the chill of air conditioning as they moved indoors.

People swarmed around her, barking orders, calling queries, their voices jumbling and echoing in the high-ceilinged lobby. Ebriel's two escorts never loosened their hold on her arms. Other cold-eyed officers joined them in their swift progress. As a group, like a school of predatory fish, they moved down a broad hall and into the enormous office where the InCo flag hung beside the black desk, and the flickering panels filled the wall.

And Ebriel came face-to-face with Commander General George Glass.

She felt for a moment that she could not breathe for hating him. He was deep-chested and strong-looking on Newnet, but she saw now that he was a short man. His hands, his fingers, his ears and nose, were coarse. She thought she detected an odor about him, something dank, like cold, wet metal. She took a ragged breath, and the tainted air filled her lungs. Her fingers curled, longing for the knife she had left in the grass of Ariana Park.

Glass lifted an eyebrow at Ebriel as if she were no more than a nuisance. "Did you get some grunts out there to clean up her mess?" he growled to the adjutant at his elbow. His lip-mike was almost invisible in the thick flesh of his lower lip.

"Yes, sir," the soldier answered briskly. "And the medic's on his way up from the clinic."

"What about Newnet?" Glass snapped.

"Got the memory stick out of their camera, sir," said one

of Ebriel's escorts. He held it out between his fingers.

The flat bit of gray plastic held all her efforts. Glass took it in his hand and bent it between his thick fingers, over and over, until it broke in two pieces. He dropped the fragments to the marble floor.

Ebriel's heart lurched. There would be no report on Newnet, no video of a colorful martyr to enrage people, to remind them. It had all been in vain. She had failed.

"*Assassin,*" she hissed. "The deaths of my family are on your head! I know this!"

He shrugged. "It's a tragedy, ma'am, that's for sure," he said. His voice was too high for his heavy body. She had never noticed that on Newnet. It weakened him somehow. "Security Corps is sorry about your loss," he went on. "But there are greater issues here than you could ever comprehend."

An officer said in a low tone, "There was an underground camera out there, sir."

Glass flashed a look at his adjutant. "Did they get that one?"

The adjutant shook his head.

"Underground?" Ebriel breathed. There was a chance, then, still a chance. She tried to pull away, and the two Corps-men yanked her back.

Someone said nervously, "We'll issue a statement."

Glass nodded. "We can blame this on the muds, right?"

"Of course, General. Terrorists. And the poor woman has evidently gone out of her mind with grief, that sort of thing. She'll receive the best of care in a private sanitarium, InCo expense, her family will be kept informed, and so forth. All right?"

"I will destroy you," Ebriel whispered. "I swear on the lives of my husband and my daughter. I will destroy you."

"Yeah, well, good luck with that, lady." Glass made a gesture with his head. "Get her out of here," he said to the officers holding her. "I don't need this." He pointed his forefinger at one of the other officers. "And I want to know how she got this far without being stopped."

"What about the medic?" the woman on Ebriel's right asked. "She's bleeding, sir."

Glass turned to the officer. "Use your judgment, Lieutenant," he said softly. His eyes were a flat black, the lids dropping ominously, and Ebriel felt the woman's hand tremble. "Patch her here, or patch her at the nuthouse, I don't give a damn. Let's do it, people."

The two officers pulled Ebriel out of the office and back down the long corridor, past the majestic lobby, and out through a small door at the angle of the expansion wing. A medic joined them, trotting to catch up. The officers thrust Ebriel into the backseat of a van, and the medic climbed up beside her. She glanced out over the plaza toward Ariana Park. The Security Corps guards still ringed the Palais, and the people strolled over the grassy park. They were all too far away to see one bloodied Frenchwoman being hustled away.

The driver backed and turned the truck and headed down the Rue de la Paix, moving north and west, out of the city.

The medic bent over Ebriel's wrist, pressing the torn edges of her skin together, applying a bandage. He held an ampoule under her nose for her to sniff.

She jerked away. "What is this?"

"Antibiotic, antiviral," he said. "Take it, ma'am, please. The—the ashes—"

Ebriel laughed in his face. "*Cretin!* What virus could survive the crematorium?"

He paled, and whispered, "You're right, ma'am, I know that. But my orders—please, ma'am. I'm supposed to give it to you."

He was hardly more than a boy, his cheeks smooth, his chin beardless. He couldn't be more than twenty, she thought. She heard the insistent chatter of orders from his earplant, and his eyes flicked from her to the officers, and back to her, pleading. For the sake of his youth, she sniffed the ampoule. He gave her a rueful smile of thanks. She shrugged, and looked away.

They rattled along the streets of Geneva and out of the city. Beyond the windows, the cityscape melted into grassy fields of flowers, but Ebriel hardly noticed. She nursed her hatred, and prayed the underground nets would broadcast their video.

Captain James Bull, Security Corps, signed out a truck from the Malmstrom Storage Depot, where he was on temporary duty from Colorado Springs, and drove north from the windswept city of Great Falls.

Shreds of winter snow lay in the hollows of stubbled wheat fields, but the air sparkled with the brief magic of a Montana spring, just as James remembered it. On the eastern slopes of the Rocky Mountains the new green of tamarac blended with the deeper evergreen of pine and fir. The Two Medicine River, swift and cold, carried glacial runoff and snowmelt down to the plains. James encountered no other traffic as he drove. The InCo-maintained road was a smooth river of concrete, a model of government efficiency, but the surface roads, dirt and gravel and decades-old pavement flanking the highway, were cracked and rutted. And cell vehicles cost money, though the energy to run them was virtually free. InCo dollars were scarce here.

Just a few miles outside Browning, James overtook a wagon pulled by two Clydesdales, still rough-coated from the winter. The wagon was loaded with round bales of hand-tied yellow hay. The dark-skinned, black-haired man at the reins could have been James's brother, the same high cheekbones, long

*narrow eyes, arching nose. A youth sat next to him and stared
with hungry eyes at the truck as James pulled out to pass.*

A glimmer of reflected sunlight flashed from one of the
dozens of ice fields that nestled between the jagged peaks.
There had been a great park there, overlooking the old home
of the Blackfoot Nation. Strip and surface mining had gouged
the last deposits of oil shale out of Glacier Park. The gashes
in the mountainsides had filled now with green, but the glacial
arêtes would never recover their old grace.

At noon, James topped the last rise. He stopped and stood
beside the truck to gaze down at the town he had left in a fury
eighteen years before.

It looked smaller than ever to the grown-up James Bull, the
buildings flatter, more dilapidated. Several had collapsed,
roofs falling in, windows buckling, abandoned chimneys standing like dismal sentinels in the spring sun. The neat pavement
of the road made the remnants of the town look even worse by
comparison. When Browning was the center of the Blackfoot
Nation, tourism and hunting and cultural preservation had
energized it, but its day had passed. Indian tribal reservations
and privileges had vanished along with states' rights. James's
father blamed InCo for the loss of his cultural heritage and had
provided his son with the perfect expression of his rebellion.

James climbed back into the truck and drove slowly down
the gentle grade. He passed a bar, where two men sat on the
slanting porch, booted feet propped on a weatherworn rail. A
grocery store fronted a huge parking lot with only two vehicles parked in it. The only new-looking building was a prefab.
A van in front bore the silver and black globe on its door, beneath the title Social Services. James drove on, out into the
fields dotted with ranch houses and barns.

The last time he had traveled this road he had been on
horseback, fleeing his home as soon as his father passed out.
With bruises discoloring his cheek and his arm aching from a
cracked bone, received in a collision with their old Kenmore
fridge, he had stolen his father's gray gelding and tooled
leather saddle, both remnants of better days. He had rolled a
shirt, a sliver of soap, and a toothbrush into a blanket and tied
it behind the cantle. He had ridden away in the small hours, a
light snowfall powdering his thin shoulders.

Now, eighteen years later, he drove a shining, modern vehicle over land his family had inhabited for a century. He pulled it up in front of the ranch house and turned off the motor.

It had never been much of a house, and it hadn't improved. A wheelless pickup truck, useless since the last of the gasoline had disappeared, was gradually collapsing into the grassless front yard, blackberry vines growing through its windshield. Gray tape sealed a huge crack running across the front window. A domestic fuel cell, provided no doubt by Social Services, lay unused on the porch. James took all of this in, standing in the yard, listening for sounds of occupation.

He circled the house. In back he found a depleted woodpile. A dented stove, half a bicycle, and a punctured water heater littered the yard. The only thing in good repair was a telepanel receptor neatly screwed to a side wall, its internal power indicator glowing. The room that had been his boyhood bedroom faced the fields. His mother, before she died, had sewn curtains for its window, but they were long gone. Thick grime layered the glass to the sill.

James completed his tour, took a deep breath, and stepped up on the porch. Now he could hear a patter of dialogue, the practiced laughter of a commercial production. A panel was on inside the house. James lifted his hand and knocked on the bare wood of the door.

A stranger's face appeared in the doorway, dark, heavily wrinkled, long gray hair, eyes blurry with cataracts. James's heart leaped into his mouth. His lips parted, but he couldn't think of a thing to say.

"Whattaya want?" the old man rasped. When James didn't answer, his voice rose. "Whattaya want? You from Social Services again?"

"Uh, no," James stammered.

There was no doubt. The stranger was his father.

"No. It's . . . I. Me. It's me, James." He was taller than his father now by at least four inches. It was strange, looking down on him.

The old man peered at him through the screen. "Jimmy?" he quavered.

"Yes, Dad." He wriggled a little in his InCo uniform, self-conscious in a way he hadn't been in a decade. He hadn't needed to wear the uniform. He had done it deliberately. His earplant and lipmike felt enormous, signposts on his body.

His father still hadn't opened the screen. He glared, his chin up. His head trembled on his neck, and his hand on the frame of the screen door was thickly veined. "Jimmy," he repeated.

"Yes," James said again. "Can I come in, Dad?"

The screen door suddenly swung wide, banging against the side wall. The yeasty sour smell of old beer swept out into the fresh morning. "Jimmy!" the old man rasped. "You little bastard! Ya bring back my fuckin' horse?"

4

When the medic finished with Ebriel, he and everyone else in the truck subsided into silence. No one spoke until they reached the outskirts of the town of Leysin, and the woman officer began giving orders, directing the driver through Leysin and up a twisting mountain road. Twenty minutes later they pulled up in front of a rambling building with steep roofs, nestled among tall evergreens and surrounded by a waist-high wall of old stone. A mountain ash spread its wide branches over a wrought-iron gate, and over a windowed kiosk with a guard in InCo greens. He came out at their approach, speaking into his lipmike as he walked. The officers conferred with him and then turned to bring out their passenger.

Ebriel's legs shook. The young medic jumped out beside her, poised to catch her if she fell. A white-jacketed attendant came through the gate to take her arm, and the medic watched with a woeful expression. He even lifted his hand as the attendant led her away, but then he glanced uneasily at the officers around him and lowered it again. Ebriel tried to smile at him, but her lips trembled. She pressed her free hand to her mouth.

"This way, madame." The attendant put his arm behind Ebriel's back, not pushing, but making it clear he meant her to

obey. They went through the iron gate and up a brick path that
cut through a manicured lawn. Alpine peaks glimmered pink
and gold in the sunset as Ebriel and the attendant passed
through the double doors and into a graceful foyer with tiled
floors and a curving staircase.

They walked beneath the staircase and down a narrow hallway to a small room with shining steel and porcelain fixtures
and a high, paper-sheeted bed.

The attendant helped Ebriel onto the bed and clamped restraints on her arms and her ankles. Weakly, she pulled against
them.

The attendant shook his head. "Never mind, madame," he
said. "It won't be for long. We're not going to hurt you."

Ebriel was shaking all over, abreaction from the long,
strange day, from her injury, from her hatred. She let the
padded headrest catch her as she leaned back.

The attendant opened a locked drawer and took out a
transparent sleeve with a new memory rod. He slipped it into
a programming module before he turned to Ebriel to unwrap
the young medic's hasty bandage. As he worked he said,
"You'll be fine, madame. Perfectly comfortable. The Clinique used to be a boarding school. You'll sleep well." He
gave her a mirthless smile. "Mountain air." She felt like a
mouse facing a fox. She turned her face away as he began
working on her wounded arm. When he put his hands on her
left ankle, she wanted to kick him, but the restraints immobi-
lized her.

Half an hour later, she found herself in a tiny apartment,
with a loft bedroom and a balcony overlooking the mountains. A metal bracelet on her right wrist held her new memory rod. Her left wrist was neatly rebandaged. She wore a
slender anklet with a tiny receiver pressed against her skin. A
powerful sedative coursed through her bloodstream, making
her eyelids heavy, slowing her thoughts, dragging at her
limbs.

She had heard the lock snick shut on the outer door. The
balcony door, when she tried it, would not open. She was secured. The flame of resistance flickered dimly in the fog of the
drug. Glass had won.

* * *

James Bull transferred most of his savings to his father's account. In the afternoon he installed the fuel cell on the slanting roof of the ranch house, connecting it to the lights, modifying the old furnace to use the power. When that was done, he drove back into Browning for groceries.

The grocery clerk didn't recognize James at first, but as he counted out money, she glanced up at him once, and then again as she caught sight of the tattoo on his left cheekbone. She put a hand to her own face. The same tiny claw had been inked into her skin. Her eyes widened as she spotted his name badge.

"Bull?" she ventured. "That your name? But aren't you Jimmy Walking Bull?"

His neck warmed. He hardly recognized her weather-worn face, and he couldn't think of her name. Her black hair was short, falling just below her chin. In school they had all worn their hair in long braids, affecting beads and bits of feathers woven into them. And the whole class, all nine of them, had tattooed each other at the end of middle school, a sort of tribal unity gesture that had been as short-lived as it was futile.

"I'm sorry," James said. "I can't remember . . ."

"Omigod," the woman breathed. "We thought you were dead! Jimmy! It's me, Linda Joseph. Omigod!"

"Hi, Linda," James said stiffly. "Good to see you again." He just stopped himself from saying, "ma'am." He reached for his groceries.

"Jimmy," she cried. "How long are you here? Are you staying at your folks' place?"

"Just a day visit," he said. "My dad. My mom's . . ."

"Oh, right, I remember. God, how long has it been?"

He stood awkwardly, the bag on his hip. "It's been eighteen years," he said.

"Eighteen—it can't be." She shook her head wonderingly. "Jimmy, you're—well, I wouldn't have known you. Except for the—" she pointed at her own cheekbone, the little ragged handpricked claw beginning to sag slightly as her skin aged. She gave a breath of a laugh. "Weren't we stupid?"

"Kids," he said lamely. He took a step back.

"Yeah, I guess. You're in the service, then," she said.

"Yes." He hesitated, feeling as if he were being rude, but he couldn't think of anything to say. He took another step. "Uh, see you, Linda."

"Yeah, sure. Jimmy, Jimmy Walking Bull," she repeated. She shook her head as he moved away. "We all thought you were dead."

When the moon rose over the plains to the east, James stood in the doorway to the living room of the ranch house. The old man was watching a Newnet broadcast. "I have to get back, Dad," James said. He shrugged into his uniform jacket and canted his flight cap on his head. His father hardly seemed to notice that the lights were bright around him, that the old refrigerator hummed from the kitchen, or that James had cleared away the newspapers and dropped beer bottles, cleaned the woodstove, and swept up the shavings and chips that littered the floor. "You have power now, Dad," James repeated.

The old man squinted up at him. "How come your badge says 'Bull'?" he demanded. "You ashamed of your name?"

James touched the badge with his fingers. "I was just a kid when I went in," he said. "I wanted to be someone else." He hadn't wanted to be Jimmy Walking Bull, runaway. He hadn't wanted the Corps to know he was too young to enlist. And he hadn't wanted Social Services looking for him.

"You're still a Blackfoot," his father said.

"Yes, Dad," James said. "I'm still a Blackfoot. I'm not ashamed."

When he had turned up at the InCo base at Malmstrom, scrawny, hungry, and none too clean, he had lied about his age and signed on as a recruit. On the entrance form, he marked the box that said "Amerind," and no one asked him any further questions. How could he explain to his father that it had been a great relief to know what was going to happen every day, to eat regular meals, wear good boots, let others make the hard decisions? He was sixteen. By the time he got into the officers' training program, he was James Bull, of the North American polities. Browning, the Blackfoot Nation, these names were not linked with James Bull. But he had kept the claw on his cheek to remind himself that a moment of foolishness could mark a man forever.

The old man snorted, and turned his gaze back to the panel. The image on the screen caught James's attention. It was the picture of a woman, a lovely woman, with long auburn hair spilling over one shoulder. Her dimpled cheek and full, shining lips were not those of a fashion model, but those of an artist. James took a step closer to hear the voice-over.

". . . the famed flutist Ebriel Serique. She is in seclusion at the Clinique de Leysin, in shock over the loss of her husband and daughter. A spokesman for Commander General George Glass has issued a statement from Geneva expressing InCo's sorrow over this tragedy . . ."

The old man swore. "Oh, sorrow, is it?" He looked up and saw James watching the broadcast. "You wanta see what your precious InCo is hiding? Take a look at this!" He hit the remote, and one of the underground net broadcasts sprang up on the screen.

James said, "Dad, you really shouldn't watch those. They're not authorized, and you can't believe anything they—" He broke off, staring at the video.

"Look at that!" his father cackled. "You think you'd ever see that on Newnet?"

It was the same woman, her hair wild and her eyes haggard. She dug at her wrist with a knife, and blood flowed over her arm. There was a gap in the video, and then, in slow motion, she turned a gray container over, spilling its contents into the air, across the grass, the cloud of it enveloping her before two InCo soldiers—Security Corpsmen—stepped forward and blocked the view of the camera.

The old man struggled out of his chair and turned to James. "Now what do you think of fuckin' InCo? See that?" He pointed back to the screen. Small sandaled feet showed between the two guards as the woman, the flutist, was hauled away.

The next shot was of Frank Dimarco, the opposition leader, a thin, tall man. He had a habit of leaning toward the camera, distorting his features. "This is an outrage," he intoned. "Not only against the bereaved mother, but against the people of the French polity, and InCo citizens in general. If we allow the present leadership to . . ."

"I—she shouldn't have—" James struggled to find words. It was a shocking scene, a disturbing scene. He knew the story, of course, had heard it last night at mess, but to see the poor woman this way . . . "Dammit, Dad, that's exactly why the underground nets shouldn't be permitted to broadcast. They take things like this and blow them up, twist them, exploit people's suffering. And you shouldn't let that feed into your panel."

The old man snorted and gave a dismissive wave of his trembling hand. "Shit. Permitted! Fuckin' InCo, same old, same old, tell you what to do, how to live, keep quiet and we'll take care of you, bunch o' fuckin' bullshit, always the same . . ." He fell into his chair, and punched the remote again. "I tell you, Jimmy, InCo ruined this country, ruined the Nation— looks to me like they ruined you!"

James gritted his teeth. It was an old, old argument. His earplant had already reminded him of his upcoming duty shift, and it was past time he needed to be on the road. "Listen, Dad," he said. "I'm reassigned to Honolulu the end of this week. My tour at Hickam is three months. But I'll come back next time I'm at Malmstrom. Give you a hand around the place."

"Sure," the old man said. "You do that. But forget the uniform."

James stared at his father's grizzled head for a long moment before he turned and strode out of the ranch house without saying good-bye. Same old, same old. Nothing had changed.

By the time twenty-four hours had passed, Ebriel knew the routine at Leysin. It was not, of course, a clinic. It was a prison.

Every inmate received the same treatment, drugs, clean beds, meals, supervised baths. There were about thirty of them, torpid men, a few women, in loose shirts and trousers of blue reworked rayon. The fabric chafed Ebriel's skin, but she hardly noticed. She had to wear the same rubber sandals as the others, their feet silent in their dazed rambling over the tiled floors and scattered stepping stones of the garden. The illusion of freedom was marred only by the flicker of a power grid just beyond the low stone wall, the locked doors at night, the sealed balcony doors. The sedative was served with breakfast and dinner.

In the lounge, a wide space with aged pine panelling, a large panel was on from early in the morning until lights-out in the evening. On her first afternoon at Leysin Ebriel saw her own face on the panel, the Villette publicity shot. The reporter informed the Newnet audience in sympathetic tones that Ebriel Serique, prominent flutist, had suffered a nervous breakdown and was hospitalized. He didn't say where. He didn't mention *L'Oiseau blanc*. The other inmates stared at the screen, not reacting to Ebriel's image looking out at them.

Ebriel's pain pierced the cloud of sedative. She stood and left the lounge, staggering slightly, her coordination destroyed by the drug. She walked with uncertain steps into the garden, wandering to the stone wall, leaning with both hands on the cool old stone. She breathed shallowly, tasting the pitchy scent of the old trees around her. A meter beyond the wall the power grid shimmered its warning.

She turned to her right, to walk along the wall. Her feet were clumsy in the thick sandals, and she stumbled, startling a bird that was feeding on the lawn, something small, a sparrow, or a starling. It sailed into the air to make its escape into the woods, but it didn't fly high enough.

The little creature struck the power field with a sharp sizzle like bacon frying. It fell to the grass between the wall and the power grid with an almost inaudible thud. Ebriel stared in horror. "Oh! Oh! *Pardon, ma petite!*" Weak tears stung her eyes. With a wavering hand, she reached over the wall to retrieve the tiny blackened body.

In a heartbeat, an attendant was at her side, a little flat shovel in his hand. He scooped up the dead bird and flung it effortlessly over the power grid and into the wood beyond. "Cursed birds," he said crossly. "Please, madame, go inside. It's almost time for dinner."

Ebriel shuffled back into the foyer, walked past the dead

faces of the others in the lounge. She sat at dinner, but she couldn't eat. Her mind whirled with images, her own face on Newnet, the charred feathers of a little bird on the grass—a row of bodies on the deck of a white yacht. She felt as lifeless as the dead bird, oppressed as much by her powerlessness as by the drug.

The director of the Clinique was a thin dry woman with a string of initials after her name. She made daily rounds through the lounge and the garden, giving impersonal greetings to the inmates. On the second day of Ebriel's sojourn in Leysin, she called Ebriel into her office. "Madame Serique," she said. "You have messages from Paris. Sit down. I'll read them to you."

"I wish to see them myself," Ebriel managed to say. Her lips and tongue felt clumsy and thick. She had to struggle to sit upright, to lift her eyelids.

The director gave her a cool smile. "Your messages have been routed through my private screen. They are text only. Please, allow me to read them to you."

Ebriel's mind churned through the explanation with maddening slowness. The director raised one eyebrow. "Shall I begin? Your father writes that your mother is better and has left the hospital. They send their love. Your orchestra wants you to know they will hold your position. All of them send their best wishes for your early recovery. And your InCo representative in the 19th arrondissement has arranged a new apartment for you, when you are ready to return to Paris."

Ebriel swayed in her chair. In her mind she leaned across the desk, pressed her fingers into the supercilious throat of the director. In actuality, she could barely move. She dug her nails into her palms, trying to rouse herself.

The director said, "Would you like to answer your messages?"

"*Non,*" Ebriel croaked.

"But, Madame—I don't know when other messages will come. Surely you should answer these? It would be better if you responded, better for everyone. At least say something to your parents. Come, just a couple of words, and I'll send them on."

Ebriel tried to snap, "Let General Glass do it." But the

words slurred in her mouth and fell drunkenly from her lips.

The director looked amused. "Very well," she said. "I'll put something together for you, something polite. Perhaps you will feel better tomorrow." She waved a dismissive hand, and an attendant came to shepherd Ebriel away.

As far as Ebriel ever knew, there were no more messages.

She slept a great deal, dozing for hours in a lawn chair in the garden. She ate a little at each meal, but never remembered what the food had been. She lost count of the days of her incarceration. There was nothing to mark them, no variance in the routine, no event to mark the sameness. When a new 'patient' arrived, his advent made hardly a ripple in the stillness. Ebriel never saw her picture on the telepanel again. In the early mornings, when the sedative had worn off a bit, the agony of her loss returned, and with it her hate, and the slight energy it gave her. But when the drug was administered again, she found it hard to remember what that had felt like. Once she tried to refuse the drug, but two attendants held her arms while another pressed an ampoule to her arm. She slept almost all of that day.

When she could stay awake, she wandered in the garden, going around and around the inside of the stone wall, looking beyond it at the flickering power grid, imagining ways to throw herself at it. But if she paused, or leaned against the wall, an attendant appeared as if from nowhere to pull her back.

Once one of the other inmates put a leg over the wall, and then fell back onto the lawn, writhing and squalling. The director stalked out of her office to lecture them all, reminding them the anklets they wore were to warn them if they got too close to the power field. For their own good, she repeated. They stared at her. Ebriel's fingers twitched helplessly.

One afternoon, making her circle of the stone wall, Ebriel heard a buzz and saw a flicker of silver above the power grid. She looked up, expecting another fried bird, but whatever it was made a swift circuit of the garden, soared above the power field, and vanished.

An attendant hurried out of the building moments later to lead Ebriel inside. She went, but she looked back over her shoulder, hoping for another glimpse. She tried to tell the attendant about it, mumbling something about a silver bird. The woman tugged at her arm. "You're confused today, madame," she said. "You'll be better tomorrow."

Weeks passed in a stream of tedium, too much sleep, too few dreams. Only in the early mornings could Ebriel feel the pain that was rightfully hers. The days were no more than dark eddies in the flow of time. When she looked beyond the stone wall and saw that the needles of the ash tree at the gate flared gold and bronze among the evergreens, she felt a little shock. She had been confined in Leysin all the summer, in stasis, not moving, hardly feeling, under the complete control of her enemy. Frustration pierced her drug-induced fugue.

She went inside, to the lounge. The only weapon she could find was a lamp, with a porcelain base and a linen shade. The lamp was cold in her fingers, and far too heavy for its size. Ebriel looked down at her shaking arms, finding them appallingly thin, her hands bony, the skin almost transparent. She blinked hard. She panted, taking in too much oxygen, but it brought her a little wave of power, and she used it to throw the lamp at the glowing panel.

The porcelain split into a dozen shining shards. The shade fell off to roll across the tiled floor. The flexible polymer of the screen ripped like the skin of an overripe fruit, exposing the circuitry beneath. The program broke off with a squawk of static as the connection erupted, and Ebriel, arms hanging, mouth open, stared in exhausted triumph at the naked sticks and wires and rods of the circuit board. She was satisfied. She had done something.

The others gaped at the ruined panel, and at Ebriel. They shoved themselves out of their chairs, knocking some over, and shuffled backward, dissociating themselves from the disaster.

Three white-jacketed attendants converged on the lounge, chattering loudly into their lipmikes. The director stalked up to Ebriel and seized her arm. "What are you doing?" she shrilled, pulling her away from the litter of smashed porcelain that covered the marble floor. "What's the point of this, madame?" She dragged at Ebriel, shoving her awkwardly up the staircase toward her room. "Now we have to wait for repairs!" she snapped. "What will they do now, how will they pass the time? What am I going to do with them? That was not considerate at all, now was it? Not at all."

The director's distorted features turned red. Perspiration drenched her white collar.

"Non," Ebriel said. A laugh rose in her throat, joy at the gleam of intelligence that had shined out of the murk of her anesthetized mind. "Considerate," she chortled, as the director thrust her into her room and palmed the lock. *"Non,"* she said, talking to herself now, going to lean her forehead against the locked balcony doors. "Not considerate. *Mon Dieu,* not considerate at all." She hugged herself, relishing the sweetness of her rebellion while she could, before they plied her with the sedative again and her spirit subsided under its weight.

Ebriel was dozing in the garden when the repair service arrived. She lifted her heavy eyelids to peer at the figure in a black coverall that was admitted at the gate and came up the walk with a flat toolkit in one hand and a roll of polymer fabric over one shoulder. The figure looked familiar, the broad shoulders, the height. A flat-billed hat covered most of the hair, but rough blond wisps stuck out beneath it. Ebriel tried to focus her eyes, but her head lolled, and she couldn't rouse herself all the way to curiosity.

When she opened her eyes again, it was already dusk. She had slept the day away. One of the attendants came for her, lifting her to her feet, half-carrying her across the grass and into the building. In the lounge, the telepanel was still in pieces. The roll of polymer fabric lay on the floor beside it. Several of the inmates sat in their usual chairs, staring at the exposed circuitry, their faces no more or less blank than usual. The attendant guided Ebriel up the stairs and locked her in her room. She fell onto the bed and slept again.

She woke to complete darkness and a sharp scent in her nostrils. Abruptly, she sat up. She hadn't moved so quickly in weeks, and her head spun.

"Sh-sh," someone breathed. Ebriel jumped, and a hard hand came down on her shoulder. "Sh-sh." A deep, feminine voice said, "Give yourself a minute, ma'am."

Instantly Ebriel realized who was in her room. She also recognized the stinging scent of giallo, a strong and illegal stimulant. She had breathed an ampoule of giallo, and the person in her room was the tall blond woman she had noticed in Geneva. In the Auberge du Saconnex, and outside the Palais des Nations, she had worn a gray jumpsuit. Earlier today it had been a black coverall.

"Who are you?" Ebriel breathed. For the first time in weeks, her lips and tongue worked properly. The only light in the room was that of the moon reflected off the snowfields of the mountains. All the lights of Leysin had been extinguished. Where were the attendants?

She pushed herself off the bed, wavering on her weakened legs. Her balcony door was open! The smell of giallo competed with the fragrance of spruce and pine and cedar.

"Tell you later," the tall woman said. "Get out of here first. Fucking general has eyes in the back of his head." She threw a thick jacket around Ebriel's shoulders. "Cold in the mountains," she said. "Come on, this way."

Ebriel followed her without hesitation. Under the effects of the stimulant she felt fearless. The open balcony called her to freedom.

The tall woman had hung a fire ladder over the edge of the balcony, and she guided Ebriel's feet and hands as they descended. The stranger was silent in her movements, but Ebriel slipped and bumped things from time to time. She sucked in her breath, fearful of detection, but the other woman shook her head. "It's okay," she said. "They're asleep."

Ebriel, her senses heightened, her wits artificially sharp, thought they were probably dead, but she didn't care. At least she was moving again, her mind working, her eyes clear. If it was all a dream, she welcomed it. If she were actually waking from the dream, the slow nightmare of the past weeks, she would seize her chance.

There was no movement anywhere that she could see. Ebriel and the strange woman reached the ground, and the stranger touched a button to reel the ladder into a neat coil that she hung over her shoulder. With a gesture of her head, and a hawkish grin that showed the gleam of white teeth in the moonlight, she indicated their route. Ebriel followed, pulling the loaned jacket close against the chill. Her sandals whispered on the stepping stones as they crossed the lawn to the brick path.

The gate opened at a touch, and Ebriel saw that the guard was slumped to one side, mouth open, eyes closed. She looked up at her guide. "Dead?"

The woman grinned again. "Just unconscious," she chuckled. She flashed a tiny pulse pistol, as illegal as the giallo, its composite case unscannable. "Little dose of their own medicine."

Ebriel felt the beginnings of the fierce headache that the giallo would leave behind. She wanted to get away before it wore off. She staggered through the gate. "Where will we go?"

The stranger pulled the gate shut and took a last look around before she answered. "First, we're getting off the grounds," she said. "Move out. I disabled the surveillance, but when they wake up, it'll be back. We'll get to the bird—copter, I mean—get your hardware off, and get up over the mountains. Then we'll explain."

"We?" Ebriel looked around into the trees. "There is someone else?"

"Guarding the bird. Come on, ma'am, please."

The tall woman strode off into the woods, checking over her shoulder from time to time to see that Ebriel was following.

Ebriel did. Her headache was growing sharper by the moment, but its pain was far better than the half-death of sedation. She had no idea what lay ahead of her, but she was certain her escape would displease Commander General Glass. For the moment, that was enough.

5

Ebriel stumbled and gasped for breath as she and the tall woman broke out of the trees and into a clearing where a silver-blue copter waited in the moonlight. Its drooping rotor blades glinted above another woman, also wearing the gray jumpsuit, who appeared in the open door. It was strange, Ebriel thought blurrily, how the neutral fabric made the women hard to see. The woman in the copter called, "Ty! It is almost dawn!"

Ebriel's rescuer took her arm, urged her forward. "I know you're tired, hon. You're lookin' poorly, too. But you can rest in the bird. We gotta go while the goin's good."

Ebriel understood only 'rest' and 'go,' but it was enough.

The moon made the clearing as bright as day to her drug-dilated pupils. She could make out the second woman's soft brown hair, the white hand she stretched down to help Ebriel up. Ebriel took the hand, but she had no strength. The woman called Ty had to put her own long arms around Ebriel's knees to boost her into the copter.

Steadying herself against one of the seats, Ebriel stared at the interior. She had seen such craft whirring through the skies above Paris. She had never expected to be in one.

The brown-haired woman helped her to sit. *"Hola,"* she said. "I am Pilar Alavedra."

Ebriel answered weakly. *"Bonjour.* I am Ebriel Serique."

Pilar smiled at her. "Yes, I know." She turned toward the cockpit, where the tall woman had taken the right seat. "Ty, have you asked her?"

Ty shook her head. "No time. Ask her now."

Pilar nodded and took one of Ebriel's hands in both of hers. "Ebriel. Do you wish to leave with us? To go away from Leysin, and from InCo?" Her accent was elegant, softly trilled *r*'s, lingual consonants limpid against her teeth.

Ebriel managed to nod.

"Si?" said Pilar.

Ebriel croaked, *"Oui."*

Ty said over her shoulder, "She's beat, Pilar. She needs food, drink, probably something for a nasty headache."

"Bueno," Pilar said. She pointed to Ebriel's wrist and ankle. "And what about these?"

"Oh, yeah." Ty came back with a tool of some kind in her hand and bent over Ebriel. A moment later, both bracelet and anklet clattered to the floor of the copter.

Pilar picked them up and hurled them into the woods with surprising strength. She touched a button to close the copter's door. "Lift off now, Ty. I will care for our new friend."

The rotors over their heads began to turn, and then to spin with a muffled whine. In a rush of displaced air, the craft rose into a hover. Pilar buckled a webbed belt around Ebriel and took her own seat. The copter tilted, straightened, and then flew east, toward the first fingers of dawn raking the horizon. The forest flowed beneath them, blurring as they picked up speed.

Ebriel's head blazed with pain, and she closed her eyes. She had passed from InCo's control into the power of some other agency. Who or what it might be, she couldn't guess, and she was too exhausted to care. A cup touched her lips, and she drank a sweet, thick juice. She lifted her eyelids enough to see Pilar move up into the cockpit. Her dark head and Ty's blond one made silhouettes against the rosy sky. Ebriel's headache receded all at once, and with it the tension in her muscles. She slept.

* * *

Ebriel startled awake, confused about where she was, about the whirring noise above her head. She blinked, and then remembered.

In the cockpit, Ty lounged in the pilot's seat, arms folded, one long leg hooked over the armrest. Pilar's head barely showed above the left-hand seat, brown hair falling over a small white pillow. She seemed to be asleep. Ebriel looked around at the interior of the copter.

A little galley filled the rear, a tiny stove, a sink, a little fridge. Storage cubes filled the space behind the seats, stuffed with weather gear, tools, a tangle of wires and cables, a coil of rope. One large carton, stamped with the InCo globe, held stacks of foilpacks.

Below she saw only ocean, waves stretching to the horizon, dancing with sunshine. With a wave of pain she remembered the images of *L'Oiseau blanc,* blue hull bobbing on the water, stubby motorboat tied to the stern. The pain was unbearable, until reawakened anger smothered it. She drew a sharp breath between her teeth. Ty turned in her seat.

"Hey," she said, flashing her toothy grin. "Feelin' better?"

Ebriel lifted one shoulder, a Gallic shrug.

Ty's freckled brow creased. "Yeah. You've had a bad time. We're sorry about that."

"Do you know about the—the time I have had?"

"Sure. And we caught your little show in Geneva."

Ebriel shook her head, struggling with the colloquial English. "I do not understand."

Ty shoved herself up out of her seat. She touched Pilar's shoulder as she passed, and the smaller woman woke, glanced back at Ebriel, then turned forward to face the controls. Ty came to lean on the seat next to Ebriel. "We're gonna explain everything," she said. "Promise. You want to hit the head first?"

"*Comment?* Hit my head?"

Ty grinned again, pointing to the back of the aircraft. "Head. Bathroom. Toilet."

"Ah." Ebriel nodded. "*Toilette.* Yes. *Merci.*"

When Ebriel emerged from the tiny toilet, Ty was waiting for her with two coffees and a foilpack marked InstaMeal in black print. InCo issue. Ty zipped the foil and laid the pack on the seat tray. "Military rations. Not fancy, but filling," she said, pressing a fork into Ebriel's hand. "It'll be warm in a minute."

Ebriel looked into the other woman's weathered face. "How do you know me?" she whispered. "Why did you come for me?"

"I'll explain," Ty said. She touched the foil and nodded. "It's ready. Eat, please. You're awful shaky."

Ebriel dug into the foil pack with the fork, bringing out a chunk of something pale green in a thick sauce. She eyed it doubtfully, her stomach quivering. Ty laughed.

"It's okay, actually," she said. "Soy protein, vegetables, flavoring. When we get to Siwa, we'll have a real meal, but I don't think you should wait that long."

Ebriel put the food in her mouth and found that Ty was right. It was bland and smooth-textured, and her stomach quieted. Ty picked up a square of plastic from the side of the little tray, slit it, and brought out a slice of flat brown bread. She handed it to Ebriel, with a gesture to indicate she should soak it in the sauce.

"Okay," Ty said, leaning back with the coffee mug in her hand. "I'm Ty Astin, by the way. Ty, short for Tyra." She lifted her cup as if in salute. "American, formerly with InCo Forces. We knew about what happened to your family. That was big news, all over the nets." Ebriel swallowed and looked away, laying down the fork.

"Yeah," Ty said quietly. She sipped her coffee, giving Ebriel a moment before she gently pressed the fork back into her hand. "It was your trip to Geneva that caught Papa's attention."

Ebriel's eyebrows went up. "Who is Papa?"

"We'll get to that. Anyway, I followed you to Geneva, because we thought you might be up to something. And then, at the Palais—we've seen this before, somebody does something, InCo disposes of 'em. Well, Security Corps specifically. Your little show got squelched from Newnet, but one of the underground nets got a great shot."

Pilar looked back over her shoulder. "I saw it," she said. "It was very beautiful, and so sad. They showed it over and over."

Ebriel said, "It seems long ago. As if it happened to someone else."

Ty reached for Ebriel's left wrist and turned it over to show the ragged white line where her memory rod had been. "Happened to you, all right," she said. "And you made your point."

"C'est bon," Ebriel said. She felt a little swell of satisfaction, but it quickly subsided. She bit her lip and put her fingers over the scar. "And now, what is there for me to do?"

"Maybe we have something for you," Ty said, releasing her hand.

"But—what would this be? Who are you?"

"We—and the others—we're the Chain."

"Pardon? The Chain?"

"Si," said Pilar, smiling. "We are the little shrub that trips the soldier—what do you call it?"

Ebriel exclaimed, "Ah! The *maquis*? You are the *résistance*! The maquis!"

Ty grinned. "Yeah. Resistance. Opposition. Whatever you want to call it." She put down her coffee cup and stretched her arms until her shoulders cracked. "We're opposed to the International Cooperative Alliance—well, to its isolationist policies, anyway. Opposed to the quarantine of the so-called latent countries and the Line of Partition. Opposed—" Her blue eyes sharpened as she looked into Ebriel's face. "Opposed to George Glass and his mob."

Ebriel saw that Ty had a foilpack, too, and had eaten everything. She pushed her own away. *"Pardon,"* she murmured. "So much has happened . . ."

"Si," Pilar said quietly. "It is enough for now, Ty. Let her rest."

"Okay," Ty said. She took Ebriel's cup. "Okay. Lean back then, rest."

"But you are going to ask me—" Ebriel began.

"Sure," Ty said softly. She patted her shoulder. "We're gonna ask you. But later."

Ebriel slept again. When she woke she saw waves of sand instead of sea, brown and beige and white ridges under a hot pale sky. The windows on the right side of the craft had darkened in response to the lowering sun. They must have left the European polities. Ebriel stiffened, her shoulder belt tightening at her sudden movement. "The spybugs!"

Ty was in the pilot seat again. "Did you see one?" she demanded over her shoulder.

Pilar said, "I do not read any."

"No, I did not see anything," Ebriel said. "But they—I mean—are we not past the Line of Partition? Would the spybugs not catch us?"

Ty chuckled and relaxed. "Oh, there's lots of gaps in the deployment pattern. Not enough spybugs in the world to cover the whole thing, fortunately. We scan for 'em. And Pilar's got a neat little ol' bug zapper right under her hand, just in case."

"Zapper?"

"It's a laser, actually. Burns out their opticals."

"Oh." Ebriel undid her shoulder belt and rose to go to the toilet. When she reemerged, she saw Ty watching out for her, nodding with satisfaction as she refastened the belt.

A quarter of an hour later Ty began talking to someone through her headset. The control panel flickered with numbers. The copter skimmed over a low ridge and dropped down into a shallow valley dotted with palm groves and dusty green olive and date trees. In the distance an enormous lake glistened, mirror-smooth in the setting sun. Below them spilled the flat-roofed houses of a desert village, but Ebriel saw no people, no movement.

"Siwa," Ty said with a wave of her hand. "Oasis in the desert. Hardly anybody home anymore." She pointed to the east, where toppled monuments and statues topped a hill. "Ruins of the Oracle of Amoun," Ty announced. "Where Alexander the Great wanted to be buried, except that somebody stole his corpse along the way."

The copter skirted the valley and topped the next rise into a second. Asymmetrical strips of dark pavement stretched beyond a cluster of rectangular buildings that looked as empty as the village. The copter banked and circled. A noise beneath Ebriel made her jump, but Pilar looked back and smiled. "The tri-gear is now extended."

Ebriel had no idea what that meant. Strangeness piled upon strangeness. Her life of music and comfort and security was only a faint memory here in this hard-edged world, the sere landscape, the strong women, the swift copter. They hovered and then settled onto one of the landing strips, the tarmac silver-gray in the slanting sunshine. Abandoned containers and bits of equipment studded the empty ground between two long hangars and along the landing strips. Ebriel felt heat sweep up from the ground even before the door opened. Her ears throbbed in the sudden silence when the blades wound down their rotation.

A dark-skinned, plump woman in loose white clothing, a dark scarf over her hair, appeared at the nose of the craft and smiled up at them.

"Hey, Nenet." Ty jumped down to the tarmac. "Success! Meet Ebriel Serique."

The single-story, rectangular buildings they passed appeared long abandoned. Broken windows were left un-mended, and sand covered sills, floors, the tops of cabinets. It drifted in doorways and over cracked sidewalks, covering everything with grit. Ebriel wasn't certain, but she thought the markings painted on the doors were Arabic characters. Nenet led the way to the very center of the complex, up the only clear sidewalk, and into a large room that appeared to be both kitchen and living area, with simple plastic furniture. The room was blessedly cool.

"Please, sit down," Nenet told them. "There is *kharoub* in that pitcher on the table, and fresh carrot and orange juice in the refrigerator. Shall I prepare dinner now, or later?"

Ty held a chair for Ebriel. "A little later, thanks, Nenet. We better talk first. Ebriel's gonna have a few questions."

Nenet nodded and took the chair opposite Ebriel. She poured the clear dark beverage into thick glasses as Ty and Pilar sat down.

"I am Nenet Nasser," she said with a nod to Ebriel. "*Marhaba,* Ebriel. That is 'welcome' in my language. Did you agree to come away with Ty and Pilar?"

Ebriel sipped the cold drink. It was surprisingly refreshing. She lifted her chin. *"Oui,"* she said firmly. "I agreed."

The dark woman smiled. "That is good," she said. "We never take anyone against her will." She spoke English easily, but with a strong accent, prominent lingual-dentals, throaty vowels. She was a plain woman with beautiful eyes, deep and black and long-lashed.

Pilar said, "We have already told her that we are the Chain. The resistance."

Nenet leaned back in her chair and waved one broad, short-fingered hand. "So. As you have seen, we use InCo's own infrastructure to strike back at them. There are not many of us—"

"How many?" Ebriel asked.

Ty laughed. "Never enough."

Nenet looked grave. "Our friend Ty is always—ah, jocular, I think is the word in English. But what she says is true. There are never enough of us. At this point, perhaps thirty."

"Zut!" Ebriel said weakly. "But InCo, it is everywhere. It is—" She struggled for a word.

Nenet nodded. "Yes. It is enormous."

"Ebriel," Pilar said, "the Chain came in search of you for two reasons."

Ty folded her arms and said with great relish, "First of all, to cause the Commander General as much grief as possible."

"And second," Pilar finished. "To invite you to join us. To be part of the Chain."

Kanika held tightly to her brother's hand, pulling him along beside her. Manu, only five years old, whimpered, but Kanika was relentless. She knew these men, who had massacred their entire village, wouldn't hesitate to put an end to a trouble-some child who lagged behind. Machetes hung from the men's waists, great ugly knives still rusty with bloodstains.

There was no sound as they trudged through the banana groves except the harsh breathing of the bandits. Kanika kept her eyes on the path ahead. She had no delusions that some-one would come after her and Manu, stop the bandits from taking them over the mountains. There was no one left alive to rescue them.

The bandits looked very much like Kanika and Manu, the same dark skin, narrow shoulders, kinky hair. They could even have come from the same tribe. Civil wars had divided the people of Sierra Leone for years. The giant refugee camps had become lawless cities, and marauders pillaged small commu-nities at will. Kanika's village had rifles and machetes, but the bandits had surprised them, caught them sleeping in the early dawn. The attackers had discovered Kanika and Manu hiding under a pile of rugs and had hauled them out of their house.

They had tripped over the bodies of their parents, stepped in the pool of their blood.

Kanika heard a buzzing, off to her left. She didn't turn her head, but she wondered how the silent men around her couldn't hear it. They made too much noise with their feet, perhaps, trudging on the bare dirt with their thick boots. She and Manu were barefoot. The sound came again, swooping above around to the right. She let her eyes flick sideways. She caught a flash of silver and black that went by very fast, like a firefinch, and then was gone. Manu sobbed, and she squeezed his hand.

Kanika knew this path. It wound to the west, out of the banana groves and up to the tall cliffs. The people of her village came this way sometimes, climbing down the cliffs to the beach to set the nets for shrimp, and the pots for lobster. There would be a place, a break in the thick brush. She and Manu could seize their chance.

Kanika knew why the two of them had been spared. Orphaned children in the camp cities could be valuable, sold into prostitution or used as decoys in battle. It was better for her and Manu to throw themselves over the cliff to the rocks below, to join their parents in death.

Kanika was eleven years old.

She scanned the tangle of bushes and scrubby trees that lined the path. At last she spied a sliver of blue sea sparkling through a narrow clearing, just at the edge of the cliff. She wanted to sob, like Manu, but she gritted her teeth. It would only hurt for a moment, she told herself. A moment, and it would be over. One sharp, terrible pain to reunite them with their family . . .

When she saw two people emerge into the clearing, surprise made her stumble. How had they gotten there? Behind them was only the cliff, and the sea. And what were these people? Their bodies were covered in smooth gray cloth, and they wore wide black belts hung with mysterious objects. Their skin was ghost-pale. Kanika had never seen anyone with light skin.

The leader of the bandits cried out and brandished his machete. One of the figures in gray lifted a hand, and Kanika heard a brief humming, as of a passing swarm of mosquitoes. The bandit leader fell as if his legs had dissolved, and he lay *on the path without moving, his arms flung out, his mouth open, his knife useless beside him. The rest froze, staring at the strangers.*

The strangers kept their weapons trained on the bandits. One of them said in bad Krio, "Stan bak, noh dai. Stan bak." Her voice was high and clear, a woman's voice. Kanika looked at the other and saw that they were both women. Were they real? She didn't understand. How could this be? And where had they come from?

There was a moment of stillness. No birds sang. Even the insects ceased buzzing. One of the bandits at the rear, a wild-haired man with only one hand, jumped forward, machete flailing. Again the little weapon hummed. The man fell hard in mid-leap, one leg bent under him. He didn't move. He didn't appear to breathe. Joy blazed in Kanika's heart.

The yellow-haired woman spoke again. "Stan bak pikin. Go go nab rod." The words weren't quite right, but the men seemed to understand. Breathing hard, angry and afraid, they backed away from her and Manu.

The woman nodded to the children. "Noh geht wohri, pikin. Kam. Kam."

Kanika could barely understand her, but she understood the gesture, the hand held out, the fingers open. It was a strong white hand, with long fingers and clean nails. Tugging Manu with her, Kanika took a cautious step toward the women, but she looked beyond them to the gap, the place where she and Manu could reach the cliff.

"Noh geht wohri, pikin," the woman repeated, as if she had read Kanika's mind. The moment she and Manu came close, the women reached for them, lifting them as if they were babies. Kanika felt the muscles in the woman's strong arms, ridges of it against her legs, her shoulders. "Go go nah rod," the yellow-haired woman snapped. And harshly, in some other language, "Get out of here!"

She leveled her weapon. The men scrambled backward, turned, and ran, leaving their two comrades lying where they had fallen.

The two strange women stepped out onto the path, still carrying the children as easily as if they were bundles of feathers. They moved forward to the point where a branch of the path turned down toward the beach. It was steep, and they put the children on their feet, but still held their hands. They climbed down together, without speaking. Kanika cast fearful eyes up into the white faces. The women smiled, and the first one repeated, "Noh fred, pikin. Noh geht wohri." Kanika guessed she knew very little else in their language, but the way she said it was somehow comforting. The whole scene was so queer, and followed upon such a horrific experience for the two children, that Kanika thought perhaps she and her brother were actually dead, and these white-faced women had come to lead them into the afterlife.

But on the beach a very real aircraft waited. Kanika had once spotted a silver airplane flying high above her village and off toward the mountains, but this was smaller, and silvery-blue. It looked like a giant dragonfly, with a drooping rotor on the top and strange welts underneath. As they approached, a door slid open in its side, and the women lifted the children up into its cool interior. Moments later, Manu and Kanika were belted into cushioned seats, and the two women sat in front of them, doing incomprehensible things with their hands and their feet. The little craft rose from the beach with a soft clatter and a stomach-lurching tilt.

Manu wailed anew, but Kanika didn't cry. Elation blazed through her grief and shock and confusion. She hoped with all her being that the two men lying on the top of the cliff were dead. She wished the two women had left the whole band lying on the stony path. She wished she had one of the mysterious silent weapons so she could go after the others, the other half of the bandit gang, and shoot every one of them until they all lay still on the rocks.

Kanika looked down at the sere waves of brush flowing beneath them as they left the green of the peninsula and flew east and north over the high plains. She took her brother's hand again. "Don't cry, Manu," she whispered. "Don't cry. We're safe."

6

Ty, Pilar, and Nenet regarded Ebriel in a waiting silence. Daylight faded quickly beyond the windows. The last slanting rays of the sun sharpened the edges of the furniture, defined each of the clean-swept floor tiles. A geopolitical map filled one wall of the common room, painted directly onto the cement. Ebriel rose and went to it, as much to avoid the intent gazes of the women as out of curiosity.

Nenet left her chair and followed her. "This map is fifteen years out of date, I'm afraid," she said. The legends were in Arabic, but Ebriel recognized the outlines of the African continent. Nenet pointed with her blunt forefinger to a symbol in the northeast corner. "We are here," she said. "The Siwa Oasis in the Western Desert. An old military airfield."

"I am in Egypt?" Ebriel asked.

"It used to be Egypt," Nenet said. "When InCo interdicted all of Africa, the Egyptian government collapsed." At Ebriel's surprised glance, she gave a short laugh. "No, they do not tell you such things, do they? But it is true. Egypt, Ethiopia, Algeria—they could have made it. Even after the Crash. But it is a hard thing for republics to stand alone in the midst of chaos. Arabia, of course, Iran, Iraq—they destroyed themselves and their people with the biochems. Still, Egypt had a chance, even with the contamination—but our chance is gone now."

"And you are Egyptian?"

Nenet nodded and tucked a strand of black hair under her white scarf. "I was born in Cairo. My parents were killed in the food riots. My sister and I fled into the desert, and we ended up here. Siwa was once a tourist destination, with a grand hotel and swimming pools. There was food stockpiled at the air base. Most of the people left when the food stores ran out, but a few of the old Siwans still live in the city. They eat olives, dates, donkey when they can get it. Their water comes from the springs. They speak the old Siwan language. They are afraid of the copters, and a little afraid of me. Sometimes I go into the village to buy olives or bread." She waved her dark, thick-fingered hand. "Of course, all their women practice purdah, so they are shocked to see my face uncovered. They make finger signs against evil when they see me."

"Where is your sister?"

"She was part of the Chain. She was lost on a mission."

"I am sorry, Nenet."

"Thank you, Ebriel. I miss her."

"Come on," Ty said, uncoiling her long body from her chair. She jerked her thumb toward the door. "Let's all go outside."

Darkness had fallen, cooling the dry desert air. The moon had not yet risen, and stars jeweled the desert sky. Ebriel exclaimed at the sight. *"Mon Dieu!* So many!"

Pilar said, "There is only one place to see more stars."

Ty said, "Easy, Pilar. Give her a minute."

Ebriel looked around at the three women, then put her fists on her hips. Her ear had caught the rhythm of their English, and she understood Ty much better. She looked up into the tall woman's face. *"Bien,"* she said. "Tell it all, now. Not in a minute. Now."

Ty grinned. "You bet," she said. She pointed at the sky. "Look up there, Ebriel. Among the stars. You see that bright one, right over the equator?"

Ebriel followed her finger. *"Mais oui,"* she said. "The star hotel. We see that in Paris, in the southwestern sky."

Ty said, "Yes. Ethan Fleck lives there."

"I know this."

"Yeah. Well, he's the one we call Papa."

Ebriel raised her eyebrows, waiting. Ty folded her arms. "So. Papa suffers from a neurological disease. Idiopathic sclerosis, the doctors call it. Years ago, when he began to lose the use of his arms and legs, he decided to live in space, in microgravity, where he would have a little more strength, be more comfortable."

"Why are you telling me this?" Ebriel demanded.

Ty gestured again at the blinking lights of the space habitat. "That's where we live, Ebriel, all of us in the Chain. Starhold. Home."

A corridor leading from Nenet's common room opened onto small rooms that had once been crew quarters. Each of the Chain members had their own. Nenet supplied Ebriel with a shift to sleep in, toiletries from a storage room full of cartons labeled by InCo, even a few stamped by the old United Nations. She smiled at Ebriel's surprised expression when she handed her a package of soap and toothpaste and skin cream bearing the black and silver globe. "Oh, yes," she said. "We use everything we can get our hands on. Of course, the Siwans have taken all the food stores, but they have no interest in toothbrushes and toilet paper. They live as their ancestors did, a thousand years ago. They left the medicines, too. They did not know how to use them."

"But how do you get these? They tell us the embargo is absolute."

Nenet nodded, her face grave. "It is, Ebriel. No food, medicines, goods, nothing. And so we—the Chain—supply ourselves directly from InCo stockpiles. We know where the warehouses are. We bribe, we steal, we trade, whatever is required."

"I do not see how you do it. Why you are not caught."

Nenet pulled the door of the stockroom closed. "We are quick, and almost invisible. And we have help—Papa's network of people, many who have worked for Fleckcell, or still do."

She led Ebriel to a room with a cot, a stained sink, a

cracked but intact window. Nenet smoothed the blanket. "The sheets are fresh," she said. "I put them on this morning."

"How did you know I would be here?" Ebriel asked her.

"Papa told me."

"Oh. Papa. It seems—forgive me—it seems very odd, that you call him that."

Nenet stood leaning against the doorjamb. "Papa," she said with a little smile, "is not only a genius. He is the most wonderful man in the world. You will meet him, if you decide to join us." Her heavy lids lowered slightly. "Ebriel—even if you decide against us—this information is given to you in trust. A sacred trust. We are sisters, all of us, whether you join us or not."

"Are all the Chain women?"

Nenet shook her head. "No. We have a few men, but somehow it seems women are more amenable to our purpose. Our mission seems hopeless—and yet we hope for change."

"I understand this very well. We French have a history of *résistance.*" Ebriel sat down on the cot and kicked off her sandals. The tiles were cool under her soles. "I must think, Nenet."

"Of course. *Salam,* Ebriel Serique. We will talk in the morning." Nenet withdrew, closing the door softly behind her. Ebriel tensed, but there was no sound of a lock. She was a guest, then. Not a prisoner.

She took off the blue rayon uniform of Leysin. As she drew the shift over her head, the touch of air on her bare skin reminded her of Paris. She concentrated, as she lay down, on the specter of George Glass, his coarse features, his unpleasant voice. She lulled herself to sleep by thinking of ways to win her revenge.

In the morning, Nenet served a breakfast of olives and dates and flatbread. She showed Ebriel how to dip triangles of the bread into a shallow bowl of thick green olive oil.

"The Siwans make it," she said. "In the old way, crushing the olives with stones."

Ebriel had almost no appetite. She managed some dates and a sheet of the flatbread, and drank *kharoub.* Ty insisted she drink an enormous glass of water, too, warning her of the dryness of the desert air.

During the night, Nenet had washed the Leysin uniform. Ebriel found it folded and ready beside her door when she rose. She held the material in her hands for a moment, smelling the scent of soap, touched by the care of a woman she hardly knew, who didn't know her.

After the breakfast things were cleared away, Nenet took Ebriel on a tour. At one end of the barracks a fuel cell installation sparkled in the hot sun. "And over there," Nenet said, pointing to another low rectangular building, "we collect biomass for the spaceplanes. The copters only need fuel cells. They can recharge right on the landing field, or anywhere in direct sunlight."

Ebriel felt so inundated with new information that she hardly knew what questions to ask.

Nenet handed her a scarf. "The sun is dangerous," she said. "You must cover your head, and then I will show you Siwa." She gave her a pair of dark glasses as well. Ebriel put everything on and followed her guide up to the low ridge that separated the air base from the town.

"You see, beyond the city," Nenet said, pointing. "That is Amoun, the Oracle, or at least the ruins of it. Alexander the Great came here to ask the Oracle if he was the son of Zeus."

"And what was the answer?"

Nenet chuckled. "Alexander never said. Perhaps he did not want people to know he was not in fact divine."

Ebriel tried to smile.

"And there—" Nenet pointed in the opposite direction. "There was a great hotel, a resort. This was a rich tourist attraction, for the Americans and Swiss, the Germans, the Japanese."

Nothing was left of the hotel but the blackened empty cliffs of supporting walls, broken girders dangling from them like giant tree roots. *"Zut!"* Ebriel breathed. "What happened to it?"

"When InCo drew the Line of Partition, a band of protesters took control of the hotel, with a few InCo citizens inside. Not many, but enough, they thought, for InCo Forces to pay attention." Deep grooves appeared around Nenet's full-lipped mouth. "There were not enough. The protesters blew up the hotel. More than a hundred died, the rebels, the InCo citizens, all the Siwan staff. And so it has stayed."

She turned her back on the gruesome sight and waved her arm at the desert. "The Great Sand Sea. It cares not for the foibles of human beings. Its waves of sand go on forever."

Ebriel, her mouth and throat dry, followed Nenet back down the ridge and through the abandoned complex. Ty and Pilar sat before a panel in the common room. Ebriel drank another glass of water, standing alone beside the window. The women joined her, one on either side.

"And so," Pilar said gently. "You have learned some things?"

"*Oui*," Ebriel answered. "Interesting things. But not what it is you do, you of the Chain."

Pilar put a small hand on her shoulder, very gently. "We resist, Ebriel," she said softly. "We work for change in small ways, sometimes bigger ways. If you wish, you can join us. If not, we will take you back to Switzerland, or to Paris, and wish you well."

Ebriel had to ask. "Do you not fear that I would give you away?"

Ty laughed. "Who'd believe a poor crazy Frenchwoman?" she asked. "You gonna point at the sky and talk about Ethan Fleck? You've been in a mental hospital, after all!"

"But how do you keep it secret?" Ebriel pressed. "You fly the copters, you live in Star Hotel One—"

"Starhold," Ty said.

"Oh, yes. But what about the spybugs? Security Corps?"

Smile lines fanned across Ty's freckled cheeks. "See? It sounds insane."

Nenet set a tureen of bean stew on the table and brought out a fresh pitcher of *kharoub*. "Never mind for now," she said. "Let us eat, and talk of other things. Let Ebriel do her thinking."

On her second night in the Siwa barracks, Ebriel lay sleepless. Through the cracked window the stars blazed from a black sky. She turned and turned till the sheets were tangled and her hair twisted around her neck. Not even her litany of ways to win revenge against General Glass made her drowsy.

At last she got up. She opened her door with caution and listened for a long moment to the quiet in the barracks. Wearing only her borrowed shift, she slipped on her sandals and tiptoed down the corridor, through the common room, and out into the cool night.

A mild breeze blew from the groves beyond the ridge. Ebriel wandered without direction, down the sand-covered sidewalks, across the runways. The moon rose to light her way. It made deep shadows behind the bits of abandoned hardware and sharpened the edges of the long grasses. She climbed the hill beyond the airfield. The silence, as broad and deep as the great desert, filled her ears. She sank to the ground to sit crosslegged, staring over the ocean of sand.

Her eyes burned, without tears. "What am I to do?" she whispered into the emptiness. "What is the point of any of it?" No answer came to her.

When she felt a hand on her shoulder, she jumped. *"Merde!"*

"I saw you leave," Ty said quietly. "I didn't want you to get lost out here. Big desert."

Ebriel put a hand to her throat, her pulse thumping. When she could speak, she murmured, *"Oui.* Very big." She turned her eyes back to the expanse of ridged sand. "I am trying to think, Ty, but I am confused. Terrible things have happened to me."

"I know." Ty hunkered down next to Ebriel and sat with her elbows on her knees, staring out over the desert. Empty minutes passed.

At last Ebriel blurted, "All I want in the world is to make George Glass pay for what happened to my family." Ty didn't speak. Ebriel's hands twisted in her lap. "If I were to join you," she ventured, haltingly, "it would be for my own reasons. Not for yours."

"Probably true for most of us," Ty said. "Want to hear my story?"

Ebriel turned her head to examine the American woman's bony profile. *"Oui."*

Ty nodded. "Yeah. Well, it's pretty short. I'm from North

America. Parker, Oklahoma. Only way out of my little town was InCo Forces, and I sure did want to fly. I was on my way up through the ranks. Captain already. I liked the life fine, travel, interesting experiences.

"Then I got orders to fly to Nassau, in the Bahamas, with fancy eats for some InCo meeting between Glass, Takanagi, the European Federation people. They were dickering about where to draw the Line to separate the South American polities from the North American. All this food, and wine, and other bullshit, and all the time on this little island no more than four hundred miles to the southeast, people were suffering. There was a big storm, and they were out of water, out of food—caught between a rock and a hard place. They weren't InCo, but nobody else claimed 'em either. They ended up on the wrong side of the Line."

She shifted, stretching her long legs in front of her, leaning back on her hands. "I disobeyed a direct order. Dropped my shipment on Caicos Island instead of Nassau. And that was it for InCo Forces and Captain Ty Astin! Nothing I could do but take that bird and hightail it out of there."

"But where did you go? What could you do?"

Ty lay back on the sand and looked up into the stars. "I was already over the Line. I had a full fuel cell and a bird, and I lit out for Taiwan. In Oceania. Neutral territory."

"A very long flight."

Ty chuckled. "Long, and lonely. But I'll say this for InCo Forces, they know how to build a copter. I made it, and the Chain knew I made it. I went to the Fleckcell plant there, with an idea of looking for work. Someone was waiting for me when I got there."

"It seems a very sudden decision," Ebriel murmured.

"Yeah, seems like it. But it isn't really true." Ty sat up and faced Ebriel. "I wanted to fly, and I wanted out of Parker, Oklahoma. I wanted a better life. But people were starving. People no different from those in Parker, with kids and houses and pets and problems. I learned pretty quick that Takanagi and the rest really meant what they said. If you were on the wrong side of the Line when they drew it—that was too bad. Your tough luck."

"But what about the bombs? And the chemical warfare, the diseases?" Ebriel asked.

Ty shook her head. "I don't have an answer. Except that quarantine isn't the way."

"We thought it was," Ebriel whispered. "Paul and I. We thought it was the way to keep our daughter safe, our world . . . we didn't know any other. When we heard Dimarco speak against the embargo, we thought he was a fanatic. A dangerous liberal, Paul called him."

"You know what Glass and the like call the latents?" Ty said. Ebriel shook her head. "They call them the muds. Like they're not even human beings."

"I suppose that naming them so makes it easier."

"You got it."

For a long time, they listened to the immense silence.

At last, Ebriel sighed. "What will I do, Ty, if I join the Chain? How will I be useful?"

"That depends. Papa usually has an idea."

"Are you fighters?"

"Sometimes. Sometimes we are."

Ebriel asked, carefully, without inflection, "Do you kill people?"

Ty's eyes glittered. "Try not to," she said. She looked away, her irregular profile sculpted by moonlight. "But I have."

Ebriel turned her face to the desert. She didn't speak again until she was certain she could control her voice. She didn't want Ty to know how much she wanted to learn to kill people.

7

The sun was rising as Ebriel and Ty returned to the barracks, and the heat with it, folding the base in a stifling blanket. Pilar and Nenet were in the common room, the panel open between them. Nenet glanced up. "It's time, Ty," she said. "Unicorn is leaving Xiao Qaidam. And a copter is coming from the coast with four aboard."

Ty nodded. "Four? That's great! Success, then. We're ready. Ebriel's with us."

Pilar stood up immediately, smiling, stretching out her hands to Ebriel. *"Si?"* she said. "You have decided? Then welcome to the Chain, *amiga*." She touched her cheek to Ebriel's.

Ebriel, abashed by her easy warmth, mumbled, *"Merci.* I hope I will be an asset."

Nenet said, "Each of us has something to offer. It only remains to find out what it is."

"She needs clothes," Ty said to Nenet. "Lose those blue pj's."

Ebriel had trouble with the idiom, but she guessed that Ty meant the Leysin uniform. She would be glad to rid of it. Pilar brought three of the gray utility jumpsuits from the storeroom, and Ebriel went to her bedroom to try them, one by one, settling on the one that was most comfortable, not too long in the legs and sleeves. The thin fabric felt tough as canvas, but it seemed new, some manufactured material, and it felt slick against her skin. It was anything but fashionable, designed for movement. She didn't know how to close the front panel, accustomed to seamless tunics and flowing dresses that simply dropped over her head. Almost by accident she touched both ends simultaneously, and the two edges sealed themselves neatly with a little zip of suction. She stepped back to look in the mirror.

Her appearance startled her. Never in her life had she been so thin, her breasts shrunken, her hips fleshless. Streaks of silver had appeared, as if overnight, in her hair. She was, she thought, no longer beautiful. Michau would not like that! *Eh bien,* it no longer mattered. There would be no more publicity shots.

She looked down at her fingers. She had been proud of them, long fingers for a small person, tapering at the ends. She curved them now as if to place them on the keys of her flute—but no. That was in the past. She had a different concern now.

"Zut," she told her reflection. "No one ever looked less a fighter than you, Ebriel Serique."

Ty, however, seemed satisfied with her appearance when she returned to the common room. "Okay! That's better, isn't it? Up for some grunt work?"

Ebriel nodded and followed her out through the heat to a storage building. They spent a hot hour transferring parts and supplies to a wooden shed near the airfield. They stacked cartons of zeolite, for the air purifiers, Ty said. They dollied canisters of liquid oxygen and nitrogen. They moved a whole pallet of boxes with InCo labels. "Whenever we go up, we take as much as we can," Ty told Ebriel. "We bring a lot down, too. Papa maintains his neutral status by supplying both InCo and Oceania with his latest creations, engineered seeds, new medicines. Those come from Starhold. And the Fleckcell plants churn out the fuel cells."

Ebriel helped lift and stack and push as best she could, but she had to stop often to rest. When the work was finished, her arms and legs trembled, and she was glad when they returned to the kitchen for breakfast. For the first time in weeks, she was hungry. The exercise, she supposed. And the feeling of purpose.

She startled at the sound of a voice over a speaker. Ty touched her shoulder. "It's okay," she said. "It's the shortband. Bird's comin' in."

They trooped out to the landing field again. The heat had intensified. Shimmering waves of it rose from the runways, suffocating the bit of breeze from the ridge. Ebriel felt the dryness in her nostrils, in the pads of her fingertips. She stood behind the others, shading her eyes as they did and watching the western horizon.

A copter identical to the one that had brought her to Siwa whirred across the expanse of sand toward them, looking like some great blue insect, its rotors invisible as they spun. It extended complex, flexible legs toward the ground as it hovered, air from its rotors whipping the sand around the field, lifting the strands of Ebriel's hair, tugging at Nenet's headscarf. The copter settled smoothly, hydraulics hissing. The rotors slowed and stopped, and the door slid open.

A stocky woman with chin-length yellow hair waved at the group waiting beside the field. Ty trotted across the field toward her.

Before Ty reached the copter, a second woman came to the door. Her hair was light brown, her figure tall and narrow. She held a dark-skinned, curly-haired child in her arms.

Pilar and Nenet hurried forward. Ebriel couldn't move.

The tiny child's arms and his dangling legs were painfully thin. His eyes rolled, showing the whites as he took in the alien surroundings. As Ty reached up to lift him down, a second child appeared in the door.

This one stood on her own feet. Her full dark lips pressed hard together as she glared at the strange scene. This one, Ebriel thought, though so young—this one looks like a fighter.

Ty turned with the little boy in her arms. Ebriel felt as if she couldn't breathe.

Children. Their soft skin, their wide eyes, their vulnerable faces—she couldn't bear it.

She stepped back as they approached, and Ty cast her a questioning glance. Pilar, leading the older child by the hand, didn't notice. Nenet brought the two new Chain members directly to Ebriel and introduced them.

"Ebriel Serique," she said with a gesture. "Georgia Barry. Astrid Sorensen."

An hour later, the receiver in the barracks crackled again, and the Chain members began to gather their things. Nenet had laid food out for the two children, and they had eaten everything and submitted to being washed and petted and soothed. The little boy, whose name they learned was Manu, slept fitfully in the arms of Georgia Barry. The young girl, Kanika, stood watching over her brother, wary whenever anyone moved suddenly. Astrid Sorensen stayed close beside her. Occasionally she murmured a few words in an odd singsong language.

Ty said to Ebriel, "That's Krio. It's a creole they speak on the coast." She laughed. "I don't think Astrid's accent is too good."

Ebriel was speechless. The two children could be hardly more confused than she herself was. Children? Why children? Her mind reeled.

"Ready?" the American asked. She held something out, and Ebriel was surprised to see that it was her own shoulder bag in Ty's hand, its scarlet and black brocade looking out of place.

"*Mon Dieu*—where did you get it?" she breathed. "I have not seen it since—since . . ."

Ty said, "Since Geneva. I picked it up in Ariana Park. Thought you might want it."

Ebriel couldn't think what was in it. It had belonged to someone who no longer existed.

Ty shrugged. "It's okay," she said. "I'll haul it along. If you want it, it's here."

"*Merci*," Ebriel said softly. "I do not know if I want it or not."

"That's okay."

"What will happen now?"

Ty pointed with her thumb at the airfield. "*Unicorn*'s about fifteen minutes out."

"*Unicorn?*"

Ty flashed a grin. "*Unicorn* is one of the spaceplanes. There are two, *Unicorn* and *Troll*."

"Spaceplane," Ebriel repeated.

Ty nodded. "Yup. Coming from Xiao Qaidam. We're going up tonight."

"It is true, then—about the star hotel."

"Did you think I made it up?"

Ebriel made a shaky sound that was almost a laugh. "*Non*—I hardly knew what to think. InCo tells us there are no resources, no fuel, no money—if the polities cannot build such a thing—"

"Right." Ty stuffed a few last-minute items into a duffel. "Well, they'd already built the hotel, meant for tourists. And one spaceplane. The Flecks built the second one on the same model." She straightened. "Since the Mars disaster, none of the polities will expend a dime on space. Except the microsats, of course, for communication, and even those are falling apart. Papa fixes 'em now and again. They're useful."

They walked out to the landing field in a little ragged line. Georgia still carried the boy, Manu. Kanika walked close behind, with blond Astrid on her right. Ebriel came last, keeping her distance from the children. The afternoon sky was pale blue, utterly empty. Standing in the dry grass, Ebriel followed Ty's gaze to the northeast.

The sound reached them first, a muted roar, a thrumming deep in the ear as if someone were plucking the low E string of a double bass. A black dot appeared above the sand hills, growing swiftly, the sound deepening impossibly as it came nearer. Ebriel startled when Ty touched her arm. Everyone else was moving into the shed. Following Ty, Ebriel took shelter with the others. They stood just inside and watched the craft come.

The spaceplane was a great vee shape, painted a deep black. It appeared above the old city and sank toward the airfield. Ebriel's ears ached with the sound of the engines, the low-pitched, intense noise as of a gigantic pot on the boil. The great cylinders of the fuel cells fitted neatly under the swept-back wings. The slender fuselage made a slight arch from nose to tail.

The little boy woke and whimpered. His sister quieted him.

Four squat cylinders appeared beneath the wings of the spaceplane, swiveling out of their nests beside the fuel cells, thrusting with powerful air-jets. The craft settled onto the field with an enormous rush of air and a deep metallic groan. Flexible joints meshed, adjusted, came to rest.

Ebriel took a swift breath, stunned by the power, the weird beauty of Ethan Fleck's spaceplane. Ty, beside her, made a deep assenting sound in her throat. "Oh, yeah," she said. "I remember what it's like, to see it for the first time. Straight out of the history books."

It was indeed, Ebriel thought wonderingly, history come to life. Such craft had not been seen since the manned mission to Mars when Ebriel had been only a child. Space tourism died with the Mars astronauts, and the end of significant sources of fossil fuels triggered the Crash. Ebriel had grown up knowing that spending resources on space was pointless.

Except for Ethan Fleck's habitat. Without Ethan Fleck, the citizens of InCo might have been working by candlelight, burning what was left of the forests, dying in the cold. At the end of the oil age, after the Crash and the quarantine, only Ethan Fleck could straddle boundaries, live in space. What must such a man be like?

The spaceplane's doors opened, and a stair extended. It seemed she would find out.

8

Weightlessness, Ebriel thought at first, felt like swimming in the salty waters of the Mediterranean. Her body felt buoyant, and her hair lifted to float before her eyes in thick strands. Then her stomach seemed to invert, and the fluid in her ears rocked, making her dizzy. She grasped at the wide webbing holding her in her cushioned seat.

Next to her Ty said, "Not to worry, it doesn't last long. The docking program has us now. We'll be in electrogravity before you know it."

Ty had just returned from the flight deck. The other passengers had been quiet throughout the atmospheric journey, the children lulled to sleep almost immediately by the dark, monotonous roar of *Unicorn*'s drive. Ebriel had watched mother Earth fall away, breathless with wonder at the curve of the planet's mass, at the blue and white and gray swirls across its face. As *Unicorn* rose into the almost-black of space, all the problems of the planet below, the particulate-laden atmosphere, the damaged croplands, dying rain forests, the tainted oceans, seemed to drop away. Even Ebriel's grief was diminished by the marvels around her.

A burst of power pushed her down into the accommodating seat and then, again, she floated. Her stomach quivered.

Her ears popped. She closed her eyes and pressed her hand to her lips, afraid she would be sick.

Ty tapped her shoulder. Ebriel opened her eyes and followed Ty's pointing finger.

It was tiny at first, a star among stars, flickering with yellow and amber and gold lights. As short bursts of power brought it nearer, its ovoid shape became clear, spiraled with layers of fuel cells like the whorls of some enormous seashell. The long delicate wings of its rectennae spread around it, soaking up the rays of the sun. Ebriel forgot her discomfort.

Long docking arms lifted out from the habitat, reaching to embrace *Unicorn*. Weight returned, pulling Ebriel in the other direction, the webbing pressing against her chest. Ty said, "Deceleration. Almost there now."

"It is beautiful," Ebriel murmured. "I did not know it would be beautiful. It is like—" For a moment she forgot her grim purpose in the wonder of it. "It is like a castle among the stars."

Ty grinned. "You bet," she said. "Papa would love that. A castle." She waved a hand in a grand gesture as *Unicorn* settled into place. "Starhold," she said with pride. "Welcome, Ebriel."

Ebriel felt anything but at home as she stood in the cramped docking bay, waiting for the inner door to the habitat to open. Her stomach had settled soon after she felt the pull of gravity, but she felt weary and disoriented. Robot arms and cranes and upended dollies crowded the narrow, high-ceilinged space. Ty and Ebriel stood shoulder to shoulder with *Unicorn*'s flight crew, the yawning children, the other Chain members. Pilar rubbed her eyes and stretched, and Astrid whispered calming words to the fretful little boy. Ebriel felt fretful herself, her skin itchy from the pressurized air, her eyes dry from sleeplessness.

With a hiss, the inner door slid back. Several women, and one man, in colorful relaxed cotton shirts and trousers, called greetings and reached to help Astrid and Georgia with the children. Pilar smiled at Ebriel over her shoulder as she left the bay. Ty said, "Watch the sill," and led the way. Ebriel followed her out, stepping carefully over the rubbery rim of the airseals.

It was like walking into a kaleidoscope. She found herself in an arcade splashed with blue and violet and red, with greenery everywhere. Vines trailed from the high ceiling, airplants clung to the brightly painted walls, flowers and shrubs bloomed in containers of every size and shape. The swirl of color surrounded a translucent tube perhaps three meters in diameter. Two people soared upward as Ebriel watched, touching the sides with their feet, briefly seizing flexible staples set into the sides. A third person, either very young or very small, passed in the other direction, head to foot. Ebriel took a hasty step backward to lean against the wall behind her.

Ty put a hand under her elbow. "You'll get used to it," she said. "No gravity in the tube, but there is everywhere else, except in Papa's level." She swept out her arm. "This is the gallery. Living quarters—cubbies—are the next level down, and below that, the gardens."

"It is so large—bigger than I thought it would be."

"Hardly big enough." Ty pointed to the ceiling. "Above this is where Papa lives."

Ebriel blinked, trying to resolve the jumble of colors and shapes into some sort of order. She kept a steadying hand on the wall as a gray-haired woman approached her. The woman wore brown cottons, the first dull color Ebriel had seen, and she spoke in an oddly flat voice. "Ty, I'm sorry I'm late. I got held up." She held out her hand to Ebriel. "You must be Ebriel Serique. I'm Semaya Fleck. Welcome."

"Merci, madame." Ebriel shook the thin white hand.

"Difficult flight?"

"Non," Ebriel said. She straightened, trying to hide her weakness.

The older woman's gaze assessed her. "Give it time," she said. "Ty will take you to your cubby. I've put clothes there for you. If they don't fit, we'll dig up some others."

"Merci," Ebriel said again. The woman nodded and moved on to speak to someone else.

Ty led Ebriel to the tube. She stepped sideways into the metal and plastic cylinder that led into it and grinned back at Ebriel. "The slip," she said.

Ebriel sidled into the cylinder after her, one cautious step.

The next led to empty air, to nothingness. Her weight vanished, and she gasped and clutched at the edge of the slip.

Ty nodded. "Okay?" she said. With a wave of her hand, she reversed her direction and floated upward. "Come on," she said. "This way."

Ebriel clung to a flexible staple, her cheeks hot and her spine rigid. Ethan Fleck's room, the control center, filled the hemispheric top of Starhold. Ethan Fleck floated in a null-grav chair, his wasted arms and legs restrained by straps, his head supported by a molded cushion. His fingers flicked ceaselessly over tiny keypads set into the arms of the chair. When he spoke, his voice seesawed up and down the scale like the tortured scrapes of a beginning violinist. Only his bright brown eyes seemed unaffected by his illness.

"Madame Serique." The chair hovered in front of Ebriel's handhold and one corner of his mouth pulled up in a cheerful grimace that was meant to be a smile. "You're angry."

There were children on Starhold, dozens of children. They dashed past her as she toured the cubbies, swirled around her in the gallery like a flock of tropical birds, brightly dressed, every color and size, laughing and chattering, overflowing with energy. With life.

She said through a tight throat, "I did not understand about the children."

Fleck's fingers danced on his keypads. His chair turned abruptly on its side as he looked at one of the many glowing monitors that lined the round room. The cubbies on the level below the gallery were tiny square bedrooms set in quadrangles, four to a side, but this room modeled the curvature of the hull. Screens and input devices bristled from every surface. The lights were dim, and a small space window, distanced from vacuum by the depth of the habitat's shielding, glistened with a thick field of stars.

The chair turned upside down, from Ebriel's perspective, making her feel as if she were falling. She clung hard to the staple, swallowing, gritting her teeth. A moment later, the chair completed its circle, and Ethan Fleck faced her.

"I'm sorry you're upset."

Ebriel closed her eyes briefly. When she opened them she saw warmth in Fleck's eyes, a sympathy his voice couldn't convey. She tried not to give in to it. "Ty should have told me."

"It's a security issue," he rasped. "If InCo knew, my neutrality would be compromised." His chair hung in front of her, briefly stationary. "They tolerate my spaceplanes because they want my ideas, my gadgets, even my help from time to time. If they knew of our other activities, they would certainly interfere. You see, Ebriel," he said. "We hide in plain sight."

"But Ty knows that I—" Ebriel's voice broke. She looked away.

"I know, too," he croaked in his tortured voice. "You've had a great sorrow."

"I do not think I can be with children."

Above Ebriel's head, a monitor chimed, and Fleck's chair shot upward. Minute spurts of air puffed from tiny jets in its frame. Ebriel glanced up at the monitor, and then around at the others. Some played Newnet broadcasts, some were text-only. Others had the odd perspectives of spybug cameras, with numbers and symbols flowing beneath them. Fleck made a circuit of the room, then rotated his chair to match her position. "Always busy."

"Dr. Fleck, I understood the Chain to be—to be the maquis. The *résistance.*"

"And so it is." When his crooked smile relaxed, it left his features slack, and Ebriel saw that he was indeed very ill. "When we can find them, we take children from perilous circumstances. From almost certain death. We give them lives of purpose. We do our best to give them the power of information, the strength of knowledge. And when we have done that, we perform our most difficult task: we restore them to their homelands."

"But why? What good can it do?"

Fleck's lopsided smile returned, and his brilliant eyes twinkled beneath their sagging lids. " 'Never doubt,' " he said, " 'that a small group of thoughtful, committed citizens can change the world.' Do you recognize the quote?"

Ebriel shook her head.

"No, I suppose no one remembers Margaret Mead now. A

shame. But we believe that. We're small enough, and committed enough. I hope we're thoughtful. We're reseeding the latent countries through their best resource—theirs and ours."

Ebriel couldn't bear to look into those brilliant eyes anymore. She glanced away, to one of the monitors. It showed a
wobbling picture of a beach, waves crashing, a boat bobbing
at anchor. The picture changed as the spybug flew along the
coastline. It responded to movement, dipping down toward
the water when a flock of birds rose from it, cutting inland to
scan a quiet village scene. It was, most certainly, not a scene
from one of the InCo polities.

"You—you have spybugs!" she stammered.

"Yes," Fleck squeaked, and then rumbled, "We have a few
spybugs of our own, and we monitor the ones InCo sends out.
We're hacked into the microsats."

"Then—did you—" She could hardly speak through her
stiff lips. "Did you see what happened to *L'Oiseau blanc*? To
my—my—" she couldn't finish her question.

His voice was incapable of expressing his emotion, but his
eyes darkened. "We didn't see it. It all happened too fast, and
we had no one in the area."

"But—do you know what happened?"

"We know some of it."

"Was it true, Dr. Fleck?" Ebriel's voice rose, louder than
she had intended, hot with emotion. Fury. "Was *L'Oiseau
blanc* over the Line of Partition?"

For a moment she thought he would not answer. Slowly, he
said, "I'm not sure. You mustn't torture yourself. There was
nothing anyone could do."

Tears spilled, all at once, from Ebriel's eyes. They floated
in the microgravity, clear droplets glittering in the green and
blue and amber lights. A drop struck Fleck's withered cheek.

"Je regrette," she whispered, and looked away.

"Don't apologize. You have every right to grieve. Semaya
and I grieve for every child we bring to Starhold, for the past
that has hurt them, for their uncertain future."

"Why did you bring me here?"

He didn't speak, but a thread of music spun into the dim
space from some hidden speaker. It was familiar to Ebriel,

very familiar. Mozart. The Flute Quartet in D, the *adagio*.

"That is my recording," Ebriel whispered. "With the principals of La Villette."

"You can bring something to our children that none of us can," he answered. "Music."

She shook her head vehemently. "*Non*. I am sorry. There will be no more music for me. Had it not been for my music—" She broke off. The Mozart stopped. "Dr. Fleck. I came here to learn to—to resist." She kept her eyes down, afraid this strange man would read her true thoughts. "You can send me back. Perhaps that would be best."

There was a silence. The monitors around them glimmered, the lights flashed.

At last he spoke again in his harsh, uneven voice. "No, Ebriel, I don't want to send you back. I'll put my plan aside. Do you want to join us?"

Ebriel looked at him from beneath her eyelashes. "*Oui*. If you will have me."

The distorted smile flashed again. "We're agreed, then."

"*Merci*. Thank you, Dr. Fleck."

"And Ebriel. Do you think you could call me Papa? Everyone else does."

A vine overhung the door of the cubby assigned to Ebriel. She ducked to pass under it and saw that it was heavy with purple grapes. Ty, coming behind her, reached up to pick a handful and stood eating them, leaning against the wall.

The tiny room held a bed set into one wall, with a closet and shallow drawers built into the opposite wall. Someone had hung clothes in the closet for her, the simple, vivid tunics and trousers everyone seemed to wear. Ty had laid her brocade bag on the bed.

Ebriel opened the trundle drawer under the bed and dropped the bag in.

Ty said, "Will you remember it's there?"

Ebriel shrugged.

"Listen, Ebriel, I'm sorry about not telling you everything. We can't. It's not safe."

"I know. He explained it to me."

"So now you've seen everything except the gardens. Do you want to go down there?"

"Will there be—will we be alone?"

"Alone, probably not. Hard to be alone here, to tell the truth. But if you're worried about kids, they won't be there. It's past 2030, and they're in the crèche now. Bedtime."

Ebriel's vision blurred, and she turned abruptly away. The memory surfaced before she could stop it—Renée, dimpled cheeks rosy, flushed from her bath, soft quilt pulled up under her chin. Bedtime. Stories, kisses, hugs, glasses of water, night-lights. Simple joys, gone forever. She blinked her tears away. Tears would not win her revenge. She lifted her chin and turned back to Ty with a smile that felt as brittle as ice.

"*Oui.* If you are not too tired, Ty. I would like to see the gardens."

The tube would take practice, Ebriel knew. Others soared past her with deft kicks and touches, while she worked her way from staple to staple, hesitant, her stomach quivering. Ty went slowly, waiting for her. When they reached the slip on the garden level, it was a relief to put her feet on the floor again.

The gardens were thick with hydroponics and aeroponics, the air pungent with the sharp scents of tomatoes and peppers and the sunny sweetness of berries. Ty picked a dark bean and held it in her palm for Ebriel to see. "Do you like chocolate?"

"I used to."

"This is a bioengineered cocoa bean—to grow in cooler climates. InCo loves this one."

They walked on, Ty pointing out other plants, talking about hybrid seeds, hydroponics mediums, protein content. Ebriel stopped listening. Beyond the tangle of vegetation, she caught sight of an enormous space window. The circle of Earth swelled beyond it, haloed with refracted sunlight. Ebriel hurried forward, crunching dry rock foam beneath her feet. She looked down on the night-dark globe.

To the south and east, where the edge of the window

blocked the perimeter, the planet was dark, but a lace of lights spread across the European continent. Ebriel bent forward to trace the lights with her finger, north from Italy, east from France.

Her enemy was there, somewhere in the starlit night. He was there. She would find him.

9

In the dining hall on the gallery level, Ebriel stood before the assembled residents, weary and frustrated. Her thighs trembled from her first session in the dojo. The simplest things the sensei had asked of her, that everyone else in the class seemed to do without effort, had been all but impossible for her. The flight simulator confused her utterly. The cramped spaces of the habitat made her claustrophobic. There was no place to hide, and no place to escape.

Only her new duty belt comforted her. It carried simple tools—a micro-light, an aid kit, a tiny laser cutter—and it had a sleeve for a pulse pistol. Vee Eyckart, the Tacticals instructor, showed her one of the little weapons. "Invisible to scanners. That's why it's illegal." She pointed it at a target: "At this distance, you can disable your enemy. It interrupts the nerve impulses." Vee was the oldest Chain member, a military veteran, gray-haired and thickset, still strong at sixty-five. She took several steps toward the target until she was within a half meter. "At this distance, he's dead. Or she is." She glanced over her shoulder at Ebriel. "Disrupt the field long enough, body forgets to breathe. Heart forgets to beat." Ebriel nodded, keeping her face impassive. "But keep track of your charge

count," Vee added. "No good if your charge is depleted."
Ebriel nodded again. She would not forget.

Now, in the dining hall, faces of every color turned up to
hers. Already she could guess which were the Chain, muscu-
lar, straight-shouldered, clear-eyed women, a few men. Ebriel's
advent made their number thirty-three. There were also three
nurses, a dozen teachers, a karate sensei, a judo shihan, a hydroponics specialist, and several technicians. They were seated
at long tables, and in and around them were the children, more
than sixty children, ranging in age from four to seventeen,
representing twenty-two different countries. At the end of one
table stood a makeshift bassinet, not much more than a padded
box on legs.

Semaya held up a hand. A child chattered loudly in the
sudden silence, and someone hushed her gently. The infant in
the bassinet cooed, a small, poignant sound. Behind Ebriel
and Semaya ran a narrow space window, but the brightness of
the interior lights dimmed the stars. Artificial stars of some
silvery material were fixed on the wall above and below the
window.

The room overflowed with vines and small fruit trees in
pots. The greenery masked the molded panels, bolts and cable
cases, struts and seams of the habitat's superstructure. Ebriel
took it all in, beginning to understand that despite the abun-
dant color, Star Hotel One—Starhold—was first and foremost
a space station. If there was charm, it was in its simplicity, its
spareness. There was nothing extra. There was nothing unnecessary. She thought with a pang of the polished glass and shining tile of her Paris apartment.

"Good evening, everyone," Semaya said. Her toneless
voice reminded Ebriel of the clunking of a broken piano key.
She held her hands linked together, the fingers still, palms a
little apart. "I would like to introduce to you Ebriel Serique,
our newest Chain member. She comes from Paris. Please
make her welcome."

Several people spoke quiet greetings, and everyone nodded, smiled. Ebriel nodded stiffly in return, grateful not to be
expected to say anything. Semaya took a seat at the head of
one of the tables, and Ebriel made her way to Ty, to sit beside
her as a plump woman with an apron over her cottons brought

out the meal on large resin platters, green and yellow vegetables, round loaves of bread, a steaming stew of tofu and fish. Talk and laughter bubbled up to fill the hall.

Ty helped herself and passed the dishes to Ebriel with a grin. "It's a simple diet—only get meat planetside."

On Ebriel's left, Ty discussed repairs to one of the copters with a technician. On her right, a teenaged girl, dark-skinned and intense, described a book she had found in her language program to one of the teachers. Ebriel ate in silence, hungry after the unaccustomed exercise. After the stew, platters of fruit appeared, scarlet berries, green grapes, something pink that tasted like a salty cherry. A platter of cookies worked its way down the table. The Chain passed them on to the children, who devoured them, scavenged the crumbs from the empty plates, and licked their fingers.

Ty winked at Ebriel. "Sugar's kinda scarce," she said.

The older children cleared the dishes and stacked them in bins. Semaya Fleck rose and went to a large wall panel, murmuring a command.

A map of Earth appeared, looking strange to Ebriel without the Line of Partition. There were no dark countries, no illumined polities of North America, Europe, Todokai. There were only the silhouettes of the continents, the spaces of sea and ocean, the islands, the polar caps, nothing to show the great nations there had once been or the fragments they left behind—China collapsed into squabbling provinces, India and Pakistan poisoned with nuclear fallout, the Middle East and Africa afire with biochemical contamination and disease.

A hush settled over the room. Even the children were more or less still. Semaya touched the map, lighting an area of South America. She said, "Marina, Pedro, ChiChi, Nuncia."

With a brief rustle and scraping of chairs, four youngsters stood up.

Semaya said, pointing to the map, "This is Brasilia. The mayor of the city died yesterday as the result of a bullet wound. No one has succeeded him. Everyone who might step into the office of mayor, we're supposing, is afraid of being the next to be assassinated. The water shortage in the city is critical, and those who can are leaving the city to move into the countryside. One man is drilling a well in the middle of

the city, and his neighbors have formed a barrier around it to
protect the workers. People are congregating in abandoned
buildings."

At one corner of the panel, an inserted spybug video
showed faces looking out of broken windows, people in
ragged clothing lounging in doorways. "A priest from the Cat-
edral Metropolitana has been working to create some sort of
order. Police are arresting black market water sellers, but they
can't jail them because they can't feed them. The bodies of
three street children were found yesterday in the business district." The video showed a badly focused picture of two men
wearing uniform shirts and denims carrying something between them. The Brazilian children, solemn-faced, sat down.
Ebriel's stomach clenched.

Semaya touched a different part of the map, the west coast
of Africa. "Kanika, Manu."

The two children from Sierra Leone stood up. "Our newest
students," Semaya said.

A wavering picture of an empty beach fringed by jungle
sprang up in the corner of the panel. "This is your homeland.
We still have spybugs there, and they've shown more bandits
on the coastline. One gang set fire to a village here, in the
farmland south of Bonjimba. The fire destroyed the rice har-
vest. A few villagers reached Freetown, and the underground
nets picked up the report from them."

A sibilant whisper reached Ebriel's ears. She turned her
head and saw that a teacher was translating for the two dark-
skinned children. The little one, Manu, clung to his sister's
hand. Kanika held her head high, her eyes blazing as if she
understood every English word.

"A Red Omega ship with medicines and infant formula
sailed for Sierra Leone, but it hasn't been heard from. InCo
denies interfering with it. Our spybugs never picked it up, so
we don't know what happened."

The children sat down, and Semaya went on to another
part of the map, repeating the ritual. Ebriel's feeling of hope-
lessness intensified with each recitation.

At the end, Semaya crossed the room to stand before
the space window. She touched one of the silver stars set into
the wall. "Aisha Udin," she said. There were nods and a few

affirmative words around the room. "Aisha is working on an agricultural project outside Jerusalem. She reached Nenet on the shortband, saying that the drought-tolerant sugarbeet is doing very well. And—" Semaya's pale, wrinkled face showed no expression. "Aisha found some people from her old kibbutz, people who knew her parents."

A sigh passed through the room, acknowledging good news.

Semaya pointed to another star. "Catarina Pellar. She's only been back in Peru for six months, but already she has a small school organized, in Tingo Maria. She has nine pupils studying English and math, and learning to read and write English and Spanish."

Again a little breath of satisfaction swept the long tables. Ebriel bowed her head, unable to share it. Such tiny triumphs, in the face of immense evil. How could they bear it, the swell of hope and optimism? How could they bear to send these children out into an uncertain future?

The hall emptied. Ty went off with the technician to look at some schematics, and Pilar went to the crèche. Ebriel, left alone, crossed the room to the wall of silver stars. Names and places had been engraved in them. Chun Shaiming, Xing'an, Hunan Province. Meryem Sivas, Cankiri, Turkey. Alile Kabir, Tajarhi, Libya. Edvalda Pereira da Silva, Itaboca, Brazil. Names as alien to Ebriel as if they belonged to another world.

When she turned away, she saw Semaya Fleck standing by the door to the gallery, watching her. "What are you thinking as you look at our wall of stars?"

"I am thinking how few they are."

"There will be more."

Ebriel glanced back at the display. "They are very sad."

"It's a sad world." Semaya walked across the room to join Ebriel. She traced a star with her finger. "This is Graciela. She was ten years old when she came to us, one of our first students. The Chain was only half-formed when one of them pulled Graciela out of Manaus. She was about to be sold as a prostitute."

Ebriel almost couldn't bring herself to ask. "Where is she now?"

"She's home again in Brazil. She's twenty years old, and

she runs a clinic near her old home. She teaches family planning. Birth control. And hygiene, infant care, basic things. Things we take for granted. Her people once had cattle, coffee and banana and orange plantations. When the rain forests were burned to free up more land, the smoke interrupted the cycle of rainfall, ruined everything. The embargo has made it infinitely worse, because they can't trade what they have left for what they need."

"How do you keep in touch?"

"Each of our students has a shorthand radio, and a backup. And Ethan has friends all over the world. Some still work for Fleckcell. We try to have a contact for each of our children."

She stroked a star set very near the space window. "Jawhar. A very brave boy. He was abandoned at the age of eight in the mountains of Afghanistan. He went back three years ago, and the militia forced him into enscription. We tracked him for a year before we lost him."

"And you never knew—"

Semaya shook her head. "No." She pointed to a star set close to the floor. "Agnessa's village in Kuwait was wiped out by nerve gas. Agnessa was four, a lovely child. She made it to Starhold, but it was too late to save her." Semaya's voice and face remained neutral as she recited the terrible stories. "It was Agnessa who began calling our students starchildren. We don't use the word, really, but the children do. Agnessa wanted so much to be a starchild. We put her star very low, so she could see it. She died not long after."

"Four," Ebriel breathed. *"Nom de Dieu."*

"We no longer bring ill children up. We simply can't. There isn't room."

This pragmatic cruelty silenced Ebriel completely.

Semaya said, "We're disappointed that you won't be teaching music. A pity."

"I cannot," Ebriel murmured.

Semaya linked her hands before her, looking out the space window at the faint blur of the stars. " 'The man that hath no music in himself . . . is fit for treasons, strategems, and spoils.' "

Ebriel lifted her eyebrows. Semaya made a small gesture with her linked hands. "I'm sorry. I can't say it in French, and I misquoted it in any case. Shakespeare."

"For me there is no more music," Ebriel said. "That part of my life, it is finished."

"A pity," Semaya repeated. "Ethan loves your recordings."

Ebriel went out of the dining hall, past the classrooms with their rows of study hoods, past the dojo, the clinic, the empty kitchen. The walls seemed to close in on her, every space chokingly small, every surface cluttered. She went into the slip and struggled away from the gallery level. The lights had been extinguished, except for small amber guiding lights.

She closed her cubby door behind her and opened the trundle drawer under the bed. She pulled out the shoulder bag and stared at it, tempted to stuff the whole thing in the recycle chute. That last morning in the Rue Georgette, she had poured out her score discs and stuffed in—what? Clothes, the knife she had left lying in the grass of Ariana Park, a little money— abruptly, awkwardly, she tore open the bag. The clothes were there, a purse, a flat wallet of still photos. And her flute case, smooth brown leather, as familiar as her own skin. The urge to put her fingers to the catches and release them was still there, a habit. She had played since the age of five.

But what she had told Semaya was true. That part of her life had died.

She dropped the bag into the trundle drawer and closed the drawer with her foot.

10

The scattered flakes of snow falling on the Montana highway melted as they touched the pavement, but James peered through the truck's windshield at the lowering sky, worrying about the storm. He was supposed to fly out to Colorado Springs in the morning. In November, as James knew from experience, snowfall on the northern plains could thicken to a blizzard with little warning. He and his friends had been caught by just such a storm when he was only twelve, hunting deer in the hills above Browning. He rubbed the back of his neck, remembering.

By the time he reached the ranch house, snow mounded the hood and roof of the derelict truck in the yard. The blackberry vines had dried to brown sticks, frosted now with snow. He parked the cell truck and lifted the carton from the seat beside him. He had shopped at the PX before he left Malmstrom.

He looked up at the house. His father stood in the doorway, watching him as he crossed to the porch. He didn't smile, but he held the door open as James climbed the steps.

"Jimmy," he said. "You shoulda called. I would've fixed up your room."

"That's okay, Dad." James stepped past his father into the

house and nodded at the wave of warm air that swept out. "Fuel cell's working, I see," he said.

"Oh, yeah, sure," his father said. He closed the door and followed James into the kitchen. "What've you got there?"

James set the carton on the table and took off his flight jacket. He hung it over the back of a chair. "Brought you a few things," he said. He glanced at Gil. The old man looked a bit better than on his last visit. He had shaved, and his hair was trimmed. His shirt was worn, but it looked clean. "You're looking pretty good, Dad," James ventured.

Gil shrugged, avoiding his eyes. "Yeah, ya know. Clean up my act a little."

Feeling a little foolish, James held out the shirt. The plastic casing crinkled under his fingers. "I thought this might be your size."

Gil's eyes flicked over his son. He hesitated, and then he took the package.

"It's reworked fabric, but it's okay, I think."

Gil slid the shirt out of the plastic. His veined hand lingered on the plaid flannel. "Yeah, Jimmy. Looks like my size," he said gruffly.

James emptied the carton, putting foilpacks in a cupboard, setting a packet of instant coffee on the counter. He brought out three chocolate bars and laid them on the table.

"What's that?" Gil asked, picking it up. "Chocolate? Real chocolate?"

James laughed. "Haven't seen that in a while, have we? There's a new strain of beans. They grow it in Greece now, and Mexico."

"That's nice. That's real nice, Jimmy. Gonna share it with Otis."

"Otis is still around?"

Gil moved to the sink to fill a kettle with water and set it on the stove. "Yeah. Otis and me, we've been fixing up the Tribal Office. Thinking about a pow-wow in the spring."

"That's good, Dad. Good idea." James moved the empty carton to the back porch and came back to sit at the table. He glanced around the kitchen. It still looked bare, but it was fairly clean. A grocery sack half-full of empty beer bottles leaned against the wall by the back door. Gil's hands trembled as he spooned instant coffee into two mugs, poured the boiling water, handed James a cup.

Gil sat down with his mug between his hands and squinted at his son through wisps of steam. "We heard, down at the Nation, that Red Omega lost another ship out there. Across the Line."

"I can't talk about that, Dad. I'm Security Corps, and that's classified."

Gil set the mug down with a thud. Drops of black coffee spotted the bare wood of the table. "Yeah, well. Wouldn't be surprised if General Glass himself sank that ship."

James stiffened. "You shouldn't say that. The Line protects the InCo polities. Protects you!"

"Yeah, well, they don't do me any favors. And that guy's too slick for his own good. That ship was probably full of medicines for people who need 'em."

"Dad—"

Gil's reddened eyes narrowed with the old anger. "Fuckin' InCo! Can't trust 'em, Jimmy, I'm tellin' ya. Especially that George Glass—his father was no good, either!"

"You don't know that!"

"Oh, no? Listen, Jimmy, you was just a kid when they drew that Line, and I'm tellin' ya, there were a lot of stories goin' around. Glass got that job because his own father was in Dirty Tricks Corps, and he—"

"There isn't any Dirty Tricks Corps, Dad. Nobody believes that old story."

"Oh, no? Well, I do, and so does Otis, and a bunch of other people." Gil's voice shook with the old rage, undimmed with the passing years. James watched his shaking hand swiping at the spilled coffee. It occurred to him that what Gil wanted was a drink, but that he was putting it off while James was there. His heart softened. "Look, Dad. Security Corps protects all of us, the Nation, too. That's why I joined. You want biochems here, or nukes? The world was coming apart when they drew the Line."

Gil snorted and wiped his mouth with the back of his hand.

James drew breath to say more, but the chime of his earplant interrupted him. "James? Michael Chang here. It looks like there's a storm coming down from Alberta. We'll have to fly out tonight. Can you make it back to Malmstrom in three hours?"

Gil watched with narrowed eyes as James tongued his lip-mike. "Hi, Michael. Yes, if I leave now I can. On my way." He tongued it off again, and drained his coffee mug. "Sorry, Dad. I'll need to get going. There's a storm coming south from Canada."

Gil watched him shrug into his flight jacket and adjust his cap. "This Michael—he's a buddy of yours?"

"He's my flight instructor."

"You're gonna stay in the service."

James nodded. "It's good work. And plenty of opportunities."

His father rose stiffly. He set the coffee mugs in the sink. "Yeah," he said hoarsely. "Not much of that up here, I guess. Not for a young man." He looked up to meet James's eyes. There seemed to be nothing to say. Their years of estrangement hung between them, a gulf as wide and unpassable as the Line of Partition.

James shuffled his feet, feeling awkward. "Look, Dad—" he began.

Gil said, "You ever think of getting married, Jimmy? Marriage is a good thing for a man.

James looked away, out the window where the snow was falling faster. How could he tell this old man about his loneliness? His father was a stranger. Michael Chang was the closest thing James had to a friend, and not all that close. As for women . . . there had been women. But the kind of women Michael and the others spent their off-duty hours with didn't appeal to James. Such encounters seemed pointless and empty.

"No, Dad. I never think about getting married. I guess I'm on the move too much."

"You oughta think about that."

James didn't answer.

The old man walked him to the door and stood on the front porch as James crossed the yard to his truck. As James opened the door, Gil called to him, "Jimmy!"

"Yes, Dad."

"Thanks for the shirt. It's real nice. It was a real nice thought."

James smiled through the falling snow. "You're welcome."

"Stay in touch, son, okay?"

"I will. You take care."

James backed and turned the truck and drove away. He knew how much his father wanted—needed—a drink. But the old man stood in the open doorway, framed by the yellow light from the kitchen, until James reached the end of the long drive and turned onto the highway.

When *Unicorn* landed at Siwa, Ty and Ebriel were the first to climb out. Stars glimmered from the violet sky of early evening, and the rush of heat from the landing field was startling after the coolness of the spaceplane's conditioned air. Nenet Nasser hurried out of the wooden shed as soon as the engines powered down, and she stood before Ebriel, her hands spread wide in amazement. "*Marhaba,* Ebriel," she exclaimed. "I would not have known you."

Ebriel pushed her fingers through her hair. With the help of one of the cooks, she had cut it as short as Ty's, though it still curled around her ears and over her forehead. It had gone completely ash-gray. "I know," she said to Nenet. "It is very different, *non?*"

"Not just your hair," Nenet said. She put her hand on Ebriel's arm, where her small, hard bicep bulged under the material of the utility suit. Her thighs, too, were developing ridges of muscle. Nenet smiled. "Only three months, and you have begun to look like one of the Chain."

"*Shukran,*" Ebriel murmured.

"And using the language programs! You are welcome, Ebriel." She turned back to *Unicorn,* her face expectant, dark eyes alight in her plain face. "And now, where is our girl?"

Pilar appeared in the door of the spaceplane. At her side was eighteen year-old Tawia Omu, whip-thin, full-lipped, with smooth skin like dark chocolate.

Twelve years ago, Tawia had been rescued from Ethiopia's Great Rift Valley, her family and her entire city lost to a flood. The evening before she had put up her star in the dining hall of Starhold. Tomorrow, she would be repatriated. She returned to her homeland armed with a hundred *birr,* a few gold coins, her fluency in Amharic, a thorough understanding of hygiene and nutrition, and as much other knowledge as her mind could hold.

Nenet hurried forward to give her a hand down from *Unicorn,* to embrace her.

"*Marhaba,* Tawia," she said. "We met only once, when the Chain brought you here—so long ago, a tiny and frightened girl! And now here you are, grown-up."

The girl nodded. She had been silent on the flight, speaking only when spoken to, gazing out the windows of *Unicorn* as Starhold dwindled and disappeared. Ebriel had sat as far from her as she could. She had skipped Tawia's farewell the night before, and the placing of her star.

Nenet drew Tawia away toward the barracks, an arm around the girl's slender waist, head bent to talk to her. The flight crew, two women Ebriel didn't know well, began the post-flight check. Ty said, "It gets cold at night here in November, and right quick, too. Let's help cover *Unicorn,* Pilar. We can off-load the empty containers tomorrow."

Ebriel picked up Tawia's duffel and followed Nenet and the girl.

Ebriel had been allowed on this flight only as an observer, under Vee's strict orders. She refused to allow Ebriel even to carry a weapon. "Three months training isn't enough," she said flatly, when Ebriel objected. "Too much you don't know."

Before dinner, Ebriel and Ty walked out to the copter's hangar to proof the fuel cell. A chill darkness had settled over the desert when they finished, and they strolled back to the barracks under a thickly starred sky. Ebriel looked up, trying to find the habitat.

Ty pointed. "Looking for home? It's right there."

Ebriel followed her finger to find the lights of Starhold blinking on the western horizon. She now knew that its geostationary orbit held steady at zero latitude, thirty degrees longitude, sparkling down on the Atlantic Ocean, often visible from western Europe and Africa and eastern South America. But she didn't think of it as home.

On Starhold she had fallen into her narrow cot every night

exhausted in mind and body by hours in the dojo, sessions under the study hoods, terrifying turns in the flight simulator, and the exacting training with Vee in Tacticals. In the three months since she had joined the Chain, not only had her physical muscles grown, but her understanding of languages and weaponry and economics and history. She was a different woman from the one who had been La Villette's principal flutist, had lived a comfortable life in Paris—had spent helpless weeks at Leysin.

Nenet had one of her bean stews ready in the barracks kitchen. The Chain members, the flight crew, and the quiet girl gathered around the table. Nenet stayed close to Tawia, filling her bowl, pressing her to try the fresh flatbread, to drink more *kharoub*.

When everyone was served, she asked the girl, "Where will you start?"

"It's called Dire Dawa," Tawia answered softly. "There is nothing left of my home."

"I know," Nenet said. "I remember that. And what is in Dire Dawa for you?"

"There's a place they make faffa, the blended food. They speak English and Amharic there. I will have a job, and a place to live."

"And you have your shorthand?"

Tawia nodded. "I do," she said. Her voice grew stronger. "It's in my things. And I have the right clothes, we saw them on the spybugs. The copter will land five miles from the factory, where there's an empty field. I will walk from there."

"This is so exciting for you," Nenet murmured. Ebriel wished she could leave the table, but everyone sat on, listening to Tawia, watching her with shining eyes, nods of encouragement.

"Yes," Tawia said. She glanced around at the circle of faces. "I—I miss Starhold already, though. I'm afraid I'll be lonely."

"Ah," Nenet said. She rested one hand on the arm of Tawia's chair. "At first you will be, naturally. I was lonely here, too, but I got to know people in the old town, and I found ways to fill my time. You will be busy, and you will meet people—young people, others like yourself."

Tawia's full lips curved. "Not quite like myself, I think."

Nenet laughed, her dark, rich voice filling the common

room. "No, of course not! No, indeed. You're a starchild, Tawia Omu. No one can be quite like you."

The field baked in the hot African sun, hectares of dried soybean stalks that crackled and sent up clouds of gritty dust as the copter settled among them. Tawia had grown silent again, sitting in the back of the copter with her bag clutched in her hands. Ebriel, in the copilot's seat, had flown the bird part of the way to Dire Dawa, listening to Ty's instructions, her palms greasy with perspiration.

"You don't want to pull on the collective too hard, or your ascent's too steep," Ty said. "Remember, from the simulator? And now the cyclic for the attitude, easy, easy, there you go. Just like in practice, only—" Ebriel saw with relief that her hand hovered over the other stick, ready to correct a mistake. "Only this counts for real."

Papa had sent out spybugs the day before to ensure that all was peaceful in Dire Dawa. The faffa factory was busy taking deliveries of soybeans and sorghum and shipping out truckloads of the product to be distributed. The town, a few miles away, was sleepy and quiet, with no sign of unrest. They had the go-ahead for Tawia to be dropped.

When they stepped out of the copter, Ebriel's nose wrinkled. "What is that smell?"

Ty pointed in the direction of the food factory. "Gasoline," she said tersely. "Never smelled that before?"

Ebriel shook her head. Ty was helping Tawia down from the bird. "Guess they still have some," she said. "And the combustion engines to use it."

Tawia shouldered her duffel. She was dressed in the local costume, a loose robe with deep pockets, her head covered, her feet sandaled. Under the robe she wore a belt that held a pulse pistol, the tiny shortband transistor, and most of her money. In the duffel were more clothes, a few books, and a new formula for the faffa, to help correct protein-energy malnutrition. She had a memory stick with a letter to Ethan's associate in the factory.

Ty put a hand on her shoulder. "Are you ready, Tawia?"

"I'm ready."

"Go then. Good luck to you." Ty hugged her, then stepped back.

The girl looked at Ebriel, her brows raised expectantly.

Ebriel steeled herself to look up into Tawia's young face, her clear eyes, her firm mouth. For an awkward moment it seemed as if Tawia were the adult, and Ebriel the child. "Be well," Ebriel managed to say through a tight throat. She forced herself to put out her hand.

Astonishingly, the girl smiled, a wide smile that flashed white teeth in her thin dark face. Her eyes shone as she shook Ebriel's hand. "And you," she said. She saluted them with a lift of her hand, then wheeled and strode away through the crackling stalks of last year's soybean crop. Ty watched until she was out of sight, but Ebriel turned her back and jumped up into the copter.

They remained one more night at Siwa. Ebriel went with Nenet to walk out through the old town, to pick up a basket of olives and jars of oil to take to Starhold. The cold wind was a shock after the heat of the day, but it was delicious to walk freely, with unlimited space, to feel she could stretch out her arms without hitting someone or bumping something.

After they made their purchases, they strolled up to the ruins and stood looking out over the reaches of rippled sand. Ebriel said, "Nenet, do you listen to Newnet reports?"

"When I can get them," Nenet answered.

"Have you heard anything about me? Of what is supposed to have become of me?"

Nenet's eyes glinted in the starlight when she turned her face to Ebriel. "No, Ebriel, I am sorry, I have not. I suppose everyone is to believe you are still at Leysin."

"But Security Corps—General Glass—they must know I am not."

"They know. But they do not say. News of you stopped when you left Geneva, I think."

Ebriel pulled the padded jacket she wore more tightly around her. "Do you suppose there is any way I can let my parents know . . ."

"I think not," Nenet said gently. "Secrecy is so important. Why have you not asked Papa, or Semaya, these questions?"

Ebriel hesitated. She felt Nenet's eyes on her, and then her thick, strong hand on her shoulder. "Are you sorry, Ebriel, that you chose to join us? Do you not like Starhold?"

Ebriel looked into Nenet's strong, plain face, clearly visible in the starlight. "I do not fit in. Everyone is so dedicated, so—convinced. They believe. I am not sure that I do." She paused, and the silence of the desert night echoed in her ears. "I do not want to be near the children."

"And why would that be, Ebriel?"

Nenet's voice reminded Ebriel of the dark music of a cello, or a bassoon. A fresh wave of hate swept over her at the loss of her music, and made her speak sharply. "That part of my life is over, Nenet. Children. Family. Music. All in the past!" She paused, and struggled to moderate her tone. "I am sorry. I hardly know myself." She tipped her face up into the starlight. "It seems I have begun my *ménopause,* even, and I am only thirty-two. Dr. Nordstrom says it is because I am so thin, and because of the stress of my—of what—"

Nenet's hand, firm and warm, stayed on her shoulder. "Your loss is still new, my friend. Still fresh. You must give yourself time."

Ebriel realized Nenet thought she was being sad. She wasn't sad. She was furious. She drew a slow breath, tasting the cold dry air, the sandy tang of the desert.

Nenet released her shoulder and looked back over the old town sleeping in the starlight. "I wish I could offer you comfort, Ebriel. Perhaps if I were a religious person, I could think of something to say. For my own grief, action was the answer. I joined the Chain. I served here in this lonely place, and my grief faded, in time."

Ebriel craved action, too. Vee was making her wait, making her practice every small detail over and over, when what she wanted was to break free, to take what she already knew and go in search of her enemy. But she could tell Nenet none of that. She only said, with feigned calm, "*Merci.* I appreciate your kindness."

Nenet smiled at her. "Shall we go back now?"

*   *   *

Before they all went to bed, the flight crew accessed Newnet. They chuckled over a comedy and listened to the latest news. Ebriel sat across the room, reading a book from one of Nenet's shelves. When she heard the familiar tenor of George Glass, she looked up.

He stood beside the great black desk with its inset InCo globe, aides to either side. Ebriel stiffened. Her nostrils flared, remembering the odd metallic odor that surrounded him. Ty and Nenet crossed to the panel to watch with the flight crew.

Glass was speaking directly to the camera. ". . . and these latest accusations of Red Omega's are completely unfounded. The disappearance of this vessel is of course an outrage, but it demonstrates the futility of attempting to interfere in the latent countries. The risk of having a ship return contaminated with biochemical residue is too great to be tolerated."

He leaned slightly toward the camera. "My fellow citizens, the situation is regrettable. But we must allow the latent populations to develop at their own pace."

Ty growled, "Guess they taught him not to call 'em muds."

"Shh-hh," Nenet murmured.

Glass said, "Our duty is to keep our own homes and families safe. I've devoted my life to this, as have all Security Corps officers, and all the men and women who serve in uniform. The Line of Partition is there to keep the scourge of disease and warfare out of our homes."

The picture deliquesced into a peaceful scene of children playing in a schoolyard. Ty made a disgusted sound in her throat. Ebriel found she was gripping the arms of her chair so hard her fingers had gone numb.

Yasmine Ananda stared across the empty fields to the black skeletons that had once been the city of Srinagar. The bombs had destroyed the city before she was born, turning the business towers into slumping hulks, collapsing the apartment buildings, infecting the sugarcane fields. In the abandoned study hoods, half-buried in the ruins, the histories stopped with the war. Yasmine knew nothing of the world since that time.

The fields were fertile again. Even now the first green shoots of the rice planting trembled in the spring breeze. And the old customs ruled.

Yasmine was fourteen. Five days ago the women of her family had stained her palms with henna and dressed her in beads for her marriage. The day after her wedding, the warlord of a neighboring village attacked. Three men of her town were killed, among them her new husband. Four days after that—today—was to be the sati—the immolation of her husband's body.

And hers, of course. Against the white silk of her sari, her hands looked red as blood.

For two days after her husband's death, Yasmine had lived in terror. On the third day, when she could bear it no more, she drew a dark curtain across her mind, the dark curtain she had known was there since her childhood. She shut out the fear, and with it all other feeling. She remembered being afraid—remembered imagining the flames, the pain, the darkness awaiting her—but it was only a memory. She was as if already dead.

Her husband's funeral pyre was built, his corpse laid on the wooden bier. There were three such pyres, one for each of the men killed in the raid. Three wives who would accompany their husbands into death. The other women were older and had children who would be left motherless. Yasmine had been sad for the children. Now she felt nothing.

When the unfamiliar buzzing passed her window, she didn't turn her head. Even her curiosity had deserted her, the restless thirst for knowledge that had driven her mother to distraction, shamed her father, caused them to give her away in marriage to the first man who would take her.

Voices sounded in the house, the cooks giving orders, the women preparing the funeral feast. Villagers walked beneath her window on their way to the funeral pyres. It must be soon now, Yasmine supposed. Soon they would escort her to the burning ground, her and the other widows, wrapped in their white saris, their veils pulled down over their heads to hide their supposedly grieving faces—or to hide their agony.

The buzzing came again, some odd creature flying around the house. It faded. Doors opened and closed. Yasmine's was locked from the outside, until the time they would come for her, to lay her beside her husband on the pile of dry wood. Yasmine had seen funeral pyres. She had heard the screams as the women burned, the unwanted women, the useless women.

She heard the tap at her window, but she didn't react. She could not. She stared at the broken skyline of Srinagar, her eyes open, but her mind securely veiled.

Distantly, she heard the crack of metal as the lock broke, and the screech of the sash against the wooden window frame as the window was pushed up.

A head appeared in the open window, the face of a pale-skinned woman with short ashen curls. In awful Hindi, the woman said, "Ana, bacha! Ana!"

Yasmine watched clouds drift over the toppled towers.

"Bacha! Ana, kripyaa!"

Yasmine didn't move.

The woman put her leg over the windowsill and pulled herself inside the room. She had something small and gray in her hand, and she cast a hasty glance around before she leaned out and hissed, "Ty! I must have your help!"

The woman put the gray thing into her wide belt, then bent over Yasmine to lift her in her arms. With a grunt of effort, she carried Yasmine to the open window.

Another woman, bigger, with yellow hair, reached up to receive her in long, hard arms. She snapped, "Ebriel, hurry! They're all standing around those damned bonfires!"

"I know this," the ashen-haired woman said. "I am coming."

She leaped down from the window. The taller woman, hardly seeming to notice Yasmine's weight in her arms, set off at a run away from the house. The ashen-haired woman loped after them, the little weapon again in her hand. Her face was smooth and young-looking, despite her silvery hair. She glanced behind her as they raced for the border of juniper trees that protected the village from the mountain winds. Yasmine jounced with each step, her head lolling, her arms hanging loosely. Her white silks fluttered in the breeze created by their flight. The tall woman's breath came harsh and fast.

Tumult rose behind them. Yasmine's brother-in-law leaned out the broken window and shouted after the fleeing women.

Others took up the alarm. Heavy feet pounded on the hard ground. The tall woman reached the juniper trees and raced through them, breathing harder, twice shifting Yasmine's weight in her arms. A weapon cracked. The smaller woman stopped and whirled, pointing her little weapon at their pursuers. It hummed briefly, and a man cried out.

The metallic clank of a sword being drawn cut through the racket of running footsteps, and the gun cracked again. Something jerked at Yasmine's foot, and the tall woman panted, "What's happening, Eb?"

Her companion said tersely, "Go on! I will be right behind you." She knelt behind a tree as the tall woman went on, slowing to a walk now with Yasmine growing heavy in her arms. The little weapon sang its muted song one more time. The pursuing feet faltered. Men shouted, swore, threatened, but they stopped running. A moment later the ashen-haired woman caught up with the tall woman and Yasmine.

"They have fallen back," she panted.

The tall woman said, "Two down, Ebriel."

Her companion muttered, "Bon," and dashed ahead of them through the wood.

There was a ruin beyond the grove, a long-abandoned temple centuries old. Yasmine had played there as a child. Snakes and rodents slid through the underbrush that grew around the crumbled walls, and the roofless chambers made perfect hiding places. The two strange women circled the temple. Behind it a silvery-blue aircraft waited, a propeller drooping above it like the petals of a thirsty silver flower. The ashen-haired woman pressed a button on her belt, and a door opened in the side of the vehicle. The tall woman lifted Yasmine up to set her inside, then exclaimed, "Dammit, Ebriel, look at this! Those bastards hit her! They weren't supposed to have projectiles!"

The woman named Ebriel bent over Yasmine to look. "Bon Dieu!"

Ty climbed up into the vehicle. "Better take care of it in the air. Don't want to be on the receiving end of that old AK47 or whatever the hell it was."

Ebriel strapped Yasmine into a seat, then scrambled to the back. Behind her sheltering curtain, Yasmine was vaguely aware that her foot was bleeding, dripping her blood on the clean metal floor. She felt no pain.

As the craft lurched off the ground, the ashen-haired woman bent over Yasmine's foot. In her bad Hindi she said, "Tum achchey," and looked up into Yasmine's face. Yasmine saw that the woman was lovely, with delicate skin, full lips, and unusual eyes flecked with brown and gold. There was something in those eyes that was familiar to Yasmine. It was an emptiness, a void, like the hollowness in her own spirit, that numbed her mind and froze her tongue.

The tall woman said, "I hope she's not witless."

The gray-haired one, Ebriel, said tightly, "She is only frightened."

"Here we go."

The craft rose straight up into the bright morning sky. Yasmine saw the temple ruin fall away beneath her, its square *outlines softened by spilling ivy and brambles. It shrank swiftly as the little machine banked, soaring off toward Srinigar as easily as a bird might fly. Yasmine didn't know what was happening. She didn't think about it. If she allowed herself to be curious, to wonder, to begin to hope—the awful fear could return. No. No. Being dead was better.*

11

Ty disengaged the neural network and pulled the collective lever to lift the bird faster than the neural net would allow. Ebriel kept her eyes on the ground, worrying about the weapon. A projectile weapon could pierce the skin of the copter if it was within range. The tri-gear retracted as they cleared the treetops and banked sharply to the northeast. When they were out of range, Ebriel pulled on a pair of anti-septic gloves and pressed gauze over the girl's bloody foot. Ty pushed the cyclic forward, and they whirred swiftly toward the wreckage of Srinagar.

Ebriel kept pressure on the girl's wound as they flew over the mass of broken concrete and steel that had once been a city. Vines now grew over the tumbled buildings, and trees thrust up between slabs of buckled pavement. Ty searched the horizon and grunted satisfaction. "There's Burzil Pass," she said over her shoulder. "Hour and a half, we'll be out over the Plateau." She tapped on a keypad and waited for the response. "Okay," she said. "Papa's got us. Four hours to Xiao Qaidam. You need help back there?"

Ebriel peeled away the blood-soaked gauze. *"Merde,"* she muttered. "This must hurt."

The bullet had gone in through the sole of the girl's foot,

and through, its exit leaving a ragged star-shaped tear. Extruded tissue glistened wetly in the sunlight. Ebriel swallowed nausea, soaked up blood with more gauze, and felt carefully with her gloved fingers for bone fragments, as the field aid course had taught her. It seemed to her that the bullet had missed the bone. She hoped it was true. There was no doctor at Xiao Qaidam. She spread the wound with antibiotic paste, smoothing the pieces of torn flesh back into place as best she could. Ty joined her, putting her hand to the girl's forehead. The dark-skinned girl didn't move. She slumped in her seat, her veil slipping from her head, her hair hanging about her shoulders, midnight dark against the white silk. Her hands lay open in her lap, fingers turned up to show palms stained rust-red. The hem of her sari, spattered with blood, tangled about her thin legs.

"She's out of it," Ty growled.

Ebriel sealed a pressure bandage around the girl's foot and then looked up into her lifeless face. She knew how bad her Hindi was, despite the study hood. Her English never seemed to improve either. Still, she tried. *"Bacha,"* she said. *"Tum achchey. Achchey."*

The girl's heavy eyelids flickered and lifted to show pupils contracted to pinpricks.

Ty said, "Give it up for now. At Qaidam, we'll reassess."

Ebriel cleaned blood from her fingers and used the antiseptic towel to mop it from the floor. She stripped off the gloves and spoke again to the blank-faced girl. *"Bacha, aapka naam kya hei?* What is your name, child? Your name?"

There was no response. The control console chimed, and Ty moved back to the pilot's seat. Ebriel took a folded blanket from one of the storage shelves and wrapped it around the girl, tucking a pillow under her head. She turned to follow Ty to the cockpit. As she moved forward, she glanced back over her shoulder and saw the vague movement of the girl's eyes following her movement. Ah. Not blind, then. A small grace.

She took the copilot's seat and looked out over the rugged peaks of the Himalayas. Ty glanced at her. "Want to fly for a while?"

Ebriel nodded. Ty re-engaged the neural network. Ebriel

had already logged more than thirty hours of flight time, she who had never even driven a cell car. The neural net made flying deceptively easy, controlling airspeed, direction, lift. Ebriel liked feeling the collective alive and responsive under her hand. Relinquishing the controls now, Ty reminded her, "Keep your eye on it. Don't assume the neurals will handle everything."

"Oui." Ebriel pulled on the stick. The copter rose sharply, and the neural network clanged a warning.

Ty's long arm reached to push it down. "Okay, Eb. We're not gonna fly over K2, right?"

Ebriel laughed and leveled the copter. *"Non.* I am sorry. Straight to Xiao Qaidam."

"Please," Ty muttered.

"Ty, the girl should drink something. Because of the bleeding."

"Got it."

Cabinets opened and closed in the back. Ty murmured something, and Ebriel looked back to see her holding a glass to the girl's lips. A rivulet of scarlet fruit juice ran down her chin. Ty's freckled brow furrowed. "This isn't good," she said.

Ebriel turned back to the controls. The copter flew at a steady altitude. She leaned her chin on her hand and watched the Tibetan Plateau flow past. The Roof of the World. Only nomadic tribes inhabited the frigid plains, and if they looked up and spotted the silver craft, there was no one for them to report it to. Xiao Qaidam, the abandoned missile silo, nestled in the great arid basin of Qaidam Pendi. The nearest InCo base was Seoul, in the Todokai polities, more than twenty-five hundred kilometers farther to the east.

Ty came back to the cockpit with a steaming cup in each hand. Ebriel engaged the autopilot and cradled the warm mug in her hands, keeping an eye on the telemetry. She glanced back at the dark features of their passenger, the thin, curving nose and sharp chin, great dark eyes staring at nothing. They might be beautiful if some life glowed in them.

Ty said, "If she's over the edge, Eb, we can't take her up. No point."

"I know this." Behind them towered the ice and limestone cone of K2. Below, sparse stands of conifers gave way to a few desiccated fruit trees in the river valleys, with fields of frozen grass between. Spring came late to the high desert.

"I mean it," Ty said.

Ebriel glanced over at her. "I have not argued with you."

Ty squinted into the pallid sunshine. "Yeah. But you haven't agreed with me either."

Ebriel sipped the coffee. She knew what would happen if they found the girl's mind was broken. It had happened before. There was little enough room on Starhold, and none for damaged children. It was not a question of sympathy, but of necessity.

Ty sighed. "Look, we'll wait till we get to Qaidam, okay? Then we'll see."

Ebriel shrugged. "As you say." But the dark-eyed girl stirred something in her, some half-remembered and somehow unwelcome feeling. She drained her coffee, set the cup aside, and took the controls again.

Ebriel had been to Xiao Qaidam twice in her eight months with the Chain, but the expanse of the great basin and the loneliness of the site struck her anew as they approached from the west. At the sound of the copter, Perk, the caretaker, came out through the blast doors and stood beside the landing field to watch them settle on the cracked concrete. His wispy gray ponytail blew in the wind, and his wrinkled eyelids narrowed against the glare.

Perk's home was a circular bunker, forty feet in diameter, with walls twelve feet thick and a yard of dirt above the ceiling. A similar bunker served as a hangar for the copters. At Xiao Qaidam nothing was visible above ground. A few dozen meters away from the bunkers the Dong Feng missile still nestled in its silo, defanged now, its liquid propellant pirated away.

Perk helped Ebriel and Ty lift their charge to the ground. His eyes flicked over the girl's limp arms, her blank face, and he raised his eyebrows. Ty lifted the girl in her arms, careful of the bandaged foot. Perk jabbed his chin toward the bunker as he climbed up into the bird. "Tea's ready," he said. "Go on in." The lonely wind gusted around them as they moved away.

The girl's head lolled, and Ebriel put out her hand to support it, staying close to Ty as they walked down into the steel-ribbed passageway. She guessed the girl must be no more than fourteen or fifteen. She could hardly weigh more than forty-five kilos.

The spartan lifestyle Nenet Nasser practiced at Siwa was not for Perk. He had stuffed his living space with lacquered chests and carved chairs, mingling his treasures with an assortment of metal and plastic stools and tables left behind by the Chinese missile crews. Mismatched appliances lined the walls, and thick cables wound around the perimeter. A row of bunk beds, neatly made up with blankets and pillows, filled one side, with a communal bath beyond them.

Perk came in from the passageway and rolled the blast door shut behind him. "All stowed," he said. He eyed the silent girl. Ebriel had settled her in an armchair, wrapped her in a blanket, propped her bandaged foot on a stool. "She said anything?"

"Nope," Ty answered. She was at a panel, reporting to Papa.

"Looks bad," Perk said.

"She is in shock," Ebriel murmured. "We must give her time."

"If we have time," Ty said over her shoulder.

Ebriel tucked the blanket tighter. "She spent three days waiting to be burned alive."

"Yep," Perk said. "Looks bad." He crossed to an old electric stove that sat between a listing refrigerator and a battered rice steamer. He began preparations with a clatter of pots and spoons and the hiss of foilpacks. A smell of frying meat filled the bunker, and Ebriel's mouth watered. She could not remember the last time she had eaten meat.

After the meal, Ty and Ebriel put heavy jackets over their jumpsuits and shoved the blast door aside just enough to let them pass, using pencil flashes to find their way up the stairs.

The April air was cold and sweet. An opulent skyful of stars arched over the great basin. Ebriel sighed, tipping her head back to admire the splash of the Milky Way across the spangled blackness. "*Zut.* I can almost understand why Perk wants to live out here."

"Not me," Ty answered, stretching her long arms over her head. "Too lonely. And who wants to live with a DF5 at their back all the time?"

"Do you mean the missile? But surely it is harmless now."

"Yeah, but all it needs is a little go-juice . . . and kaboom!" Ty laughed.

"More than a little, I believe. And it is so old. *Merci à Dieu,* they never fired it."

"True." Ty shivered and pulled up her jacket collar. "They considered it, you know, when China started to fall apart. War is a great way to retain power. Helped pull Japan and the Koreas together. And the European polities." She shivered. "As if it weren't bad enough when India and Pakistan blew."

"*Mais oui,*" Ebriel said. "We could all be dust by now."

"Eb—"

"What?"

"If our girl doesn't wake up, we're going to have to leave her. Perk'll take her to Xining. There's an orphanage there."

Ebriel avoided Ty's gaze. Something in her could not let go of this girl, this damaged child. "Ty—how can I explain? When I was in Leysin, helpless, drugged—it was like being dead."

"It's terrible," Ty said gently. "I know. But if her mind's gone, we can't keep her."

Heat flooded Ebriel's cheeks and her jaw clenched. "I would like to go back and kill them all," she said tightly. "For what they have done to this child. For what they did to the others."

"Not our mission to kill people, Eb," Ty said mildly.

"But I saw them fall. Two of them."

"I doubt you killed anyone. Not at that range."

Ebriel put her cold hands to her face. "Would you care, Ty? If I had killed those men?"

"Of course I would."

Ebriel's voice dropped. "I would not care. I would not care at all."

"You'd be surprised at how it feels."

"But you have killed, Ty."

Ty looked away. "I have. There's no joy in it, Ebriel. No matter what they've done."

Ebriel kicked at the frozen ground with her boot and didn't answer.

12

Yasmine lay in the unfamiliar bed, listless. There had been a meal. The gray-haired woman—Ebriel—had coaxed her to take a little in her mouth, something green and salty, something else tender with fat. She had accepted the spoon, her young body craving food. When she swallowed, Ebriel's beautiful mouth curved, and the black curtain over Yasmine's mind drew back a little. She turned her head away, frightened by the ray of light threatening her safe darkness. She didn't eat any more.

The others—those other women of her village—had they suffered, the way she, Yasmine, had been meant to suffer? It was an honor, they told her. She was to support the illusion that it was her own choice, to join her husband in death, to win the approval of the gods. The priest had told her to breathe the smoke, when it was her time, to breathe it in hard, and then she wouldn't feel anything. But Yasmine trusted neither the priest nor his gods.

She slept at last. When morning came, the tall woman, Ty, helped her out of the bunk, bathed her, dressed her in a loose shirt and trousers, careful of her bandaged foot. Yasmine submitted, let her body be moved here and there, her hair be washed, her hands scrubbed, her bandage changed. Ty's English was slurred and casual, difficult for Yasmine to follow.

Ebriel's English was precise, in the way of a second language. Yasmine understood almost everything she said.

"Ask Semaya to give us a day," Ebriel was saying now, at the table.

Ty said something about time and then some other words indistinguishable to Yasmine.

"It seems a waste," Ebriel said. "After all that we did."

Ty said something about life, and the old man with the ponytail grunted and added something. His English was even more difficult to follow than Ty's.

Ebriel said, "Ask her, Ty."

"Okay, okay." The tall woman left the table, moved to the panel and spoke to it.

Ebriel bent toward Yasmine to give her a searching look. Yasmine stared back, fascinated by the golden flecks in Ebriel's eyes, the short, silvery curls that fell over her forehead, entranced by her musical voice. *"Ma pauvre,"* Ebriel murmured. *"Tu es là?"*

Without intending to, hardly knowing she did it, Yasmine answered her in a whisper. *"Oui, Madame. Je suis ici."*

Light blazed in Ebriel's hazel eyes, and she slapped her hand on the table, making Yasmine jump. "Ty!" Ebriel exclaimed. "Tell Semaya the child spoke to me. *In French!*"

Yasmine shrank back in her chair. Suddenly she felt pain in her foot, lancing up her ankle to her shin. Tears stung her eyes, and she groped for her veil to hide them. Her veil was gone.

"Where," Ebriel demanded of Yasmine. "Where can you have learned French?"

The tears slipped over Yasmine's cheeks, and she pressed her palms over her eyes. Her throat constricted. "Srinagar," she stammered, hiding behind her hands. "S-s-study hoods." She said the words in English, the only name she knew for them.

She had discovered a half-collapsed library under the rubble of a school. It had been her undoing. She cringed, expecting their fury at her revelation.

The offense had maddened her parents, but her mind had been hungry. She who would not play with other children, who could hardly speak to anyone outside her family, had been ravenous for information, for stimulation. And now she had revealed herself. What would become of her? Slowly, she lowered her hands, and looked into Ebriel's face.

Ebriel's voice shook a little as she said, "*Pas de danger ici, ma pétite.* You are safe."

Yasmine could not believe it. She dared not believe it.

"Ebriel," Ty said. "Are you sure?"

Ebriel laughed. "*Oui,*" she said. "Of course I am sure." She put out her hand to touch Yasmine's arm. "*Comment t'appelles-tu?*"

"*Je m'appelle* Yasmine," Yasmine whispered.

"Yasmine. *Belle,*" Ebriel answered. And to Ty, "Her name is Yasmine. Tell Semaya."

"Well," Ty said doubtfully. "I s'pose . . . it's Yasmine?"

Yasmine forced her eyes up to Ty's cool blue eyes. "I am Yasmine," she said in cautious English. "Yasmine Ananda."

The blond woman's uneven features split in a grin. "You speak English, too, then?"

"A little, madam."

Ebriel sat back in her chair. "Study hoods," she breathed. "In Srinagar."

Ty asked, "Did Papa's contact in Srinagar know that?"

Perk, from a little distance, said, "I never heard about it."

Trembling, Yasmine said, "It was forbidden."

"Why?" Ebriel asked.

"The war. Such—knowing. No, knowledge. Such knowledge made the bombs."

"So what did you learn, Yasmine, under the study hoods?" Ebriel asked.

"Languages." Yasmine glanced around at their faces. None seemed angry, only curious. Surprised. "History. Geography. Mathematics."

"And it was forbidden."

"Yes. I hided—hid. I hid in buildings where are the study hoods. My father did not like."

The man, Perk, came to stand beside Ty and stare down at Yasmine. She covered her eyes again, anxious that he, a man, would be furious with her. But perhaps not. These women knew so much, how to fight, how to fly, and to speak languages. And what else? What else did they know? The little flame of curiosity sparked in her mind, familiar and dangerous.

And then the man said, "Too bad about the others."

Ty said, "Nothing we could do, Perk. Papa's contact knew about this one, the young one. His spybugs caught the building of the pyres. Ugly business. We were lucky to get this one."

Yasmine looked up into Perk's wrinkled face, into Ty's craggy one. Renewed horror rose in her. She gripped her hands together and turned back to Ebriel. *"Madame,"* she choked. *"Mortes? Toutes les deux sont mortes?"*

Ebriel's eyes darkened. *"Oui, ma pauvre. Elles sont mortes."*

They had burned them. While she flew away in the wonderful silvery copter, they had wailed and suffered on the burning ground, the smoke from their charring flesh and bone and hair blowing down the village lanes. While she, Yasmine, escaped, as she had escaped to the study hoods, escaped to the old temple, leaving her duty to her family unfulfilled, her duty to her village, to her husband. She had not chosen him, but she had not meant to dishonor him.

It was too much. She curled into a ball, her face in her lap, her fists under her chin. She pulled the dark curtain over her mind again. She lost touch with her body, with her sight, with her hearing. The pain of her foot receded. She hid, safe again in the darkness.

Ebriel and Ty went topside to argue, standing just beyond the entrance to the bunker. The dry wind of the Plateau beat around them, whipping bits of gravel past their feet, making their eyes tear and their cheeks redden. Ty folded her arms and squinted against the wind.

"She doesn't pass, Eb."

"She will," Ebriel insisted. She had said it twice already. "I have a feeling about this."

"Great," Ty said. "Semaya's going to love your 'feeling.' "

The sky stretched vast and empty over their heads. Ebriel stared out over the empty plain. "There is something special about her, Ty."

Ty turned her back to the wind and faced Ebriel. "They're

all special," she said. "Every one of them is special to the
Chain. But they aren't all suited to Starhold. You've seen what
the training is like, the discipline. How would this one—"

"Yasmine," Ebriel interjected.

Ty spread her hands. "Yasmine. How would Yasmine handle the dojo? Or Tacticals?"

Ebriel shook her head. She didn't have an answer, didn't
know how to answer. She was still shaken by the spybug pictures of the funeral pyres that had been bounced from Papa's
contact in Srinagar to the panel in Perk's bunker. The white-
garbed figures, veils bound tightly around their faces, had
been thrown into the flames by strong men while the villagers
stood watching. She supposed the women had screamed, and
was grateful the spybugs had no audio. She supposed the
smoke that billowed out over the watching people and clouded
the spybug's optics had reeked of roasting flesh. The thought
made her gorge rise.

Ty's eyes on her were hard. "She'll live, at least," she said,
her words clipped and clear under the whine of the wind. "In
Xining. She'll have her life."

Ebriel struggled to think of a rational argument. "She is
bright, Ty. Can you not see?"

"Intelligence is important, of course. But to be a starchild—
it takes more than intelligence."

"I know this, Ty."

"It's reaction times, vision and hearing, strength,
coordination—"

Ebriel expelled a breath through her teeth. "I know, but—
how can I explain? I think we should—I think Starhold should
make an exception. This time."

"Starhold can't afford to make exceptions."

Ebriel lifted her chin. "This is not true."

Ty lifted her brows and waited for her to explain.

"The baby. The infant from Gansu Province."

"Ah." Ty unfolded her arms. "Yeah, you're right. That was
an exception, because she was so young. But she seemed
healthy to the Chain members who found her. They did an Ap-
gar test. She responded, she ate, she cried, she behaved normally for a newborn."

"But still, she was an exception. And Semaya allowed it."

Ty nodded, and her face softened. "Babies. We don't get to see babies on Starhold." She eyed Ebriel with ironic amusement. "And you've never been near that one. Bet you don't even know her name."

Ebriel pulled her jacket closer about her. "You are right, Ty. I am sorry."

Ty's hard hand rested on her shoulder. "It's okay, Eb. I understand. But why this one? Why now?"

Ebriel could only shrug.

Ty dropped her hand. "Look, I'll talk to Semaya, okay? See what she says."

They stood side by side in the cold for a moment. When Ebriel shivered, Ty said, "Better get inside." And as they turned toward the bunker, she said, "It's Xiao Sying."

"What?"

"Xiao Sying. The baby. Little Star."

"Xiao Sying. Such a lovely name."

"She's beautiful. Almost a year old now. You should get to know her."

Ebriel stopped before the blast doors to face her partner. "I cannot," she said bluntly. "I hope I have not disappointed you, *mon amie,* or disappointed the Chain."

Ty grinned. "Hey, Vee's gonna be thrilled with your performance out there. Cool as a cucumber, maybe a little reckless. But under fire! Like you'd been on a hundred missions."

Ebriel nodded. "I have told Vee I was ready."

"Right." Ty pushed open the blast door. "Well, that can't hurt your cause, Eb. Come on, we'll get on to Semaya. I'll do my best. Promise."

13

In the morning, Yasmine curled in the armchair in the bunker, her face buried against her knees. Ebriel brought the quilt to cover her and returned to stand beside Ty at the panel, listening to Semaya's emotionless voice. Ty spoke a few more words and ordered the panel off.

"Semaya's a tough sell," she said.

"Comment?"

Ty stood up. "Semaya doesn't find anything in your argument that convinces her. She says if the girl's that withdrawn—" Ty jerked a thumb toward Yasmine. "Eb, she's catatonic."

"No, she is not," Ebriel said stubbornly. "Her arms are flexible, her eyes move. She is only—" She made a helpless gesture. "She is running away. She is escaping inside herself. She needs time, and attention."

"How far are you ready to go for her?"

"Pardon?"

Ty leaned her hip against the desk and folded her arms. "Look, Eb—personally, I wouldn't do this. But Semaya said, if you'll take responsibility for her—we can bring her up. But you have to take care of her. And you have to bring her back if it doesn't work out."

Ebriel's breath caught in her throat. "I?"

"Yeah. You."

Perk left the sink and crossed the room to join them. "Look, I've taken several children to Xining," he said to Ebriel. "The Children's Home. Nancy Chao is the director. I give them some clothes, sometimes food or medicine. They do the best they can for the kids."

Ebriel's cheeks grew hot. "And how often does the Chain discard children?"

Ty made a wry mouth. "Discard is kind of a nasty word, Eb. They're all kids who would have died if we hadn't taken them."

"Not running a nursery," Perk said. "More like a college." He turned and stalked away.

Ebriel stared at his stiff back, the thin ponytail hanging to his shoulder blades. He clattered dishes and flatware, no more noisily than usual, but it sounded angry. Ebriel had never before seen him show any emotion. She wondered how he came to be here, to live on this lonely plateau, utterly solitary for weeks on end.

Ty touched her arm. "Come on, Eb," she said. "Let's take a bit of a walk while we can."

With *Unicorn* expected in a few hours, they were already dressed in their utility suits. They pulled on jackets and rolled back the blast door.

They strode away from the buried bunkers under thin spring sunshine. A sharp breeze whistled in their ears, but new growth softened the ground beneath their boots. The high desert bloomed with the pink crowns of stonecrop, fragile yellow Chinese poppies, red clusters of pedicularis nestled among stones. They stepped on cushiony growths of rock jasmine. For twenty minutes they hiked. Faces reddened by the wind, they stopped in the shelter of an outcropping of gray stone, shelved layers jutting a meter out of the earth. Ty sat on one of the rock shelves, her back to the wind, her face turned up to the sun.

"When I was a kid," she said, "my mother made me wear a hat whenever I went out, even for a few minutes. Used to take it off sometimes when I got away from the house, but the slightest touch of sunburn got me a licking, so I didn't leave it off long. Hated it, though. Damn good thing for the planet when the fossil fuels ran out."

Ebriel leaned against the rock, gazing off to the west, where the distant peaks gleamed white. "Ty, do you know why Perk lives out here?"

The sun sparkled gently on Ty's sharp, freckled cheekbones. "Perk," she said, "escaped from an InCo jail. In North America."

"He escaped? Or the Chain rescued him?"

Ty chuckled, opening her eyes to squint up at Ebriel. "Oh, no, the Chain had nothin' to do with that! Perk was a bad 'un in his youth." She shut her eyes again. "A couple of years ago, Perk and I came out here, right here, on a summer night. He had a bottle of sake and we drank it all. Damn, it was cold that night!" She laughed. "A drunk Perk is a very different animal, I can tell you. Talks a lot. Waves his hands around. Even laughs. Or cries."

"Why was he in prison, Ty?"

Ty sighed and sat up. "I hate to tell you, Eb. You're not gonna like it."

Ebriel leaned her back against the rock and folded her arms. The stone was warm from the sun, warmer than the air. "Tell me."

"Perk was in prison for murder. Two murders, actually."

"Mon Dieu!" Ebriel murmured.

"Yep. Said he went to prison for one, then killed somebody else inside. Said if he didn't get away, he was going to do it again, so he rigged an automatic gate to malfunction, and he slipped away one night. Clever with machines, Perk. And weapons, I guess, though he won't touch 'em now."

"Did he tell you the story?"

"Yeah. Seems Perk opposed the abolition of private gun ownership in the North American Polity. Stockpiled a bunch of projectile weapons—pistols, semi-automatics, hunting rifles—and when InCo came after him, he fought back. Killed an InCo soldier, a private. Kid was only nineteen. Then, in prison, he killed somebody with a knife. Self-defense, sounded like, but he didn't want any more lives on his conscience, he said. So he skedaddled."

"How did he reach the Chain?"

"He had to get out of the InCo polities. He stole a boat out of some port in Washington State and sailed and motored across the Pacific, if you can believe that. By himself. Got to the Philippines, neutral territory, but some Security Corpsman got onto him, so he went on into China. Ended up in Xining. A Chain member found him, working with street kids."

"Penance," Ebriel said, half to herself.

"What?"

"He was doing penance. Expiation."

"Yeah, well, maybe. He's a tough nut, Perk. Calls 'em as he sees 'em." Ty straightened, and fixed her hard gaze on Ebriel. "Eb. Is that what you're doing? Penance?"

Ebriel scanned the horizon. The Himalayan peaks seemed only hilltops at this altitude. "I did not intend to have a child," she said, her voice almost lost in the whine of the wind. "My music was all I cared about, my concerts, the orchestra—my life was full. Paul's work occupied him many hours each day. We wanted nothing else." A painful knot grew in her throat. "When we realized, Paul and I, that I was *enceinte*—I made an appointment—to terminate."

"But you didn't do it," Ty prompted.

"*Non*. I could not. I awoke on that morning with such a strong feeling—I knew. I stayed in my apartment, I played my flute, I paced from room to room, I watched the traffic in the Rue Georgette—the hour came and went. I missed the appointment. I never made another."

"Feelings again."

"I do not have the word in English for this feeling, Ty. It is more than a feeling, *vraiment*. It is a—more like a *croyance*— a belief. Irresistible. And when I saw my little daughter, my Renée, when I held her in my arms—" Ebriel shuddered under her padded jacket. "I understood it then. I began to go to church again, to mass, because I thought the church must be right, that life is so precious, children so precious, they are worth any sacrifice. And then I lost her after all." She lowered her gaze, down to her booted feet on the sparse desert grass. "There will be no more children for me. I could not live with the risk. The fear."

Ty pushed herself up from her stony perch and stood watching, listening.

"It was like a punishment." Ebriel heard her English pronunciation, the *r*s, the *th*s, the closed *n*s, deteriorate. She sounded like a cartoon of a Frenchwoman. "Ty—how can I take responsibility for this girl? How can I bear it?"

Ty answered quietly, "I don't know, Eb. Only you can know that."

When they went back in through the blast doors, they found Perk huddled over a panel, speaking urgently. "Use the zapper, blind the damn things!"

There was a crackling response, and Perk said, "Okay, Simon, then you'd better abort. Get the hell out of there." Another response, unintelligible to Ebriel. Ty strode swiftly across the room. In the armchair, Yasmine Ananda stirred, but she didn't lift her head.

"What is happening?" Ebriel asked.

Ty held up a commanding hand. "Where are they, Perk?"

"Sea of Japan," he growled.

"What? Damn it!" Ty crouched beside his chair to see the panel display. Ebriel came to stand behind them, peering over Perk's shoulder. "What are they doing there?" Ty demanded.

"Boat people. Trying to get into InCo polities," Perk growled.

It wasn't easy identifying the images. The screen had divided into four views, all from spybugs. Ebriel saw a flimsy wooden boat rocking on a choppy sea, a sleek molded-hull cutter marked with the InCo globe coming up on it fast. The other two frames were delayed, slightly behind the action, and Ebriel guessed they were being bounced from the microsats through Starhold, down to Qaidam. They showed two clear views of one of the Chain copters, a harnessed Chain member dangling beneath. On the boat she saw four children. One was very small. The oldest looked like a teenager.

"Pull up!" Perk rapped. "Get him out of there!"

"Who is it?" Ty said, her voice flat with tension.

"Simon Blake," Perk said, and then again, louder, "Pull up, Johna! There's nothing you can do! They've spotted you!"

And Papa's voice overrode everything, shrill and cracking, but perfectly clear. "Scrub the mission, now. Security Corps's scrambled their own long-range from Hokkaido. Get out of there, Johna. No more delays. Pull Simon in when you're away. Now."

The spybug views rocked sickeningly as the little automatic fliers tried to follow the copter's evasive maneuvers.

"What's with the laser?" Ty asked.

"Don't know. Not working," Perk muttered.

They were all silent as they watched the screen, saw the children on the pitiful wooden boat, saw the cutter slicing the water toward it, saw their own people, their own copter, angling away to the north, and in the distance, a new one approaching. The dangling harness retracted, and a moment later, they heard a woman's voice. "He's in," she said. "We'll head over Vladivostok. We're going to have to set down, recharge the cells."

Perk had another panel at hand, and he spoke into it rapidly, watching the screen. He addressed the Chain copter again.

"Johna, you getting me? Listen, when you're over Vladivostok, turn due east, to Dunhua. I don't think they'll follow you over the boundary. But it looks like you'll have cloud cover, they won't get a good look if you can stay ahead."

There was a little pause, and then the woman's voice came again, the tension in it easing slightly. "Yeah, I think I can." She paused. "Yeah. Got a visual on Vladivostok. The InCo bird's dropping back."

A male voice joined in. "Still got the bloody spybugs, though."

It was true. The delayed images, fuzzy and distorted, were still coming through the microsat relay.

Ty said, "Try your pulse pistol. You might be able to disrupt their electrical systems."

Simon Blake answered, "I already did. The range must be too long." And a moment later the frustrated exclamation, "What a balls-up!"

Ebriel listened to all of this with half of her mind, the other still on the portion of the screen showing the wooden boat. The InCo cutter had tied up to it now and was pulling it through the choppy sea. The children huddled beside the mast, their single sail furled. The perspective gave no details of their faces, but the attitude of their bodies, the way they clung together, spoke of their desperation.

"What are they doing with them?" Ebriel breathed. No one answered her.

Perk bent over his second panel, giving orders, scanning the information. "Got it," he said abruptly and returned to the first panel, unceremoniously pushing Ty's arm out of the way. "Simon," he snapped. "How much charge do you have left?"

Simon's voice came back after a moment. "Perhaps one hundred kilometers, perhaps less. Bloody low."

"Right." Perk glanced back at the second panel. "Okay, Johna, turn south fifteen degrees. You should be in thick cloud."

"Okay." Johna's voice sounded thin. "Pea soup here, Perk."

"Right. Here's the deal. The fog's dense there, but it's low-lying, according to the weather feed. When you're sure the bugs are with you, pull your collective all the way, steep climb. If you pop out of the cloud suddenly, the optics in the bugs won't have time to adjust. You'll burn 'em out. Same effect as the zapper. Give 'em maybe thirty seconds, then get your asses on the ground."

Papa's voice sounded then, squeaky and calm. "Very good, Perk. Johna and Simon, you're now over a ridge of about 2,500 meters. Watch your telemetry on descent."

"Affirmative," Simon said. "Climbing now."

The transmission from the InCo spybugs turned gray, the bobbing view of the copter obscured by roiling clouds. Water droplets rolled across the view, even as the optics in the spy-bugs compensated for the diminished light.

Papa's spybugs, deployed from Vladivostok, were several seconds ahead. Their screens blazed white, optics burned out, just as Johna cried, "There! We're out!" The InCo transmission still showed the silver-blue copter in a sharp ascent, like a reverse dive, its spinning rotors invisible in heavy fog. Then those pictures, too, erupted in a wash of light and disappeared.

"Thirty seconds," Perk reminded them.

The air in the bunker was thick with tension, with silence, with waiting.

"Beginning descent," Johna said tensely. "Are the pictures gone?"

"Absolutely," Perk said.

"Watch your pitch," Ty called out.

Simon responded, "Right-o."

There was silence for a minute, two minutes, three. Ebriel hardly breathed, nor did she think Ty or Perk did. They bent over the now-blank panel, waiting. At last Simon Blake's voice came again.

"We're down! Found a flat place on the ridge. I don't see any buildings, or much of anything, but it's rather foggy. We'll proceed with care."

"Got 'em," Perk said. He struck the desk with his closed fist. "Made my damn day!"

"But what about the children?" Ebriel said.

Perk glanced up at her. "InCo's towing their boat back over the boundary. They'll prob'ly pull 'em out of the current, the Japan Current that flows to the northeast. Then they'll set 'em adrift."

Ebriel bit her lip and glanced over her shoulder at the Indian girl still curled, mute and unmoving, in her chair. "Ty," she said softly. "Our cell is charged, *non*? Let us go after them."

14

The agent in Vladivostok deployed his last two spy-bugs as Ebriel and Ty flew east. Perk monitored their transmissions from Qaidam. In between his reports, Ty gave Ebriel a terse lecture on air-sea rescue. "We're supposed to have a winchman, but I can run the cable from the cockpit. Problem is," she said, "I've never done this. Blind leading the blind."

Ebriel studied the sling harness in her lap as they flew. The cable reeled out of a modular compartment between the seats and the galley. Ebriel had collected extra straps and ties and found the tight-fitting cap that would block out the ancillary noise of the rotors but allow her to communicate with Ty. The marine system blanketed the ground in gray cloud. Ty flew at altitude until they reached the coast, where the fog melted away, and the green waters of the Sea of Japan flickered with late afternoon sun.

"We haven't got much daylight left," Ty muttered. "Guess that's good in a way. Papa will pitch a fit if we pick up InCo spybugs again. But we don't want to risk this in the dark."

"I will do it," Ebriel said.

"Not in the dark, you won't."

Perk was following their path, with Starhold's help. "Turn twenty degrees to the right," he said tersely. "You're about fifteen kilometers away from the boat, near as we can tell. Looks like their sail is gone and they're drifting. Gotta be damn cold down there."

Ebriel was already stepping into the harness. Her hands trembled as she fastened the straps around her chest, but she wasn't áfraid. It was—what? Excitement? Anticipation? She hid a grin as she tightened the sling. She knew she was intoxicated with adrenaline, but she didn't care. She could hardly wait to test herself, to face the wind and the water. She adjusted the cap. The receiver tucked under one earlobe and extended its cushioned wire into her ear. Pads fitted over her ears, and the transmitter curled under her jaw. "Ready."

Ty moved the collective down cautiously, losing altitude bit by bit. The rotors blew radiating patterns in the opaque surface of the sea.

"There they are," Ty said, her voice made tinny by the receiver.

Ebriel followed her pointing finger. The wooden boat, its sail hanging in shreds, drifted on the choppy sea. "Hurry, Ty," Ebriel breathed.

"Pedaling as fast as I can," Ty muttered.

"What?"

"Never mind. Be there in a minute."

The copter slowed. Ty flew a large circle around the little boat, and Ebriel saw the Chain spybugs glinting in the slanting rays of the sun as they sensed the copter and lifted out of its path. The four figures on the boat huddled around the mast, the torn sail flapping around them. Abruptly, the sun dropped below the horizon. Long cloud shadows stretched over the water.

"Damn it, Eb, this is tricky," Ty said in a low voice. She brought the copter to hover over the boat, her fingers playing on the cyclic, trying to stabilize her position. "I'm not sure we can get 'em all before it's too dark to see."

"Let us begin!"

"Watch yourself, now," Ty said. Ebriel felt the bubble of a laugh rise in her throat and quickly suppressed it. If Ty thought she were hysterical, she would cancel the whole thing.

When the door slid back, a frigid wind swirled through the

copter, making it dance like a marionette on a string. Ebriel gasped as the harsh salt air sucked the breath from her lungs. She eased herself backward out the door to lower herself over the edge, gripping the handholds set into the curving bulkhead. It was an eerie feeling to stretch her feet out and meet only empty air. The rotors beat a wild rhythm, their downdraft competing with the squall of the wind. The spotlight spearing the little boat threatened to blind her, and she blinked. The flow of adrenaline surged to a flood, her muscles singing with it, her belly clenching. She shouted, "Now!"

The harness began to lower. Ebriel swung in a stomach-lurching arc, the sling biting into her thighs. The children's pale faces turned up to her, mouths open. What would she say to them? She didn't know a word of Russian. *"Zut,"* she muttered. "You foolish Frenchwoman, too late for that now!"

"What?" Ty said.

"Non! Nothing! Go on!" A grin tugged at her lips, and her bared teeth dried immediately in the cold wind.

When her booted feet hit the deck of the wooden boat, she slid across the spray-wet surface, flying right over the low railing. She cried out and clutched at the harness. Her feet danced above the choppy water, and a swell wet the bottoms of her boots. The salty wind stung her cheeks and eyes as she swung back toward the boat. She grabbed at the railing and hauled herself onto the deck. She reeled and staggered across the deck to the children.

The smallest of them appeared to be no more than three or four years old, bundled in layers of dark clothing. The biggest was a youth, surely not more than fifteen, with a fuzz of adolescent beard on his chin and a tangled forelock of black hair showing under a thick knit cap. He struggled to stand, gripping the mast, and reached down for the little one. He lifted the child in one arm and thrust it out to Ebriel, saying something in guttural Russian.

His eyes were bloodshot and desperate. His courage made Ebriel's heart twist with pity. She gritted her teeth, resisting anything that might temper her rush of excitement. She reached out for the child.

"Courage," she said to the black-haired boy. "I will be back."

The child weighed hardly anything, an anonymous, genderless bundle of dark clothing, head covered in a knit cap. Ebriel clasped the child to her middle and wound a strap around both of them. She spoke into the transmitter. The harness tightened, and the cable began to retract. They rose jerkily off the deck, and the child screamed and clutched at Ebriel, grabbing at her arms, her neck. Ebriel murmured, *"Chut, chut, mon pauvre. Tout va bien."*

The three left behind watched them go with wide eyes. The harness bit into Ebriel's thighs as they rose toward the copter. The strap held the child close to her, warm against her breasts and stomach. An old image flashed in her mind. She saw herself struggling along the Rue Georgette, groceries in one arm, one-year-old Renée in the other, a wriggling, kicking Renée, almost making Ebriel lose her hold on the shopping bag. She had been impatient, snapping at her daughter. Renée had burst into tears.

The copter lurched in a gust of wind, and the memory dissipated in the dizzying swing of the cable. The child shrieked above the roar of wind and water, the clatter of the rotors.

They rose steadily up, out of the cloud shadow and into the fading daylight. The copter bobbed in the wind, and the boat below dipped and rocked on the roughening sea. Ebriel swallowed a sudden nausea. The lift seemed to take forever, though it was probably no more than three minutes before she hoisted the child and herself up over the edge of the door. She unwound the strap that had held them together and belted the little one into the nearest seat. Ty glanced back at her, her face tight with tension.

"Going back now," Ebriel said breathlessly.

"Hurry!" Ty said. "Getting dark fast!" Sweat darkened her cropped hair.

Ebriel slid out of the copter again for the swaying ride down to the boat.

The temperature had dropped sharply. This time, Ebriel gripped the rail the moment she was close enough. The deck slanted beneath her feet, this way and that. The children watched her with mute fear. She hooked one boot behind a rail support, bracing her thighs against the rail as she wriggled out of the harness. Darkness made the straps hard to see, and her fingers grew stiff with cold. She used hand gestures to try to make the boy understand what she wanted. At first he shook his head, confused, chattering at her in Russian.

"Non, non," she shouted over the wind. "You go up, carry the little one, and then I will come up with the last. Come now!"

At last he seemed to understand, nodding, glancing up fearfully at the hovering copter. Ebriel staggered across the deck to clutch at the mist-slippery mast while she helped the boy into the harness and fastened the straps. She lifted one of the children, a child of perhaps five. The smaller child clung to the older one, face buried in his chest. Ebriel strapped the two of them together, holding up the fastenings for the youth to see, hoping he would understand how to undo them once they were in the bird. When they seemed as secure as she could make them, she spoke into the transmitter. "Ready, Ty! Pull up!"

She watched the boy and his small charge lurch upward through the darkness. Frightening as it had been to make that ride, it seemed impossible from this vantage point. The boat pitched and the sea drenched everything with salt spray. The remaining child clung to the mast, sobbing. Ebriel bent and tried to shout over the racket, "It will be all right. *Mon pauvre,* it will be all right." The child cried harder.

In her ear she heard, "Damn it, Eb, what were you thinking? What if he couldn't get into the bird? I've got my hands full up here! Lucky for you, I've got him. Here comes the harness. Now get a move on!"

The harness dropped, but without any weight it flew sideways in the wind, out of reach. Ty had to bank and circle, once, a second time, a third, before Ebriel could get her hand on the cable and pull the harness in. She struggled with the straps, her hands freezing, everything greasy with cold and saltwater. In the pitch blackness of a night at sea, she finally picked up the last child. She wound a strap around them both, but her fingers were too stiff to fasten it. *"Merci à Dieu,"* she muttered, and then cried into the transmitter, "Pull up, Ty."

The moment they were off the deck, Ty banked the copter to the west. The wind made Ebriel's face ache. Her biceps burned with the effort of holding the child, terrified she would lose her grip. She panted through clenched teeth, sparing no breath to try to soothe the frantic wailing. There was still some light once they were off the sea, enough that Ebriel could look up and see the open door of the copter, and the black-haired boy, cap and coat gone now, braced against the sill, waiting for her. Ebriel pushed and he pulled, and the last child was safely inside.

Ebriel crawled up into the copter. As the door slid closed behind her, the relief from the bite of the wind and the roar of the sea was overwhelming. For a moment she simply lay on the floor, panting, waiting for her icy hands and feet to warm. When at length she sat up, she found Ty's eyes on her, freckled brow creased. "You okay back there?"

Ebriel pulled off the tight cap and took the receiver wire from her ear. She ran her fingers through her wet hair and rubbed her cold, burning cheeks. She grinned at Ty, at the boy, at the weeping children. "I am wonderful," she cried. *"Magnifique!"*

Ebriel's rush had receded by the time they landed at Xiao Qaidam, leaving her headachy and tense. She helped the children and the older boy down from the copter. Perk was waiting to shepherd the children into the bunker while Ebriel and Ty rolled the bird down the ramp into the hangar. It was past midnight, and Ebriel hurt all over.

The bunker was warm and brightly lighted. Perk already had the children out of their sodden clothes and wrapped in blankets. Soup steamed in a big pot, and he was setting out bowls and spoons. In the shadows, Ebriel saw Yasmine tucked into one of the bunks.

Ty went to help Perk, and Ebriel followed with reluctant steps. The children, all boys, were quiet now, exhausted. The eldest watched everything with wary eyes. All four were sun-burned, bedraggled, big-eyed with fatigue. They smelled of saltwater and other things, fish and wet fabric and unwashed hair. Ebriel could hardly make the connection between these pitiful scraps of humanity and the exultation she had felt as she dragged them off their sorry craft and up into the safety of the copter.

"Where's *Unicorn*?" Ty asked Perk. She was cutting slices of dark bread and placing them before the children, pantomiming that they should eat. The youth spoke to the younger boys. They picked up their spoons and started on Perk's thick soup.

"Siwa," Perk said. "They held for a day. Pilar and Astrid didn't get their target."

"They didn't? What happened?"

"Too late, sounds like."

"Where?"

"Brazil again. River country."

Ty rubbed her face with her big hands. "God," she said. "That stinks."

"Well, you got these four. That's something. Come on, eat," Perk said. "Ebriel?"

Ebriel hesitated. Now that the children had faces, features, she found she didn't want to be near them. She didn't know what would happen to them. She didn't want to think about it, nor did she want to think about Yasmine.

The black-haired boy, his wispy beard bedraggled, his eyes reddened with exposure, looked up as she approached the table. He looked even younger without his heavy coat, narrow-shouldered, thin-faced. Ebriel took a chair at the end of the table and ate a spoonful of soup. The boy said something, looking at her. She shook her head, and spread her hands.

"I am sorry," she said. "I do not understand."

He said something else, and Ebriel looked to Perk for help, but he shook his head, too. "Russian," he said. "Don't know a word."

And then, from the shadows beyond the kitchen, Yasmine Ananda shuffled into the circle of light, her hair tumbled around her face, a blanket wrapped around her shoulders. Her dark eyes glittered beneath her heavy eyelids.

"*Madame*," she whispered, directing her words to Ebriel. "*Merci. Il vous dit 'merci.' *"

Ebriel put down her spoon. "He said, 'thank you,' " she translated for the others. Her mouth was dry. "Yasmine says that the boy said, 'Thank you.' "

Ty exclaimed, "Russian, too? Good lord."

Yasmine opened her mouth again, then closed it. She

blinked as if she didn't know where she was. Mute again, she turned back to her bunk, the blanket trailing behind her. Weariness washed over Ebriel. How could she abandon this fragile, flawed, brilliant girl?

The smallest refugee was now sound asleep, his little head tipped back against the arm of his chair, his lashes long and dark against his round cheeks. Perk came to lift him out of the chair and tuck him into one of the bunks. The older boy half-rose, then sank back into his chair as he saw what Perk was about. When Ty picked up another of the little boys, Ebriel made herself do the same. They took them into the bathroom, and put them to bed. The black-haired boy followed, but he wouldn't lie down until he had checked on the others.

"They must be brothers," Ty said to Perk when they rejoined him.

Perk was stacking bowls in the washer. "Looks like it," he said. "When Johna and Simon get their cell charged, they'll be here. Then we'll know. Simon's Russian is fair."

"What did Papa say?" Ty asked. "Are they going to Starhold?"

"Nope. Two middle ones have scoliosis. Youngest one is probably deaf."

"Oh, no," Ebriel breathed. "Are you certain, Perk?"

"Not completely. But close enough."

Ty's voice was unemotional. "What are we going to do with them?"

Perk dried his hands and turned to lean against the tilting cooker. "Gonna slip 'em into the neutral polities. Huberto'll take 'em."

Ebriel said, "Huberto? Who is this?"

Ty said, "He runs a mission in Quezon City. He and Papa help each other out."

Ebriel shook her head in amazement. "How is this possible, Ty, that Papa knows so many people, all over the world? On both sides of the boundary, and even in the neutral polities?"

Ty chuckled. "Fleckcell is a big company," she said. "And it's made a lot of people wealthy. A lot of 'em are still loyal to Papa."

"And Huberto—he worked for Fleckcell?"

"Yep."

"And who else? Who else is in Papa's network?"

Perk draped his dish towel over the cracked sink. "Almost everybody." His seamed face creased in a grin. "Even me, briefly. I assembled proton-exchange membranes."

"I did not know this," Ebriel said.

"Didn't ask," Perk said. He turned off the light over the table, casting the bunker into shadow. The array of panels blinked steadily on their side of the room, and light from the shower room cast a narrow slice of illumination from the opposite side. "Better get some sleep," Perk added. "Got a houseful. Lots to do tomorrow."

Obediently, Ebriel dragged herself out of the chair.

"I'm for a shower first," Ty said.

"I, too," Ebriel agreed.

When she stripped off her utility suit, Ebriel found that her thighs were bruised from the sling, her arms abraded in several places from dragging herself over the sill of the copter door. She soaped her hair and stood under a stinging flow of hot water for long minutes, letting it soothe her aching muscles and her scraped skin. Ty held out a faded towel for her when she turned the water off at last. She dried herself quickly and pulled on a flannel nightshirt, soft and comforting, sewed together long before the advent of reworked fabric.

"Where does Perk find these things?" she whispered to Ty.

Ty, grinning, whispered back, "He's a scavenger. Best in the Chain."

"Ty . . ."

"What?"

"Could not the older boy—the black-haired one—could he not come to Starhold?"

"I don't know," Ty answered. "Not my decision." She clapped her hand on Ebriel's shoulder. "Sleep well, Eb. You've earned it. But never pull a stunt like that again, okay?"

In silence, they went to their bunks. Ty took the top, and Ebriel the bottom. In moments, Ebriel heard Ty's breathing slow to the even rhythm of sleep. But Ebriel, tired though she was, lay awake for a long time, reliving the events of the day, and those of the day before, wondering what was to come next. She didn't realize until the next morning that for the first time since Paul's and Renée's deaths, her last thought before sleep had not been of them.

15

Yasmine seemed not to notice as Ebriel fastened the webbed belt around her. Since her brief translation of the night before, Yasmine had not spoken again, though the Russian boy had tried to engage her during breakfast. Now the girl lay her head back on the headrest, staring blindly out into the gathering dusk.

Unicorn was half empty. Pilar and Astrid were morose, almost as silent as Yasmine, unwilling to speak of what had happened on their failed mission. Ty was on the flight deck with the crew. Simon and Johna had flown to Taiwan with the four Russian children.

Ebriel was quiet also. It was not only Yasmine Ananda who worried her, this burden she had accepted. She had allowed too much time to pass. In the excitement of the last days, and in the weight of responsibility for Yasmine, she had been distracted from her purpose. She stared out into the dusk and swore to herself that she would not forget.

Before their departure, Perk drew her aside, one skinny hand on her arm. "Listen," he said. "If that one—" with a jerk of his head toward Yasmine. "If she doesn't work out, gotta be tough about it. I'll see she's taken care of."

"She will work out, Perk. She must."

His pale eyes narrowed in the failing light. "Ebriel. You can't replace the dead."

Ebriel stiffened, and her cheeks flamed. "You do not need to say this," she snapped. She jerked her arm away from his hand, made even angrier by her remorse.

Unoffended, Perk persisted. "No room in the Chain for pity," he said. "We've all suffered our losses. But the kids are more important than our personal problems."

"I have told you," Ebriel said. "I have a feeling about Yasmine. It is not pity."

He nodded. "Yeah. Just remember."

Ebriel turned her back on him and went to collect Yasmine from the armchair where she waited, mute and passive, for someone to move her.

Yasmine clung to her veil of darkness, but it was difficult. Wonders unfurled about her, the graceful spaceplane with its swept-back wings, the soft material of the wide seats, the women, each speaking English with a different accent. Yasmine tried not to see, to notice, but the wealth of information beguiled her, tempted her out into the light.

Ebriel sat next to her. She put her head back, her ashen hair curling against the headrest. Her hazel eyes flicked over Yasmine.

"Ma pauvre," Ebriel murmured. "It seems we are in this together."

Such sadness in her voice, a slight throatiness, an edge of despair. But no weakness, surely. Ebriel had climbed right in her window, carried her away. Ebriel would always be strong. Ebriel would never be afraid, the way Yasmine herself was afraid. Sad, beautiful Ebriel. Courageous Ebriel. Yasmine could never be so brave.

The door to the flight deck closed, and Ty took her seat. The lights in the cabin dimmed. Slowly, Yasmine turned her head to the right, irresistibly drawn by the vista beyond the window.

When the craft lifted, the great engines' multitoned thrum vibrating in her very bones, Yasmine became aware of the depth and resiliency of her seat. In the distance the Himalayan peaks cast a shimmer of ghostly light into the evening. Stars winked in the darkening sky, and a crescent moon showed its horn just above the horizon, then vanished as the spaceplane leaped forward. Yasmine's stomach shuddered. Panic surged through her, and she gripped the armrests of her seat and closed her eyes.

After a long minute, her stomach settled under the steady lift. She opened her eyes and glanced surreptitiously to her left. Ebriel appeared to be sleeping. Again, Yasmine turned her eyes to the window, and what she saw made them open wide.

The Earth had begun to curve against the deep blackness of space. Yasmine gazed in awe, losing all sense of time passing, of the sensations of her body, forgetting her fears in the spectacle laid out beneath her. The continents carved dark silhouettes into the paler darkness of the oceans. The lights of great cities sparkled like jewels scattered on bolts of black velvet. But . . . she knew the maps, had studied them in the crumbled libraries, under the abandoned study hoods . . . there should be a city there, too. And there! Where were they? What had become of them? She sat up, trying to see farther, leaning against the restraining webbing. She put her finger on the cold glass to trace the necklace of lights on the eastern coast. She murmured to herself, in her own dialect, "But where is Beijing? And Hong Kong? And Delhi?"

Ebriel's voice startled her. "What is it, Yasmine? What are you saying?"

Yasmine shrank back immediately into the seat. If she admitted—if she said—but curiosity overwhelmed her. She spoke hesitantly, her voice slender and weak under the roar of the engines. "I see Tokyo. I see the Koreas, I know these lands. But some are not there. Their lights—where are they? I know Srinagar is gone . . . but Delhi? Lahore?"

"Ah." The older woman leaned back again, rubbing her eyes with her fingers. Strands of gray hair curled against her sunburned cheeks. "Yasmine, the study hoods in Srinagar are out of date. Do you understand the expression, out of date?"

Yasmine gave a small nod.

"*Bon.* The world has changed very much," Ebriel said. "Japan and the Koreas are now Todokai. India, China, Pakistan, many other nations are broken apart." She hesitated.

"I am not sure you should hear it all at once. Did you read about the Crash?"

Yasmine nodded again. "The markets," she said.

"*Oui.* When the international markets crashed, everything fell apart. The Middle East was first, with biochemical weapons. Then—I think then it was China, the provinces fighting with each other. Srinagar came after that, and Delhi and Lahore."

Yasmine struggled to translate in her mind as best she could. Her head throbbed.

Ebriel continued, "The polities of North America, of Todokai, and Europe, formed a protective alliance. They called a quarantine. They drew the Line of Partition to shut off all the parts of the world that they fear." At first Yasmine thought she heard bitterness in her tone, and then realized it was sadness. "We, the Chain," Ebriel said, "we are the *résistance.* The rebellion." She fell silent, her chin in her hand.

"*Madame,*" Yasmine ventured, after a time. "Where are we going in this—this—"

"Spaceplane," Ebriel said. Her voice hardened. "We are going into space, Yasmine."

In the loading bay, Semaya barely looked at Ebriel. Her eyes were on the girl beside her. She said, in her flat voice, "Ethan wants to see you. Both of you." She turned away without saying anything more, but Ebriel understood that she was angry.

Ty had already disappeared with Pilar and Astrid, leaving Ebriel alone with the silent girl. She tried to speak hopefully. "Come, Yasmine. Now you will meet Dr. Fleck."

She shepherded Yasmine into the null-grav tube, where the child surprised her. Ebriel had learned with difficulty to move in the tube, her propelling motions too strong, sending her bouncing off the translucent sides. But Yasmine sailed smoothly by Ebriel's side, her long hair floating behind her, twice just touching the sides of the tube.

Before they entered the aerie, Ebriel gently touched Yasmine's shoulder. "Yasmine," she murmured. "I must ask you for something."

The girl looked up in alarm. She pulled back. Even her pupils seemed to shrink.

"*Non, non, ma pétite,*" Ebriel said swiftly. "Do not be afraid. I only want to ask you to—please, if you can—answer Dr. Fleck when he speaks to you. Now is not a good time to—to withdraw. *Bien?* Do you understand?"

For a breathless moment, Ebriel thought Yasmine would freeze up, even now. But then her eyes slid away, and she gave a small, shuddering sigh.

"*Oui, madame,*" she breathed. "I will try."

And Ebriel thought, I can ask no more than that. It is just what I said myself.

Yasmine gazed in fascination at the wasted, pale man floating in the shining silver chair. Ebriel clung to one of the flexible staples set into the curving wall, but Yasmine drifted easily in the odd space, enchanted by the monitors and screens, the wealth of information around her. Her fingers curved involuntarily, longing to touch the keypads, to seize the voice input mikes.

Ebriel said, "Papa. This is Yasmine Ananda."

Ethan Fleck's chair hovered before Yasmine. Only one side of his face moved when he spoke, and his voice skittered like drops of oil on a hot skillet. "Yasmine," he said. "The Chain saved your life."

Mutely, Yasmine nodded, and saw the man's eyes sharpen. With an effort, she said aloud, "Yes, sir," and was rewarded with a flicker of his eyelids.

They regarded each other. It occurred to Yasmine that they were both frozen, the two of them. Ethan Fleck was frozen by illness. Yasmine was numbed by fear.

But he was right. The Chain had saved her life. Ebriel had rescued her. And Ebriel had asked her to respond. Yasmine glanced at her savior.

With the turning of her head, her body shifted in the microgravity. She compensated with a flick of her hand. Dr. Fleck's chair spun in a quarter-circle, showing its tiny pneumatic jets. He tapped at a keypad, and a monitor flashed. He jetted to another, spoke to it, and a screen shifted focus. A moment later the chair righted itself, and he gave Yasmine his distorted smile.

"Always busy," he croaked. "And now, Yasmine Ananda, tell me about yourself."

Yasmine drew breath. Her hands were waving slightly, as if she were back-floating in a pond, but this was easy, an instinctive thing, to keep her steady. She tried to think of the English words she needed, but the images she had tried to banish rose suddenly in her mind as if to drown her, the memories of her wedding, of the strange rough man who had become her husband. After their wedding, when it was still daylight, he had taken her into his bedroom and stripped every stitch of clothing from her body. She had trembled, naked and exposed. Somehow her nakedness had been worse than the violation that followed. And then had come the attack in the night, the screaming and shouting, Yasmine huddling in her husband's house with her hands over her head. The dreadful days of waiting, and then the surreal flight, Ebriel's strong arms around her, then Ty's. The copter, the bunker, the Russian children—there was too much to say. The words stopped in her mouth.

She drew another breath, and blurted instead, "Papa—why do they call you Papa? Means it—*nahi, nahi*—does it not mean father?"

"Yes, it does," he squeaked. "Your English surprises me. How did you learn it?"

These words she had practiced, and they came more easily. "The study hoods in Srinagar. They are—" with a shy glance at Ebriel—"out of date. But many languages there are. English, and also Japanese. Russian. Also French. Very much pleasure to learn."

"You speak six languages?"

"Oh, *nahi, nahi,*" Yasmine said breathlessly. "I only study. I do not speak, not rightly, because—no one to speak with. Except the programs. I speak with the programs."

"Very good," Papa said. His fingers flicked over keypads set in the arms of his chair, and signals responded around the strange room. Yasmine followed the sounds, devouring the monitors and screens with her eyes. When he spoke again, she had to force her attention back to the sound of his voice.

"Yasmine, do you know what fuel cells are?"

She nodded. "Yes. I have seen."

"Yes. Good. Years ago, before you were born, my company perfected the technology. Fleckcell is a big company, offices and plants all over the world. I wasn't so ill then, and I knew everyone in my company, visited all the different installations. I had no children. They were my family. And they started to call me 'Papa.' Can you guess why I live here, in space?"

She nodded again. "Yes. More easy, no gravity. Because you are ill."

He chuckled, his voice a thin scrape of sound. "Indeed, more easy. Exactly so."

Suddenly his chair darted to the right, where an image had appeared on a small screen. Without thinking, Yasmine gave a tiny kick with her right foot, and followed, her hands out to balance her movement. She hung beside Papa's chair with one finger on the curving wall for balance. His eyes caught her movement, and his chair swiveled slightly to allow her to see the screen. "Weightlessness doesn't disturb you at all, does it?" he croaked. Even in his strange, constricted voice, Yasmine heard laughter.

"Way—way?" she asked, not understanding.

"Weight. Less. Ness." He touched his controls, and his chair swerved back and away, to face her. "Being without weight. Because here, in my aerie—my room—there is no gravity."

"Oh, oh, yes, I see. Weight-less-ness. No, it does not disturb. Swim. Like swim."

"Yes, it is like swimming," Papa said. "I like it, but not everyone does. So we charge the other levels with electrogravity."

"Electro—" She struggled with the word. "Electrogravity?"

"Yes. Electrogravity. The hydrogen that is a by-product of very large fuel cells is useful in creating a residual electromagnetic force. Starhold's gravity is almost exactly that of Earth."

Yasmine nodded, absorbed in the concept. It was a moment before she realized that she had been talking with this man as freely as if he had been a member of her family, as freely as if all the terror that had frozen her tongue had drained away. But had it? No. But in this wonderful room with its abundance of computers and keyboards and wisdom—who could be afraid here?

She followed the jet-driven chair as Dr. Fleck—Papa—moved this way and that, scanning monitors, inputting orders. Ebriel remained where she was, watching. Papa said at last, "There. That's done for the time being." He turned his chair to Yasmine again.

"I was told you were unresponsive," he said to her in his wildly fluctuating tone. "Do you understand? Not responding. Not talking."

"With-drawn," Yasmine said carefully, remembering the word Ebriel had used.

"Yes," Papa said. "Exactly so. Withdrawn." He gave her his tortured one-sided smile. "But not with me, eh, Yasmine?"

She thought carefully through the English before she answered. Solemnly she said to him, "I am not afraid here. In this place."

"Ah. But in other places?"

She thought again, and ran her phrase through her mind before she spoke it. "Sometimes I am afraid. I am not brave. But I will try."

He winked at her. "Good girl. You do that." His chair swiveled to face in Ebriel's direction. "Ebriel, I persuaded Semaya to give you this chance. It wasn't easy." The distorted grin again. "But I can see why you took an interest. Keep me informed, please."

"Yes," Ebriel said. "Thank you, Papa."

He watched her for a moment. Ebriel's answering gaze was steady, but Yasmine sensed her tension and understood that she, Yasmine, was the cause. It filled her with dread.

"Off with you both, now," Papa said. "Yasmine, come and see me again soon."

Moments later, they were once again in the tube, floating the opposite direction through the levels of the habitat—Starhold. She did not understand the name. Starhold overflowed with greenery, like the abandoned temple, but the walls were stark, metal and plastic disguised with bright paint.

The corridors were crowded. Children in bright clothing ran everywhere, like flocks of chittering birds. Women and men, with hard serious eyes like Ty and Ebriel and the others, watched her pass, and she trembled and shrank within herself, despite her promise.

Ebriel installed Yasmine in a square room next to her own that she called a cubby. There were clothes, and a toothbrush and a hairbrush. A small mirror showed Yasmine her own face, her pointed chin, her arching nose. She looked away, wishing the mirror weren't there.

But it was the dining hall that undid her. Ty came to the cubby and stood in the doorway. "Gear all stowed?" she said. "Great. I'm starved."

Together the three of them floated up the tube to the gallery level, and Yasmine, under the gentle pressure of Ebriel's arm, went into the dining hall. A hundred faces turned to her. A thousand plants hung from the ceiling and climbed up the walls. A deep, narrow window gave onto the darkness of space.

Yasmine felt as if every eye watched her stumble over vines, weave between the tables. When Ebriel seated her on the long bench among children and Chain members, all strangers, the dark curtain fell. She couldn't resist it. She folded in on herself, her arms crossed, her chin dropped, her thighs trembling.

From a great distance, she heard Ebriel speaking to her, but she couldn't answer. Her body was lifted, carried, the clamor of voices around her receded and faded to nothing. She huddled in lonely misery behind the curtain of her fear.

16

Ty helped Ebriel tuck Yasmine into bed. The girl lay in a knot under the blanket, her knees pulled up, her hands in fists under her chin, her eyelids pressed tight.

"You'll have to stay," Ty said. "Watch for a change."

"I know."

"Sorry, Eb. Sorry it went like that."

Ebriel ran her fingers through her hair. "She was so good with Papa."

"She's unstable." They turned at the sound of Semaya's voice. "You should have known, Ty." She leaned in the doorway, arms folded over her thin chest.

Ebriel looked away, resentment flaming in her cheeks.

Ty said, "Yeah. Well, win some, lose some."

Semaya stepped inside the cubby. "Do you know how many children are on the habitat right now, at this very moment?" she asked. "Sixty-four. Star Hotel One was designed to hold fifty guests and the staff to serve them. The crèche is full. The classrooms are full. The dojo is full. Still Ethan wanted those children from Brazil, the two Pilar and Astrid lost. He still does. And now you've brought this girl here, when you knew she wasn't fit."

Ebriel's lips trembled with fury. "Do not blame Ty. It was my wish. And you agreed."

"Ethan insisted," Semaya said. "Against my advice."

"Well, Semaya, she's here now," Ty put in. "Might as well make the best."

"I will stay with her," Ebriel said. "Perhaps she will be better tomorrow."

Semaya made a noncommittal noise in her throat. "I'll send Dr. Nordstrom to see her, but time is a luxury we don't enjoy. A decision will have to be made, and soon." Semaya turned to leave, her shoulders sagging as if standing straight took too much energy. She seemed to have aged swiftly in the last months. She stepped with care in the narrow corridor.

Ebriel felt a grudging sympathy for her. "Ty," she murmured. "What am I to do?"

Ty patted her shoulder. "Look, done is done. Just have to wait and see. I'll bring us some food. Then I'm going to the dojo. When I'm finished, I'll spell you."

Ebriel pulled a stool close to the bed and sat down. She was weary herself from the events of the past days, and she was thirty years younger than Semaya Fleck. She looked down at the Indian girl's slender face, her tawny skin, her eyelashes like glossy bird wings against her cheeks. *"Ma pauvre,"* Ebriel whispered. "How can I help you? What can I do?"

All of that day, Ebriel sat with Yasmine, only leaving to spend an hour in the dojo. She returned from her workout drenched with perspiration and found Ty sound asleep on the stool, arms folded, head tipped back against the wall. Yasmine had not moved. Ebriel showered and dressed in fresh cottons, then returned to the cubby and touched Ty's shoulder. Ty woke immediately and straightened, rubbing her eyes.

"Mon amie," Ebriel murmured. "Go off to your own bed now. *Merci.*"

"Yeah," Ty said sleepily. She stood, stretching her arms with a cracking of joints. She looked down at Yasmine's still form. "Shame. Poor kid never stood a chance." She yawned as she wandered off to her own room.

Ebriel sat on the edge of the bed, tousling her damp hair with her fingers to dry it. Yasmine's head lay near her thigh, the warmth of her small body radiating through the blanket.

Ebriel put a hand lightly on her back. The girl barely seemed to breathe.

Ebriel closed her eyes. She could not save this child. She must resign herself, despite the strength of her intuition. It would be terrible if this resistance she felt was no more than embarrassment, an unwillingness to lose face with Semaya, to lose credibility with Papa.

"Zut!" she whispered. She gathered Yasmine into her arms, blanket and all, shifting so she could hold the girl across her lap. Long strands of dark hair fell over her knees, and she combed it with her fingers.

She held her that way for a long time, feeling the beat of her own heart and watching the pulse in Yasmine's slender throat.

Perk was right in one thing. There was no replacing the dead. And yet, how good it felt to have a child in her arms, to breathe the scents of clean hair and laundered clothes. Ty was right, too. Yasmine had never had a chance.

Renée, though—laughing, beautiful child—Renée had had every chance, the world at her fingertips, a future bright as morning. And George Glass had allowed it all to be destroyed. Ebriel's chest burned as she sat holding Yasmine, staring through the open door into the corridor.

An hour later, the doctor arrived and bent over Yasmine, testing her pulse, touching her arms and her legs. Emily Nordstrom was a small woman in her sixties who had been a physician in the North American polities. "This girl is asleep," she said quietly. "That's all."

"Excusez-moi?" Ebriel said. "Asleep? Not—"

The doctor shook her head. "No, not. Semaya told me she was catatonic, but she is not, at least not now. She's asleep."

"But then, what is happening, Dr. Nordstrom? Why did she—"

"I can't tell you, Ebriel. I can only guess that she shuts down in response to too much stimuli—of course, we don't know what she was like before the events of the last week. When she's awake, I'll examine her." She adjusted Yasmine's blanket. "For now, let her sleep."

"But she should not be alone, do you think?"

"No, definitely not. I'll have someone bring you some dinner, but you should stay with her. Let her waken on her own, and then bring her up to the infirmary." The doctor's faded eyes assessed Ebriel. "And you must rest, too. Not like that—lying down. We'll have a cot set up here. Eat, and then sleep. All right?"

"I suppose." Stiffly, Ebriel slid out from under Yasmine's weight and laid the girl's head gently down on the wrinkled pillow. Her left arm had gone numb.

"Call it an order, Ebriel," the doctor said. "As much of one as I'm able to give you."

Ebriel managed a tired smile. "Yes, Dr. Nordstrom, I will do as you say. Eat, sleep."

"Good. I'll see you when she's awake, then." The physician nodded and left the cubby. Ebriel stood in the doorway, massaging her arm, and watched the doctor's small figure float up the tube.

Yasmine stirred in the night and cried out. Ebriel woke immediately in the spare cot and, with difficulty, wriggled across it to Yasmine. "Yasmine? It is Ebriel. Everything is all right."

Yasmine sat up in the darkness. She reached out blindly, her fingers spread wide.

Ebriel caught her hands. "Yasmine? Can you speak to me now?"

"Oh. Oh, yes, *madame*. Oh! *Je regrette*—I am so sorry!"

Ebriel stifled her sigh. "Yes, I know, *chérie*. Do not worry about it now." She stroked the girl's hair, and said again, "Do not worry now. Lie down, sleep. Everything will be all right."

Obediently, Yasmine lay down again, and Ebriel pulled the blanket up around her shoulders, murmuring reassurances. She wished she believed her own words. In truth, she doubted that everything would ever be all right for Yasmine Ananda.

17

Yasmine struggled to answer the doctor's questions. The questions were easy. Opening her mouth, saying the words—it was like being stripped naked.

"Tell me your name again," Dr. Nordstrom said. They sat across from each other at her desk. There were only two chairs in the tiny office. Ebriel leaned against one wall, arms folded.

"My name," Yasmine whispered through dry lips. She swallowed. "Yasmine Ananda."

"How old are you?"

"I am . . . fourteen years of age." She shivered violently, unable to stop herself, wanting desperately to withdraw and resisting with all her strength.

"You are safe here, Yasmine," the doctor said. She had said it before. She seemed to understand Yasmine's spasms, and she repeated herself quietly, without impatience. She had probed and examined, manipulated, prodded. She had given Yasmine materials to touch, rough, smooth, hot, cold, sharp, and dull. She had dimmed the lights, and then brightened them, and she had given her things to taste, sweet and sour and salty and bland. Now she held up one thin white finger. "Can you follow my finger?"

Yasmine watched the fingertip as it moved from side to side, up, down. When Dr. Nordstrom's finger came straight toward her face, toward the bridge of her nose, Yasmine cowered away from it.

Again, "You are safe here, Yasmine. No one will hurt you."

Ebriel was silent, but Yasmine knew she was worried, and that it was her fault.

Dr. Nordstrom snapped her fingers. Yasmine jumped, and the doctor smiled. "Good, Yasmine," she said calmly. "That's very good. Now, do you think we could talk alone, or do you need Ebriel here with you?"

Yasmine swallowed again. The doctor's eyes were gentle. The clinic was a colorful place of cushions, posters in many languages, toys and books. "I do not need Ebriel," Yasmine whispered. It was true enough. No one's presence, not her mother's, certainly not her father's, had ever made it easy for her to talk to people. Study hoods were easy. People were hard.

Ebriel straightened immediately, and Yasmine sensed her relief, her wish to be gone. *"Je regrette, madame,"* she whispered miserably.

"Non, non, chérie," Ebriel said. She patted Yasmine's shoulder. "You must not worry."

Dr. Nordstrom nodded approval at their exchange, and Ebriel slipped out of the examining room. Yasmine wrapped her arms around herself as she watched her protector depart. She wanted to rock, to sway forward and back. She had rocked that way by the hour when she was little, using the monotonous movement to shut out new faces, loud voices, sudden sounds. Her father had beaten her for it, first light slaps, then great swats, and once, a thorough whipping with a long switch of unripe sugar cane. That was the first time she had completely withdrawn, rolled herself into a ball, head against her knees, hands locked under her chin, eyelids pressed tight. By the age of seven, she had learned to withdraw invisibly, to hood her eyes and close her ears. It was not until she was locked in her dead husband's bedroom, waiting to burn, that she found she could pull a curtain of solid black around her mind, a veil no stimuli could pierce.

"Yasmine," Dr. Nordstrom said. "Could you take my hand?"

Yasmine's body began to sway. She clenched her muscles tightly to stop it.

The doctor rested one hand on the desk, palm up. "Just take my hand."

Yasmine, almost whimpering with the effort, forced herself to put out her own hand, to lay her trembling fingers into the doctor's steady ones. Dr. Nordstrom didn't squeeze Yasmine's hand, or stroke it. She only sat, breathing lightly, gazing at a poster of children playing on a beach. Yasmine fixed her eyes on a blank spot on the wall and worked at not yanking her hand away. The doctor's hand was cool, dry, very steady. Yasmine felt a pulse where their fingers touched. She didn't know if it was her own, or Dr. Nordstrom's.

They sat on that way for some time. Bit by bit, after how long a time Yasmine couldn't guess, her tremors began to slow. Still they sat, their hands linked.

At last, Dr. Nordstrom smiled. "There, now," she said. "Feeling better?"

Yasmine managed a nod. "Yes," she faltered. "I am . . . feeling better."

"Good." The doctor released her hand and stood. She moved slowly, as if carefully planning and executing each movement, nothing abrupt, nothing disturbing. "Now, Yasmine, I understand you're quite adept at using a study hood."

"Yes. I think so. Adept."

It was a new word, a delicious word. Yasmine seized on it with her mind, turning it this way and that. It was a great relief to have a word to think about, to play with. It was clear in the context, but she wondered at the root of it, *ad* . . . and then *dept,* what might that be? Latin, of course, the *ad* meaning to, toward, and the rest? She itched to look it up, to understand. Her shoulders relaxed, her stiff ankles flexed, her rigid features softened.

"Languages especially, I think?" Dr. Nordstrom asked.

Yasmine tore her mind away from the lovely new word. "Yes, madam. Languages."

"Very good, Yasmine." The doctor moved to the side of the room and brought back a portable panel. She opened it and placed it on the desk. "Will you show me?"

* * *

Ebriel and Semaya met each other at the door of the clinic. Emily Nordstrom was waiting. Ebriel glanced around for Yasmine.

The doctor said, "Ty took Yasmine back to her cubby."

"What did you find, Emily?" Semaya eased herself into one of the chairs.

Dr. Nordstrom took the chair behind the desk and leaned forward, steepling her fingers. Ebriel stood running her fingers through her hair, tugging at the short locks in a gesture that had become habitual.

"Yasmine is very bright," the doctor began.

"Fine," Semaya said abruptly. "But that in itself—"

Dr. Nordstrom opened her fingers in a forestalling motion. "She's the brightest child we've ever seen on Starhold. Her facility with languages, math, science—it's astounding."

"Astounding? Surely you exaggerate, Emily."

The doctor shook her head. "No." She leaned back. "She's brilliant. And she's autistic."

Semaya made a small, triumphant sound. Ebriel flashed her a look.

The doctor held up a finger. "Before you make assumptions, let me explain that there are many levels of autism. There are no biological tests for it, so my diagnosis could be called an educated guess, but I believe Yasmine suffers from Asperger's, or a similar disorder in the autistic spectrum. Her difficulties with transitions, with surprises, her resistance to touch, these are common signs. Also, such patients often exhibit exceptional skill and obsessive interest in a specific area—in Yasmine's case, language.

"It's interesting that the input she receives through a panel doesn't disturb her. She finds it soothing, actually, predictable and controllable. I understand she defied her parents in order to slip into Srinagar and use she study hoods there—that would have been her coping mechanism. She is very high functioning and has taught herself to control her condition under most circumstances. But what happened to her in the last week—what she experienced, waiting to be immolated . . ." Dr. Nordstrom's eyes hardened. "This is enough to drive anyone mad. For Yasmine, her already fragile nervous system simply overloaded. But here, in my office—in less than half an hour, she was relaxed enough to work with me."

"What are you saying, Emily? That we should keep her? Despite her problems?"

The doctor gave Semaya a searching look. "How can we not keep her?"

Semaya gave a weary sigh. Ebriel felt a welling of emotion in her breast. Some moments passed before she realized that, for the first time in almost a year, she had felt joy.

When Yasmine and Ebriel came into the aerie, answering Ethan's request to visit him, they found Semaya clinging to his null-gray chair. The chair hovered opposite a live screen, but upside down to its perspective. A man's face, fleshy, worried, looked out of the screen at Papa, who slumped in the chair with his head at an awkward angle, braced against the headrest. Yasmine's eyes widened with alarm. "What is wrong?" she whispered. "Papa is ill, I think."

Semaya glanced up, and signaled for them to stay where they were.

Ebriel had learned that it was better not to touch Yasmine. She held up her hand in a forestalling gesture. "Wait, *ma pétite*," she murmured. "Let us wait until they are done."

Semaya was speaking in a brittle voice. "No, it's impossible," she said to the fleshy man.

He looked uncomfortable. For him, Semaya too was upside down. He said, "Couldn't Dr. Fleck just—"

"No," Semaya said again. "Can't you see for yourself how ill my husband is?"

"But—" the man tried again. "General Glass wanted me to ask—"

Ebriel stiffened.

"He knows Ethan doesn't receive visitors," Semaya said. "Now you do, too."

"Dr. Fleck . . ."

"Please, let me attend to my husband. You'll hear from us. Off," she said to the screen.

The moment it blanked, Ethan's erratic cackle rattled through the aerie. Yasmine jumped, and she and Ebriel floated backward, freefalling until Ebriel's feet touched a hard surface.

"Got 'em," Papa cried, winning a tired smile from his wife.

"Yes, I expect that will keep them for a while. But you'll have to come up with something, Ethan."

Papa's distorted grin was gleeful, his eyes shining. "Don't worry," he croaked. "I've got a couple little tokens I've been saving. Cold weather tobacco, for one! They can grow it in wheat country. Should keep 'em off our backs for months."

"Tobacco," Semaya said. "What good is tobacco, Ethan, when people are hungry?"

"You underestimate the pressure of addiction," Ethan rasped.

Semaya sighed. "Ethan, Ebriel and Yasmine are here. I'll let Ebriel explain everything, all right? I'm going to rest."

She floated awkwardly past Ebriel and Yasmine to the slip. Ethan's sharp eyes followed her, then turned to Ebriel. "She's not happy with me."

"I think it is I who have made her unhappy," Ebriel said.

"Not your fault," he answered. "Mine. Semaya's worried about me."

Ebriel saw how emaciated he had grown, the hollows over his eyes deepened, his hands skeletal. In the muted light, he appeared even more sallow than on her last visit. Only his crooked smile seemed as cheery as ever. "Papa," she said. "Who was that man? What did he want?"

"Our esteemed General Glass wants to send someone to Starhold. Got the wind up, I should think, after the little *contretemps* in the Sea of Japan." His sunken eyes glittered. The right side of his mouth stretched up. "Right word, Ebriel? *Contretemps?*"

Ebriel couldn't help smiling at him. She wondered for the dozenth time how such a cheerful man had married a woman like Semaya. Ebriel had never heard Semaya Fleck laugh. *"Oui,"* she said. "It is the perfect word."

"Glass has always wanted us to let someone come, look around." Fleck paused to swallow, with difficulty. Ebriel tensed, wondering if he needed help. He winked at her. "Bit dry," he croaked. "That's all." His chair tilted, and he examined a monitor, then spun to face her again. "We keep InCo satisfied with bits of tech, little inventions. It's their choice, you know. They choose to have earplants and caseless ammunition and spybugs instead of spaceplanes. So they want to use ours. But we don't have to let them do it."

He stopped, swallowing again, appearing fatigued by the long speech. Ebriel moved forward, concerned, but then was distracted by Yasmine, who dropped suddenly and nimbly past the null-grav chair. A projection of the Earth spun slowly in the dim light, masked with swirls of cloud. Papa's chair dipped to follow Yasmine.

"Would you like it larger, Yasmine?" Fleck rasped.

Yasmine glanced up at him with shining eyes. She turned back to the spinning image to examine it from all sides, to peer beneath it at the projection console. "Larger," she said, experimenting. The globe swelled by half, and Ethan chuckled. Yasmine repeated, with more confidence, "Larger."

The globe bloomed to a meter in width, the continents clearly etched, the oceans blue and green and gray. As they watched, a storm system prowled across the face of Asia. The image turned, showing the coastline of Europe, the expanse of the Atlantic Ocean.

Yasmine turned to Ethan. "How?" she demanded.

"Microsats," he said with satisfaction. He tapped a command into the pad on his chair arm, and a section of the image zoomed outward. "Florida," he rasped. He tapped again. Another extruded itself, alive with swirling clouds. "Mexico. Big storm in the Gulf."

Ebriel watched the globe turn. The Pacific passed, and the Asian coastline appeared. She thrust away from her handhold, moving too quickly, having to stop herself with a hand on another staple. She watched intently as the globe spun, majestically, ponderously. There!

"Geneve," she muttered.

Yasmine's dark eyes turned to her. *"Madame?"*

Ethan said, "Geneva? Are you interested in Geneva, Ebriel?"

Ebriel hadn't realized she had spoken aloud.

Ethan said, "Of course. Ariana Park."

"Oui," Ebriel said. "Ariana Park."

And the Palais. George Glass. It was time, and past time.

18

The Tacticals room on the gallery level glimmered with the blue and green lights of simulation screens. Vee stood at Ebriel's shoulder and watched as she took her practice with the pulse pistol. "Good, Ebriel," she said. Her English had the short vowels and thick consonants of her original Dutch. Vee Eyckart had been one of Fleckcell's first employees. She had also competed in the Olympics with small arms three times before the Games vanished after the Crash. No Chain member was allowed on a mission without her approval.

"Now faster," she told Ebriel, standing at her shoulder. "But don't lose your precision. See the target, breathe, aim, fire, one continuous—yes, yes, good. Exactly. Very good." She stood back and let Ebriel finish her drill. When Ebriel finished, took off her visor and fit the practice pistol back into its sleeve, Vee said, "Come into my office, please."

Ebriel followed Vee into the brighter light and cramped space of a room the size of Dr. Nordstrom's office. A narrow vertical window, almost completely covered with grape vines, opened onto the gallery. Beyond the tangled green strands, the tiled corridor curved around the tube. A few children in bright cottons circled the corridor, small soft brushes in their hands.

Ebriel recognized Kanika, the girl from Sierra Leone.

Kanika had grown several inches, her shoulders broadening, her thighs long and strong. She bent to brush a plant with pale white blossoms, then cupped the brush gently in her hand as she moved to the next plant to transfer the pollen. In the dojo, the girl was anything but gentle. Ebriel had watched her spar with girls older than herself, her fists quick and hard, the reach of her kicks growing every month. Like herself, Ebriel thought, Kanika was impatient, and eager for revenge.

Vee Eyckart indicated a chair, and Ebriel slid into it gratefully, her tired thighs trembling. Ethan had invited Yasmine to stay with him for a meal in microgravity, and Ebriel had seized the chance to attend a class in the dojo and the practice drill in Tacticals. As she had for the past year, she sought, and welcomed, physical fatigue. Now her legs ached from practicing roundhouse kicks, and her left cheekbone stung, threatening a black eye where her sparring partner's padded fist had penetrated her block.

"So," Vee said. She propped her short, strong legs on her desk and regarded Ebriel above her booted toes. "Your first mission was a success."

Ebriel caught a note of something in her voice, a warning timbre. "I think so," she said. "I believe that from a tactical standpoint, we were successful. What will happen to Yasmine—the girl who was our target—this I do not know."

"I only deal with tacticals," Vee said. "And I want to talk about your second mission."

"Pardon?"

"The Sea of Japan."

"Ah." Ebriel straightened. "You are going to scold me," she said. "But this mission was also a success." She lifted her chin. "We saved four children. Their boat was in trouble, and the sea rising."

"And if you had not made it back? If the child you put in your harness had not been able to climb up into the copter?"

"But this did not happen!" Ebriel exclaimed. "Vee—four children who might have drowned are alive! And—and it was—" She remembered the exhilaration, the rush of well-being she had felt once she was safely inside the copter. "How can I be sorry I did such a thing?"

Vee lifted her feet from her desk and set them firmly on the floor in a fluid motion that belied her age. She leaned forward, her hands on her desk, and looked into Ebriel's face. "You put Ty at risk. You put the children at risk, the ones already in the air, and the remaining one on the boat. Worse, you ignored Ty's orders, and she is senior to you."

Ebriel stared back at her. "Do you wish me to say I am sorry? It would not be true." She knew her accent intensified, heard the nasal consonants.

Vee eyed her for a moment, and her leathery face creased in a frown. "No, Ebriel," she said, shaking her head. "I'm not either. But next time listen to your senior partner, okay?"

Ebriel lifted one shoulder, expressively.

Vee's frown deepened. "You did some great work. But if you get cocky—"

Ebriel raised her brows, not understanding the word.

"Cocky, cocky—" Vee searched for a synonym. "Overconfident," she supplied. "If you're overconfident, you make mistakes. I don't want you to forget—" She pointed one stubby finger. "You can die down there, Ebriel Serique."

Ebriel shrugged again.

After dinner, Ebriel floated up the tube to fetch Yasmine. Semaya and Ethan were watching a Newnet broadcast, and Yasmine floated easily at the foot of the null-grav chair. Ebriel caught sight of the image on the panel as she came through the slip. She took a sharp breath between her teeth. Yasmine's dark eyes flashed at her, and Semaya said, "Ah. Ebriel."

Ethan said, "Someone's finally noticed you've gone missing, Ebriel. Security Corps says you've fled the clinic in Leysin and that you may be dangerous, to yourself or to others."

Ebriel stared at the screen, at the face that no longer existed. The dimpled cheek, full lips, the auburn curls were those of a fantasy. Yasmine looked from the old stillphoto to Ebriel, and then back again.

"Madame," she whispered. *"La différence—"*

Ebriel looked down at her own strong fingers gripping Papa's chair. Slender ridges of muscle stood up on her forearm. *"Oui."*

Yasmine's gaze took in the bruise on the orbit of Ebriel's eye.

Ebriel touched it gingerly, and then ran her hands over her cropped silver hair. Even she could hear the bitterness in her short laugh. "*Oui*. I am greatly changed."

The broadcast left the subject of Ebriel Serique, the missing flutist. Ethan touched the keypad under his hand, and the panel blanked.

"Did they say—was there any mention of my mother? My father?"

Ethan's chair turned, gently, the puffs of air that propelled it no more than breaths. His eyes, so expressive in the slack muscles of his face, shone with sympathy. "There has been no change," he croaked. "Your mother is in a sanitarium. Your father visits her, they say, and continues in his work, and waits for news."

"Is there not something we can do? Some way to let them know?"

Semaya said, "Ebriel, you're as lost to them as your own child is to you."

"Semaya, my dear," Ethan rasped. "That's harshly put."

"It's the truth," Semaya said. "She knew that when she joined the Chain."

"They are suffering," Ebriel cried out. "My parents are suffering!"

"So many are," Semaya said. "It is why we do what we do." The muted light of the aerie softened the lines in her face, but her voice was hard.

"Ebriel," Ethan said. She saw his difficult swallow, how his throat muscles struggled. "You couldn't go back," he said. "Semaya is blunt, but she's right. They would put you back in Leysin, and you would still be lost to your parents. I'm sorry for you and for them, but this is the truth for all the Chain. Ty, Pilar, Astrid, all have left their families, their old lives, behind."

"But, surely," Ebriel tried again, knowing they were right, fighting it. "Surely I could at least send a message to my father, some word . . ."

"Would you risk all of us for that?" Semaya said. "The Chain? Our children?"

Ebriel couldn't look at her. She whispered, after a moment, *"Non."*

"We knew that," Ethan said. "Of course."

And Yasmine whispered, *"Je regrette, madame. Pauvre madame. Je regrette."*

19

James Bull and Michael Chang had the big twelve-seater to themselves, nothing to worry about but staying in loose formation with three other copters as they made their way from Colorado Springs to Hawaii. James was halfway to earning his wings, and Chang let him fly the bird for hours. Brilliant August sunshine gilded the polycarb windows. Occasional clouds made fleeting shadows across the ocean's surface. James gloried in the clear sky, the vast ocean, the feeling that his customary solitude was right and natural.

Tropical heat filled the cabin as they hovered over the tarmac at Hickam. By the time they retracted the door, humidity wilted their collars and softened the creases in their uniforms. Stepping into the fragrant Hawaiian evening was like stepping into warm bath water. James's skin prickled at the change of atmosphere.

A sergeant saluted. "Welcome to Hickam, sir!"

James absently returned the salute as he surveyed the airfield. There were at least twenty copters, tied down in neat rows, and one fixed-wing airplane in an open-ended hangar. "Where do we report, Sergeant?"

"Ops is over there, sir." The noncom pointed to a one-story building. The two officers canted their flight caps and walked toward it, the heat from the tarmac working its way through their boots.

The Ops master sergeant grinned as they flicked their wrists over the sensors to check in. "You're in luck," he said. "Two days liberty in Honolulu before you're off to the parade."

"Parade?" Chang asked.

"Yes, sir." The sergeant pointed to a stillpanel displaying service bulletins. "Big meeting on Taiwan. The commander general, the premier, and President Blackfield. Lot of aircraft providing escort for the general, and lots of security. That's you."

James scanned the stillpanel. Blackfield, the leader of neutral Oceania, was hosting the InCo leaders in a summit meeting. "It's a big show, Michael."

Chang nodded. "Yeah. Security will be a bitch, though. Neutral territories! No spybugs, sloppy militia."

"Maybe." James took the data stick with their billet assignment from the master sergeant, and he and Chang went back out into the warm evening. A lone banana tree grew by the door, glossy ground foliage spreading up its trunk. Inland-leaning palm trees lined the roads, their fringed branches rustling in the breeze. A constant flow of trucks passed, interspersed with bicycles and pedicabs, and the lights of Honolulu beckoned through the twilight. James wished his father could see this scene, the power, the comfort, the security.

In the officers' quarters, Chang met buddies from other units putting together a jaunt, a round of the bars and clubs that crowded downtown Honolulu. James begged off, smiling, not wanting to explain. Chang finally clapped him on the shoulder, said, "Have it your way. See you in the morning. Not too early, though!"

Left alone, James changed out of his uniform into a pair of khakis and an open-collared shirt. He unpacked his duffel and put his room in order and then followed the signs to the Officers' Club for a brief meal. Night had settled in by the time he finished, and he strolled out through the base, sometimes passing couples or groups of three or four, laughing, talking together. James nodded to them and walked on.

The sound of the surf drew him to a small beach, a half-moon of white sand washed by gentle waves. A few people sat on towels or beach chairs, watching the foam of the surf glimmer in the darkness, the rush of the water drowning their conversation. James crossed the sand to a flat, dry rock and sat down, stretching his long legs out in front of him. He watched stars flicker to life in the night sky. Alone. He was so often alone.

He could have gone with Michael Chang and his friends, but experience had taught him that his temperance invited a lot of questions, made him feel even more an outsider.

James had taken his first and his last drink at the age of thirteen. Beer first, straight from his father's six-pack. It tasted great, and it made him feel strong, brave, a foot taller. He liked it so well he decided to try something stronger. He and a friend acquired a bottle of whiskey, and spent all of one night drinking it, shouting and singing on the banks of the Two Medicine River. While they were drunk, they were the kings of Browning, the future chiefs of the Blackfoot Nation. They ended the night throwing up. Dizzy, James had staggered home with vomit on his shirt and found his father passed out on the front porch, too drunk even to make his way inside. James stumbled around him, staggering into the bathroom to stare at himself in the mirror. At thirteen, he faced the flat truth. Alcohol would turn him into his father.

He never forgot that night. And he never drank again, or used any other drug. Never.

And so now, alone on a lovely Oahu beach, James leaned back on his elbows, face turned up to watch the few brave stars bright enough to outshine the lights of Honolulu.

On a hillside of sand at Siwa, Ebriel sat by herself, having left Ty and Nenet playing cards in the common room. To the west, the lights of Starhold shone steadily against a sparkling field of stars. Ebriel lay back on the sand, her head pillowed on her hands. Tomorrow she and Ty were scheduled to fly to Xiao Qaidam.

Today she had made her first solo flight.

She had flown out over the desert, far from the airfield and barracks and the broken landmarks of the old town. With only the flight monitor murmuring occasionally in her earpiece, she banked and descended to skim the waves of sand, then climbed, feeling the power of the copter under her toes, in her fingers. The sun blazed hot gold from a pale sky as she made a long arc over the scattered oases. Once she saw the tents of a nomadic tribe pitched in the lee of a dune. She circled to the north, and then west. She saw the sparkle of the Mediterranean on the distant horizon, and she knew that a few hours in that direction lay Geneva. Only a few hours, and he could be within her reach . . . except he wasn't there.

She had developed the habit of checking Newnet daily and found that it was a rare day that Glass's activities weren't reported in detail. He made a parade inspection of the North American bases; he conferred with environmental specialists in Washington; he met with the European Federation heads, including her own *Présidente,* to discuss boundary enforcement; he held a video conference with Ethan Fleck. Of course the Chain knew this was a mostly fictional report of a conversation with Semaya; but Newnet reported it as if it were essential to maintaining InCo's stability. And tonight, just before Ebriel and Ty and Nenet sat down to their meal, Newnet reported on the summit meeting taking place in Oceania, on the island of old Taiwan.

Ebriel stretched out her arms, wriggling impatiently on her bed of sand. Sand crept into her hair, down her neck. She thought of Ty's clear gaze following her as she left the common room, and Nenet's dark eyes full of remembered pain. She thought of Ethan Fleck, and his flock of children with their bleak histories and uncertain futures. She thought of Starhold itself, cramped, spartan, disciplined, and the people who swore loyalty to it and to the Chain, people who battered themselves uselessly against the ramparts of InCo policy. They were like insects biting at an elephant.

The stars mocked her with their light that looked like fire but had no heat. And Starhold, glowing among them, was a castle in the air, a foolish dream. The cheerful Ethan Fleck and grim Semaya were playing, indulging themselves, aggrandizing their small victories, rationalizing the tragedies that befell their people.

Ebriel closed her eyes. It had been more than a year. It was August already. She had learned what she needed to learn. She was ready.

20

Ty and Ebriel had the copter ready for the long flight to Xiao Qaidam, the cell charged, the tri-gear serviced, pre-flights completed on all systems. Nenet was to rise early with them and give them coffee and breakfast before they left.

Ebriel lay awake, staring out into the black African night. Two doors down the hallway, Ty slept soundly, trusting in tomorrow. What would she think when she woke? And Nenet, of the plain face and beautiful eyes—would they hate Ebriel's name, after this?

She tossed, twisting the blanket around her, wishing for just a few hours of rest. Around midnight, she fell into a fitful sleep and startled when her mini woke her at four. Her eyes felt scratchy and her neck stiff.

She reached into her duffel for the pair of ancient corduroy trousers and stained sweater she had found in Perk's hoard on her last trip to Xiao Qaidam. There had been no time to try sizes, and everything was too big. She tightened the pants around her waist with a bit of cord through the belt loops. The sweater hung halfway down her thighs. When she picked up her duty belt her fingers trembled with eagerness on the composite case of the pulse pistol. She slung the belt over her shoulder and thrust her feet into her boots. She stripped the bed and left her utility suit neatly folded on top of the blankets. They would understand, when they saw it. She trailed her fingers across it, wishing for Ty to understand, and forgive.

The dawn air chilled her neck where the loose sweater exposed it. She walked carefully, silently, to the open hangar where the copter waited. She touched the button on her duty belt to retract the door, and she slung her duffel inside. Then she trotted quickly to the other side of the hangar, where the second copter rested. She climbed up on the back and opened the fuel cell. With the cutter from her duty belt she severed the restraining clamps and tugged out the proton-exchange membrane. She climbed back down and propped the membrane against the tri-gear. It was repairable, but it would take time. No one would be coming after her.

When she had helped roll the copters out of the hangars, they had felt no heavier than bicycles, or very small cell cars. Their titanium alloy frames were built to be as light as possible. But rolling the craft by herself, trying not to make noise, negotiating the ramp at the end of the hangar, surprised her with its difficulty. Fortunately, the ramp sloped downward toward the airfield, and she hadn't far to go. Still, by the time she had the copter in position, and had strapped herself into the pilot's seat, the promise of sunrise already streaked the eastern sky with rose and gold. She glanced back at the silent barracks. Ty would be waking at any moment.

She touched the console. The blades began to turn, and then to spin. The noise would bring Nenet and Ty dashing out to see what was happening.

Lights flashed on in the barracks. Ebriel set her jaw and turned her face to the horizon. She lifted the bird into a hover and pushed the cyclic forward. The whine of the blades changed as the neurals compensated for the nose-down attitude, and the bird leaped forward. Ebriel pulled the collective, climbing as fast as the neural net would allow. The bird quivered under the effect of the translational lift.

She was away. Ty must be out of the barracks now, must be staring, aghast, at the tail of the copter. She would dash to the hangar to get the other copter, and she would see the ruined fuel cell. She would be helpless. Ebriel couldn't look back to see her partner's lean figure, standing abandoned on the airfield. She flew as fast as she dared away from Siwa, toward the rising sun.

The headset, hanging from its hook in the console, began a steady chatter. She picked it up and fit the earpiece into her ear. The flight monitor from Starhold called over and over, "Ty! Ebriel! You're off course. Off course! Advise, please, what heading you have? Ebriel! Ty! Who's at the controls? Advise, please. You're off course."

And then, a direct transmission from Siwa. "Eb, what's up?" Ty's laconic voice was unmistakeable. Familiar. Calm. "Where you headed, partner?"

Ebriel bit her lip so hard a bead of blood slid down her chin. She pulled the earpiece out of her ear and dropped it on the floor beside her boots. A hard sob rose in her throat, but she choked it back. It was too late for regrets.

She knew her flight plan, but she didn't program it into the console. They would have to guess at her destination. She checked her power readings and increased her speed, but not too much. She was concerned both about retreating blade stall and about depleting her power too quickly. She sat back, trying to relax her tense muscles. It would be a long flight.

She passed over the Red Sea, the sere hills of Arabia, the dry Iranian plains. The sky was a blank, pale blue, without even clouds to distract her. After an hour, she put on the autopilot and went to the galley for her breakfast. She returned to the cockpit, zipped the foilpack, and resumed manual as she waited for it to warm. The scent of the sauce reminded her of the dining hall on Starhold, its trailing vines, the swirl of conversation and laughter at meals.

"*Merde*," she muttered, gazing out her window into the empty sky. "You foolish Frenchwoman. What does that matter now?" She tugged at her hair in frustration and anxiety and impatience to be there, to do it, to have it all be over.

James and Chang flew the big copter to Taipei with four VIP's on board, five aides, and a steward to distribute drinks and meals, to service the galley and the head. It was business all the way. Chang gave James the controls for a time, but under a watchful eye.

Taiwan was new to James, with its towering mountains, forests of spruce orchards of jujube. The northern city of Taipei bustled as the players for the great parade assembled. Newnet and O-Net reporters swarmed over the city, and several waited at the airfield for the important arrivals. The highest ranking official on James's copter was only a Major General, but when. James and Chang hopped out, boom cameras dipped in front of their faces, camera lights glittered in their eyes. Self-conscious, surprised, James ducked his head, tried to straighten his jacket. He was relieved when the cameras switched their attention to his passengers.

Dozens of Security Corps personnel were posted in front of the terminal, their mirrored glasses flashing, lipmikes glistening, Glocks prominent and ready. Chang nudged James. "See that?" he murmured. "Nobody trusts Blackfield's people."

They crossed to the terminal through crowds of InCo Forces officers and enlisted personnel, civilian officials and hangers-on. An hour passed before they had their orders and were free to try to find their billet, a hostel in Nanking Road, just beyond the airport. It was another hour before they actually dropped their duffels on the floor of the dormitory. As usual, Chang headed out for beer call, and James found himself alone.

He ate a spicy meal in a noodle house and then wandered out to see a bit of the city. Its ugliness discouraged him. The edges of its potholed streets shed great flakes of cement. Its buildings leaned at dispirited angles, their windows grimy. Crowds of noisy people, gaudily dressed in flimsy reworked clothing, soon drove him back to the relative peace of the hostel.

He found a panel in the lounge. The divided screen ran Newnet in two quadrants, closeups of arriving dignitaries, speculations about the summit on Taiwan. Outside the hostel, the sirens of official escorts wailed intermittently as they rolled past.

O-Net occupied the remaining half of the screen. James tuned his earplant to its audio. He watched a video about Quezon City, in the Philippines, the capitol of the neutral polities. It ended with a brief report of the death of an ancient Visayan woman, the solitary remnant of a group of Philippine natives.

There was no one left of her people to mourn her. James thought of his father, and the Blackfoot Nation. The Nation, too, belonged to the past. Who would be the last of their people to die, unmourned and misunderstood?

When O-Net switched to an interview with Frank Dimarco, James went to bed.

Ebriel used her mini to figure her route. She did it over several times, double- and triple-checking, fearful of making a mistake. The figure of almost eight thousand kilometers daunted her. The good thing was, traveling east, she would be able to put down under cover of darkness. If she didn't get lost or fly into a mountain. She called up a map of Taiwan, and studied it.

The central mountains were the highest east of the Himalayas, and Ebriel whispered a prayer of thanks that Taipei was west of the mountains. To the east were the steep cliffs of the coast, too rocky and bleak for habitation. She enlarged the map, zoomed on locations. There had to be a place. There had to.

At her feet, the earpiece nattered. "Ebriel? Ebriel! This is the flight monitor. Respond, please." And occasionally, "Eb? D'you want to talk? You sure you want to do this? Hey, partner. Talk to me."

But Ebriel had nothing to say. She was on her own mission now.

It was midnight when she began her circuit of the leaf-shaped island. She had switched to her alternate fuel cell four hours before. Her eyes burned from scanning the sky for other aircraft. She extinguished her external lights, leaving only the dim glow of her console inside the copter. She remembered hearing that Oceania didn't use spybugs, but she kept the zapper at hand just the same. The lights of the city of Tainan glowed distantly as she approached over the Strait, but she kept well south, over the sparsely populated farmlands. Her mini reported that the island's population had exploded since the embargo began, and that the infrastructure couldn't keep up with the tide of immigrants. Most of the island country had reverted to an agrarian lifestyle.

She leaned her chin in her cupped palm and gazed down at the dark villages, the flat fields, the empty roads gleaming faintly in starlight. Here and there a glow sparked against the blackness, a solitary light shining through the darkness. Such a simple thing, a light. Such a great difference. She flew on, the burden of her loneliness intensified by knowing that communities, families, slept below her. Hours before, her nerves ragged, she had finally disabled the receiver of the headset, stopping the pleas for her attention from Starhold and Siwa, and eventually Xiao Qaidam. Cutting off the voices of the Chain made her decision irrevocable.

Ahead of her, clouds masked the mountain peaks. She banked again, to a heading almost due south. Without a flight monitor, she wouldn't dare try to pass through the mountains. She skirted the southern shore instead, where sandy beaches glowed white against the dark ocean, and then turned north to fly up the eastern coastline.

In places, the cliffs of eastern Taiwan dropped a hundred meters directly into the sea. Ebriel kept her altitude above two thousand meters, until she saw the small rocky island that was her first landmark. Rough air rocked the copter as she made her descent around the northern promontory. She flew on, occasionally skirting shreds of cloud and patches of drifting fog.

It took an hour of cautious circling, one eye on the charge of her fuel cell and one on the dark skies, to find her chosen location. A steady rain began to fall, obscuring her vision. She racked her memory for the topography of the area as she widened her arc. Her back ached with tension.

At last she spotted the modest lights of Keelung, a small city that ringed a long narrow inlet. And she found her second landmark, which she had chosen because it was large, and white, and clearly visible even in the semidarkness of the coming dawn.

The enormous statue was illuminated, spotlights gleaming off the white stone of its base and throwing the majestic figure into dramatic relief. Kuanyin, the Goddess of Mercy, soared twenty-three meters high, with Keelung Harbor at her feet. In the distance lights glimmered from the airport at Taipei. It was time for Ebriel to land her bird and take her chances in Oceania. She sighed, rubbed her eyes, and circled back, confident now of her location.

She flew above rolling hills, a scattering of beaches and cleared areas, peering at the ground until she made out a clear space in the graying light, an empty rectangle of grass in a cluster of protecting trees, backed by a slope of stone. She banked and began to descend.

The patch of grass was not much bigger than the copter itself. That meant a confined-area landing. The neurals didn't like verticals, would clang warnings at her, try to correct her. She disconnected them. She knew how to do it, she was sure she did, if she could only keep her mind clear. She took quick, shallow breaths, forcing herself to concentrate. She adjusted her angle of bank, and moved the collective gradually as she scanned the ground for obstacles.

And then she saw the lights.

At first she couldn't think what they were. They were dim at first, like spots before her eyes, and she shook her head, trying to clear it. She blinked, but still the lights didn't vanish. Instead, they grew brighter, and she saw the warning flashes of red and green, identifying another aircraft. She remembered that she had turned off her external lights, making her invisible in the darkness. A rush of adrenaline cleared her vision and sharpened her mind. It was another copter, a big one, the shaft of its forward search light brilliant white in the darkness. And coming right at her.

Ebriel gasped and reduced the collective to drop her bird out of the big copter's path.

Her descent was too steep. And she had too much power. Settling with power was one thing she was not supposed to do, she was never supposed to do it. The simulator had drilled that into her. But her options were gone.

The turbulence struck as her own downwash hit the ground and became an uprushing column of air that curled up and over her rotors. The copter bucked and yawed.

To avoid a crash-landing she needed to maneuver out of the updraft, needed to fly forward, but there was no room, and she was too low. Trees surrounded her on three sides, and the unforgiving cliff of sandstone backed the clearing. There was nothing she could do, nowhere she could go. She reduced her power, but it was too late. She was caught. She pulled the collective with little effect.

Ebriel gritted her teeth and rode the rotor wash in. The bird slammed to the ground. The tri-gear buckled and collapsed. The tail smashed against the sandstone cliff.

Ebriel was thrown hard against her seat belt. Her head snapped forward and then jerked back against the headrest. Bits of equipment flew from their fastenings and crashed to the floor. The sections of the fuselage screeched with the pressure of metal grinding against metal. Above her the blades spun, slower and slower. When at last they stopped, all was quiet.

A sharp pain spread up the back of Ebriel's skull, and she closed her eyes against a wave of dizziness. It was lovely, having her eyes closed. All was silent around her, so peaceful. She supposed she should move, should try to get out of her seat, but she was so tired, and her head hurt. Perhaps, she thought dimly, if she just rested a few moments . . .

She sighed and drifted into unconsciousness.

21

Ebriel didn't rouse until sunlight streamed in through the copter's windows. Her brow and neck and torso dripped perspiration. She put her hands up to rub her eyes and winced at the pain that gripped her shoulders and pierced the base of her neck. She didn't know if she had passed out or fallen asleep. She loosened her seat belt and tried to move her legs, worried about what further injuries she might have sustained.

At first, since everything moved, she thought perhaps she had escaped with no more than a nasty headache. The copter slanted toward the ground, tri-gear destroyed, tail crumpled against a tree. The nose faced the sloping cliff of sandstone, less than five meters away. "Merde," she said aloud, shakily. "Far too close. Vee would be furious." A little giggle of hysteria rose in her throat. She bit it back and tried to concentrate. Her head felt as if stuffed with cotton. It was tempting to put it back against the headrest, to sleep again.

She had to move. She fumbled for the button to retract the door, and pressed it. Nothing happened. She leaned over to push at the door and found that its bent frame bulged under her fingers. She stood up to get better leverage, and it was then she knew that she had sustained some injury to her leg, perhaps her ankle. Clenching her jaw against this new pain, she put all her weight against the door. Gradually, with a screech of metal struts, it slid open enough for her to squeeze through.

She gingerly lowered herself, bearing her weight on her arms and her good leg, until she felt spongy earth beneath her feet. The air smelled of tropical fruit and mold, spicy scents that helped to clear her head. She hopped on her right leg, the sound one, until she reached the sloping stone cliff. Propping herself next to the crumpled tail of the copter, she bent to roll up her trouser leg and stared in dismay at her distended ankle.

She probed it with her fingertips. It hurt, and she pulled her hands away. She frowned, trying to think. She needed ice, and pressure. These things the copter could supply, and a narcotic from the aidkit. She could stabilize her ankle enough to be mobile. She didn't have much time. It was to be this afternoon. He would be in Keelung, in the open.

She hopped back toward her broken bird and the aidkit that could get her through one more day. After that, none of it would matter.

The warm rain stopped in the early morning, leaving a haze of humidity over the distant mountains. James and Chang, with more than a hundred officers and noncoms, accompanied their commander general on a formal tour. A forty-minute drive from Taipei brought them all to Keelung, a ramshackle city sprawling around a long, narrow inlet. Ships crowded the harbor, ships under sail, ships powered by fuel cells, even simple rafts poled by Taiwanese farmers, come to ply their wares among the seagoing vessels.

James stood in the growing heat by one of the piers, scanning the crowd, listening to Takanagi and Blackfield's formal greetings. General Glass waited beside Takanagi, stiff and impassive. James wasn't comfortable with the general's exposure, but the ranking officer, a Security Corps colonel, didn't seem concerned. Technically, it wasn't James's problem. Still, he kept a sharp eye out and saw to it that his troops did the same.

The area had been cleared of its usual commerce, the food and souvenir vendors forced to close down their kiosks for the morning. Across the street from the assembled dignitaries, the people of Keelung watched the ceremony. James envied them their loose woven trousers, sandals, their broad-brimmed hats. He, like his fellow Corpsmen, perspired in his day dress uniform, white trousers bloused over gleaming boots, olive green jacket glittering with gold trim and polished service medals. Takanagi's people wore suits, brown or black or navy. Blackfield's retinue wore one- or two-piece outfits in red and blue and green.

James had never been close to the commander general before. He had seen him countless times on Newnet, but the camera angles, he now understood, were used to exaggerate the general's height. In person, he was short and thick-bodied. His voice, when he finally spoke a few words, sounded oddly high for the wide nose and blunt chin.

The officers, at parade rest, did not applaud the speeches. The Todokai staff patted their hands politely together, and the Oceania group clapped with enthusiasm. The natives stood in silence, waiting. The moment the formalities ended, the dignitaries vanished into a long car with the Security Corps colonel and two guards. James released his own troops from parade formation, and the vendors surged forward, babbling accented English as they tried to catch the attention of the soldiers before they and their money would be gone. The Taiwanese were a polyglot population, brown, white, black, all eager to profit from the influx of foreign money. James sidestepped outstretched hands offering brownish tea eggs, smelly squid balls, fragrant peanut dumplings.

Chang stopped at a wheeled kiosk to haggle over a paperweight carved in the shape of Kuanyin. James picked up two or three souvenirs from the counter, idly examining them as he waited. One was a tiny globe, with the continents of Earth laid out in green on a background of vivid blue. It had been years since James saw a globe without the Line of Partition dividing the continents. The trinket made him uncomfortable, and he set it down.

Ebriel couldn't close the copter door. Balancing on her right leg, she pushed with all her might, but it would only move partway. In the end, sweat-drenched and trembling, she gave it up. She scanned the interior for any betraying remnant of the Chain, but decided it looked just like a crashed InCo Forces craft. She left it as it was. The sun warmed the clearing, and broadleaf plants steamed gently in the rising heat. Ebriel had eaten an Instameal and drunk coffee and juice. The narcotic had begun to do its work. The pain in her ankle receded to a persistent ache.

She drew her pulse pistol out of its sleeve in her duty belt. Everything containing scannable metal, the cutter, the microlight, even her mini, she threw as far as she could into the trees, each in a different direction, then tucked the pulse pistol carefully into the cord holding up her trousers. She found a fallen bamboo stem, thick enough to hold her weight, and stripped it of leaves to serve as a cane.

Leaning on the stick, she hobbled away through the bamboo and spruce and juniper trees. When she had walked for five minutes, she looked back. Her landing place was already invisible. There was nothing left of the Chain on her person except her pistol.

In the distance, the tip of the great white statue beckoned from the eastern side of the harbor, beyond the low-roofed buildings of Keelung. She tried to set a steady pace toward it. An hour's walk, perhaps two, would take her there. If she conserved her strength, she could do it. She knew exactly where he would be, and when. She glanced down at her discolored sweater, overlong trousers, tattered sandals. She looked exactly right. She looked like a mud.

The ranks of Security Corpsmen reassembled outside the Keelung Refugee Camp while Blackfield's formal address fed into their earplants.

"Our facility here is strained to the breaking point," he intoned. "There's work available in Tainan, at Fleckcell and other manufactories, but housing is short. We've set up a receiving station here, at the north end, and at the south end are the medical facilities. The camp is designed to hold three thousand people. At this time there are forty-two hundred."

James eyed the foambrick walls and ground rubber paths of the camp. A line of latrines ran down the fence, their reek detectable even from where he stood. Listless children played in a makeshift playground of old tires and cast-off timber. Their laughter was muted, as if somehow they didn't have the right to have fun. He had thought Browning in bad shape, but this scene rent his heart. Brown-skinned people stared with a tired curiosity at the visitors from across the fence. The power grid flickered and sparked dimly in the humid air. A dozen security towers rose around the perimeter, cameras trained on the camp. Trucks and vans rolled through the nearest gate, carrying supplies in, hauling refuse and empty containers out.

Blackfield's voice droned on through James's earplant. "Fleckcell makes a substantial contribution through their distribution center, but our resources are exhausted. Last week we turned away a boat from the mainland with fifty people on it. We didn't like to do it, but . . ."

General Glass's interjection was picked up by Blackfield's microphone. "You should turn them all back. Muds! They'll overrun you."

"Commander General," Blackfield said with exaggerated politeness. "It's the policy of the neutral polities to accept and care for as many refugees as we're able. It's simply that here, on Taiwan, the camps are full."

"Just encouraging them," Glass snapped. "They'll ruin your economy, infect your children. Muds poured into Greece, brought an epidemic of cholera."

Takanagi's clipped, nasal English intervened. "The commander general has a point, Mr. President," he said.

The transmission ended abruptly. Chang raised his eyebrows at James, and James shook his head. The general's short temper was common knowledge.

A moment later, a recorded travelogue on the beauties of Taiwan began. Over the heads of the crowd James saw Blackfield gesturing, his back to the throng of dignitaries and soldiers and officials. Next to him Glass stood, his heavy chin jutting. On his other side, Takanagi whispered to an aide. The Todokai people began to slip away. James glanced up at their next stop, the huge white statue to the east. Kuanyin. Goddess of Mercy.

Across the fence, one of the refugee children trotted up to

stare at the ranks of soldiers. He was skinny, and some sort of skin disease marked his bare chest. He said something in a high-pitched singsong, and held out a dirty palm. Chang murmured, "Don't give him anything. It'll cause a riot." And James, knowing he was right, watched the child move along the fence, hand outstretched, mechanically repeating the singsong phrase.

Ebriel had never been in such a crowded city in her life. Even hobbling as she was, leaning on her makeshift cane, she felt invisible among the throngs of people. Nothing seemed real. Around her the melodic intonations of Mandarin rose and fell, with occasional snatches of English pronounced with the flat vowels and odd diphthongs of Oceania. She judged it to be midday by the time she reached the city center. Her head reeled with the din. Her nose wrinkled at the smells of fish, spices, unwashed bodies. The broken paving of the road complicated her progress as she struggled through the crowds. Through the cushion of the narcotic, pain flashed up her shin. The thought crossed her mind that she shouldn't be putting weight on it, and she laughed aloud, drawing curious glances from passersby.

As she got closer to the harbor, she saw ships and boats of every size and shape. Whistles and sirens blew. A cortege of open military trucks turned into the road, creating an instant traffic jam as other vehicles had to back and turn to get out of the way. Someone jostled Ebriel, and her cane fell from her hand. As she reached to retrieve it, a fresh surge of pain almost knocked her from her feet. She staggered back to lean against a wall between two shop windows selling telepanels. On either side of her, display screens glimmered with Newnet and O-Net broadcasts. In front of her, the line of trucks held uniformed InCo officers, six or eight in each vehicle. The InCo flag fluttered beside every windshield.

She put a hand to her waist, reassuring herself that her pulse pistol was still there, and forced herself to stand again, leaning on her stick. The summit leaders on the display screens shook hands and smiled at the cameras. Ebriel recognized Glass's thick figure and a wave of fury took her breath away. She forced her eyes away from the panel and looked into the truck just then passing before her.

A pair of dark eyes caught hers. She saw high bronzed cheekbones, a curious tattoo, a clipped brush of blue-black hair, a wide, thin mouth. For a dreadful moment she saw herself as he must see her, a small woman, gray-haired, badly dressed, unkempt, staggering drunkenly beside the road. A flash of sympathy bridged the distance between the uniformed Security Corpsman and herself.

Ebriel didn't want his sympathy, couldn't bear to feel a stranger's kindness, however random. She turned her head away.

The line of vans stopped dead in the street for several minutes, while up ahead some official tried to undo the tangle of vehicles blocking the next intersection. Ebriel pushed her way through the crowd, trying to escape that dark gaze. This was no time to see an InCo officer as a human being. He was the enemy. They were all her enemies. She limped away as fast as she could and turned at the next corner to get away from the military procession.

James watched the slender woman hobble away. Despite her derelict clothes and her tangled ashen curls, she seemed somehow youthful. Though her eyes were ringed with dark circles and her cheeks too thin, he was left with an impression of beauty, even of grace.

Keelung was worse than Taipei. The shops and cafés seemed to hang right over the road, making it almost too narrow for the cortége of trucks, and a constant stream of pedestrians moved on either side. The whole scene was noisome and hot and miserable, and the people stared at the InCo soldiers with resentment.

The slender gray-haired woman, too, had gazed at them— at him—with eyes full of anger. He didn't understand it. He and Chang, and the other Corpsmen, indeed the other soldiers in the line, were only servants of the International Cooperative Alliance. There were no open hostilities between Oceania and InCo. He glanced around at his fellow officers, who were staring ahead, ignoring the people on the street. Perhaps they had the right idea. Maybe it was better not to question. Just follow orders, stick to your guns.

But he wondered.

The InCo entourage met the Oceania one a third time on the hill east of the city. They arranged themselves at the base of the Kuanyin monument, and the net cameras took advantageous positions. The statue towered twenty-three meters, brilliant white in the hot sunshine. Two other statues flanked Kuanyin, fat golden cats with enormous toothy maws gaping over the square. They made James think of the animal totems of his own people. Like the figure of the goddess, they were hollow, and people swarmed through them, and stuck their heads out the open windows.

The colonel arranged a line of Corpsmen around the foot of Kuanyin. James paced up and down the line, making sure the scanners were working, that the troops were alert, responding to queries in his earplant. The hour was 1400, and the sun beat on his neck. Sweat soaked the band of his hat. The men and women in Takanagi's retinue held paper umbrellas over their heads. Blackfield arrived with a dozen or so of his staff, and they threaded their way past the guards while the blue neon glimmer of security scanners flashed over the crowd. The scene was chaotic, and uncomfortable, and boring.

When Glass, with the premier and the president, disappeared inside the enormous statue, to climb the inner stairs, the colonel accompanied him once again. Security Corps relaxed when their commander was safely indoors, speaking to each other occasionally, laughing. James relaxed a bit, too, though he kept the scanners in motion. A restless crowd of spectators, awaiting their own turn to enter the statue, surged closer, moved in and out of the pagodas that dotted the hill, and roamed the square behind the official visitors.

James saw her again. He adjusted his dark glasses.

It was the hair, he thought, that made her stand out. Her silvered curls caught the light. She appeared beneath the Cheshire grin of one of the fat golden cats, leaning against the stepped base, her face turned up to the white statue.

James knew she was waiting for the commander general. He couldn't have said how he knew, but he was certain. He looked at the line of Corpsmen to see if anyone else had noticed her. The blue flash of a scanner passed over the square. When he looked back at the hollow golden cat, the woman was gone.

22

Brightness dazzled Ebriel's eyes. She squinted to shut out the glare from the white surface of the statue. Her head ached fiercely. The square blurred with official visitors, throngs of vendors, knots of tourists. A constant stream of scooters and bikes flowed back and forth. Voices filled the air, commands of soldiers, children's cries, the calling of parents.

Ebriel wished she had brought more pain medicine. Her ankle drove her half mad with misery. She told herself it would all be over soon. She patted her sweater to reassure herself. Her pulse pistol was still there.

Neat ranks of InCo officers stood in the square, their hands linked behind them, their shoulders squared. For a moment, she thought she saw the same dark-skinned man she had seen earlier. But no, surely not. It must be the sun, tricking her tired eyes. She took a deep breath, and fresh pain lanced up her spine and across her shoulders. Soon now. Soon.

She didn't bother looking at the golden monument behind her. She didn't know what it represented, and she didn't care, but it was shelter, a place to lean and take the weight from her foot for a few moments. She limped around its bulging clawfeet and found a position in the fold between two of its great cement toes. She was just opposite the door through which

Glass had entered the Kuanyin monument. Security Corps guards circled the statue, facing outward, stationed about five meters apart. Their mirrored sunglasses mocked her, their holstered Glocks warned. But she had managed to thwart them before. And then she had known nothing, had been weak and unprepared. This time, she was ready.

Two Corpsmen operated security scanners, swinging the wands halfheartedly over the crowd, checking the readouts. Ebriel was invisible to them, small and plain, unremarkable.

She slipped the pulse pistol from its place at her waist. The case was cool in her hot palm. She held it under her sweater, against her bare stomach, her finger on the activator. Perspiration trickled down her ribs as she watched the door into the statue of the Goddess of Mercy, watched and awaited her chance.

James shifted his feet, wriggled his shoulders. Sweat made his back itch. His earplant, usually a constant feed of information, had fallen silent, depriving him and the others of even that diversion while Glass and Takanagi and Blackfield made their slow climb of the stairs inside the statue. They stopped at each level to wave pointlessly out the little windows, making James groan with tedium.

He glanced sideways at Chang. Michael's long eyelids were closed, and he swayed, ever so slightly, on his feet. James suppressed a chuckle. He had come back to their billet very late the night before, declaring that the women of Taiwan were wasted on the neutral polities. He had fallen into bed, still dressed, sound asleep. This morning he had slumped over a cup of black coffee, holding his head and moaning that the military had no consideration for the needs of young men. The heat, the still air, and a hangover—it made James celebrate his own temperance.

At last, when he feared Chang might actually fall over, the door in the base of the white statue opened. The ceremonial party reappeared. James stepped forward, hand lifted to command attention from his Corpsmen. They straightened as the dignitaries emerged, and the scanners swept the crowd with more diligence. But only James, every sense alerted, was watching for the gray-haired woman.

Without making a sound, the Security Corpsman to the right of the statue's door fell to the ground as if his legs had dissolved. The Corpsman on the left fell a fraction of a second later, crumpling, collapsing in a heap, his hat falling from his head.

A path opened, a window, and the official party was at the center of it, at the convergence of all sight lines.

A small, ashen-haired figure leaped forward, and time, for James, stood still.

The clatter of her cane as it fell to the paving stones seemed impossibly loud in his ears. He saw her arm come up, the wrist braced, her legs wide apart. Perfect form. She moved like a martial artist, with precision and speed. She wasted no energy. She made no extraneous movements.

No one moved for a long, agonizing beat. No one except James. He was already running by the time the second Corpsman hit the ground. He heard the strike of his boots on the pavement before the sudden intake of breath around him as the Corpsmen grasped that something had happened.

The woman was directly in front of Commander General Glass. Glass's adjutant was a step behind him. The others, Blackfield, Takanagi, the colonel, were caught in the narrow doorway. Glass's thick figure was the center of the scene, the focal point, as clear a target as a painted bull's-eye. The woman's little weapon pointed directly at his heart.

Ebriel felt as if she had all the time in the world. The length of five heartbeats felt like five minutes to her as she leaped forward.

She had learned in the dojo to move from one point to another with efficiency. It was a matter of concentration. The pain in her ankle didn't register. She fired the pulse pistol at the two guards from a safe distance, confident they would rise after a time, shocked but unimpaired, and then she took another leap forward, to the point past the line of guards, bringing herself within lethal distance of her enemy.

Her mind was stronger than her body. She saw herself there, and she was there. She saw herself closer, and another stride took her closer.

Her vision narrowed, focused to a cone of visibility with the general at its apex. Around her, people moved with nightmare slowness, their voices muted, their faces indistinct. Her muscles blazed with energy. Her brain worked at lightning speed, measuring the distance to her target, giving the command to her arm to lift, to her hand to steady, to her right forefinger, poised on the activator . . .

She saw his ugly face as if through the lens of a telescope. She was six meters away, and then four, and now two. Close enough.

Close enough to kill. The pulse pistol's wave of electricity, tuned to the frequency of the neural synapses, would dampen them forever. Extinguish them. Simple as pulling a plug out of a wall socket. Her enemy would fall at the foot of the maternal Buddhist saint, the Goddess of Mercy, the symbol of compassion.

She ordered her brain to send the signal to her finger. Push. Activate. Fire! He would fall at the skirt of Kuanyin, and he would never rise again. Fire!

But Ebriel Serique's mind betrayed her. Her nature betrayed her, and her conscience. She saw George Glass, saw how his black hair was plastered against his round skull, saw how his small eyes glistened with shock at her nearness, with recognition of the little blunt pistol so close to his heart. She tried to focus on his blunt chin and thick nose and bristling mustache, the features of the unbending man she wanted to punish.

But what her tortured mind delivered up to her was a pitiful row of still shapes under sheets of dirty canvas on the deck of a blue-hulled yacht. Death laid out on polished wood, death that stole breath and laughter and movement. The pulse pistol in her hand would turn a living human being into just such an inert bundle, a lifeless bag of empty flesh, of useless bones and sightless eyes. Into an urn of ashes.

And Ebriel knew, even as her chest burned with hatred, that she couldn't do it.

It didn't matter that she had spent more than a year planning this, that she had given up everything for her revenge. Driving the life from this man's body wouldn't restore life to her beloved Paul. It wouldn't waken her precious Renée, who slept now forever. It wouldn't restore the joy to her own soul. What it would accomplish was to condemn her to a never-ending hell of guilt and remorse and despair.

Her last wisp of hope evaporated. There was nothing left for her to do.

She took her finger from the activator, and reversed the pulse pistol in her hand. She found the button with her thumb. The mouth of the little weapon faced her, dark and empty, an invitation to oblivion.

This time when she ordered her brain to respond, nothing interfered. The signal ran unimpeded from her brain to her spinal column, leaping across the branching nerves of her arm and into her hand.

James didn't hear the shouts around him, the commotion that rose and swelled like a sudden storm at sea. By the time others began to react, he was already there. He saw everything she did. She didn't fire at Glass, and that gave James his chance. He reached her just as she turned the pistol toward herself, took aim at her own heart.

James shouted. He may have yelled "No!" or he may have cried something else, he no longer knew. It was instinct, alone, that made him call out, and it was just enough.

Her arm jerked as she fired. The pulse of destructive energy, tightly focused because of her nearness to it, went past her head, its waves spreading, dispersing into the humid air. Before the weapon could recycle, he seized her from behind, reaching past her to wrest the weapon from her slender fingers. With his other arm he pulled her off her feet, holding her tightly against him, even as they crashed together to the hard pavement. James took the brunt of the fall on his right side. The shot of someone's Glock went wild above their heads and sang off the white skirts of the monument.

James felt her cries begin before the sound reached his ears. Her body convulsed against his chest, and she shrieked something, over and over. He didn't know the language, but the words sounded like *"Mon Dieu, mon Dieu! Pardon! Pardon!"*

There was no time to think what that meant. Around them the scene was madness, Corpsmen shouting, the Oceania security people belatedly squeezing out of the statue's door, pushing each other in their hurry. James had fallen hard with the woman crushed to him and would be bruised from shoulder to hip. A Corpsman, a broad-shouldered woman, reached down to wrest the woman from his grasp.

He shouted at her. "No! Stand back!"

"But, sir,—" she began.

He struggled to his knees, pulling the small woman with him. He showed the Corpsman that he had the weapon secure, in his own hand, and he dropped it into his pocket. The ashen-haired woman's cries had ceased, but as he stood, dragging her to her feet, he saw how her face paled, and her eyes rolled back. Her left ankle was swollen, with a great bruise spreading up the shin. He tried to shift her weight, to bear as much of it as he could with his own arm. Despite her small size, she had the solid weight of muscle.

Her head fell forward. Her neck was grimy, her gray curls matted with sweat. Pity stirred in him. The Corpsman patted her down, searching for other weapons. When the woman's hands touched the swollen leg, the prisoner whimpered and jerked away with an involuntary movement. A moment later she lost consciousness, slumping nervelessly in James's arms.

Security Corpsmen surrounded James, while the Oceania militia in their black uniforms tried to get through the crowd to him. Several of Takanagi's suits stood on the steps of the statue, nattering into their lipmikes. James stood still amid the tumult of shouted orders, demands, flourished weapons. He looked up, over the head of the crowd.

General Glass still stood on the steps of Kuanyin. He scowled at the gray-haired woman, and his eyes were as flat and black as the cold glittering eyes of a snake.

Ebriel regained consciousness in agony. A rocking motion tossed her this way and that, sending white-hot fire up her leg, wrenching spasms into her neck and the back of her skull. Her throat hurt as if she had been screaming. Perhaps she had. She couldn't remember.

I am mad, she thought. My mind is gone.

But it wasn't. She wished it were. She feared the opposite, that she was sane again at last, and that was more terrible.

She opened her eyes to slits. She found herself in the back of an open truck, lying on unpadded flooring, her head jostled against a spare tire, hard plastic and metal cartons all around her. She waited a moment before trying again to open her eyes, her teeth clenched tightly to keep from crying out. In that moment, she felt a hand touch her shoulder, a broad, hard hand, but a gentle touch.

"Ma'am?"

Ebriel's eyes flew wide and then squeezed shut as the light sent fresh waves of pain crashing through her head.

"I'm sorry, ma'am, I know you're in pain. We'll be at the hospital soon."

She tried to turn her head, to shake it from side to side.

"Take it easy," the voice said again. It was a deep voice, with slurred American consonants. Like Ty's. The hand remained on her shoulder, steadying her. Slowly, letting the light in bit by bit, Ebriel opened her eyes.

It was he. It was the officer she had seen earlier that day, as she rested against a wall. Through a burning haze, she saw the same dark face, prominent cheekbones, arching nose. The tattoo, seen close, took the trefoil shape of a talon, as of a bird of prey. His eyes were dark, too, not midnight-dark like Yasmine's, but a luminous brown beneath black brows, and a short brush of black hair. There were others in the truck, but she only saw him, crouched beside her in the open cargo space, bracing her body against the swaying of the truck with his big hands.

He spoke again. "We'll be at the hospital soon. Hang on."

From somewhere in front of them, a nervous voice snapped, "Much good that will do, Bull. She's not getting away just because in the end she didn't pull it off. We got two guys only now coming to."

The hand on Ebriel's shoulder didn't move. "They'll be all right," the dark man said, his voice even. "She didn't hurt anyone."

"Tell that to your commander," another voice said, a voice with a different accent. "His orders are already on their way."

"This is Oceania," the first voice said. "Not his jurisdiction."

"We'll see about that," the second answered. "She's in our custody."

And the dark man with the tattoo said, very quietly, "Lay off. It's not our job to decide. First let's get her to the hospital."

Ebriel closed her eyes again. The truck jostled her, banging her against the cartons, but it didn't matter. The taste of failure filled her mouth.

23

The conflict followed them to the refugee hospital, where the gray-haired woman was borne away on a stretcher. The Security Corps colonel had ridden in the truck, his Glock drawn, held on their prisoner as if she might rise up and overpower them all. He had insisted on handcuffs, but James had seen to it they were not too tight, and that the woman, mostly unconscious in any case, was cuffed with her wrists in front of her, that her weight was on her right side, away from her injured leg. In the general melee of official outrage, shock, embarrassment, James had retained control of the prisoner. He had been the one to place her in the back of the truck. He laid her in the cargo space between a softsided canvas bag of tools and a spare tire, and climbed in himself to crouch beside her. Half a dozen Corpsmen crowded onto the bench seats. Several times the woman roused from unconsciousness, but she murmured things James couldn't catch.

When they arrived at the emergency room, Glass's adjutant was already toe-to-toe with one of Blackfield's staff. Oceania claimed jurisdiction, and the adjutant objected, loudly.

Medical needs came first, fortunately. James watched as the dazed woman was admitted beyond the security gate. In the waiting room, the verbal battle between the adjutant and the Oceania official raged. The colonel waded into the thick of it, scrambling to transfer guilt to the Oceania militia.

James strode out through the doorway and stood on the cracked sidewalk outside the hospital, drawing deep breaths of fresh air. He hoped the hospital's crumbling walls and dilapidated entryway didn't speak for the quality of its care. The windows were cracked as if someone had struck them with stones. The waiting room was full, harried nurses and orderlies trying to conduct triage while people tugged at their sleeves, raised their hands in supplication.

James frowned and thrust his hands into the pockets of his white trousers. Something small and hard met his fingers. He still had the weapon, her weapon. The little pulse pistol, highly illegal in InCo territories because it was impervious to the scanners. He should turn it in to the colonel, of course, but he felt a strange reluctance. Why, he wondered? Why did he feel this way? The woman had taken aim at General Glass, whom he was sworn to protect, but she had changed her mind at the last moment. They had all failed Glass today, every Corpsman present. If the woman had fired at him, he would be dead. A pulse pistol at that range . . .

But she had changed her mind. She had not fired at the general. And something about her touched James. It was ridiculous, of course. As yet he hadn't understood a single word she had spoken. She was grubby, and small, and odd . . . but she was determined, and courageous, and stoic in the face of what must have been ghastly pain. James wanted to understand her.

He tongued his lipmike and requested updated orders from Ops. There were none.

He crossed the disintegrating pavement to a teashop identified by a sign in English and Mandarin. He found a window table where he could see the hospital. The open truck he had arrived in was now blocked by one of the troop vans they had used earlier, the InCo flag hanging limp on the little staff beside the windshield. Through the cracked hospital windows, James saw Corpsmen, a couple of officers, the black uniforms of Oceania. A car pulled up, bearing the insignia of Todokai beside the InCo globe. A man and woman got out and hurried into the waiting room. James ordered tea and drank it slowly, watching and waiting.

"Jumper fracture," the doctor said, in English. There was another voice, a brief question. "Yes. Talar dome and the distal fibula. Stable enough to walk on, but my god. Must have hurt like bloody hell."

Ebriel opened her eyes to see a woman in green surgical scrubs. Strands of short reddish hair poked out beneath a frayed cap. A gray plastic mask hid her mouth and nose.

Ebriel's ankle and leg blazed, and her neck ached. She tried to move her right hand, but something stopped her. She squinted down her arm at the handcuff of dull metal that locked her wrist to the railing of the bed. She tugged at it, pointlessly. *"Docteur?"* she whispered.

"Oui," the woman answered, giving her an efficient pat on her arm. She pressed an ampoule to the inside of Ebriel's elbow, and her eyes creased with sympathy above her mask. *"Française, madame?"*

Ebriel felt the narcotic spreading through her body almost at once, erasing the agony of her leg, the pain in her head. *"Oui,"* she breathed. Her eyelids drooped, and she couldn't lift them again. She relaxed her right arm, and the handcuff clinked distantly. *"Merci,"* she breathed.

"De rien." She heard the snick of scissors as someone slit the leg of her trousers from the ankle to the knee. Gloved hands touched her, feeling cool and clean. Through the drug, Ebriel felt one sharp pain, then another, but distantly, as if the doctor were setting someone else's fractured ankle. Ebriel slipped back into unconsciousness.

When she woke again, darkness had fallen beyond the external window, but in the room, the lights were uncomfortably bright. The door was closed, but it too had a window, and she saw uniforms beyond it, olive-green and black. Stiffly, she turned her head. She lay on a narrow, railed bed facing a small sink that hung crookedly from its fixtures. A bit of curtain masked a toilet in one corner of the tiny room. Mold stained the cracked plaster walls.

Someone had removed her sweater, and she wore a hospital gown, its print pattern faded beyond recognition. Her shredded trousers had disappeared. She saw her sweater hanging in the corner, her sandals set neatly beneath it.

She lifted her arm. The handcuff bound her wrist to the bed. Of course. She was a prisoner. But whose, she wondered? Not that it mattered. Glass would win out. No doubt she would soon be on her way back to Leysin.

She plucked at the cotton sheet with her fingers. It smelled of bleach. The whole room, probably the whole hospital, reeked with disinfectant. A distant and continuous clamor leaked through the flimsy walls, sounds familiar from St. Louis Hospital, rolling gurneys, ringing call bells, wailing sirens, buzzing address systems. She welcomed the noise. Leysin, she remembered, was a silent place.

A few stars glimmered through the darkness, stars that were lost to her now, along with the colorful world she had come to know. She had thrown it all away, and gained nothing in exchange. She had failed even to end her own life. She regretted that, especially now as she lay staring at the stars, floating in a haze of drugs, her throat dry, her eyes burning, her heart numb. She had lived for revenge. Her hatred of George Glass had been a way of refusing to deal with her pain and loss. What would she live for now? How many years would she go on, without joy, without even sadness, drugged into oblivion? There would be no Chain to rescue her this time, no Ethan Fleck in search of a musician for his little castle among the stars.

She despaired.

Yasmine flicked her fingers, just enough to propel her from the space window at the top of the aerie to Ethan's side. His chair floated before the panel showing the Newnet broadcast. A two-story building, with broken windows and dingy walls, contrasted vividly with the reporter's neat green suit.

"In this hospital," he was saying, "in Keelung, in the neutral polities, lies the object of today's debate. It's the woman who attempted to assassinate Commander General Glass this afternoon just as he completed a ceremonial tour of Taiwan."

A video began, not the dipping, swaying views from a spybug, but the focused photography of a netcamera. It showed a petite woman, silvery hair vivid in the sunlight, leaping past two fallen guards. Fleck made a noise in his throat, and Semaya groaned.

The voice-over said, "An unidentified InCo officer, without regard for his own safety, threw himself on the general's attacker, bringing her to the ground and forcing her to give up her weapon before she could hurt anyone else. Two Security Corpsmen were injured by the woman's pulse pistol. They were transferred immediately to Taipei, where doctors say they are hopeful the two will make a full recovery. Meanwhile, the dispute over who has the right, and the responsibility, to prosecute the would-be assassin goes on in—"

Ethan croaked, "Sound off," and the panel silenced.

Semaya said tightly, "Ethan. She could betray us."

She didn't say, I told you so, but Yasmine heard it in her voice, sensed the tension between husband and wife. Yasmine hugged herself and cast a longing glance out the space window at the cool unchanging stars. When she felt in control again, she looked back at Ethan. He sat slumped in his chair, his eyes closed. She touched his shoulder, just a brush of her fingers, and he opened his eyes with difficulty, the lids fluttering. Yasmine bit her lip, frightened anew by his weakness. She hugged herself tighter, digging her fingertips into her arms.

"Papa," she said in a choked voice. "Ebriel would never betray the Chain. Or you."

"We don't know that!" Semaya snapped. "We never thought she would do this!"

Fleck rasped, "No. No. But I understand it."

"Understand it! She stole a copter, she tried to kill someone!"

Yasmine steeled herself to turn her head and meet Semaya's bitter gaze. "But she did not," she said hesitantly, hearing her own voice falter. Semaya always had that effect on her. Yasmine struggled constantly against her reaction to Papa's wife. She swallowed. "I mean, she did not attack the general. She was there, she was in position—if she had done it, we would know. He would have fallen. In the end, she could not do such a thing. And—" Her outburst caused her to move her head, and she floated backward, toward the curving wall of monitors behind her. She put out a foot to stop herself, and finished weakly, "—and Ebriel would never betray us."

"Yasmine." Ethan touched the keypad, and his chair swiveled to face her. "Yasmine, Ebriel would not mean to betray us. But there are ways to make a person say things they don't intend to say. Drugs. Pain. Threats. All kinds of ways."

Yasmine trembled. Despite herself, her eyes wandered to the restfulness of the stars.

"Semaya, call Vee for me," Ethan said hoarsely. "And Perk. We have to go after her."

Yasmine closed her eyes, and she felt her body begin to curl. She heard Semaya's hands touch the wall, heard the whisper of her cottons as she sidled into the slip.

"Yasmine," Ethan called softly. "You must stay with us, Yasmine. I need you."

She opened her eyes, fastening them on his wasted face, his lopsided, gentle mouth.

"I know you care about Ebriel. We'll do all we can for her," he said.

She trembled. "But what, Papa? What can you do?"

He glanced back at the Newnet panel. A constant flow of traffic moved in and out of the dilapidated refugee hospital, and the lights of Keelung threw garish shadows on the street. "We'll hurry," he croaked.

24

James received his orders just as the late summer darkness crept over the city. The trucks and vans had pulled away from the hospital, leaving only Blackfield's and Takanagi's limousines. Pedal carts and bicycles and scooters swerved around the cars. A river of people streamed in and out of the emergency room.

"Come in through Admitting on the west side." The colonel's voice in James's ear was tight with tension. "There's a sign in English. Up the stairs to your left, first door on the right. Hospital administrator's office."

"Yes, sir." James dropped money beside his empty cup and worked his way between the crowded tables to the door. He was relieved to be going back to the hospital. He had half-expected to be ordered back to Taipei, to be debriefed tomorrow. He straightened his jacket and tucked his cap under his arm.

He found the office, knocked once. The door opened immediately, and a captain stepped back for James to enter.

The room was as crowded as the tea shop had been, but every man in it was a Security Corps officer. The colonel, pale-faced, stood stiffly before a small desk. Behind the desk, in front of a bank of computer panels and stacked data towers with Mandarin and English titles, stood Commander General Glass, his mustache bristling, his flat cheeks ruddy with fury.

"How the fucking hell did this happen?" he thundered, as James found a place beside a small window overlooking the alley. Glass pointed his thick forefinger at the colonel, who grew even paler. The finger shook with rage. "I oughta strip that bit of gilt right off your damn collar!" he shouted. The glass at James's back vibrated, and James took a step away from it.

The general caught sight of him. He dropped his pointing finger and fastened the intensity of his attention on James. "What's your name, Captain?" he barked.

James squared his shoulders. "Sir. I'm Bull, James Bull."

Glass gave a sharp nod. "Saved my fucking life, Captain," he growled.

James drew a shallow breath. "Sir. With due respect to the general, I didn't."

"Whaddya mean, you didn't? Little bitch was going to shoot me!" Glass gave a short, harsh laugh. "At that range, even a pulse pistol is lethal."

"Yes, sir, I know," James said. He cleared his throat. "Except she didn't fire, sir. If she had—" He broke off. Surely everyone in the room understood that he hadn't reached her in time to prevent her firing at the general. She had, at the last minute, decided not to do it. The general stared at him, waiting. James cleared his throat again, glancing at the colonel, then around at the others in the room, two other captains, one major, the lieutenant colonel who was Glass's adjutant. "General, sir, the woman reversed her weapon without firing. She pointed it at herself, and that was when I was able to reach her. Uh, not before that, sir. I'm sorry."

The general said, "Bullshit."

"Uh, sir? Pardon?"

Glass barked another laugh and put his thick hand on James's shoulder. "Son, this is a public relations goldmine. Young handsome captain saves his senior officer."

James shook his head, confused. He fumbled in his pocket for the pulse pistol and held it out, butt first, to the general. "Sir, this is her weapon. You can see by the charge count, it was only fired three times—the last meant for herself. She didn't shoot at you, sir. She could have, she was there, she took aim. But she didn't do it."

Glass grinned, showing yellowing canines beneath his thick mustache. He folded his arms and his chin jutted at his adjutant. "Get me a Newnet team," he said. "Gonna introduce our hero here." He turned his flat black eyes back to James. "Better have a wash, Captain," he said jovially. "Comb your hair. It's your day, son, you're a goddam hero."

James couldn't think of how else to object. It wasn't true, and he couldn't allow them to say it was. Surely the memory sticks of the event would prove—

And then he saw the video playing on the hospital administrator's desk. It cycled through to the end, and immediately began again, showing the woman, her gray hair distinguishing her from the crowd, leaping past the two fallen Corpsmen. Her small hand gleamed white in the sun as her overlarge sweater fell away from her arm, and her stubby weapon pointed directly at Glass.

And then the commotion erupted around her. Arms, hands, and heads blocked the camera's view. Scrambling Security Corpsmen converged on the woman's position. And in front of it all, covering the woman's actions, before the furious wave of Corpsmen crested, James saw his own dress jacket, his cap flying off as he sprang forward, he and the woman going down in a whirl of other uniforms. The video didn't show what she'd done.

George Glass saw him watching, and the mirthless grin spread across his face again. "Shit-hot, Captain," he said. "We can spin it any way we want to."

And what he wanted was to make James a hero. Which meant that the woman, though she had chosen not to fire on the general, but on herself, would be the villain.

Stunned, unable to think what to do, James followed orders. He combed his hair and washed his face, and stood stiffly in front of the Newnet cameras as the general's adjutant described his service record, his rise through the ranks, his accomplishments. The interviewer asked questions, and James answered in monosyllables. Glass clapped James's shoulder, and made a brief speech about his confidence in the men and women of Security Corps. When the cameras turned away, James wiped his hot forehead with the back of his hand.

The adjutant was talking again. "Newnet will post a picture of the woman who tried to assassinate the commander general," he said in clipped military fashion. "She refuses to give her name. She has no ID rod. She may be a citizen of the neutral territories, or she may be an illegal immigrant. Oceania claims to have no record of her DNA signature. InCo will check it against their own rolls, but any citizen with information should contact their InCo representative."

As he spoke, a picture flashed on the inset panel. James stared in shock. The adjutant went on speaking in voice-over. "The general expressed concern about this woman's mental health, and we assured him she will receive appropriate treatment."

They had produced a picture of a woman with short gray hair, but it wasn't the woman James had held at the foot of Kuanyin, had comforted in the truck on the way to the hospital. He doubted the face looking out of the panel was of a real person at all. The room cleared as he stood helplessly staring at the unfamiliar face, uncomprehending. When he tore his eyes from the panel, he realized the only men left in the room were himself, the colonel, Glass's adjutant, and the general himself. The back of his neck prickled.

The general had turned his back to the officers, facing the window. He tilted his head to the side, listening to something the others couldn't hear, then spoke loudly into his lipmike. James thought it must be burning the ears of whoever was listening. "Get me some help," Glass snarled. "She's crossed my path for the last time. What?" He tilted his head again, then snapped, "She's not leaving this hospital, that's what I mean. If you don't get that, you're in the wrong fucking branch of the service!"

The adjutant and the colonel looked at each other uneasily, and the adjutant coughed. Glass turned at the sound. His chest swelled under his uniform. James's nose twitched at the odd metallic odor that filled the room.

"You know who that bitch is?" he demanded of them. No one answered, and Glass thundered, "It's that Serique woman! That damned flutist all the fuss was about! And the muds think they have jurisdiction. This is a can of worms I don't want opened. I don't need protesters outside the damned summit meeting in Taipei. And if that limp-wrist Blackfield has his way, she'll be tied up in legalities for years!"

"Uh, sir," the adjutant began, with a tentative motion of his head in James's direction.

Perspiration broke out on Glass's forehead, and the metallic odor intensified. The general ignored his adjutant, pacing across the small office, punching one fist into the other hand. "Damn it! The woman had her chance at Leysin, and those Swiss jackasses let her get away. We were too easy on her that time! She's not getting another shot at me, you got that?"

The adjutant stepped into the general's path. "Sir," he said. "Captain Bull can be dismissed, I think."

Glass froze in midstep, his black eyes swiveling to James as if he had forgotten he was there. And indeed, James thought, the general had forgotten.

"Right," Glass said. "You're right." His eyelids dropped as he reined in his temper, and then slowly, deliberately, he spoke to James. "Captain Bull. Excellent work today. You're a credit to Security Corps."

James could only blurt, "Uh, sir. Thank you, sir."

Glass nodded. "Dismissed, Captain. Get back to Taipei, enjoy your day off."

And James could only say, "Yes, sir," salute, turn on his heel to leave. The colonel was speaking into his lipmike, and the general had turned back to the window to stare down at the trash-filled alley behind the hospital.

James stepped out of the office and pulled the door closed behind him. He glanced to his right, down the long dim corridor. A black-uniformed guard stood with arms folded, back leaning against a door. That, undoubtedly, was the room where the disputed prisoner lay, waiting to see into whose hands she had fallen. As James descended the stairs, an InCo soldier, a man with thick Asian features and a master sergeant's insignia, was coming up. He sketched a salute, and James returned it, then pushed out through the door at the bottom of the stairwell, and moved out into the street.

* * *

The mission assembled in the loading bay as Yasmine huddled in her darkened cubby with her blanket pulled tightly around her. She had tried to be there to see them off, had wanted to speak to Pilar, to plead with Astrid to intercede for Ebriel. She had stepped out of the slip to find people hurrying around the gallery, brushing past her as they ran to collect their own belongings or fetch things for the crew. Yasmine made it as far as the loading bay, where *Unicorn*'s captain was snapping orders, and Vee was having a spirited argument with Astrid Sorensen. Semaya stood in the center of the echoing space, her arms folded, her eyes terrible. Yasmine backed out of the loading bay and crept around the gallery to the slip, hoping no one would notice her, that she would not encounter Dr. Nordstrom, or Kanika, who would be begging to go with the Chain. She let herself drop swiftly down the tube and ran to her cubby.

She lay for a long time, her eyes closed, her ears stopped by her blanket. She felt the long shudder run through the hull of the habitat. The vibrations meant *Unicorn* had been released from the docking arms. Momentum would take the spaceplane far enough away for it to power up and begin the long descent to Xiao Qaidam. Still Yasmine lay, past the hour for the evening meal, past the bedtime rituals in the crèche. At last, looking warily about her in the night-dark habitat, she tiptoed out of her cubby, careful of the tangle of bumbleberry vines that wound through the narrow corridor. She sidled into the slip and gave a sharp kick that propelled her swiftly upward, past the gallery, on to the aerie.

She didn't go through the slip until she was sure he was alone. His chair hovered before a screen where *Unicorn*'s telemetry rolled. The main illumination was off. The only light came from glowing panels and monitors. She heard *Unicorn*'s captain's voice, and then there was silence except for the faint whirr of the circulating fans.

"Papa?" Yasmine breathed.

His chair swiveled slowly to face her. "Yasmine," he rasped. His color, even in the poor light, frightened her.

"Papa, do you need something?" she asked, trying to keep her voice steady.

"Your company will do," he croaked, his distorted grin pulling up the left side of his face.

Relieved, she floated away from the gate, and came to his chair. "What shall we do tonight?" she asked.

His eyelids sagged helplessly, but beneath them his eyes were still bright. "Tonight, we monitor *Unicorn,* and the broadcasts from Newnet and O-Net and the undergrounds."

"For news of Ebriel?"

"Yes." His chair turned to the right, where the net broadcasts flickered constantly. Yasmine followed him. Newnet was showing entertainments. One underground net was broadcasting grainy pictures of people in a food line before a half-collapsed cement building. Another was blank. O-Net was replaying video of the summit in Taipei. Yasmine didn't see anything pertaining to Ebriel.

"What is happening to her now?" she asked.

"She's still in Keelung," he answered her. "In the refugee hospital." He touched his keypad, and a picture came up on a replay screen. "They're showing this."

Yasmine stared, her mouth open. "But—but that is not Ebriel!"

"No. No, indeed."

"Then why . . ."

Ethan's breath whistled in his chest. "InCo doesn't want the world to know who really attacked General Glass," he said. "They haven't admitted that she escaped from Leysin, and there are people still asking for news of her. Her family, her orchestra, her agent. This picture, if you look at it . . ." He touched his keypad, and the image grew, the perspective changed. "Look at the eyes, and then the mouth and nose— not only are they not Ebriel's, they don't belong to the same person. It's a composite. A created face."

She saw it was true. The nose of the face was long and thin, but the lips were full. The eyes were round, with heavy, half-closed lids. "What does it mean, Papa?" she whispered.

"It means Ebriel is in very grave danger."

Yasmine clutched her hands together before her. "Why?" Darkness threatened to close over her mind, but she thrust it away. Ethan waited until she had composed herself.

"If they're hiding her identity, it can only be so they can dispose of her as they wish. We don't know very much about George Glass." He drew two noisy breaths in succession, and Yasmine glanced at him with fresh concern. His voice faltered, steadied. "Except that he's a politician first, a soldier second. We can hope—" he stopped to breathe again. "We can hope his plan is to send Ebriel back to Leysin. The situation—" another breath—"is complicated by Oceania. They claim that the attempted assassin is their responsibility. Their prisoner. But Glass is a formidable opponent." Another pause. "Do you know the word, Yasmine. 'Formidable'?"

"Yes. As in the French, *formidable*. Latin, *formidare*. To dread, to fear."

He managed a hoarse chuckle. "Indeed. Your English is almost perfect now, Yasmine. And your accent is much improved."

"Papa—"

"Yes."

"If the Chain can reach Ebriel, if they can get her out of that place—then what will you—what will we—do with her?"

"Yasmine, do you understand what she did?"

Yasmine hesitated. She wasn't at all sure that she did understand. She knew Ebriel had gone somewhere she was not supposed to go. She knew the flight monitor had called and called, for hours, and Ebriel had never answered. "I—I think she took a copter. I mean—stole it."

"Yes, that's right." Ethan paused for breath. "But more than that, Yasmine, Ebriel broke our trust. She abandoned her partner, aborted her mission. And by placing herself in InCo hands, she risked the Chain itself."

"But she—" Yasmine couldn't find the words to express the complexity of her feelings. For once, what she felt was not fear, but sorrow. "Papa, Ebriel saved me."

His voice sent chills up Yasmine's arms. "Yes, Yasmine. I could never forget that. I'll always be grateful. But I have the Chain to think of, and our children."

He fell silent, and Yasmine waited, her heart in her throat. At last he said, "Sometimes we have to make difficult decisions. Even impossible ones. First, let's try to get Ebriel away.

Then we'll decide what comes next. And now." Papa's chair
darted to the opposite side of the aerie. "Tonight I will teach
you the frequencies of the microsat relay. Are you ready?"

Everything must go on. The Chain was on its way to
Ebriel. Here, in Papa's aerie, with its soft lights and muted
sounds and rich and continuous flow of information, Yasmine
was safe. But would Ebriel ever be safe again?

25

Ebriel woke to a hot bar of sunlight falling across her face. For a moment, she couldn't think where she was. Her left leg ached fiercely, and her scalp and neck were wet with perspiration. She tried to lift her right hand to wipe her brow, but it rose only a few inches before something gripped it, something slick and hard. She lifted her head, dizzy with pain and narcotic hangover, and peered at the gray metal bracelet that locked her wrist to the bed rail.

Just above the handcuff, an intravenous tube was taped to her arm, the little Y ports dark orange against the clear plastic. The drip bag was flat and empty. An inflated cylinder, with stabilizing bars visible through the gray plastic material, encased her left ankle and most of her calf. It itched. She wiped her forehead with her left palm. She couldn't see a call system, but she tried anyway. *"Pardon? Excusez-moi?"*

Nothing happened. A small carafe of water rested on a small table, but when she reached for it, the handcuff stopped her. She let her head drop back, and she stared at the fissured plaster of the ceiling, feeling as empty as the IV bag. It was the cessation of wanting that left her empty. She understood that. She had subsisted on her craving for revenge, and without it, there was nothing left. Even her grief had lost its immediacy.

An hour passed. Her mouth was dry, her lips parched. Her ankle shot darts of misery up her shin and into her thigh. The pillow beneath her head was damp with perspiration. She shifted her shoulders, trying to get comfortable, and was rewarded with fresh waves of pain.

The lock on the door was an old-fashioned deadbolt assembly. When it opened at last, it made a heavy clicking noise. The doctor who had treated her the night before came in, accompanied by a man in the black uniform of the Oceania militia. The doctor wore no mask this time. Her thin lips pinched with weariness.

"*Docteur*," Ebriel whispered, swallowing painfully. "*J'ai soif.*"

The doctor flashed the soldier a look of pure fury. "You see?" she exclaimed in Aussie-accented English. "You left her in here alone all night, and she can't even reach the water! You could have at least looked through the bloody window, couldn't you?"

The soldier took up a position by the door, his arms folded. "Orders, ma'am," he said. "No one in or out. They're worried about security. It's not like we're outfitted for prisoners."

"Dozy bugger," the doctor muttered.

The soldier appeared unperturbed by the epithet. He leaned against the wall, crossing his boots at the ankles. The doctor held the water glass to Ebriel's lips.

Ebriel murmured, "Thank you."

The doctor lifted her sandy eyebrows. "Ah, speak English, do you? Good," she said. "We've about exhausted my French." She ran her hands over the plastic cast, touched Ebriel's exposed toes. She had an old-style stethoscope, not wireless like Paul's. She put the earpieces in her ears and held the bell to to Ebriel's chest, nodded. She pulled a stool out from under the high bed and sat down with a sigh, as if glad to get off her feet.

"Now, *madame*," she said, putting one hand on Ebriel's arm in friendly fashion. "Seems you're in a bit of trouble. They're going to be in to interrogate you."

The soldier said, "Dead cert, that." Ebriel didn't understand him.

The doctor ignored him. "Probably not until tomorrow,"

she said. "The powers that be haven't yet sorted out who has authority. In the meantime, can you tell me your name?"

Ebriel shook her head.

"Do you understand my question?"

"Yes," Ebriel whispered. "I understand. But I cannot answer."

"Is that can't, or won't?" the doctor asked.

Ebriel averted her eyes. "Okay. Won't, I'll assume," the doctor murmured. She turned Ebriel's wrist and frowned over the little scar. "Well," she said. She pursed her lips. "Unfortunately all I can do is make you comfortable," she said. "We'll send you some breakfast. I expect that leg hurts. We'll give you something for that, too." The doctor stood up, saying to the soldier, "Stick your head out and call my nurse, will you?" And then to Ebriel, "The nurse will help you with a bedpan. I've been here all night, and I've got to get some sleep. I'll see you tonight when I start my shift again."

Ebriel didn't watch her leave. She didn't want breakfast, and she didn't care who came in or out of the room. She was grateful, though, when the nurse, a Taiwanese woman with small warm hands, injected something through the lowest port of the IV tube. The pain of her leg, indeed, all her pain, faded. She heard the heavy snick of the lock as the door closed behind the nurse, and she closed her eyes to float in the welcome fog of the drug. Perhaps this was what it was to be dead. No pain, physical or emotional. No sorrow. No guilt. Memories evaporated, worries irrelevant. A thick, impenetrable cloud of nothing.

James, ordered back to Taipei, had gotten as far as the train station, where he stood surrounded by crying children, tired parents, ragged men begging for handouts, one or two prostitutes soliciting business. He kept seeing the gray-haired woman's pale face, her hazel eyes flecked with gold.

"She never leaves this hospital," Glass had said. Never leaves the hospital? James knew what it meant, all right. He tried to convince himself otherwise as he stood waiting for his train. He couldn't do it.

The rumors were true. Enemies of InCo disappeared, not

into the latent countries, as he wanted to believe, but permanently. The clinic at Leysin, the work camp in Edmonton, and the rehab center in Kaesong, were not humanitarian institutions. The fabled Dirty Tricks Corps, the black ops he had believed to be fictional, was real. And InCo Forces was no more worthy of his allegiance than the tired remnants of the Blackfoot Nation.

All of this made James an even bigger fool than his father said he was. His naïveté appalled him now, as he thought of the woman's fate decreed by a man to whom she was no more than an inconvenience. And who was she, after all, to have angered George Glass? James frowned over this, trying to remember her face, wondering where he had seen it before. It niggled at his memory, trying to come to the surface, but it was elusive. The more he tried to grasp it, the more it slipped away from him, like trying to catch trout with his bare hands in the achingly cold waters of the Two Medicine River.

His head buzzed with fatigue and the aftermath of excitement, and he rubbed his temples. Where had he seen her? He couldn't remember. But he wanted to see her again. He didn't care that she was a prisoner, that she had fired her weapon at two of his Corpsmen, that she was grubby and maybe crazy and supposed to be dangerous.

He stood in the crowded train station as it emptied, as train after train came and went. When the morning sun rose over the shabby city of Keelung, James was still in the station. He tongued his lipmike and spoke to the duty sergeant.

"I missed my train," he said, with a pang at his untruthfulness.

"Okay, Captain Bull," the sergeant said breezily. "I don't have anything for you, anyway, not till the general's back."

"Where is he now?"

"Off duty for the moment. Meeting this afternoon in Taipei with the mucky-mucks—uh, sorry, sir, with the president and the premier."

"Thanks, sergeant. I'll check in later, then."

"Fine, sir."

James had been driven to the station the night before in a pedicab. Now he set out to walk back to the hospital, a walk of an hour or more. He welcomed the time, needing to think.

The sidewalks were already filling with people on their way to open their shops. Chattering housewives waited for the vendors to lift their awnings, and children passed on their way to school. The noise, James noticed, was different than in an InCo city. Fewer powered vehicles, more foot traffic, and of course, the high-pitched sounds of Mandarin. It all combined to make a white noise, a blank background to his thoughts. He walked, occasionally looking about him to see he was heading in the right general direction, and he dredged up everything he could remember hearing about Dirty Tricks Corps.

He bought breakfast at a kiosk, some sort of dumpling stuffed with vegetables and rice, and ate it from the paper wrapping as he went on. When he reached the refugee camp, he circled it, dodging the delivery vans, glancing past the foambrick fence. Lines of listless people waited outside the showers and the meal tents as the camp began its sluggish day. James slowed his steps. What was he going to do, now that he was here?

A sense of déjà vu crept over him. Years before, he had stood at a crossroad not unlike this one, a point of life-changing decision. He had decided then to turn his back, to ride away into the snowstorm of a bitter Montana night. This crossroad came in sweltering heat, on the other side of the world. But the turning he had reached was much the same.

His youth had been filled with tirades about the honor of the Indian, the bravery, the honesty, the nobility. Despite his father's example, the ideas had taken root, and flourished. They had shaped his character, turned him into a man who couldn't stand aside and allow a woman—defenseless, probably drugged, a woman who had done no real harm—he couldn't allow her to be sacrificed to the pique of one powerful man. And yet, his loyalty to the Corps—his sworn loyalty, he reminded himself—dictated that he follow his commander in chief's orders.

His hasty breakfast roiled in his stomach. He didn't know how the general's orders would be carried out, but he had an idea of the way black ops worked. Disguises, covers, substitutions. Dirty Tricks Corps was reputed to be a profitable assignment for anyone clever enough to do the work. Such a man had to be unburdened by scruples.

James moved around the refugee camp toward the hospital, keeping a circumspect distance from the guard towers and the black-uniformed militia patrolling the fence. He tried to think what action the colonel might have ordered.

What if he, James Bull, were trying to silence someone who lay imprisoned in a hospital room? His dark hair and skin would make him blend in with the populace of this city, though his height was a problem. He supposed he would wait until night, when the staff of the hospital was reduced, when most of the patients were asleep, and the emergency room less crowded. He would get his hands on the proper clothes, bribe someone, impersonate someone, work his way into the patient's room and do something that would make it look natural. Nothing that would give Oceania cause for complaint against the International Cooperative Alliance. An unfortunate occurence. An accidental death.

He walked more and more slowly as he went up the hill to the hospital. He saw no InCo uniforms at all. There were a lot of civilians, people in search of medical attention, mothers carrying babies, friends supporting the lame or the elderly. There were doctors and nurses in white coats or green scrubs. A few militia wandered around the outside of the hospital. The entrances looked even more dismal in the morning light, the walls separating from their foundations, the cracks in the windows glinting crazily with the sun.

James stood in a patch of shade, around the corner from the tea shop, feeling conspicuous in his uniform. His jaw itched, and when he put his hand to it, he felt the slow beginnings of his morning beard. Moments later he had made his decision. He turned away from the hospital to find a hotel, a shower, some different clothes. He didn't feel he had any choice. He would act according to his conscience, and deal with the consequences afterward.

When Ebriel opened her eyes the sky beyond her window was dark again. The rising pain of her ankle woke her. Her mouth was dry as cotton, but this time the glass was within her reach, and she found the straw with her mouth and drank deeply of the tepid water. Through the oblong window in the wooden door, the corridor was dim. She peered at it for several moments, but didn't see either her militia guard or any hospital staff. Dimly, she heard the bustle of the hospital going on beyond her room. When she tried to lift her head from the thin pillow, a wave of dizziness assaulted her. She had not eaten since early the previous day, but she felt no hunger. She felt only the physical pain, and the totality of her loneliness.

She turned her head to the narrow vista of stars beyond the window. "Foolish Frenchwoman," she muttered. "To think of loneliness now." She was ashamed at how glad she was to hear the heavy lock open, to see the nurse come in.

The nurse was even more harried than the night before. She hastily replaced the bag of saline. She administered more medication through the IV port, and set a bowl near Ebriel's side, noodles in broth, with a wide spoon. She touched a button that raised the head of the bed. As it rose, Ebriel's head swam again. "You must eat, now," the nurse said. She straightened the sheets and patted her patient's hand absently.

Ebriel obediently reached for the spoon with her free hand as the nurse hurried out, and the door locked behind her.

Ebriel managed to swallow a few mouthfuls. The broth was salty, the noodles thick and soft from sitting in the liquid. Her dizziness subsided, and she was glad, for the moment, to be upright. She gazed out into the field of stars. She dozed, still sitting up, the spoon falling out of her limp fingers and into her lap.

She dreamed of music. She was playing the Ravel, the flute and harp concerto. The conductor was looking at her, and the harpist, but somehow she couldn't think of what came next, what the notes were—what movement were they in? Her fingers moved, seeking the keys on her flute. The spoon in her lap dropped to the floor with a toneless clank, but it was not that that woke her. There was an alarm sounding, over and over. A klaxon, so loud—and under its incessant blare, the heavy snick of the deadbolt on her door.

She opened her eyes. There was someone in the room. Someone beside her bed, the right side, where the IV bag hung from its stand. The nurse? No, a black uniform—the militia guard? He had a syringe in his hand, she could see the

glimmer of light on it—but why would he be changing the
IV? And the alarm—surely that was a fire alarm! But the man
was reaching up to the bag, his broad shoulders blocking the
dim rectangle of light coming through the door. Starlight from
the exterior window twinkled on the steel needle as he—
whoever he was—tried to find the Y port with his fingers in
the semidarkness. He found it, and she saw the needle disap-
pear as he inserted it into the port.

A surge of adrenaline brought Ebriel fully awake. She sat
up, her spine rigid, her right wrist straining against the handcuff. She cried, *"Non!"*

The intruder whirled. Instinct drove her, reactions honed in
the dojo, in Tacticals. She ripped the IV needle from her arm
in one swift motion, tearing the tape, the plastic, and her flesh.

He grunted, an animal sound. He reached across her body
to seize her free left arm, to stop her, but he was too late. The
IV tube swung free, rattled lightly against the metal frame of
the bed. Her attacker cursed, some word she didn't recognize.
She twisted her head to see him jerk the needle out of the IV
bag. He lifted the syringe, seeking exposed skin on her shack-
led right arm.

Part of her mind found the whole scene no more than curious. Only the day before, she had made up her mind to die.
But now her body, caught by surprise, fought for survival. She
struggled. She thrashed her legs, trying to kick him, pulling
hard against the handcuff. She shouted, louder this time, and
he let go of her arm long enough to rip the pillow from beneath her head and place it over her face. Still she fought him,
kicking, wriggling, her cries muffled by the polyfill and by the
repeating blast of the alarm from the corridor. She felt his
hard hand pressing on the pillow, pushing it tighter and tighter
over her face.

She struggled to breathe. Her muscles weakened. She
would lose consciousness, and then he could take his time, in-
ject her, make his escape. But she would not make it easy.

She pulled at his rock-hard arm with her hand, she gouged
at his skin with her fingers. The pressure on her face did not
ease, though she felt her nails break his skin, his blood run hot
under her fingertips.

She had no chance. The taste of the bleached pillowcase filled her mouth, her lungs burned with the need for air, her head spun. Her head filled with the loud and toneless clanging, the alarm's racket blending with the ringing of her ears. It was almost over.

Yasmine floated beside Ethan's chair, her hand on his shoulder, her eyes stretched wide with sleeplessness and worry. Ethan was talking to Perk, at Xiao Qaidam, where *Unicorn* had landed only hours before.

"They're on their way," Perk said in his laconic way. "Doubt they'll be in time."

"Our contact in Tainan says jurisdiction hasn't been decided."

Perk squinted into the camera, and pulled at his gray ponytail with one hand. "Glass will never let it get that far, Ethan."

"The mission is over Hunan now. They'll reach Keelung tomorrow."

"Mighty risky," Perk said.

"Yes. As you say."

When the transmission ended, Yasmine said, "What will happen now, Papa?"

Ethan turned his chair to face her. "Yasmine, you've been spending too much time here. Your face is puffy."

"I will go to bed soon. But please tell me."

"Two things could happen," Ethan said slowly. His face sagged despite the microgravity, and his breathing scraped in his lungs. "If InCo wins custody of Ebriel, they could take her to Todokai, or more likely, to InCo Forces headquarters in America. But if the stories we've heard are true, Security Corps will be impatient with any court proceedings, and will . . ." he paused for breath. "Will dispose of her."

"I want to be here in the morning. When the mission arrives."

"It may be very upsetting, Yasmine."

Yasmine answered, "I have faced my own death, Papa. There are worse things, to me."

"Very well, my Yasmine," he said, his voice scraping to nothing. "And now, rest."

She touched his face with her small brown hand. "And you, Papa. Sleep."

26

InCo dollars carried a lot of weight in Taiwan. James found a shop that sold reworked clothing and bought a loose shirt and a pair of dingy beige trousers. He spent a few moments looking at a rack of recycled rubber sandals, but decided to stick with his service boots. They looked odd with the pants, but they were flexible and strong. He felt better wearing them.

A hotel not far from the refugee camp offered him a room with a hard, narrow bed and a communal bath. It was almost midday, and the bathroom, a ramshackle affair with precarious fixtures and cracked tiles, was unoccupied. James showered, shaved, and lay down to try to rest. The room was hot and stuffy, its windows painted shut.

James felt certain Dirty Tricks Corps would make its attempt in darkness. He couldn't imagine that the operative would want to appear in daylight. He himself wouldn't, not with the constant traffic in and around the refugee hospital. Nothing would happen until nighttime. Still, anxiety and the feeling of displacement, of being out of his proper environment, kept him wakeful. And when he tried to sleep, the internal debate raged behind his closed eyelids. What if he was wrong? Surely the general—his commanding officer—couldn't have ordered harm to a defenseless prisoner. But James had clearly heard him say she wasn't to leave the hospital. What else could that mean?

It meant that Gil Walking Bull had been right. That InCo Forces, at least some in InCo Forces, were liars, criminals, even murderers. James had disbelieved, had sworn his loyalty. His friends in Security Corps had done the same—Chang, the others—could they all be mistaken?

And on and on and on his mind churned as he tossed on the hard bed.

He forced himself to wait until the light started to fade beyond the grimy window. He rose, changed into his new-old clothes, and went in search of food. He ate some kind of steamed meat roll, standing beside a counter, and returned to the hospital.

He made a casual progress around it, assessing the building, which was little more than a prefabricated rectangle. He knew from the day before that each floor had a single long corridor. The windows looked out over the alley on one side, the street on the other. The emergency entrance faced the row of shops, while the admitting entrance opened toward the refugee camp. The doors were locked now, the admitting desk empty. The two exits, one at each end of the building, had fire doors locked from the inside.

James slouched along the sidewalk, one pedestrian among many. People passed the hospital on their way to the shops or into the city. Two black-uniformed militia stood at the emergency room door, chatting, eating out of paper cartons. James walked by them, peering sidelong through the cracked glass. The molded plastic chairs were full of people. A panel flickered on a side wall. The opposite wall held an ancient cork bulletin board with sheafs of printed instructions and leaflets pinned to it. Between the bulletin board and a red fire alarm lever stood a much newer telepanel with a voice-input mike, but it was blank, the power off.

Full dark fell over the harbor city as James completed his circuit. The street outside the emergency entrance was garish as day, lit by the brilliant lights from the row of shops, and more muted light spilling from the windows of the hospital. In the alley beside the tea shop James found an upended bit of broken paving stone, and he sat on it, leaning his shoulders against the wall, invisible in the shadow of the building. He settled down to wait.

In his youth, if James and his friends wanted to eat real meat instead of the canned stuff passed out by Social Services, they hunted their own, often spending whole nights in the mountains, rising before dawn to watch for signs of game. They crouched, hardly breathing, hidden by underbrush and stands of tamarac saplings, waiting for the white-tailed deer to parade delicately out into the meadows in the gray early light, their great ears twitching, white flags of their tails raised, slender bodies poised to flee at any sound. James was an expert at waiting.

The night wore on, and the emergency room began to empty. People passed the alley, going into the shops, laughing, calling out, walking in pairs or knots of three or four down the sidewalk, across the street. Sirens wailed here and there around the city, but no one seemed to pay any attention. Once or twice someone passed through the alley, unaware of James. Once a man, teetering drunkenly, relieved himself on the opposite wall. James didn't move. He watched the door to the emergency room, the only open entrance into the hospital, and he waited.

The militia guards grew bored as midnight came and passed. They leaned against the door jambs, yawning.

James had always known when the deer were close. A little tingle would grow across his scalp, across the back of his neck, a little electric warning. The others watched James to know when to be ready. His eyelids would lift, his hands come alive on the stock of his rifle. When the deer picked their way on silent hooves through the dawn-dark meadows, James had his rifle up, the stock pressed into his shoulder, his cheek against the barrel as he sighted. The passage between stillness and action was no more than a heartbeat.

Now, in the noisome alley, he felt the tingle under his hair. His eyes moved, searching.

It was 0200. The shift was changing. The two guards by the door greeted their replacements, exchanged a word or two, a brief laugh, and departed. Another man appeared from the

street and flashed a badge at the new guards, went on into the
waiting room. He approached the desk behind the wire screen.

The third man also wore the black uniform. He strode with
confidence into the waiting room, the kind of straightforward,
assured behavior that James knew very well drew less attention than acting furtive. Through the cracked glass James saw
him waiting beside the door for the receptionist to buzz him
through. James came to his feet, slowly. What was it? His
neck burned now, his heart pounded. The new man might be
only the guard, sent to relieve the one posted outside the prisoner's room, simply an Oceania grunt doing his job . . .

The door beside the screen opened for the new man, and he
disappeared inside the hospital. And then James realized what
it was that had triggered his alarm.

It was boots. James still wore his InCo boots, cut to fit, perfectly broken in, strong enough to withstand water or mud or
to shield his feet from hot pavement or freezing snow.

And the Oceania militiaman, who had just been admitted
into the interior of the locked hospital, wore InCo boots.

How many minutes were required for the man to make his
way to the second floor, down the long corridor to the guarded
cubicle that held his target? He had already delayed too long,
not wanting to believe, denying his own instinct. James
dashed from the alley, raced across the street and into the hospital, brushing past the startled guards without a word. He
slammed his fist down on the lever of the fire alarm inside the
now-empty waiting room.

A shrill electronic clanging began in the corridors and in
the emergency room itself. The receptionist leaped to her feet.
The guards at the door turned to stare at James, open-mouthed,
stupid with surprise. James pointed at the ceiling, and shouted,
"Fire! On the roof! Fire!"

The two militiamen ran out into the street to look up, and
James followed them, pointing, shouting, but when he reached
the sidewalk he darted to the right, into the shadows, around the
corner to the closest fire door. It was already open as staff
poured out, looking up and around, trying to find the source of
the alarm. They cried out to each other, Mandarin and English,
about patients and fire extinguishers, demanding of each other

to know where the fire was, what was happening, was it for real? They milled about in the darkness. A fire truck, its siren wailing, just as sirens had been wailing all day, raced up from the city. It pulled up in front of the hospital just as James slipped inside, passing confused orderlies and nurses, dashing up the stairs. Several doors stood open, patients in robes or clutching hospital sheets around them staggering to the door-ways to beg for information. James raced past a room where one patient was trying to help another into a wheelchair, but he didn't stop. He spared a moment to hope no one would be hurt in the confusion. Soon enough they would know the alarm was false. But now, for the moment, he had one press-ing concern.

The day before, he had come up the stairs on the opposite end of the building, and had seen the guard in the corridor. Her room had to be close. Where was the guard?

James slowed his steps. He would have to check every room. He passed two empty ones, then one with an elderly woman asleep, her mouth open, unaware of the commotion. The door to the next room was closed, and one glance through the window told James he had found it. He could already be too late.

He braced himself, and smashed the door with his booted foot, splintering the old wood, the flimsy deadbolt. The door collapsed just as a man in green scrubs ran past, shouting something in Mandarin, and then in English, "Out! Out! Everybody out!" James leaped through the door. He seized the man in the black uniform from behind, throwing one arm around his neck, yanking at his right hand with the other. His voice was lost in the bedlam as he shouted, "Not today, you bastard!"

Ebriel's lungs burned fiercely, craving oxygen. When the pillow suddenly lifted from her face, she threw herself away, off the bed, sucking in air as if she had been drowning. Her manacled hand still locked to the rail, she fell to the floor with her right arm extended, her right knee bent, her left leg in its cast straight out in front of her. Lights blazed from the corridor, and she saw the other figure, taller than her attacker, thinner, wearing pale loose trousers. She gasped great sweet lungfuls of air. Sirens shrieked and people shouted. She struggled to stand, levering herself with the handcuffed hand, but the cast hampered her. The light from the hall was too bright, and there were drugs in her bloodstream. She blinked, trying to clear her blurred vision.

The tall man pulled her attacker right off his feet, but not for long. He had him in a grip from behind, left arm in a choke hold around his neck, right hand squeezing the right wrist, the hand that held the syringe. The syringe fell to the floor with a plasticky clatter, but the man in the Oceania uniform was thickset and strong. He ripped himself free, and the two grappled, face-to-face. The newcomer had shouted once, but now he fought in deadly silence. The man in the black uniform was trying to free his hand, to reach something at his waist.

A duty belt, Ebriel thought. He is military, he has a duty belt. A weapon.

The men swayed together, struggling, their boots gripping the old linoleum of the floor, their rasping breaths almost inaudible under the clamor. The stakes were life and death.

Ebriel groped for the syringe. She tugged at the handcuff until it bruised her wrist, and she stretched out her left arm, reaching, reaching. She felt as if her right arm would come out of its socket. The flimsy hospital gown caught on the bed rail and tore like tissue paper.

The syringe gleamed in the white light spilling from the shattered door. It had carried her death, or was meant to. She scrabbled across the floor with her fingers.

And now she had it. She turned where she was, one hip on the floor, her back braced on the cold bed frame. With her free hand, grunting with effort, she plunged the syringe into the black-suited leg of her attacker and depressed the plunger with her thumb.

When the man collapsed to the floor, like a balloon deflating, he made no sound at all.

The tall man reached past him with strong hands, pulling Ebriel to her feet.

At the same moment, a woman shouted from the hall,

"Out, everyone out! Don't you hear the alarm? Everyone out! Are you all right in there?"

And the tall man called back, "We're coming!" as if it were the most natural thing in the world.

27

Ebriel struggled to her feet by pulling on the bed rail, thankful for the strength of her trembling thigh muscles. She found she could bend her knee above the cast. Half of the torn gown hung from her right arm, caught by the handcuff. The other half fell from her shoulders to puddle around her feet.

The tall stranger pulled something from inside his shirt and applied it to the handcuff.

Ebriel stared at the man on the floor. He lay unmoving, his Asian features blank, dark eyes open, lips already gray.

The handcuff clicked open. When the shackle fell away from Ebriel's arm, it carried with it the remnants of the hospital gown, leaving her with nothing on but her shredded trousers.

The tall man held up a little metallic object for her to see. "Universal key," he said. His voice was deep, the accent distinctly American, familiar. He grabbed her sweater from the wall hook and held it out to her. "Come on, ma'am. We'd better move."

Ebriel tore her gaze from the man at her feet. "Dead," she said stupidly.

The man glanced down at her assailant, and then back at her. His eyes were dark, too, but they gleamed with determination and intelligence. And life. "Probably, yes, ma'am," he said, his voice matter-of-fact. "Or he will be soon. And a damned good thing." He pushed the sweater over her head and gently tugged her arms into its sleeves, pulled it down over her breasts. "Don't think about it now. Better move out." He bent and slipped her sandals onto her bare feet.

Stunned, shocked, Ebriel obeyed. She leaned on him, his forearm hard and strong under her fingers, and hobbled out of the room that had been her prison.

Together, Ebriel negotiating one stair at a time, the tall man supporting her, they descended to the fire door. Ebriel's ears rang with the incessant blare of the klaxon. Her savior found an aluminum crutch abandoned in the hall, and Ebriel fitted it under her armpit, supporting her bad leg as they struggled away from the refugee hospital. The sidewalk was clogged with patients and staff. Emergency vehicles competed for space in the street. Lights flashed blue and red and white, blinding everyone, and people were shouting orders and questions, calling out names. No one paid Ebriel or her rescuer the slightest attention in the melee. She leaned on his arm with her right hand, and swung the crutch with her left arm. It took a moment to find the rhythm, and then they were off, moving almost as fast as if she were unencumbered.

Within a block of the hospital, all traffic vanished. The din of the fire alarm faded. Dawn was still several hours away, and the streets of Keelung were dark, shops and houses and kiosks closed. The white light from a half-moon stippled the road with shadows. When they were perhaps half a kilometer from the hospital, the tall man led Ebriel to the sheltered doorway of a closed office building, where a large wooden planter afforded an edge wide enough to sit on. She lowered herself onto it with a sigh of relief. Whatever pain medication she'd had the evening before was gone. Her leg throbbed, though the cast held it stable. The old sweater came only to her thighs, and the night air was cool on her bare legs. She leaned back, braced on her two hands, and looked up at her rescuer.

The little claw tattoo on his cheekbone was just visible in the moonlight. His eyes were pools of darkness.

She said abruptly, as if confessing, "I have killed someone."

"Yes, ma'am."

"The *seringue*—" she said it in French, then repeated it in English. "Syringe. It had poison in it." It was hard to take in, to comprehend what had happened. What she had done.

He nodded. "It was meant for you, ma'am."

"But who wanted me dead? Who cares about someone like me? And why did you—" She paused for breath, and tipped her head to see him better. "Who are you, *monsieur*?"

"I'm James Bull," he said. He smiled, his teeth shining white in his dark face.

"You are InCo Forces. I saw you, in the truck, with other soldiers."

"Right. Security Corps. I'll explain later." He put out his hand to her. "Now, if you're rested, we should get going. Can you go on?"

"I will be fine," she said, pushing herself erect. Her vision clouded, then cleared, then blurred again with a host of dark stars. She swayed, unsteady on her feet, gripping his hand. "I am sorry," she muttered. "If I could—just have a moment . . ."

She tried to take a step, tottered, almost fell. His long arms came about her, and he said, "Whoops!" It was a word she had never heard.

She shook her head, hard. "I am better, it will be all right."

"It's the drugs, I expect, and shock. But we need to get out of the city. I have a hotel room, but it's not safe. Both InCo and Oceania are going to be looking for you within the hour."

"*Oui*," she said. "Let us go, then. Toward the west—I know a place."

They labored on through the uneven streets, Ebriel leaning heavily on James's arm, the pain in her leg coming in hot waves. In an hour they reached the edge of the city, where the pavement was rougher, but there was cover of trees and undergrowth. Ebriel stopped briefly, panting, sweat running down her face and sides. With distaste, she realized she could smell her own body, unwashed now for three days. She pointed up the hill.

"Up there," she said when she caught her breath. "There is a little clearing, hard to see. It is where I—" She realized what she was about to tell him, and hesitated. Exhaustion and pain confused her. "Where I landed," she finished weakly.

His glance was startled, but he only said, "How far?"

"A kilometer, perhaps. But uphill."

He put his left arm around her waist to take more of her weight, and they went on, moving slower and slower as the way grew steeper. Ebriel's breath came in sobs.

The moon set just as they reached the park. James pulled a microlight out of a pocket to light their way, but it was hard to read the landmarks. Ebriel remembered where she had come out onto the paved path, how she had pushed through the bushes, but it was difficult to find the spot again. She took one wrong turn, forcing them to backtrack. When she found the place at last, the eastern sky had begun to brighten. They pushed through the underbrush to reach the clearing, and her ruined copter, just as the red disc of the sun rose above the treetops. It glimmered on the little pond and the polycarbonate of the copter's windows.

James stopped at the edge of the clearing, staring at the copter. It tilted to one side, its tail jammed against the cliff, its rotors drooping. "You flew this?"

Ebriel gave a weak laugh. "I crashed it."

He gazed down at her where she stood leaning on her crutch, and on his left arm. He shook his head. "I can't imagine it," he said. "Can we get into that bird?"

They climbed through the jammed-open door and into the interior of the copter. Ebriel, half-crawling, worked her way up the tilting floor to the back. The aidkit lay where she had dropped it. She found what she needed, pressing the ampoule to the inside of her elbow and almost sobbing with relief as the pain began to recede. A sense of unreality rose in her, as if all of it had been a fever dream. Only the tall man with the tattooed cheek made it real.

James collapsed into one of the rear seats, looking about him with wonder. "This is an InCo bird," he said. "Where on earth did you get it?"

She didn't answer.

He looked at her for a long moment, and his dark eyes

narrowed. "I've just remembered," he said, half to himself. "I've finally remembered why I know your face."

She mystified him. Her slender body was hard with muscle, and her thin face had the porcelain character of an antique doll's, with autumn-hazel eyes and long lashes. She had acted without hesitation, shoving the lethal syringe directly into her attacker's leg, right through the trousers. She had moved fast, and struck hard, to pierce that hard leg muscle. She had faced him afterward, unabashed at being half-naked before a stranger.

But James knew without being told that she had never killed before. Her skin had gone clammy at the sight of death, her pupils dilated, her breath fast and shallow.

James remembered his own first kill, a lovely six-point buck that had leaped once at the crack from his rifle, then fallen heavily to the needle-strewn forest floor. James, nine years old, had found his exhilaration colored with a grief he could never explain to his father. His shoulder had burned from the kick of the gun, and his feet had ached with the cold of the spring snow, but it was the confusion of emotions he remembered, the urge to shout with victory and also to weep for the fallen beauty of the buck.

Now he said to this beautiful, confusing woman, "I saw you on Newnet. You're a musician. And your family . . ."

Her full-lipped mouth twisted. "*Oui*. My husband, my little daughter. General Glass said their yacht was over the boundary, and so InCo did nothing to protect them. It was a lie."

Weakly, James said, "I'm sorry." He could no longer defend his commander.

She had begun to shiver with the aftermath of shock. He went to the little galley, legs bracing against the tilt of the floor, and opened the cupboard that held standard InCo issue polyfiber blankets. He took one out of its plastic bag and put it around her shoulders. As she accepted it, she said, "Ebriel. My name is Ebriel."

"Ebriel." The name was like her, delicate and strong.

Her trembling began to subside. "And you are *Monsieur* Bull, *oui*?"

"James," he said. "Yes." He stood up to climb back to the galley. "Is your bird outfitted? I'll get us some food, some coffee."

"*Oui*. And I need to get clean. I am so filthy, I cannot bear it."

"How much water do you have on board?"

"I don't know, but enough for a wash, I think."

"A spitbath," he said.

She raised her eyebrows. *"Comment?"*

He shrugged and came to help her to her feet. "Just an expression, American. It means a very small bath."

She leaned on him to make her way to the head, and just managed to fit herself inside, dragging the thick cast, already pulling off the sweater as he pushed the door closed. Her body was white, her arms and her back marked with bruises. Her breasts were small as a girl's, her hipbones sharp. She needed food, he thought, and soon.

He found two InstaMeals and zipped them open. They were just warming when she opened the door of the head and sidled out, dragging her splinted leg behind her. She had a towel around her, and she nodded toward the passenger seats. "There is a dress there, under the seat," she said. "Will you give it to me?"

He found the dress, a faded cotton shift. It looked child-sized, but she managed to pull it on. It clung to her wet body, and barely reached her knees. She fluffed her wet hair with her fingers, a small, intensely feminine gesture. It made James catch his breath.

She lowered herself into one of the seats with a sigh and said softly, "Now tell me, James Bull. Why did you do this for me?"

He stalled, fussing with a pouch of coffee. "I—I had a hunch. A feeling."

"Ah, a feeling," she said. "I have had such feelings. But the risk to you . . ."

He turned to her with the tray of foilpacks and coffee in his two hands. Her eyes caught the morning light, her damp face shining. "I'm not at risk yet. But I'm due back in Tainan tonight," he said. "If I'm late, there'll be trouble."

"You must go, then," she said. "Go back."

"But what will happen to you, Ebriel?" He laid the tray on the armrest beside her. "You're not safe. If you're apprehended again, they'll send someone else, another operative."

"Who will?" She asked the question casually, as if it were of no great importance. But he knew, he had seen, how she fought for her life.

"I'm ashamed to tell you," he answered her. "I can hardly believe it myself."

Her hand, clean now, touched his arm. "Why, James? Why should you be ashamed?"

Where her hand touched him, his skin warmed. She made him feel like a boy, gauche and awkward. He swallowed. "I'm a sworn officer," he said. "And it was my own commander who gave the order. I heard him do it."

"And who is your commander?"

"I'm a captain in Security Corps. General Glass is my commander."

Her hand lifted suddenly from his arm as if it had burned her. "Glass," she hissed. It was like a curse. The change in her face stunned him. Her features sharpened, her mouth thinned, her eyes darkened. Heat flamed in her cheeks before she turned her head away.

He moved the tray closer to her hand. "Eat, Ebriel," he said. "Then if you want to, you can tell me about it. But we have to think what to do about you."

She accepted the InstaMeal without meeting his eyes, and she began to eat as if starving. She probably was. He was ravenous himself. There were soybean cubes and vegetable sauce and puréed fruit. He took the rectangle of flat bread out of its fold of plastic to sop up every calorie, and he saw that she did the same, automatically, like any other soldier. But she wasn't InCo Forces. So then what?

When they finished, he took the empty foilpacks and stuffed them into the recycle bin under the tiny sink. He stood in the galley a moment, a pouch of coffee in his hand, marked with the black and silver globe. "Ebriel," he said quietly. "Where did you get this copter?"

It was a different voice that answered him. It said, in a strong southern American accent, "She stole it."

James whirled. He had been preoccupied, negligent, and

he hadn't heard her approach. She was tall and rangy, with short blond hair and irregular features. She wore a jumpsuit of a featureless gray material, with a duty belt of InCo issue around her lean hips. Her cool blue eyes met his. "She stole this bird from me," she repeated. "And I stole it from InCo."

Ebriel breathed, "Oh, Ty." She struggled out of her seat, and worked her way down the slanting floor to the door. She climbed down, and stood leaning on her crutch beside the tall woman. "I am so sorry."

The strange woman touched Ebriel's shoulder. "Later, Eb," she said. She nodded up toward James, still standing in the galley. "Who's your friend?"

James cast a quick glance through the windows of the copter, but he saw no one else.

The woman nodded. "Right," she said curtly. "Came alone. Landed on the other side of the hill at first light. It took me a while to walk here."

James moved down the aisle and jumped out of the copter. The blond woman—Ty, Ebriel had called her—was almost as tall as he, broad-shouldered and strong-looking. She carried herself with her back straight, her shoulders pulled back. Like a soldier.

"James Bull," he said to her, with a short nod. "Captain, Security Corps."

She gave him a wolfish grin. "Captain," she said with a nod. "Ty Astin, formerly of InCo Forces." She put out her hand. He shook it. "I don't know what you're doing here, but it looks like you've helped my friend. Thank you."

Ebriel asked quietly, "Am I still your friend, Ty?"

The tall woman looked down at her. "Yeah," she said briefly. "With problems." She folded her arms. "Ebriel, we saw the video on Newnet. You had him in your sights. It was what you wanted. Why'd you wait? Why didn't you fire?"

Ebriel's cheeks blazed again, spots of fiery red against her white skin. James fought an urge to step forward, to shield her. He forced himself to stand still and listen.

"I could not," Ebriel said, her eyes on her bare feet, her voice choked. "I could not do it. And yet now I have—" Her eyes came up to the other woman's. "Now I have killed, Ty. You were right. It is a terrible thing."

"He was going to kill you," James said. "Another thirty seconds, and he would have."

Her eyes, enormous in her thin face, found his. She nodded wordlessly.

"You can tell me later." Ty Astin stepped around Ebriel and peered into the copter. "Don't know what to do about this bird, Eb. It's not gonna fly, that's for sure."

"The locals will strip it," James said. "When they find it. It's pretty well hidden out here. Visible from the air, I suppose, but InCo pulls out tomorrow, when the summit's over."

"Yeah. We'll just have to leave it," Ty said. She straightened. "Come on, Eb, we're getting you out of here. Can you walk?"

"*Oui*," Ebriel said. "Are you going to take me away, then, Ty?"

"Can't leave you here."

"But—" James began, and then hardly knew what to say. "Where will you go? Where did you come from? And where did you get this bird?"

"No offense, Captain," Ty said offhandedly. "None of your business."

"But it is, Ty," Ebriel said. "He saved me. The man in the hospital would have killed me, except for James." She gave James a trembling smile. "He had a feeling."

James's heart turned over at her smile. Ty made a small noise in her throat. "Feelings," she said in a flat tone. "Great. Well, it's still none of your business."

"Maybe not." James touched Ebriel's shoulder. "Listen," he said in a low tone. "Will you let me know that you're all right, at least?"

"*Oui*. If I can."

Ty had climbed up into the copter and was in the galley taking things out of drawers, stuffing them in a pack. She spoke over her shoulder. "No contact with InCo Forces, Eb. It's not safe."

"She's right," James said. "But I'll give you a place where you can leave me a message." He found a scrap of paper near the copilot's seat and wrote his father's address on it. "This will be secure, I promise."

When she took it from his hand her fingers were cold against his. "North America?"

"Far north," he told her. "In the mountains. Montana."

"I will try to get word to you."

"Promise?" he said.

She smiled again, her head tilted to one side. "*Mais oui*, James. I promise."

Ty climbed out of the copter. "Ready?" she said to Ebriel.

Ebriel answered, "Ready." She looked up at James, and then she stood on tiptoe to kiss his cheeks, first one, then the other. Her lips were soft and smooth, and his throat went dry. She whispered, "*Merci beaucoup,* James. *Cher* James. Thank you."

He couldn't speak. Her hand lay on his arm, and he covered it with his own.

"James," she said. "We must go. And so must you."

"Yes," he said.

Her eyes glistened in the morning light. "*Au revoir,*" she said softly.

He lifted his hand, releasing her.

Ty shouldered the pack. "Come on, Eb. Let's hit it."

He watched as they left the clearing, Ty leading, Ebriel following. He waited a few moments, and then he headed out in the opposite direction, for the long walk back to Keelung.

28

The Chain copter waited on a hill overlooking the eastern coast, settled neatly among a stand of spruce trees, its fuel cell open to the sunshine. Ebriel's armpit was raw from using the crutch, and her ankle throbbed. The last few meters of the climb took all her strength. Astrid Sorensen, Pilar Alavedra, and twelve-year-old Kanika lounged on the grass near the tri-gear. They rose, Astrid nodding coolly, Pilar murmuring, *"Hola,* Ebriel." Kanika stared, openmouthed, at the sight of the prodigal in her worn shift, hobbling toward them.

Ebriel collapsed into one of the passenger seats, her leg sticking straight out into the aisle. Astrid closed up the fuel cell and took the pilot's seat, with Ty next to her. Kanika sat across from Ebriel, Pilar behind. They were in the air in moments. They flew south around the island, retracing Ebriel's own journey, but then turned westward to cross the strait well south of Taipei, out of the path of other air traffic. Kanika began to pepper Ebriel with questions, but Pilar turned in her seat and said, "Kanika, we will hear Ebriel's story at Xiao Qaidam." Kanika subsided into reluctant silence, but Ebriel felt the girl watching her.

Once over the coast of the mainland, they banked to the

northwest for the long flight over Guangdong Province. Ebriel propped her chin on her hand and watched the green and brown of the Chinese landscape flow beneath. She dreaded facing Perk. She had proven him right, and Semaya, too. Ty had interceded for her, and been betrayed for her pains. And Ebriel feared for Yasmine. She prayed the girl had not crumbled under the news of her deception.

Yet despite these dark thoughts, her mind felt clear in a way she hardly remembered. It was as if she had broken through a wall, from the darkness of grief into the light of a new day. She touched her pocket with her fingers, feeling the scrap of paper with James Bull's address on it. She felt reborn. Her loss was unchanged, and yet her body had spoken for her, her nature had driven her to fight for her life.

She glanced at Kanika, sitting beside her, leaning toward the window to take in everything she could see. The girl embodied all the promise that training, nurture, education, and health could give a child. She, and the other starchildren, held the future in their young, strong hands.

Ebriel touched the cool polycarb of the window with a fingertip. She heard Kanika's every breath, Ty's murmured comments to the flight monitor. When Astrid touched the controls, Ebriel's fingers twitched. When Pilar, without speaking, handed her an InstaMeal, she ate it all. *Zut,* she thought, as she folded the empty foilpack. Foolish Frenchwoman. It seems you are to live after all. You had better decide how you are going to go about it.

Her life stretched out before her, a darkling plain, empty as the barren Tibetan Plateau. But still, a life. Days to live. Work to do. A destiny to discover.

Perk said little as they stowed the copter, except, "Ebriel, we'll do this: Get some clothes out of the locker before you freeze."

Ebriel obeyed, feeling out of place and unwanted. Leaning on her crutch, she limped across the landing field to the bunker. Even in August, the wind off the plateau was icy, and the cotton shift left her skin exposed. Goose bumps rose on her bare legs as she hobbled down the ramp into the living quarters.

She raided Perk's stores of scavenged clothing, trying several things on before settling on an ancient pair of blue denims with legs wide enough to fit over her cast, and a linen shirt, once white, now dimmed to a spotty beige. She dropped the soiled shift into the wash pile. She laid the clean clothes on a bunk and went to the showers to stand for long, blissful minutes under a stinging stream of hot water, the plastic cast carefully propped against a drain so she wouldn't slip. She soaped her body, rinsed, lathered again. She washed her hair and found a disposable toothbrush and used it. When she dressed, she tucked James Bull's note into the shirt's single breast pocket and buttoned the age-yellowed plastic button. Thoroughly clean for the first time in days, she felt stronger. She felt ready to face the Chain.

She hobbled out of the shower room, past the bunk beds to Perk's eclectic kitchen. Pilar and Astrid sat talking at the table in a pool of light from the overhead fixture. Kanika ran from appliance to appliance, demanding of Perk that he explain each to her, what it did, where he had found it, who had made it. Her chatter ceased when she saw Ebriel approaching, and she sank into a chair next to Pilar. Pilar and Astrid also fell silent. Perk, stirring something on one of the stoves, put down his long spoon and went to sit beside Kanika. Ty was using a panel. She ordered it off and came to stand at one end of the table, her face in shadow.

Five solemn faces watched Ebriel come. It was a tribunal, and she knew it.

Her feet felt like lead, but she limped steadily across to the kitchen, the rubbery strokes of her crutch against the cement floor loud in the silence. She heard the beat of her own heart and felt the flaming of her cheeks. When she reached the circle of light around the table, she stopped.

"You are going to judge me now," she said, not a question. Kanika's eyes stretched wide with awe. Astrid looked angry, Pilar sympathetic. Ty linked her hands behind her back.

Perk spoke first, pragmatic as always. "Did you tell anyone about the Chain?"

"*Non*," Ebriel answered. She didn't elaborate. Either they believed her, or they didn't.

And Pilar, her voice gentle. "Did you mention the habitat, or Papa?"

"Of course I did not."

Kanika's head turned, following the questions, the answers. Her full lips glistened as she touched them with her tongue.

Astrid spoke with icy contempt. "We have only six copters, and you destroyed one."

"I know this," Ebriel said quietly. "I am sorry for it."

"What will you do about it?"

Ebriel lifted one shoulder in her Gallic shrug. "What can I do, Astrid?"

Ty lifted her face into the light. "Forget it," she said. "The bird isn't what matters now."

"*Oui*," Ebriel answered, looking into her former partner's clear eyes. "I know what matters, Ty. I can make no argument for myself." She let her gaze move from one to another of them, opening herself to their scrutiny. Only Kanika's face held no reproach. Her eyes burned with excitement. Ebriel regretted her own naïveté, so long vanished.

She lifted her chin. "I betrayed you all, in principle and in deed. I failed my partner, and I am certain you believe that all your training was wasted on me. Perhaps it was." She dropped her eyes to her bare toes sticking out from beneath the wide denim pant legs. With her fingers she touched the pocket of the old shirt, where the slip of paper crackled. It gave her courage, and she looked up again. "I could try to explain, but it would not matter. I did not mean to harm the Chain, or Papa. I would undo it if I could, but then I would not have learned—" She broke off.

"Tell us," Perk drawled. He fingered his stringy gray ponytail, his gray eyes sharp in their web of wrinkles. Ebriel remembered that he, like herself, had made terrible mistakes in his life, and had worked through them. Perhaps, despite his dry tone and his hard eyes, Perk understood. Perhaps he understood better than she did herself.

She took a deep breath, tasting the scents of stewing meat, simmering vegetables, the underlay of soap and old wood and clothes dried in the open sun. She directed her words to Ty, speaking slowly. "I learned," she said, "that I could not kill to avenge my loss, though I wanted to very much. I learned that even in the worst of days, there is good waiting to be discovered." Her hand slipped to her pocket again, to the talisman of James Bull's handwriting. "I learned that although I thought my life had ended, I am still alive. And I want to be."

Ty gave a slow nod. Perk leaned forward, elbows on the table, and looked at Pilar and Astrid. "Ethan wants us to decide," he said. "Right here. He said we'll know the right thing."

"Decide what?" Ebriel asked.

Perk cocked an eyebrow at her. "Decide whether to accept you back into the Chain."

"Mais non," Ebriel exclaimed. "You cannot!"

"What d'you mean, Eb?" Ty demanded, straightening. "Don't you want to come back?"

Ebriel tried to smile, but it was a pallid attempt. Her lips trembled. "Oh, Ty, my friend. I do want to come back. I do, but I cannot. I am not—" she fumbled for a word. "I am not right for the Chain, not now."

Pilar and Astrid both nodded.

"And," Ebriel said, her voice steadying, "I must choose my own path. Not have it chosen for me."

"But what will you do, then?" Ty asked stiffly. "Where will you go?"

"I have thought," Ebriel answered, "of going to Xining. To the orphanage. To work there. Perhaps to—let us say, redeem myself."

"How long?"

"Oh, Ty. How can I say? But when it is enough—when it is finished—I will know it."

Ty put her hands on her hips and looked down at the others. "Send a shortband with her. And a weapon. Perk, you take her to Xining, be sure she makes it okay."

Ebriel thought that there might be a slight gleam of approval in Perk's eyes. "I'm willing," was all he said.

"Merci," Ebriel said.

"Pilar? Astrid?" Ty said sharply. And then, "Kanika?"

Kanika gaped at her. "Me?"

"You will be a starchild," Ty said. "Would you trust Ebriel with a shortband, with our names and the locations of our bases?"

Kanika looked back at Ebriel, and her eyes narrowed in her childish features. "If you ever hurt the Chain," the girl said, "I would come after you."

Hands came up around the circle, hiding the adults' smiles. Ebriel kept her own face solemn as she nodded to Kanika. "Of course," she said. "I would expect you."

Pilar and Astrid put their heads together, conferring. When they looked up after a moment, in perfect unison, Ebriel saw how close they were, how much they operated as a unit. She and Ty might have become that close, might have become a team of great power. She was infinitely sorry to have wasted the opportunity. But she could not change it now.

At last, Pilar spoke. "We will give you a shortband," she said. "But no weapon. The director of the orphanage knows of the Chain and its work. No one else must ever learn of it."

Ebriel nodded. "Very well. I thank you all. May I speak to Papa, just once?" And, she hoped, to Yasmine.

When the news had come that Ty, with Ebriel injured but safe, was on her way to Xiao Qaidam, Yasmine had slipped out of Papa's aerie and floated down the tube, buoyant with relief and an unaccustomed feeling of absurd happiness. She went to the storage area where slatted shelves held stacks of the cottons they all wore. She unfolded shirt after shirt until she found a very long one in azure, and then went through the trousers until she found a pair in the same color that fit her. The shirt flowed around her, sari-like. She intensified the effect with a long scarf of reworked yellow silk from a loose bag of odds and ends. She tied it around her, from her left shoulder to her right hip. She did her long hair in a knot behind her head. She used the space window in the corridor as a mirror, and nodded satisfaction at her image.

Semaya frowned when she reappeared in the aerie. "Yasmine?" she said, a bit querulously. "What is this?"

Ethan turned his chair to hover before Yasmine. "It's beautiful," he croaked. His eyes were bright, though his skin was gray and slack. His lips drooped helplessly on one side.

Yasmine said, "I wished to look like Yasmine Ananda. Like my mother's daughter."

"How lovely," Ethan said.

Semaya objected. "Ethan, it's too different. It sets her apart from the others."

"She has always been apart," Ethan rasped. "You know that, my dear. Yasmine will always be set apart, and now she has decided that for herself."

Semaya turned her head abruptly to the side, the motion sending her careening in the opposite direction. She seized a wall staple. Yasmine stared at her in bewilderment.

"Papa," she said slowly. "Is there something wrong? Is Ebriel . . ."

"No, Yasmine, nothing is wrong. Ebriel is on her way to Xiao Qaidam. She will be there tonight, which will be morning for us."

Semaya took a ragged breath. "Go to dinner, Yasmine. I'll see you there."

Yasmine hesitated. "Could I not—may I have dinner here, with Papa?" She almost never went to the dining hall, though she managed it fairly well now. Today, knowing Ebriel was safe, she felt she could do almost anything. But there was something going on between Papa and Semaya, and it worried her.

Ethan's voice was so thin as to be almost inaudible. "Yasmine. Please go down to dinner this time, and I'll see you in the morning. All right?"

Yasmine flicked her hand, to come close enough to his chair to kiss his cheek, and, surreptitiously, look into his eyes. What she saw there alarmed her. "Of course, Papa," she whispered. "In the morning, then."

She left the aerie in a heavy silence, but she paused in the slip before going out into the tube. Ethan and Semaya were arguing.

"She's too young, Ethan," Semaya said in a low tone. They were both facing the space window, their silhouettes outlined with the white sparkle of the stars.

And Ethan's croaking voice. "She can do it, Semaya. With your help."

"I don't know how I can face it." Semaya's voice choked. Yasmine thought the sentence ended in a sob.

Silently, she dropped out of the slip and glided slowly down to the gallery, the yellow scarf trailing behind her.

Yasmine was back in the aerie as soon as she woke in the morning. Semaya was not there. Ethan floated in front of a panel where Ty's face, tired and grim, looked out.

"Eb's in the shower," she was saying. "We'll talk to her, and get back to you afterward."

The panel blanked, and Ethan turned his chair to face Yasmine. "Sleep well?" he asked.

"Yes, thank you, Papa," she answered. She hovered before him. "You do not look as if you have slept at all."

His hoarse chuckle did not convince. "Oh, I slept, Yasmine. As much as I ever do."

She put out her hand to touch his face. "Oh, Papa," she whispered. "Are you very ill?"

His eyes turned to the space window and the cool stars beyond. "Yes," he said at last. His voice was even thinner than it had been the night before, and she feared the sclerosis would seize his vocal folds at last, steal the last vestige of his independence. She had plans for a device, a voice synthesizer, that would speak for him. The parts were in the storage area, and she had been saving memory sticks and rods from bits of discarded equipment.

"Yes." His voice grew a bit stronger. "I am very ill. We always thought, Semaya and I, that a cure would have been developed by now, but the world's troubles pushed this bit of medical research off the priority list. Adapting the solar fuel cell was much more important, in a global sense, than trying to cure the handful of people suffering from my disease. And now—" His voice weakened again, marred by gaps and scrapes. "Now it is too late."

Yasmine wanted to curl into a ball, to hide from this hard truth. But she could not indulge herself. Instead, she let her small hand cover his, feeling the fine bones under his wasted skin, the last remnants of muscle and fat devoured by his illness. "What do you want of me, Papa?" she said in a small, steady voice.

His eyelids fell and rose, a slow movement that she guessed required great concentration. His voice was no more than a thread. "I think you know, Yasmine."

Carefully, so as not to fly away from him, she nodded.

When Ebriel's face appeared on the panel, the ragtag furnishings of the Xiao Qaidam bunker behind her, Yasmine and Ethan were side by side, watching. Yasmine saw in Ebriel's eyes the same strength, the same patient courage, she had seen in Ethan's. How had Ebriel achieved it? She hoped that someday she would find out. She, too, would need courage.

Ebriel thought her mind had never felt so receptive, so sensitive to every nuance. Though the Chain members spoke little, she understood their feelings about her with a powerful sense of intuition. When she saw Ethan on the telepanel, she knew instantly that his illness was approaching its final stages.

Yasmine's eyes lighted at the sight of Ebriel.

"Yasmine," Ebriel said with a smile. "You look beautiful."

Yasmine's grave smile softened her sharp features. "Hello, Ebriel," she said. "It is hard for Papa to speak just now. I will try to speak for him."

"*Bien,*" Ebriel said. "I wanted to say I am sorry. About the copter, about everything."

Yasmine glanced down at Ethan, whose head lay limp against the back of his chair. "We think we understand," Yasmine said. She looked infinitely older than the last time Ebriel had seen her. At fifteen, she carried a weight of knowledge many people never acquired in a lifetime. "We care about you, Ebriel, yet we understand that you cannot come back at this time. Papa is content with your decision. And the Chain—" Her eyes moved to where Ty stood behind Ebriel.

Ebriel nodded. "There is a question of trust. Yet I thank the Chain for coming for me."

Yasmine's eyes glinted with sadness. "They could not leave you there," she said. "Because of the danger to them. To us."

"Of course," Ebriel said. "I understand this. Still, I am grateful. But you must know, Papa, I would never have betrayed you."

Ethan took a harsh breath and rasped, "Drugs. Torture."

Yasmine put in, "Vee said you were not yet ready to deal with such things. You were not meant to be carrying out missions where you could be captured."

Ebriel spread her hands. "I cannot undo what I have done. Perk will take me to Xining, and I will find work. In the orphanage, if I can."

"But you speak no Mandarin."

Ebriel shook her head. "No. But Perk has said many speak English there, for business. I will learn. And—" She shrugged. "In Xining, no one will know where I am, and there will be no risk to the Chain."

Ethan breathed again, a whistle in his thin chest. "Perk will know. You're not alone."

Ebriel's eyes stung. *"Merci,* Papa," she whispered. *"Merci beaucoup."*

She and Perk went out to watch the Chain depart. The copter was on the landing strip, packed and ready. Ebriel's hair was still damp, and her scalp chilled in the sharp breeze. Astrid nodded to her as she climbed up into the bird, but Pilar put out her hand. "Good luck, Ebriel," she said. "Take care of yourself."

Ebriel braced herself on her crutch and shook the proferred hand.

Kanika had already hopped up into the copter, but she hopped out again and dashed across the cracked tarmac. "Good-bye, Ebriel," she said breathlessly. "Next time you see me, I'll be a starchild!"

Ebriel smiled at her. "I know you will, Kanika." Kanika grinned, bouncing on her toes, and ran back to the copter, her frizz of black hair waving in the wind.

And then Ty was beside Ebriel, her tall figure blocking the wind. Ebriel squinted up at her. "I will miss you, Ty," she said.

Ty nodded. "Me, too." She had a bag of dark fabric slung

over her shoulder, and she slipped it off now and held it out to Ebriel. "Remember this?"

Ebriel took the bag in her hands, shaking her head in wonderment. The old brocade was soft, its deep color fading, the seams fraying. Its contents spoke to her probing fingers. "Of course," she said. On the tarmac, the copter's engine started, and the rotors began to turn. "Why did you bring it to me?" Ebriel asked.

"I don't know when I'm gonna see you," Ty said stiffly. "I just had a—" she laughed a little, uncomfortably. "I had a feeling, Eb. A feeling you should have it."

Ebriel put her hand on her partner's strong arm. "Ty. A feeling? I can hardly believe it."

Ty laughed again, more easily this time. "Yeah, me neither. Hey, Eb, you take care, okay? Stay in touch with Perk?"

"*Oui,*" Ebriel said. "I will. And you, Ty."

"Yeah." Ty shifted her weight from one foot to another, then bent quickly and pressed her leathery cheek to Ebriel's. "Bye, partner."

Ebriel stood at the side of the runway, shading her eyes with her hand, as the copter lifted to hover and then took off. She shivered in the breeze, watching until the craft disappeared into the west over the high plateau.

29

Perk kept a battered van in one of the empty hangars. It was a vehicle he had cobbled together, boasting varicolored panels of plastic and metal, big bald tires, a shining new Fleckcell fuel cell. It reminded Ebriel of a circus van she had seen as a little girl. The morning after the Chain departed, Perk brought out the van, rolling it down the ramp and onto a patch of dry grass. He had hardly spoken since the day before. In silence, he piled a few cartons in the back and went to close up the bunker while Ebriel settled herself in the single passenger seat. She propped her cast on a bundle of spare clothes.

Perk climbed into the driver's seat and started the engine. Ebriel was trying to fit her brocade shoulder bag behind the seat.

Perk raised an eyebrow and nodded at the bag. "From the old days?" he asked.

He put the van in gear and set out over open ground. Ebriel had to raise her voice over the creaking of the axles. "Yes," she said. "Yes, Ty brought it to me."

"Anything good in it?"

She started to shrug, but then, glad Perk was talking to her, she pulled the bag back into her lap. Perhaps there was something in it he would want, Perk the great scavenger. She opened the bag and saw the deep red lining she had been so fond of when she first bought it. What a long time ago that seemed now!

The van bumped and jostled. Ebriel drew the little purse out of her bag. "There is some money," she said, turning it out on her palm. "InCo dollars."

"Those're useful. What else?"

She reached in and felt soft fabric under her hand. It came out in a soft spill of white silk. "It is a *chemise*—a blouse I took from Paris, when I left." She stroked it. "New fabric, Perk, not reworked. Feel how soft." She held it out, and he touched the material with one gnarled forefinger.

"Nice. French?"

"Mais oui." She draped it over her shoulder and put her hand back into the bag to bring out a hairbrush. She laughed over the long auburn hairs tangled in its bristles. "My hair was long," she said. "And almost red." She tugged a short gray curl that fell over her forehead. "Look at me now!"

They reached the road. Perk drove up over the edge and onto the pavement, the van creaking as if pieces of it might fall off. "That all that's in your bag?" he asked. "Hardly seems worth hauling all this way."

"No," Ebriel said. "Not all." She pulled out a little wallet and held it in her palm for a moment before she opened it to look down at the stillphotos. Paul's face, slender and sensitive, looked up at her. Renée dimpled at the camera through her halo of auburn curls. Ebriel closed the wallet gently. Her pain had not diminished, but it had, in some way, withdrawn. The blunting of her sense of loss was a new sadness in itself. The part of her life that had been her family receded farther from her with each day that passed.

She turned her head to gaze at the distant Himalayan peaks through a sparkling haze of tears. Perk kept a sympathetic silence.

At length she said, "I miss them. Every moment of every day."

He nodded and said simply, "I know." She believed he did.

She put her hand back into her bag and rested her fingers on the smooth oblong of the flute case. "There is one thing more."

He drove with his right hand, left elbow resting on the open window frame. "Let's see it."

She drew out the flute case, letting the shoulder bag slide to the floor between her feet. The silver fittings on the case sparkled in the sunshine that streamed through the windshield. Perk whistled. "Is that leather?"

"It is," Ebriel said, caressing the glossy brown surface. "The case is old, though the flute is not." She touched the locks, and they released. She lifted the lid.

Her little black-and-silver instrument lay sectioned in velvet pockets, glittering delicately, the maker's name embossed in gold. Matit. The company had made the flute to her special order, in the Louis Lot tradition, with the French sound, the offset G, the slender carbon fiber barrel perfectly suited to her small hands. Automatically, without thinking about it, she found herself fitting the sections together, the metal cool and familiar under her fingers, the length so comfortable, the slight weight of it like taking the hand of an old friend. But she didn't put it to her lips. She only held it, thinking of Ty, and how Ty had wanted her to have it, had thought she should have it. Had had a feeling.

"Gonna play?" Perk asked, with a sidelong look.

"*Non*," she whispered. Swiftly, more swiftly than she had put it together, she uncoupled the sections and fitted them back into the case. "It has been too long. My *embouchure*—I am out of practice."

They rode on in silence, winding down the steep eastern slope. The road's paving was rutted and broken. In many places it had worn right through to the dirt underneath. They drove through fields of grass browning in the cool sunshine. Several times Perk had to stop as a line of shaggy, thickset yaks straggled across the road, curved horns bobbing, spring calves trailing behind. Dozens of Tibetan antelope leaped away at the van's noisy passage. Once they saw the moveable huts of some nomadic community nestled in a grassy meadow.

The descent took hours. When they reached Dulan, a hamlet of wooden houses on the edge of Qaidam Pendi, Perk pulled up in front of a slope-roofed building. "Lunch," he said. He got out and went to open the fuel cell to the light.

Stiff from sitting, and from bracing against the rough ride,

Ebriel retrieved her crutch from the back of the van and hobbled after Perk. The inn had a dirt floor, and unshuttered windows on three sides that let in the afternoon sun and a buzzing host of flies. An open brazier flamed in the center of the room. A man with the very dark skin of the Tibetans, his hair in long, thin braids, hurried out to bow to them. He had flat cheekbones, a broad nose, and eyes so narrow Ebriel could not see their irises. Perk chattered to him. Ebriel didn't understand a single word. They were the only customers.

A woman brought them bowls of noodles and a platter of meat rolls, smiling without reticence over her missing front teeth. Perk drank an enormous glass of beer. Ebriel drank water, and they both had cups of strong green tea. Perk scooped something thick and brown into his cup, then held out the shallow dish to Ebriel. "Yak butter," he said with relish. "Want some?"

She shook her head, but she smiled, surprised at how cheerful she felt. Not cheerful enough to try yak butter in her tea, perhaps, but peaceful.

Perk said, "These people would love some of your InCo dollars."

Ebriel put down her cup. *"Vraiment?* But—what good are InCo dollars, here?"

He tightened the band around his thin ponytail. "Not a lot of any kind of currency around here. Mostly they barter."

"I will go and get the money. What do you usually pay with?"

"Whatever I can come up with. InstaMeals. Medicines. Small fuel cells, if they have any appliances. Sometimes we have some *yuan* or *ren min bi,* people's money. InCo dollars are the most prized, though I doubt they know what their real value is. Probably trade 'em."

That night, InCo dollars bought them a room in a similar inn, this one on the shores of the huge, salty Qinghai Lake. Thousands of birds swirled above the water, gulls and cormorants, black-necked cranes, wild swans. They ate the region's specialty, a fish called naked carp, and then were led up a dark stairwell by candlelight. They each took a bed. Another traveler already slept in a third. A sharp breeze from the lake filled the air with a salt tang. Not till morning did Ebriel see the tapestries and murals that hung on the unpainted wooden walls of the inn, the little carvings in yak butter for sale on the first floor. Their fellow traveler was already gone when they woke. Ebriel and Perk took turns in the outhouse behind the inn and washed their faces and brushed their teeth in icy water from a pump. Ebriel was becoming adept at swinging her cast and used the crutch less and less.

They reached the provincial capital of Xining, three hundred kilometers farther on, in the afternoon of the second day. They drove through lush farmlands, rich with late-summer greenery. The air was mild, and farmers in their fields of highland barley and wheat stopped to watch them pass. They saw no other traffic until the city sprawled before them in a jumble of stucco and stone houses, shops, apartment buildings with upper windows broken and gaping, lower ones crossed with boards. They passed a few high-rise buildings on their route, but it looked to Ebriel as if only the first floors were occupied.

Perk turned down one narrow street after another. In the city center they passed a building that looked as if it had been hit with a bomb. Ebriel asked Perk about it.

"Bad masonry," he said. "It just fell down."

There were a few cell vehicles, but mostly they saw pedicabs and bicycles and scooters carrying working people home. On the eastern edge of Xining, Perk parked the van before a five-story, flat-fronted building with a sign in front in Chinese characters.

"This is it," he said with a nod of his head. "Children's Home. It used to house sixty, seventy children, but now it's half that. Been here forever."

It looked like it. Its stucco walls were dingy and chipped, its windows smudged. An old-fashioned fire escape ran up one side. On the other side a fuel cell sparkled, sun on metal. A patch of worn grass stretched between the front door and the street, and a stone fence circled the back courtyard. As Ebriel climbed out of the van, a woman came out into the courtyard with a child in her arms, crossed to a waiting wheelchair, and settled the child into it. The child's thin arms and wasted legs made Ebriel's stomach clench.

"Coming?" Perk asked. He was already halfway to the front door, a bag of clothes in one hand and a carton of first-aid supplies in the other.

"Yes." She pulled her crutch out from behind the seat, slung the brocade bag over her shoulder, and hobbled up the short walk to follow him inside.

In the short hallway, their steps were quiet on much-dented linoleum. Ebriel sniffed, smelling mildew and disinfectant, other things she couldn't place.

Perk said, "Nancy's expecting us." He led Ebriel into a long, low-ceilinged kitchen. The biggest table she had ever seen ran down its center, with mismatched chairs and high chairs ranged around it. Here the air smelled distinctly of cooking vegetables. A woman standing at an enormous stove exclaimed when she saw them. "Perk! *Ni hao!*"

He dropped his bundles. *"Ni hao,* Nancy." She tugged a padded glove from her hand and came to them, a small Asian woman with graying wisps of straight black hair framing her face.

Perk said, in English, "Here she is, Nancy. This is Ebriel Serique. Ebriel, Nancy Chao."

Nancy Chao took Ebriel's hand in her dry, rough-skinned one and held it as she searched her face. *"Huan ying,* Ebriel," she said. "Welcome. Perk tells me you wish to work with us."

"Yes, I do."

"Our work isn't easy." The older woman gestured to Ebriel to follow her as she moved to a window. It overlooked the back courtyard, a pleasant place with a children's climbing structure, a swing made of an old tire, the plastic slide ending in a box of sand. The branches of a tall dragon spruce hung over the stone wall. The courtyard was full of children.

There were perhaps a dozen running back and forth, brown knees flashing, calling and laughing. Others could not run. They watched, or slept, several in wheelchairs, several on blankets in the shade. A variety of deformities marked them, an enlarged skull, a missing leg, arms and legs that twitched with palsy. Several wore heavy swaddles of diapers.

Ebriel's heart sank, but she lifted her chin. "I want to help," she said.

Nancy Chao hesitated, looking down at Ebriel's cast. "You're injured," she said.

"It will heal," Ebriel told her. "I walk quite well."

The older woman looked into her eyes for a long moment as if reading something there. Ebriel smiled, and Nancy nodded. She turned away to speak to Perk.

Ebriel turned back to the courtyard. The children were mostly Chinese, but some had the deep color of the Tibetans. As she watched, a girl who had been sitting under the tree struggled to her feet. She wore metal braces on her legs, and she staggered to the window to stare up at the stranger. Ebriel gazed back at the uneven features, the running nose, the black oily strands of hair. When the girl limped away, her metal braces glinted, and Ebriel saw that her calves were thin and wasted.

Ebriel closed her eyes, thinking of the healthy, active, beautiful children dashing through Starhold's gallery, absorbed under the study hoods, chattering in the dining hall. She thought of Paul. Paul could have done so much for these children—but would he? Paul would not have approved of the *résistance*.

She opened her eyes. This work would be more than difficult. It would be painful. But she needed to do it. She could do it. The odd sense of cheerfulness rose in her once again, and she left the window to go and help Perk unload the van.

Stories raged through InCo forces, and Security Corps in particular. Newnet didn't report the disappearance of the prisoner from Keelung, but the underground nets joyfully and repeatedly returned to the story, examining every scrap of evidence, exploring every rumor, speculating about who the woman might have been, where she came from, how she escaped. The nets also covered the false fire alarm in some detail, but never mentioned the man who died in Ebriel's hospital room.

James never mentioned him either. He assured Chang, with only mild compunction, that he knew nothing more. He counted the weeks until his next tour ended, and he could go home.

The simple thing, of course, would have been to route the

message on to him from his father's panel, but he didn't want to risk it. Any Newnet message could be traced. James doubted Ebriel would be in danger, vanished into the latent polities, flown off with her strange friend. But he himself could come under scrutiny. Gil Walking Bull, of course, would never report any message he received, not to InCo. Should Ebriel find a way to send James a message, it would be safe in the old ranch house in Browning.

James watched the calendar, and waited. From Taiwan he flew to Honolulu, and then on to Colorado Springs. He sent a message to his father through the Social Services ground mail that ran once a week. He spent his days training privates and corporals, drilling with other officers, developing contingency plans and sending them out to the various arms of InCo Forces. He accumulated flying hours. He watched Newnet, scanning for news of the latent and neutral polities. And he spent every spare minute of off-duty time digging through the archives, searching for the truth about Ebriel Serique.

The vast archival stores were new territory for him. It was like wandering through a maze, a confusion of paths leading in all directions. It took days for him to learn how to follow a nugget of information, such as a report on a boundary violation, or a reference to the Red Omega smugglers. Misdirection, redundancy, filing errors distracted him, wasted his time, led to dead ends. It took weeks to delve down to the information he sought, figures for latitude, longitude, personnel, equipment, cached video clips. He downloaded some of these onto his mini and generated a few reports as proof of his diligence. August wore into September, and then October. He thought he was drawing closer to the incident, the seizure and destruction of the yacht *L'Oiseau blanc*, the information buried under security protocols. But by the end of October, and his leave, he still hadn't reached it.

He flew from Colorado Springs to Malmstrom, and drove north to Browning. The rusting aluminum roofs appeared bleaker than ever against the gold and red glories of autumn. New snow capped the mountain peaks of the old park, but the plains had dried in the heat of Indian summer. The dirt lane leading to his father's house swirled with dust, a cloud of it rising behind the truck like a brown contrail in the afternoon sun.

James parked in the yard. At first he couldn't think what was different, and then he realized that the hulk of the old pick-up, which had been settling into the dirt for years, was gone. He strode swiftly up onto the porch, his duffel bag on his shoulder. No sound greeted him. He knocked on the door, and there was still no response, even after he knocked again, and waited a polite five minutes. Finally, after trying to peer in through the windows, but seeing only the glare of the sun on the dirty glass, he tried the handle on the front door. It was locked.

James went around back, passing the fuel cell he had installed. The abandoned washer and stove and other things were gone, too, leaving the crumbling dirt of the backyard bare. The kitchen door opened under his hand, and he stuck his head through. "Dad? It's me. It's James."

The smell of stale beer had faded from the house. James wandered through the rooms, finding the same old worn furniture, cracked linoleum, and ragged carpet, but no stack of empty beer cans. Vaguely anxious, James hurried back to the bedrooms. He was relieved to find his father's room looking lived in, the bed made, toiletries scattered on the bureau.

In the kitchen cupboards he found stores of canned and boxed food marked by Social Services. There was even a stack of InstaMeals, but he passed those over in favor of soup and a package of crackers.

It was after five when James heard the purr of a cell motor in the yard. He had been making up his old bed, the same sagging mattress he had used as a boy. He left it and came out to the living room to see his father give the driver a short wave, then step up on the porch. James opened the door.

The old man stood with his hands on his hips, looking at his son. "So," he said.

"Hi, Dad." James made a gesture to include the house, the yard. "Place is looking good."

"Saw you on Newnet," his father said without preamble. "You're supposed to be a hero."

"Well . . ." James shrugged and stood aside for his father to enter. "Mostly hype."

"Yeah? Could have mentioned you're Blackfoot. Mentioned the Nation."

"Dad, they—that is, the Corps—they don't know anything about where I come from. I told them I was an orphan when I joined up, and never set it right."

His father walked past him, through the hall and on to the kitchen, where he took a pitcher out of the refrigerator. He saw James watching him. "Tea," he said shortly. "On the wagon."

James pulled a chair up to the table. "How long?"

The old man sat down, too, but he didn't answer for a moment. He poured a glassful, and sipped the tea, and James saw how his gums had retracted, how the years of alcohol and smoking had stained his teeth. Gil rolled a cigarette with unsteady hands. He said, "Two months, I've been dry two months. I'm not promising anything. But we're working at the Tribal Office, me and Otis Blackhand. Every day."

"That's good, Dad," James said. "And did you get my message? Back in June?"

"Yeah. No return address, though, so I couldn't answer you."

"Right. I think it's better the Corps doesn't know about you. This place."

The old man squinted through the yellow stream of tobacco smoke. "They're dirty, aren't they? Told you so."

"I know you did." James leaned back, balancing the chair on two legs. "Yes, Dad. There might be a problem. I need a place to get messages. Someplace confidential."

His father nodded with satisfaction, the skin of his seamed neck folding like worn fabric. "You got one, son," he said. "No problem."

30

"The children speak no English," Nancy Chao told Ebriel. "Some don't speak Mandarin either. They learn, though. You will, too." Nancy's English had taken on the musical lilt of Chinese, odd words popping up in pitch here and there, reminding Ebriel of plainsong. "How much longer will you need your crutch?"

"I must make a guess," Ebriel said. "Perhaps three weeks? I—I had an accident."

If Nancy knew anything about Ebriel, she didn't reveal it. It seemed Ebriel was to be as anonymous as she wished. Nancy only asked her, "Can you cook?"

"Yes, a bit."

"You won't be able to clean, not till you're out of the cast. Wash clothes?"

"Yes. Whatever you would like."

Nancy paused in her stirring. She lifted a dripping wooden spooon out of the big pot and tapped it against the rim. She had a peaceful, tired face, dark eyes warm with intelligence. "Ebriel," she said casually. "Such a lovely name. French, isn't it?"

Ebriel leaned against the counter, taking the crutch from her armpit. "I was born in Paris," she said. She glanced out the window. The motley gang of children swarmed over the court-yard, all of them in mismatched bits of clothing, like those in Perk's locker. "I grew up there."

"A beautiful city." Nancy laid her spoon on the counter and opened a cupboard stacked with pottery bowls and plates. "Could you manage to set the table, do you think?"

Ebriel picked up the crutch again and limped to the table. One-handed, she set out the plates and bowls and then hob-bled around again, setting spoons beside them. Somewhere above, she heard a thin wail. She stopped, listening to the lonely sound. "How many children are here, Miss Chao?"

Nancy Chao stopped on her way to the stairwell. "It's Nancy," she said. "We have twenty-six children just at the mo-ment. One infant, and eight children with serious illnesses or disabilities. There are only three of us. Occasionally someone comes to stay and help out for a while, like yourself. But it's discouraging, and they don't last long." She started up the stairs, saying over her shoulder, "I'll just fetch the baby, and I'll be right back."

Ebriel finished setting the table, and cast about for some-thing else she could do. She was laying out napkins she found in a drawer when Nancy came back with an infant in her arms.

"And so, Ebriel, you have left the Chain?"

Ebriel put down the napkin in her hand. "Do you know about them?" she asked.

Nancy patted the infant's blanketed form, cuddling the child's head under her chin. "I worked for Ethan," she said. "In London. I had relatives in Hong Kong, and I was touring the provinces when the embargo went up. I missed the win-dow to be allowed back. So—here I am."

"I am sorry," Ebriel said lamely.

"There is no need," Nancy said calmly. She laid the now-silent infant into a rattan bassinet under the window. "This is the work I wanted to do. My only regret is that InCo cut us off from so many resources. Children die because of it."

"*Oui.* I know this."

And so began Ebriel's work at the Children's Home. That first day, and the long, trying days that followed, she worked in a sort of isolation, doing anything Nancy asked her to do, but unable to communicate with either the other helpers or

any of the children. Slowly, she began to pick up bits of
Mandarin as she learned the routines. By the time she took off
her cast, she was doing six loads of laundry every day in the
slant-roofed, screened porch on the side of the house by the
fuel cell. She folded diapers, sorted donated clothing, sat with
the children at mealtimes. She spooned soup for a child with
palsied hands, combed lice nits from the hair of a newly arrived toddler, wiped noses and bottoms, soothed coughs.

Because of the crutch, Nancy had given her the only first-
floor bedroom, a room only slightly larger than a cubby on
Starhold. She fell into the hard bed each night, her head
aching from struggling with the language, her heart heavy
with loneliness. In the brief moments before sleep, she watched
the stars through the four-paned window and thought of the
Chain, and Yasmine, and Ethan Fleck. She missed Ty. The
scrap of paper with an address scrawled on it lay at the bottom
of her brocade bag, as if forgotten.

But she hadn't forgotten. In her dreams, James Bull sometimes made an unexpected appearance, and she woke from
those dreams confused, her body throbbing with a vague and
guilty longing. Once she rose and fished in her bag for her
wallet with the stillphotos of Paul and Renée. She slept again,
holding it between her hands.

Her ankle was weak when she first took the cast off, and
she used the crutch for a few days while the muscles strength-
ened again. A week later, she put it aside completely. By the
next day, it had been pressed into service for one of the older
girls, who had a crippling clubfoot and had outgrown the stick
she used.

Ebriel no longer noticed the miasma of unwashed diapers
and baby formula that persisted in the house. She learned to
make Nancy's homemade remedies, vinegar for head lice, potato and flaxseed paste for boils, tar soap for treating ring-
worm. She got over her shock at the multitude of ailments that
afflicted malnourished and neglected children. She felt only a
passing longing for the cleanliness of St. Louis Hospital, with
its pristine sheets and disposable gloves and refrigerators full
of medicines.

She became accustomed to other things, too, as time
passed. The two others who worked with Nancy Chao were

native to Xining. Ting was an unskilled peasant, middle-aged, never married. When her parents died, she desperately needed a place to live and work that she could do. She did everything Nancy asked of her with an almost pitiful willingness.

The other was a strong-backed creature called Ruan, slow-witted, inarticulate. Nancy treated her with the same pragmatic patience she used with everyone. Ebriel never saw her get impatient with having to repeat her instructions to Ruan, and she never heard Nancy raise her voice to any child. Ting was devoted to Nancy, leaping up to help her, scurrying to save her any extra effort, refusing to eat until Nancy was seated at the table, insisting on washing and folding Nancy's laundry herself. This, too, Nancy Chao accepted. At first it set Ebriel's teeth on edge, until she realized that Nancy behaved in exactly the same way toward herself. If she was curious about Ebriel, she didn't express it. If she suspected that Ebriel was in some kind of trouble, or had done something wrong, she kept her thoughts to herself.

The work never ended. Ebriel was so busy, from early morning until late at night, that she hardly noticed when the weather began to change. One morning, while she was starting breakfast, a glancing flash of light in the courtyard caught her attention. She went to the window, a measure of uncooked rice in her hands.

Ice rimed the branches of the tall dragon spruce that sheltered the house and shot beams of reflected sunlight into the pale blue sky. The brick walkway sparkled with ice crystals. Even the dry spears of grass shone with a glassy sheen. Ebriel put the rice in the steamer and filled it with water, then pulled on one of the utilitarian jackets that hung near the back door and stepped outside into the bone-numbing chill of early Himalayan winter.

The jacket was InCo Forces issue, with an English label, but that no longer surprised her. Perk, she had learned, kept the Children's Home supplied with a steady flow of InCo goods lifted by Chain members from various storehouses. Once, when there had been neither fish nor yak nor goat meat to be had, Nancy had gone down to the cellar and carried up a carton of InstaMeals to feed the house.

Ebriel stood beside the sandbox, her nose and ears tingling

with cold. The courtyard faced west, toward Qaidam Pendi, and the distant peaks smothered in snow. Cookfires sent ribbons of gray smoke into the crystal air above Xining. "Winter," Ebriel murmured, and then, practicing the word in Mandarin, *"Dongtian."* She went to the wall and stood on tiptoe to look into the yards of the nearby houses. Woodpiles had been stocked, pipes wrapped, hoses uncoupled. Winter on the Roof of the World was at hand.

When she went back inside, her cheeks stinging, she was grateful for the warmth of the fuel cell. How long had she been here? She had not once used the shortband. Nor had she sent the promised message to James Bull.

Perk answered sleepily, and Ebriel thought she must have wakened him. *"Ni hao,* Perk," she said into the mouthpiece of the little radio. "I suppose I have called too early."

"Who's this?" he mumbled.

"It is Ebriel. From Xining."

There was a pause, and she heard the sound of a great stretching yawn. She waited, looking around her little ground-floor room. By the time her leg had healed, everyone, including Ebriel, thought of it as hers. As she took over more and more of the early-morning kitchen duties, it seemed natural. Nevertheless, the room appeared neutral, white curtains, mended coverlet, rattan chest to serve as a bureau. She had added nothing personal. Anyone could be living here.

"Ebriel!" Perk finally said. "Thought I'd never hear from you. Everything okay?"

"Yes," she said. "I only just realized that the autumn is over. I promised Ty—" She felt a stab of loneliness as she said the name. "I promised to check in. I am—I am checking in, Perk."

"Good," he said. He sounded awake now. "How's Nancy? How do you like Xining?"

"Nancy seems well. As to Xining—I have seen little of it. I go to the market, near the river. Once I walked past the business district when I took one of the children to a clinic, but it seemed there was no business."

"Most of it moved away after the embargo. No markets."

"It is strange to see, Perk. The houses, the buildings, so

many dark and empty. And there are no doctors, no medicines to care for the children."

"Nope. All went away. There wasn't a lot to begin with."

Ebriel hesitated, wanting to ask for news, wondering if she had the right. Perk seemed to sense her doubts. "Ty's fine," he said without prompting. "They got the children from Peru. Boy and a girl. They're on Starhold now."

"And Yasmine?"

"Well, every time I talk to Ethan, she's there beside him."

Ebriel closed her eyes, picturing Yasmine in her blue cottons and yellow sash, sailing up the tube. The spartan environment of Starhold seemed luxurious compared to the Children's Home. She heard doors above her beginning to open, footsteps sounding on the stairwell outside her door. "I must go, Perk," she said. "Perhaps you will be coming to Xining soon."

"Yeah," he said. "I might. See you, Ebriel."

"Yes," she said, reluctant to end the conversation, the contact. "Good-bye." She pressed the button with her finger, and the radio went dead. She put it back in the rattan chest and hurried out to the kitchen.

Nancy, with a baby in her arms, was at the stove, stirring a pan of infant formula that she made from powdered yak's milk and boiled water. "Zao shang hao," she said.

"Zao shang hao," Ebriel answered. "The rice is almost ready."

Nancy nodded. "Good. Could you hold Li Li for me while I finish this?"

Ebriel came forward and took the infant in her arms. The child had come to them the month before. A man had thrust her into the hands of the first person to open the door, and then fled. They had unwrapped the handmade blanket to find a little cloth bag containing a few yuan snuggled under the bend of the infant's knees. They had wondered at the time why she didn't cry, but soon they knew that this one would rarely cry, and in fact would not live long. It was all they could do to get her to take a little formula. Mostly they simply held her, whenever anyone had a free pair of hands. Profoundly retarded, was what the one physician at the clinic said. They called her Li Li because physically she was perfect, with large luminous eyes, exquisite skin, a little triangular face. Sometimes Ebriel held her, looking into her face, and whispering to her, "Li Li? Can you even hear me, Li Li?" The child never responded.

Now Ebriel cradled the silent baby against her shoulder and watched Nancy stir the formula. "Nancy," she said. "How long have I been with you?"

Nancy glanced up at her with a smile. "Why, Ebriel, I haven't thought. The time goes so fast, doesn't it? I think—well, it's November now."

"Is it? Truly?"

"Yes, and I think you came in August, or early September."

"Mon Dieu!"

Nancy chuckled. "Indeed."

Ebriel patted Li Li's tiny back. There was no answering movement. "Nancy, may I send a message? From your panel?"

Nancy pulled the pan of formula from the stove and set it on a wooden board to cool. She reached for Li Li again and pressed her cheek against the infant's glossy black hair.

"Of course you may use the panel," Nancy said. "And if you would like to talk . . ."

Ebriel regarded the older woman with affection. Nancy was always busy with some task, her hands never still. But she had a special quality, a talent for patience, of giving her full attention to the matter at hand. It was as if, for Nancy, the world around her could always wait while she attended to what was important.

"Do you watch the news, Nancy?" Ebriel asked.

Nancy nodded. "Once in a while. Sometimes Newnet comes through. And the underground net from Beijing. O-Net, if the microsats are working."

Ebriel busied herself taking rice out of the steamer, taking teacups from the cupboard. "I was made an InCo citizen when I was sixteen. We didn't know—we didn't understand."

She felt Nancy's eyes on her wrist. "You have a scar," Nancy said matter-of-factly. "Where your identification rod would have been."

Ebriel put down the saucers. Absently, she rubbed her wrist. "I cut it out," she said.

"That must have hurt."

Ebriel shrugged. "I didn't feel it," she said. "My hurt was already so great, that this little cut—" She traced the pale scar with her finger. Nancy cradled Li Li and waited. "George Glass destroyed my family," Ebriel said at last. "My husband. My daughter."

Nancy stepped closer to Ebriel. "Oh, my dear," she murmured. "How tragic. I thought I knew your face when you arrived. You are she, aren't you? You're the flutist from Paris, the one from Ariana Park. It must be almost two years since that happened."

Ebriel, overwhelmed with memory, could only nod.

"Yes," Nancy went on. "They played that video over and over. It was a terrible, an unthinkable thing. I am so sorry."

"Thank you," Ebriel said.

"But do you really think—you really believe Glass is responsible?"

"I know it," Ebriel said simply. Nancy watched her, neither agreeing nor arguing.

There were footsteps on the stairs, the clamor of high voices. A flood of children inundated the kitchen. Nancy touched Ebriel's arm with her work-worn hand. "Use the panel whenever you wish, of course," she said.

"I need to send a message to North America," Ebriel said. "Is that a problem?"

"No," Nancy said. "You'll have to route through Quezon City, through O-Net. A return message is more difficult. InCo sets up a lot of blocks. The O-Net people try to erase them, though. I think they like having the opportunity—it's one way of getting back at InCo."

Nancy turned away to supervise the seating of the ambulatory children at the table, and to help Ting and Ruan with the wheelchairs. Ebriel filled bowls with rice and poured warmed yak milk over them. This morning there were also some pears Nancy had found at the market, and Ebriel sliced them. It was a busy half hour, soothing squabbles, cleaning up spills, watching over the children who had difficulty swallowing and had to be carefully spoonfed. Then, while Ebriel set about cleaning up, the children were bundled in an assortment of scarves and jackets and trundled outside to spend the morning in the courtyard. Nancy sat at the table with Li Li in her lap, trying to coax her to swallow a few mouthfuls of formula.

When they finished the chores of the day's first meal, Ebriel swept the long kitchen, and Nancy nestled Li Li into her bassinet under the window, where the sunshine could reach her.

"Do you need help with the panel, Ebriel?" she said, watching Li Li's peaceful, unresponsive face as the infant fell asleep. "With the language?"

"No, I think I can do it," Ebriel said. "*Merci,* Nancy. I mean, *xie xie.*"

"*Bu ke qi.* Don't mention it."

Ebriel climbed the stairs to Nancy's office, which she maintained in one corner of an orderly storage room on the second floor. Donated clothes, baskets of mending, stacks of diapers and blankets and towels, even a few odd appliances crowded the floor and the wall shelves. The office itself was windowless, merely a desk that had once been a piece of lacquered hardwood, but which now showed bare wood through a hundred cracks, a decrepit file cabinet of bamboo, and a rocking chair resting in front of the panel. Ebriel went into the room, shut the door behind her, and sat down in the rocking chair.

She had James Bull's little scrap of paper in her hand. She had looked at it so often the numbers were in danger of wearing away, but it wouldn't matter. She had them memorized, the InCo zone code, the routing symbol, the personal designation number. She checked a directory that lay beside the panel for the Oceania symbols, and then spoke to the panel.

"Voice only," she instructed. The light over the camera went dark, and the panel flashed its green ready light. It looked a bit like the one she had had in Paris, the bank of indicators, the input mike, the camera on its flexible wand beside the screen. There was a tiny ideographic keyboard, and a mini attached with a slender cord.

She said the code, the routing symbol, the number, and then, "This is a message for James, from . . . his grateful friend. Please tell him I am well and I am safe. He should not worry for me. I would—I would welcome news from James, if he is able to reply. Thank you. Good-bye." She hesitated, and then added, *"Au revoir, mon ami."*

She made the panel play back her message, and she sat thinking about it for a moment. It seemed pallid, empty of meaning. But there was so little she could say. She didn't know him, not really, though she remembered his dark face, the little tattoo on his cheekbone, the strength of his hands. *"Zut,"* she whispered, frustrated. The query light flashed, and she said, "negative." She shook her head at her own foolishness. "Send," she said clearly. When the lights told her it was done, she almost said, "Off," but she hesitated again. She heard an infant crying, and the voices of the children calling from the courtyard. She should get back to the waiting piles of laundry. She bit her lip for a just a moment, and then said, "Newnet."

She didn't know if it would come through, but it did, immediately. The panel was not divisible, so she could only watch what was being broadcast, though she knew it had to be meant to propagandize the latent countries. The muds.

And there he was. He was speaking from that same office where she had first seen him, where she had been dragged by the two Security Corpsmen. She watched his coarse features, the bristling mustache, the flat black eyes. Nothing had changed. What she had done made no difference, except to herself. The banked embers of her hatred flared at the thought of the damage this man might yet do, the people he might harm.

She ordered the panel off and slowly left the storeroom and descended the stairs to her bedroom. She reached into the rattan chest for her flute case. She opened it, took out the sections, and put them together, the silver fittings glimmering in the sunlight, the black cylinder of the instrument cool in her hand. Absently, she put the mouthpiece to her lips.

It had been so long. A year and a half since she left the rehearsal at La Villette, left her life behind. The small muscles of her *embouchure* were stiff and unresponsive. Her upper lip trembled as she tried to focus her tone, and the sound was breathy, lacking the sweet, firm core that had been the trademark sound of Ebriel Serique. But it was a note, a real note. And then there was another, and another. She played a scale, an arpeggio, another scale.

She lowered the flute and went to stand by her window, looking out into the empty street. "I am still here," she whispered. "After all of it, I am still here. And I will learn to play again." She glanced up into the wintry sky. "What next?" she wondered aloud. "What is coming next for me?"

31

James took a short leave in December. He had sent a note for his father to expect him, but still, when he parked in front of the ranch house, the blaze of light in its windows and the cheerful stream of smoke rising from the old brick chimney surprised him. The ground was bare and dry, though heavy snow clouds hung over the valley. A slender column of western cedar seedlings now marched along the side of the yard. Gil Walking Bull came to the door as James pulled his duffel out of the truck.

James nodded toward the trees. "Few years, those will make a good windbreak, Dad."

Gil made a dry sound in his throat that might have been a chuckle. "Yeah, well. Shoulda done it a long time ago." He held the door open for James to enter and took his duffel from him.

James shrugged off his denim jacket, sniffing a rich fragrance that filled the house. "What's that cooking, Dad? Turkey?"

"Yeah. Social Services sent a whole truckload of 'em." He snorted. "Just like the old days." He led the way back through the narrow hall to the kitchen. "Want some cider, Jimmy, or some coffee? I didn't buy any beer."

"That's okay. I don't drink, Dad."

Gil turned to look at his son. "Not at all?"

"Nope."

Gil nodded, his leathery face somber. "Smart."

James watched as his father took a pitcher of cider out of the refrigerator. There was no sign of tremor in his wrinkled hands. "You're looking good, Dad."

"Doin' okay." He avoided James's eyes. "It was good for me, seeing you again, Jimmy." He poured two glasses of cider and handed one to James. "Busy down at the Nation. Gotta get the word out about the spring pow-wow."

"No trouble over the pow-wow?" They sat together at the table. Gil had spread a cloth on it, and James ran his fingers over the little flowers embroidered on the corners. He wasn't certain, but he thought it could be his mother's needlework. He wondered what closet or chest it had hidden in through the years.

The old man's almost-chuckle sounded again. "We'll see, son," Gil said. "Otis and me are trying to convince Social Services it's good for the people."

James lifted his glass. "Good luck to you, then."

They sat in silence, sipping. Occasionally Gil rose to baste the roasting turkey, the aromas of sage and pepper sweeping out into the kitchen when he opened the oven door. Steam clouded the windows, and the white curtains over the sink clung to the cold glass. When Gil went to the pantry and pulled out a bag of potatoes, James jumped up. "Here, let me do that."

At the sink, wielding a peeler, James said, "By the way, Dad. I got promoted."

Another space of silence followed this announcement. James concentrated on the potatoes, peeling them, dunking them in a cool water bath, putting them in a battered aluminum pot. Gil, shaking flour and water and salt in an old Mason jar, said at last, "So. A promotion. What does that make you now, a major?"

"Yes." James dried his hands and lifted the pot of potatoes onto the stove. He wiped the sink with a towel. "Major. With a higher security clearance, a bit more money."

"Because of that hero thing?"

James snapped the towel against his thigh. "It could be, Dad. You can never tell with the Corps. But it does mean I'm going overseas. Stationed in the neutral territories."

"Yeah? Where?"

"Quezon City, in the Philippines." In fact, his father probably had it right, and James knew it. Not all promotions brought improved security clearance. But James Bull was a hero, supposed to be a model for InCo Forces and especially Security Corps.

"You can send me messages there, Dad, through O-Net. I'll give you the routing."

Gil folded his arms. His eyes were hooded by his dark, wrinkled lids. "You got a message here, Jimmy. Came a month or so ago. I saved it."

James stopped snapping the towel. He straightened, slowly, and he felt his face go still. "A message? Did you listen to it?"

Gil stood up, scraping his chair against the scratched linoleum. "Huh-uh. Your business. It's in memory, on the panel."

"Thanks, Dad." James folded the towel with deliberation, hung it over the edge of the sink. "Excuse me for a minute."

He went straight to the living room and the panel. He called the message up, and felt a pang of disappointment that it was voice-only. He played it through, played it through again, and then another time. It was so little, just a few words, but the liquid consonants, the slightly nasal vowels brought her face back to him, the full lips, the thin cheeks, the silvery curls. "You should not worry for me." But how could he find her again? He wanted to find her, wanted to very much. He hadn't wanted anything so much in a long time.

Otis showed up for dinner, and made much of shaking James's hand, calling him captain until Gil corrected him, and then using the title 'major' many more times than was necessary. The turkey tasted wonderful, with mashed potatoes and gravy and green beans grown in Browning and frozen by Gil himself. The cranberry sauce came from a

Social Services can, but there was not a trace of tofu or mystery sauce in the whole meal. James ate until he could hold no more and then sat sleepily listening as his father and Otis smoked their hand-rolleds and talked about the Nation, the pow-wow, and the government until his eyelids drooped and closed.

It was George Glass's name that woke him from his drowse. He heard his father say it, and he came immediately awake, though he kept his eyes shut. He listened. The men's voices had dropped, whether because they thought James was asleep, or because of the subject, James wasn't sure.

"Son of a bitch turned all those people back from Cairo. Said they had plague."

"Can't believe a word he says. Dimarco's got the right idea. Biochems wouldn't have lasted this long—what is it, eighteen years since that war?"

"Something like that. We're just lucky the Nation wasn't on the wrong side of the line when they drew it."

James had heard similar discussions a hundred times as a boy, though usually they had been accompanied by the clinking of beer bottles. Now his father's complaints and Otis's stories took on a new complexion. James sat, arms folded, eyes closed. A little knowledge made everything look different, though he wasn't ready to admit that to his father. When the conversation finished, James opened his eyes, yawned, and said good night to the older men. He lay awake in his bed, looking out into the night made brilliant by moonlight reflected from the mountain snowfields. For more than an hour he wrestled with the undercurrents of the society he had pledged to serve.

In the morning James rose early and walked outside. His boots crunched on the frosted earth when he stepped off the porch. He smelled the coming snow in the chilly air. A perfect day for hunting, with the deer wandering down below the tree line in search of fodder, elk descending from the hills to crop the dry grass of the meadows before the snow buried it. But James had no time to go hunting. He was due to fly out for Quezon City in three weeks, and he had work to do, briefings to attend, reports to study, the language program to complete.

And he hoped to finish his search for the fate of *L'Oiseau blanc*.

He went back into the ranch house, opening and closing the door quietly so as not to disturb his father. He went to the panel and called up Ebriel's message to copy the return by hand. He recognized the O-Net routing symbol, but he didn't know what the final designation numbers meant. He would wait until he was in Oceania, in the neutral polities, before he sent a response, and not risk alerting the Newnet tracers. Maybe, from Quezon City, he could find her.

"The big push," Colonel Corliss said to James at his final briefing in Colorado Springs, "is to get Oceania to join the Alliance. Security Corps isn't directly involved, of course, but it's a political hot potato. Anything we come across that bears on the issue takes top priority, by order of the Commander General."

"Are we expecting information like that to crop up in Quezon City, sir?" James asked. He sat stiffly across from the colonel, selfconscious at the newness of the major's insignia pinned to his collar, the crispness of his completed pilot's license lying on the desk between them.

Corliss was a handsome black man, fit and clear-eyed. He relaxed, leaning back, his legs crossed at the ankles. His office looked out over the old Academy grounds. Beyond, the Sierra Nevada rose in snowy splendor into a sky so blue it seemed to burn. "Ostensibly, James, you're in the neutral polities to maintain secure communications between InCo and Oceania. And dispatch security details whenever the brass come in from Todokai or Europe. But keep your ear to the ground. When the Aussies took that contaminated grain shipment a few years back, they tried to keep it hushed up, but Security Corps got the word on it. It was useful information, to put pressure on the neutral polities, reassure our own people. It's that kind of thing they'll be looking for."

"Yes, sir. I see."

"And, of course, anything that comes up regarding Red Omega. We'd love to draw a bead on that organization."

James kept his face carefully still. References to Red Omega were everywhere in the files he had been digging through, but all the leads ended in blanks. "Red Omega, yes, sir. The ones that smuggle medical supplies." He hesitated, chose his words carefully. "Sir, wasn't there a connection between Red Omega and that yacht in the Mediterranean, couple of years ago? I forget the name . . . White Bird, something like that."

Corliss's eyes narrowed. "Better stay away from that one, Major."

"Sir?"

The colonel uncrossed his legs and leaned forward with his hands on the desk. He seemed to consider, then sat back, turning up his palms. "Nobody knows what's up with that. A lot of people got transferred, and some got booted after that incident. It's done now, no help for it. Just between us, and off the record, it's better to let that story die."

James's neck began to tingle. "Yes, sir."

"But look for anything to do with Fleck."

"Fleck, sir?"

"General Glass thinks if we can get Fleck to fall in line, Oceania will, too. Fleck does a lot for the neutral polities, too much. Churns out fuel cells on Taiwan, and in New Zealand, the production as high there as in North America." Corliss turned in his chair to look out over the parade grounds, where the assortment of statues and old airplanes poked out of a blanket of unblemished snow. "Fleck has a lot of influence. He gets away with things nobody else could. Goes across the Line of Partition and nobody says a word."

"Sir?"

The colonel glanced back at James. He was only a few years older, perhaps forty. His chuckle was rich and dark. "Haven't you heard the speculation, James? About the spaceplanes? The general goes apeshit about the spaceplanes."

The tingle spread up James's scalp. "What about them, sir?"

"Some people think Fleck is smuggling valuables out of the latent countries, like gold or paintings. I can't see that myself. Seems like Fleckcell has plenty of cash. The general thinks it's secret weapons, though we don't say that where anybody but Security Corps can hear. No matter what it is, Glass wouldn't like it. If you want one of these—" he touched his colonel's insignia and laughed again. "Get the general something on Fleck, something he could use to bring him in line."

"Sir—" James hesitated, choosing his words carefully. "Sir, what difference does it make? I mean, if Fleckcell hands out fuel cells in the neutral polities? That doesn't hurt InCo, does it?"

Corliss frowned. "You're talking politics now, James. I'm just a soldier."

"Yes, sir."

The colonel pushed a mini across the desk to James. "Last-minute details are recorded for you," he said. "Your office staff, equipment, supplies. Good luck with it, James. You'll find life quite a change in the neutral polities."

James stood up. "Yes, sir. Thank you, sir."

By the time he left the office, his neck and his scalp burned with that premonitory itch. He rubbed his neck with his hand, but the sensation didn't go away until he was out of the building and on his way back to his quarters.

Ebriel knew Perk was coming. She felt an absurd pleasure at the prospect of his visit, at seeing almost any face besides the thirty inhabitants of the Children's Home. It was too cold to send the children outside. Keeping them entertained within doors had strained everyone's patience. She busied herself with small chores, listening for the van. She finally heard its clatter of metal and plastic coming up the street in the late afternoon.

Ebriel dropped the diaper she was folding into the basket and hurried into the kitchen, where the older children were working around the table, busy with paper and scissors, their hands covered in flour paste. Nancy looked up to give Ebriel her patient smile. "Why don't you get the door for Perk?" she said. "He's probably carrying all kinds of things."

Ebriel smiled back. What a joy to have a little variety in the procession of grim winter days! She almost ran down the short hallway and threw open the front door.

Perk was there, his hands full as Nancy had predicted.

"*Ni hao,* Perk!" He nodded to her, and stepped inside, grunting a little with the weight of a bulging cloth bag in his arms. Ebriel moved to the door to close it.

She glanced up and stopped with her hand on the doorknob.

Ty stood on the doorstep, wearing a ragged down jacket and frayed denims. Ebriel stared, openmouthed.

Ty grinned and shifted the small carton she was holding to her other arm. "Hey, Eb. Gonna let me in? Damn cold out here."

Ebriel tried to speak, stammered something, then laughed. "*Zut, mon amie.* I am speechless!" Impulsively, she stood on her tiptoes and kissed Ty's weathered cheeks, first the right, then the left.

Ty laughed as she followed Ebriel into the warmth of the house. "People aren't usually that glad to see me," she said. Ebriel laughed, too, knowing she was blushing, not minding at all.

Nancy Chao and Ty shook hands, and then, while Perk handed out small treats of candy to the children, Ebriel gave Ty a tour of the house, from the laundry room on the first floor to the nursery on the second, all the way up to the two bedrooms on the fifth floor reserved for the oldest girls. Ty carried her jacket over her shoulder and trudged after Ebriel, looking into the rooms, sniffing the distinct odors of the place.

"God, Eb," she finally said as they walked back down the flights of stairs. "I can't believe the work you do. How do you stand it?"

Ebriel lifted one shoulder in her old Gallic shrug. "It is not so bad. Every time I scour a floor—cook a meal, wash a diaper—I feel I am a step closer to—to finishing something. I cannot explain it."

Ty shook her head. "Seems to me you're wasting your talents."

"Well, never mind. I am here now. And here is my bedroom," Ebriel said, opening the door. "Come in. You will have to sit on the bed, though, I have no chair."

Ty looked around the plain little room. "Like a cubby," she said.

"So I have thought," Ebriel agreed. "Everything here is very plain, as you see."

Ty picked up the wallet of stillphotos from the rattan chest. "Your family," she said.

"Yes," Ebriel answered. "Paul, and my Renée. That was in my bag that you brought me."

Ty sat down slowly on the narrow bed, holding the pictures in her big hand. "Ebriel," she said after a moment. "You don't have anything to make up to them. To Paul, and to Renée."

Ebriel shook her head. "No. It is you—and Ethan, and the Chain—it is to you I owe my—penance, if you will. For betraying you."

"Listen, Eb." Ty seemed to search for words, her narrow lips pressing and releasing, her fingers tracing the photographs. "You were kinda crazy. We should have seen that. I was your partner. I take some of the blame."

Ebriel leaned against the wall beside the bed and watched her friend. She felt, suddenly, that it was Ty who needed comforting, and not herself. It was a relief to feel sympathy instead of heartbreak, to sense another's feelings instead of only struggling to survive her own. Perhaps she had learned something from Nancy. She straightened and went to lift the lid of the rattan chest.

"Look, Ty," she said. "Look what you did for me."

She brought out the flute case. Ty watched her fit the pieces together and put the silver mouthpiece to her lips. Ebriel blew one experimental note, and then another. She moistened her lips, and played a riff, liking the silvery tone, pleased with her returning *embouchure*.

When she reached the end of the phrase and stopped, Ty said, "Wow. You're really good, aren't you?"

"Well, I have begun to practice, at least. Those are the first bars of a Mozart flute quartet that I have played since I was a girl. It is hard now."

Ebriel swabbed her flute and replaced it in its case, aware of Ty's close regard.

"Listen, Eb," Ty began.

"Yes?"

"I wish you could come back to the Chain."

Ebriel looked down at her flute case, caressing its glossy brown surface. She chose her words carefully. "I wish I could, too, Ty. Although I doubt they would have me."

"Well, I don't know about that. But I'd like to have my partner back."

Ebriel glanced up, startled. "Surely you have a new partner."

Ty shook her head. "Nope. Kanika went with me to Peru, me and Astrid and Pilar. And Vee and I did one mission." She grinned. "Made a little foray into North America. Snuck over the pole and into the Great Lakes Storage Depot. Had a great time, and swiped a lot of stuff."

Ebriel smiled at that. "I think I have seen some of your 'stuff,' Ty. All over the Children's Home." She heard sounds from the kitchen and said, "It must be time to start preparing dinner. Come, you can help. I will show you how to fill the rice steamer."

"Gee," Ty drawled. "Sounds like fun."

Ty and Perk spent the night at the Children's Home. In the morning, after breakfast, Ty asked Ebriel if she had seen the Newnet and O-Net reports about the new attaché to Oceania.

"No, Ty, I have not. Should I?"

Ty's craggy features wore an odd expression. "I think you'll be interested," she said. "You'll recognize him."

Ebriel had a stack of bowls in her hands. She stood very still, watching Ty's face. "It is he, is it not? It is James."

Ty said, "Major James Bull now. North American hero. And a new addition to the Security Corps office in the neutral polities."

Heat crept up Ebriel's throat. "Where, Ty?"

"Quezon City." Ty laughed. "Yeah, I thought you'd be interested."

Ebriel put down the bowls and pressed her hands to her

cheeks. "I sent him a message," she said softly. "Because I promised. But he did not answer."

Ty rose from the bed and patted Ebriel's shoulder. "He will," she said. "Count on it."

32

James couldn't accept the colonel's warning. His faith in his own loyalty, in his judgment, rested on proving to himself that the blame for what had happened to *L'Oiseau blanc* did not lie at Commander General Glass's feet. Or finding out that it did.

With two days left before his reporting date in Quezon City, he huddled over a screen in the archives at Security Corps HQ. It was late, and he was alone. Deep December snow silenced the old Academy grounds, its crusted surface sparkling with the light of a waning moon and a riot of stars. Tall, narrow data towers forested the dim library like the tamarac pines of Montana. The windows bore half-moons of frost in their corners, and the ranks of dormant panels gleamed with reflected light.

James was hunting, and when he found the trail, he knew it.

The file was coded Security Clearance Three, James's level. His neck began to itch. He froze before the screen as if the file could turn and flee if it became aware of him. He spoke the commands slowly, clearly, tracking the file, getting it in his sights, drawing a bead. It was filed under Red Omega. It fell right into his hands, a cache of spybug information, statistics, dates, hours, names. But something was missing.

It was the terrorist incident off the coast of Menorca, in the Mediterranean Sea. The French yacht, *L'Oiseau blanc,* the Serique boat, the tragedy, the lives lost. But the latitude and longitude, the vessel's position with regard to the Line of Partition, had been erased.

Security Corps—Commander General George Glass's command—had the information. The report that *L'Oiseau blanc* was involved in a Red Omega operation was still there in the file. But where was the proof? Where was the operative's name? All that was left was the spybug video, with all locational data deleted. Someone had altered it.

There was more, a change of spybug routes, monitoring patterns. James copied the original routes, and then the new ones, to ponder later. It was a classic cover-up. A dead end.

Ebriel, wrapped in two sweaters, a jacket, and a shawl of woven yak hair, her feet in fur boots and her head swathed in an enormous muffler, trudged home from the market in Xining, pulling a flat wagon behind her. She had bought yak curd and meat, a burlap bag of rice, and a catch of fish netted the day before beneath the ice of Qinghai Lake. Her exposed cheekbones and the tip of her nose tingled with cold, but she didn't hurry. She paused to watch a baker twist strands of noodle dough into long ribbons, then pile them on greased paper circles for wrapping. She walked among people riding shaggy ponies, pushing bicycles. She nodded at the Muslim women in their thick headscarves, and dropped her eyes when the men in their white cloth hats passed her. The Buddhists greeted her with wide smiles, their faces barely visible under thick fur hats. She walked past the old Christian church, empty now, its roof fallen in, its interior gutted for firewood and furniture. The fresh winter air bit her lungs with cold.

She circled the Children's Home to pull the wagon through the back gate. Nancy saw her coming and came out to help. As they carted the supplies up the single step to the back door, Nancy said, "You had a call, Ebriel."

Ebriel stopped, a pottery jar in her hands. "Perk?" she said. But something in her knew it had not been Perk. Or Ty, or any of the Chain.

"He didn't use a name," Nancy said. "And there was no video."

"Do you know where the call came from?"

Nancy lifted the last straw-wrapped parcel of fish from the wagon and went up the step to the door. "It was O-Net," she said over her shoulder. Her eyes sparkled at Ebriel, taking pleasure in the little mystery. "I happened to be in the store-room, at my desk."

Ebriel followed her inside. "What did he say?" she asked. Her throat had gone dry.

"He said he would like to speak to you. I suggested he call back tonight." Nancy took the yak curd from Ebriel's hands. "Don't look frightened, dear," she said. "It's only a call."

"Yes, I know this," Ebriel said. "But—Nancy—" She turned away to unwind the heavy muffler and pull off the thick layers of clothing. Her cold cheeks stung as they began to warm.

"Tell me, Ebriel," Nancy said. "This is someone important to you, I think."

"I do not really know him," Ebriel answered. "But he is—he seems—it might be—"

Nancy chuckled.

Ebriel went to pick Li Li up, to change her diaper, to try to coax her to take a little formula. With her hands thus occupied, she told Nancy Chao her story, about the refugee hospital in Keelung, about the man who attacked her. She described James Bull coming to her rescue, her heroic savior, even though all he knew about her was that she had planned, and then failed, to shoot General George Glass with her pulse pistol. She told Nancy how he looked, how brave he was, how kind. And then, after a pause, she said, "But I cannot—surely I cannot—betray Paul's memory, or my Renée's, by anything so foolish—if it were to happen—I mean to say, if this man—" She broke off, staring at her feet in their thick woolen socks.

"I think," Nancy said, "that you have your life to live." She turned to look into the courtyard, where the dragon spruce dripped fragile, glassy icicles. "It's been a long time, but I remember what it is to be in love."

"Oh, Nancy, I am not—I could not be in love. I hardly know him. James."

"No. But there is something in the way you say his name, in the way you talk about him. Perhaps you could care for him."

"Perhaps. But he is InCo, and I am not. Not anymore."

"No. And you're not safe in InCo territory, either, it seems. It's a problem."

"Nancy, you have never married?"

"No." Nancy turned away to the cupboard and bent to fit the burlap rice bag under the counter. "I would have married, but he—the man I cared about—didn't want to do this work. I had to do it. I couldn't live in England, safe, while these children had no one, and nothing."

Ebriel bit her lip, appalled at the thought of years of living in the Children's Home, endlessly performing the same chores over and over. She marveled at Nancy's courage and patience, and her wisdom. She supposed Nancy was right. Paul's and Renée's lives had ended, and though she would willingly have put herself in their place, have gone with them, it was too late. The days stretched endlessly ahead, a future empty of their love and company.

But James Bull had called.

James had found the shop with its commercial telepanels in the Makati Market. Before he left his office in Quezon City Hall, he changed his uniform for a reworked linen shirt and cotton trousers. He caught one of the retrofitted buses the natives called Jeepneys. It was crowded, and he stood gripping a hand loop as it wended its way through throngs of people, bicycles, pedal carts, past shop fronts draped with scarlet bunting, gates overgrown with bougainvillea. The heat lay over everything, a thick, humid cloud. Since his arrival a week before, James had worn a constant sheen of perspiration on his face and chest. His staff sergeant told him he would get used it, but he longed for a breath of clean, cold, dry air.

The comm shop nestled in one corner of the lower section

of the Market. It swirled with languages, Tagalog, English, French, Spanish. The panels, each behind a bamboo curtain, had slots for Philippine centavos or the heavier InCo coins.

James found a free panel and drew the curtain. He had tested the system from the office, trying through the microsat feed and through Newnet to hack into O-Net's public communication service. His failure gave him confidence he could contact Ebriel Serique without being traced. It was no wonder InCo chafed at Oceania's refusal to join the alliance. The slack security of the neutral polities left a huge hole in the dike InCo had tried to erect between itself and the turbulent seas of the latent countries. A year before, such carelessness might have irritated James. He felt differently now. But he didn't know what he was going to do about it.

Ebriel sat in Nancy's makeshift office in the corner of the storeroom, waiting. Crowded wall shelves and stacked cartons loomed behind her, shadowy sentinels, vague lumpen shapes in the gloom. The panel's lights glowed stubbornly blue, ready. The amber advisory light was dark. She fidgeted, watching for the white flash that signaled a call.

Perhaps he wouldn't call. Maybe it hadn't been James after all, or maybe he hadn't meant to call back, and Nancy had misunderstood. Or work could have intervened, the duties of his new office. He was Security Corps, she understood that. A policeman, essentially, though with a high rank.

And what did she know about him? Only that he couldn't allow an innocent woman to be murdered in a hospital bed. He might still be a patriot. He could be loyal to InCo and its policies, just as she herself had been, in her privileged past.

The labors of her long day began to catch up with her. She leaned back in the old rocking chair. She felt sleepy, and a bit foolish. He would not call, and she would have wasted a valuable hour or two, sitting here, when she could have been doing something useful.

She startled at the panel's tinny chime, disoriented. A twinge of pain pinched the back of her neck. A white light flashed steadily on the panel, its small light dazzling her eyes, the little bell ringing softly.

"Oh!" Ebriel exclaimed. She rubbed her eyes, and stretched them wide. "Oh. *Pardon*—I mean, on! Panel, on!" The screen came to life, startling her with its brightness.

Ebriel stared at the face of James Bull, a face she had seen so often in her memory. Now, in its reality, it seemed that of a stranger.

The glaring light of the commercial panel's camera made his cheekbones sharp, his dark skin darker, the little claw tattoo only a deeper shadow. He was out of uniform, but his hair was military-short, his shoulders straight. Behind him an odd background, as of woven grasses, blurred into grayness. He leaned forward. The perspective changed, softening the strong line of his jaw, the straight heavy eyebrows.

"Excuse me," he said, looking into the camera. "Is it possible to speak with Ebriel?"

Ebriel's lips parted. For a crazy moment, she thought of simply shutting off the panel, escaping the storeroom, pretending it had never happened. Her camera was off. James couldn't see her. He didn't know who was answering his call.

She put her hands to her hair, trying to comb it with her fingers, and then she laughed at herself. How silly! She was a grown woman. She had been lonely. It was good to hear from a friend, however short their acquaintance.

"Visual on," she said to the panel. The camera's ready light glowed, and she smiled into it. "*Bonjour,* James," she said. "How good it is to see you."

James's pulse beat faster at the sound of her voice. The visual lagged, but she was there. The picture coalesced bit by bit, a glimmer of light, then a silhouette, at last the pixels resolving to show her white face, her full pale lips, her tousle of ashen hair.

"Hello," James said, feeling awkward and boyish. He cleared his throat. "You look well."

"And you." Her smile widened. She, at least, seemed unselfconscious. "It is good of you to call," she said. "I have thought of you often."

"Have you?" James leaned back a little, took a deep

breath, tried to relax. Even through the grain of a second-rate net system, she was beautiful. That ghost of a dimple in her cheek, those wide eyes, her slender throat . . . He remembered the feel of her solidly muscled small body leaning on his arm, the touch of her lips on his cheek. "I've thought of you, too. I've wondered if you were all right, what happened to you."

"I am fine. I am working with children, in an orphanage."

"I know where you are, I think," he said slowly. "Because of the routing symbols."

"Yes. Very far from you."

"Right." Now he did relax a little. "And what kind of work are you doing?"

Her laugh was like a riff of music. "Oh, I am very privileged!" she said. "I wash diapers and scrub floors and cook rice." She spread her hands. Her fingers were white and slender, tapering at the ends. "And so I use my classical education!"

He chuckled, too. "At least you have a classical education."

"*Mais oui*. And you? What is your education?"

"Let's just say if we're ever lost in the woods, you'll be glad you brought me along."

She searched his features through the badly focused picture. She said carefully, "You are all right? There are no—I do not know the word. No problems for you, after . . ."

He shook his head. "Repercussions, I think is the word you want. No, everything's fine for me." He wanted to assure her that she was safe, too, that Security Corps would never cross the Line, come after her, but he was no longer certain it was true. "I have questions for you, too," he said. "How did you get to—where you are? Who was that woman who came for you?"

She tilted her head, considering how to answer. "Some of this I do not think I can say," she said. "It is not for myself, James, but for others."

He nodded. As he suspected, she had been well-trained. He wondered by whom? "Can you leave, if you want to?"

"Yes. I am not a prisoner."

"Good. And your ankle healed all right?"

"Yes. *La docteuresse* was wonderful. And here—" she made a vague gesture at her surroundings. "The crutch has been useful."

"Are things very difficult for you? For the children?"

Her face grew grave. "For the children, yes. There is no medicine, James. Few doctors. The people have little to spare."

"I wish I could help."

She lifted one shoulder. "We all do what we can." He heard a vague sound, as of a baby's cry. Ebriel glanced over her shoulder, and then looked back into the camera. "I must go, James. I am needed."

"Ebriel—I'll call again, okay? Next week. Will you be there?"

She sighed and tugged at her hair. "Oh, I will be here. I will certainly be here."

James sat on after she broke the connection, staring at the green query light on the panel. His centavos had not yet run out. He was tempted to send a message to his father, but decided it was better not to try it. No one needed to know that James Bull was using a commercial panel, when the InCo office in Quezon City Hall sported a dozen of them, with microsat monitors and a staff of secretaries and aides. He sat listening to the ticking of the meter as it ran down, wishing he could hold Ebriel Serique's thin, strong arm once again, see that vague dimple in her cheek as she laughed. What did this mean, that he, a major in Security Corps, wanted more than anything to be where she was—Ebriel Serique, outlaw and fugitive? That he dreamed of taking her home to the pine forests, to show her the meadows and valleys of his boyhood?

James had known women, but he had never known one like this. He had never fallen in love. He suspected this was what love felt like, and it embarrassed him.

When the screen blanked at last, he got up, pulled back the bamboo curtain, and walked out into the hot Philippine night, the garish lights of Metro Manila, the racket of night life. Pedal cart drivers who spoke to him in Tagalog and English— "Ride, Mister? Too hot to walk, Mister!" He shook his head.

He bypassed the Jeepney stop, too, and set out on foot toward his billet.

He passed a little knot of teenagers, boys and girls who clung together as they walked down the street. They laughed up at him. He grinned back, feeling strangely lighthearted.

33

Yasmine lifted Ethan's wasted hands to slip her gift beneath them. She had fashioned clamps out of moldable plastic, and she secured the voice synthesizer board over the arms of the chair and placed Ethan's fingers on the sensors.

"There now, Papa," she said as matter-of-factly as she could. "Now you can speak to us."

She watched his thin fingers find the little speaker, the icons, the clamps that left the controls of his chair free. He explored the sensors and found the raised symbols with his fingertips. The synthesizer spoke. "Thank—you," it said, in an American accent. Ethan's eyes danced, and the side of his mouth pulled up.

Semaya, watching, asked, "Yasmine, how did you do that? The voice?"

"I downloaded it from Newnet," Yasmine said. "And digitized it. It is the voice of a broadcaster." She turned back to Ethan. "Do you like it, Papa?"

The synthesizer spoke for him again in the resonant voice. "Yes. It's—beautiful."

"It's wonderful, Yasmine," Semaya said. "We could have brought something from one of the Fleckcell plants, but you did a lovely job of this. Better than any they're building on Earth."

Yasmine felt a glow of pleasure. "Yes," she said. "I used the neural network of the copters as a model. A memory stick will record Papa's most common expressions, and code for them. And there is a programmed list, of everyone's names, all the Chain, all the staff, all the children." She laid her hand on Ethan's emaciated arm. "With practice, Papa—it will speak almost as quickly as you do. Did." She pulled her hand back, her little swell of confidence subsiding. She cast Semaya a helpless glance. "Oh, I am sorry," she blurted. "It is so—"

The synthesizer interrupted, the words coming slowly, separately. "Yasmine. My dear. I—love it. I will be—an expert— by tomorrow. I—promise."

Yasmine smiled at Ethan through a mist of tears. "I know you will, Papa," she whispered. She wiped her cheeks with the back of her hand.

Semaya handed her a handkerchief from her own pocket. "Don't be upset, Yasmine. We know how hard it is to talk about."

And the synthesizer said haltingly, but pleasantly, "Much easier—today—than yesterday!"

Yasmine blew her nose and dried her eyes. She patted Ethan's shoulder and then floated away, leaving Semaya and Ethan to explore the synthesizer. Yasmine hovered before a monitor. At Siwa, Nenet Nasser was working to coordinate a meeting between a Red Omega boat, loaded with smuggled vaccines, and the representatives of three African tribes. The alliance between the tribal emissaries was uneasy, the landing point disputed. It had been tricky, but between Nenet and Starhold and Red Omega, the parties had reached agreement. Yasmine watched and listened as the rendezvous approached.

The boat had already slipped through the spybug net off the Greek coast. Now it approached the agreed-upon landing fifty kilometers east of Misratah. Nenet was in touch with both parties by shortband, and with Starhold by the secure channel. Yasmine listened to her switching from Arabic to English, and back to Arabic, giving directions, reporting, guiding. One of Starhold's spybugs deployed from Siwa and reached the isolated bay just as the boat, a vessel bristling with fishing poles, dropped anchor. A dinghy lowered and forged the choppy waves toward the beach. Nenet's voice came softly from the monitor.

From behind her, Yasmine heard the synthesizer. Already it had begun to seem that it was Ethan's own voice speaking. "Are they—there, Yasmine? The—yacht? The—emissaries?"

"Yes, Papa. Nenet is speaking with them."

The exchange went smoothly, the cartons offloaded, the dinghy bouncing on the waves as it returned to the boat. The spybug circled the beach, where men in desert robes sorted the boxes and loaded them onto camels kneeling among the dunes. Yasmine watched with her hands linked beneath her chin. How beautiful, to see the ungainly animals with their long knobby legs lumbering away from the coast, laden with boxes full of hope.

"Starhold? All is accomplished."

Yasmine said, "Wonderful, Nenet. We will send back the spybug now."

"Good. I'll be watching for it."

And from Ethan's chair, in resonant tones, "Congratulations—Nenet."

Nenet's face appeared on the panel. "Who was that? Who spoke?"

Yasmine shifted to one side, to allow the camera to focus on Ethan. His chair moved forward, little jets of air spurting white in the gloom of the aerie. His lips didn't move, but his fingers did. Slowly, the words came. "It was—my voice—Nenet. My new voice."

Nenet smiled uncertainly. "Your new . . . What does that mean?"

Semaya floated beside Ethan, one hand anchoring her to his chair. Wisps of gray hair floated about her face in the microgravity. "Yasmine has made a voice synthesizer," she said.

"Ah. Well. *Tamam*, Yasmine."

Yasmine nodded to the panel. "*Shukran*, Nenet," she said gravely.

Nenet's chuckle was like dark velvet. "Your Arabic is good, Yasmine. And now, I had better go out to watch for the spybug. *Salam*, Starhold."

The voice synthesizer spoke in tones as rich as Nenet's own. "Peace, Nenet."

Yasmine floated down the tube to the gallery to fetch Ethan's dinner. The cooks prepared the same food for him as everyone else ate, a soy and fish casserole, a purée of fruit. They ground it, mixed it with a little broth, and packed it into paper cones that Semaya, or sometimes Yasmine, could hold to Ethan's lips. Yasmine gathered the cones of food and sailed back to the aerie, her vivid cottons fluttering like butterfly wings. She had assembled three combinations of cottons and scarves, all with the sari-effect. The pleasure the simple clothes gave her surprised her, and she often felt that her choices reflected her moods. She wore scarlet on her best days. On thoughtful days, there was a set of indigo shirt and trousers, with a scarf of white. Her first outfit, the blue and yellow, gave her courage when she wanted to do something new.

She delivered the meal to Semaya and then went back to the dining hall for her own dinner, sitting at one end of a long table, listening to the chatter around her. Across from her the engraved stars sparkled. She knew every name on that wall now, every story. Often it was her task to monitor the starchildren, to trace their movements, receive their communications. Only the night before, there had been messages from Rio de Janeiro, from Ukraine, and from a hilltop near Ankara. Yasmine had answered them all. One, Tawia in Dire Dawa, had requested a formula for making a medicine, and Yasmine had secured it from the clinic, transcribed it, sent it on with detailed instructions, all within twenty minutes. She imagined the sick child getting better, being helped, and she, Yasmine, had been a part of it.

A boisterous ten-year-old boy from Peru sat across from her at the table. As she ate the casserole, he bounced in his seat, reached across his neighbor for bread, joking loudly in Spanish and in English. Yasmine dropped her eyes, put down her spoon, and waited for him to subside. She almost always ate in the dining hall now, and most of the inhabitants of Starhold knew she preferred to be silent. It had been weeks, perhaps even months, since she had withdrawn, had to flee the stimuli of the crowded room. But she couldn't eat with the boy shouting like that, banging his fork against his plate. She stared down at her folded hands.

One of the Chain came to admonish the boy in rapid Spanish. Yasmine looked up gratefully into Pilar Alavedra's eyes.

"Yasmine, you could have spoken to him," Pilar said. "Your Spanish is perfect."

Yasmine dropped her eyes again. "Yes, I know," she said. "I will try. Next time."

She saw Pilar's hand reach out, strong and brown, as if to pat her shoulder, but before it touched her, Pilar withdrew it, no doubt remembering. Yasmine looked up again. "I am sorry, Pilar," she murmured.

Pilar shook her head. "That's not necessary, Yasmine. I understand. Next time."

Yasmine managed a smile. Pilar winked at her as she went back to her seat.

As soon as she finished her meal, Yasmine hurried around the gallery to the slip and up the tube to return to the aerie. Ethan had eaten and was drowsing in his chair.

"I think I must go get some sleep, Yasmine," Semaya whispered. "I'm exhausted. You're going to stay?"

"Yes, I will stay," Yasmine whispered back. It was almost unnecessary to say so. Most nights she stayed with Ethan until past midnight, watching the monitors, scanning the net broadcasts. Time of day meant little in the aerie. The stars twinkled endlessly through the space window. Yasmine had visited the garden level and seen the great window overlooking the planet. She preferred the dimness and peace of the aerie. And she liked to be with Papa.

"Thank you, Yasmine," Semaya murmured. She touched Yasmine's hand, just a brush of her fingers, as she floated awkwardly to the slip. Yasmine tolerated Semaya's touch fairly well, and she touched Papa all the time. The Chain had come to understand her special requirements, and to accept them. Only rarely now did she have to pull away from some unwanted contact, and she had not withdrawn, not really withdrawn, in a very long time.

She drifted to the bank of monitors. The Newnet broadcasts

were all propaganda. O-Net was showing an entertainment, something with nude bodies painted in bright colors and playing strange instruments. Yasmine found it silly. She much preferred to listen to Papa's recordings, especially Ebriel's. One of the underground nets was broadcasting a protest demonstration on the island of Crete, just inside the Line of Partition, but it seemed tired and hopeless. Yasmine glided away to the space window to soothe her eyes with the unchanging vista of stars.

"Yasmine?" The voice startled her, and for a frozen second she couldn't think whose it was. But how silly! Of course, it was her own creation. She turned toward it.

"You are awake, Papa."

"I am." His fingertips moved on the sensors of her device. The rest of his body was as somnolent as if he were still asleep. Only his eyes moved, following her as she floated toward him. "All is—quiet, it seems." Already the words came more quickly from the synthesizer. Yasmine believed he was right, that he would be expert with it in a day. The memory stick and code system should integrate soon, and he would speak almost as quickly as anyone else.

"An underground net is showing a protest on Crete. I have seen nothing else of interest."

"The Red—Omega ship?"

"It's back in Greek waters. Your associate in Athens is waiting at the harbor."

"Good." Normally, Ethan would have moved his chair close to the banks of monitors, to scan for himself, send messages to his people, feed his boundless hunger for information.

"Is there something wrong, Papa?"

His fingertips moved. She waited, listening to the background murmur of Starhold's machinery, the muted voices of the panels, the occasional creaking of the shields. The voice came at last, mellifluous, halting.

"Yasmine, your—gift will be most—useful to me." A silence. "You are a gift in—yourself."

Yasmine couldn't answer, couldn't find the words to pour out her feelings about him, about the work she was allowed to do, the unlimited access to the study hoods, to the panels, to the wealth of information that was the Chain. She, who had never been happy in her life, was happy on Starhold. She was happy here, in the aerie, with Papa.

Ethan's fingers moved. "I can see the—end now, Yasmine."

"Papa?"

His fingers flicked over the synthesizer. "I'm—tired. Trying to—breathe. Trying—to eat."

Yasmine's body stiffened, and her hands found each other to twist and twist her fingers. The beginnings of a great grief burned in her chest, but she bore it, for his sake, and she did not withdraw. "Oh, Papa," she said softly. "I wish there were something I could do."

"There is," the voice synthesizer said after a time. "Something—very important."

Yasmine waited in silence. She knew. She knew what Ethan was going to ask, and it was both what she dreaded and what she wanted more than anything. She let her eyes wander to the distant stars, but she wasn't avoiding. She was accepting.

"Will you—do it, Yasmine? You understand—everything."

"I am not clever like you, Papa."

"You are clever in—different ways."

"Yes." Yasmine moved her fingers, propelling herself to the window. She clung to a staple and gazed out into space. "I cannot run Fleckcell, Papa."

"Semaya will—do that. That, too—is important. We want to—supply fuel cells." A pause while his fingers found the new words. "But . . . the Chain is important—too. Our—special project. The—starchildren. You and Semaya—together—you can do—this work."

"I understand, Papa." Yasmine splayed her fingers against the space window.

"Vee is building me—a module. A—pod."

Yasmine concentrated on the coolness of the glass. She allowed the pain to fill her body and her mind. She would grow used to it. She had grown used to so many things. She had become accustomed to the crowded habitat, the strangeness of her cubby, the company of Semaya Fleck. "You are going to leave, then."

"Not just yet. Soon." The chair's tiny jets puffed, and Ethan sailed to the window to hang suspended just at Yasmine's elbow. "The stars. I—always wanted to see them."

"But, Papa, you'll be alone."

"Some things—we have to do—alone." A little rasp of a chuckle came from Ethan's own vocal cords.

"You are a brave man, Papa." Yasmine spoke with care, breathing around the pain.

"You are a brave girl—Yasmine."

"No. No, I am a coward."

Ethan's fingers searched out the words. "Cowards do not—overcome their fears. Cowards—give in to them. You are—the most courageous—starchild, Yasmine. Remember that. Show them—the way."

"Yes, Papa. I will try. For you." Yasmine put both her hands on the staple and leaned her forehead against them. She said with a little sob, "I will miss you always."

A rasping breath came from his throat, and his synthesized voice said, "Don't cry—my dear. You are the—daughter I never had. Remember!"

Yasmine choked, "Yes, Papa. I will remember."

34

When James seized the final piece of the puzzle, he felt the same mix of triumph and grief as when he took his first white-tailed buck.

He had plenty of free time to search. Corliss had been right about the neutral polities. Work hours were relaxed, and the Security Corps officers wore short sleeves and went without their jackets. They socialized with the Philippine civilians from the office, attended parties, trooped out together after work for drinks. James's solitary habits isolated him in Quezon City even more than on InCo bases. He spent most of his evenings poring through the data towers, digging for information. Only his weekly calls to Xining relieved his loneliness.

He had been late calling once or twice and had spoken the routing symbols hurriedly, anxious that she might have given up and gone to bed. But each time, she was there, often looking sleepy, but smiling into the camera and saying, "It is good to see you, James," in that musical tone that made his skin tingle and his heart quicken.

"Ebriel." Speaking her name delighted him. "Ebriel, you look tired." He had come to know her face well, the curve of her pale cheek, the ghost of a dimple that flashed if he said something to make her laugh. He wished he could laugh as freely as she did. He worried that his reserve made him seem dull. If only he could touch her, hold her hand—yet their talks had the feel of intimacy, James in his bamboo-curtained cubicle, Ebriel in her dim storeroom.

"Yes, I am tired," she said. "We have had a sadness here. A child died today, a little baby—Li Li. We knew she would not live long, but still, we grieved. We will miss her."

"I'm sorry." James struggled for something to say. "I wish I could help." He leaned closer to the camera. "I wish I were there with you."

She leaned her chin on her fist and smiled into the camera. She had gained a little weight, and it softened her face, rounded her cheekbones. "Oh, James, it would be funny to see you here! You would tower over everyone! And with all these children, and piles of laundry, stacks of dishes—" She pointed one slender finger. "I would give you a broom and make you sweep away the last of the snow in the courtyard!"

"I'm good at snow," he said. "But I use a shovel."

"Ah." Ebriel nodded. "*Mais oui*. Montana."

"Yes. Though we usually just leave it to melt in the spring."

Her smile disappeared. "I think this snow will not melt for a long time. I am so weary of it." She shrugged. "I am sorry, James. I am not good company tonight, I think."

"You're always good company." He said it with more intensity than he intended.

She tilted her head, smiled again. "I do wish you were here, with a broom or a shovel or with empty hands."

"What would we do together, you and I?" he dared to say. "If I were there?"

"Oh, James! Such fun we would have! We would take a sick child to the clinic, perhaps, or we could shop for very smelly yak meat, perhaps stroll along the river, which is frozen solid!"

He chuckled. "Yak meat sounds good."

She wrinkled her nose. "*Zut!* I am so tired of it. Yak butter. Yak milk. Yak fur!"

He laughed aloud, then quieted, remembering he was not

alone in the comm shop. "I would eat it," he said. "Probably tastes like venison."

"I would not know," she said. "What is venison?"

"Deer meat. At home, we ate venison a lot."

She sighed. "Oh, James, I wish I could show you this place. I was an InCo citizen, and I, too, thought the Line of Partition was necessary. But these children—they pay a high price."

James heard himself saying, "I'm sorry, Ebriel. I'm really sorry," as if it were all his fault. Again she tilted her head, smiled gently at him. He repeated, lamely, "I wish I were there."

Restless after their conversation, feeling as if he had somehow not acquitted himself well, he went back to the office, and spent another hour digging through records. It was then that he found it, the crucial, damning bit of evidence.

He had discovered an enormous library of O-Net reports, filed in the Security Corps offices by order of the Commander General. One of his jobs was to review and categorize O-Net broadcasts, to forward anything interesting or suspicious on to Colorado Springs. It was a simple thing, while scanning each week's reports, to delve into older files. He devised a sampling pattern and dug deeper and deeper into the past until he found the broadcast, almost two years old, of the terrorist incident in the Mediterranean.

O-Net had borrowed heavily from the underground nets for its coverage of the loss of the French yacht *L'Oiseau blanc*. They had broadcast the underground video of Ebriel's demonstration in Ariana Park, the one James had seen in his father's house. He put the memory stick in a nearby panel and ran the video.

How different she looked, with her long auburn hair fluttering around her shoulders. Her blood, when she applied the little silver knife to her wrist, spattered her clothes. And the guards—Security Corps, his own people—had hauled her away by the arms like a criminal.

James had sworn an oath, but he was going to break it. He told himself that InCo, that General Glass himself, had violated the promise made to him, made to all citizens. He tried to believe that invalidated his own pledge, but it was a challenge.

What he found that night was the spybug video. The original.

One of the undergrounds had hacked into the microsats, caught the spybug's transmission in their own system. No one had doctored this one. The data stream in the corner supplied the missing numbers. Latitude 42° 5' 36" North. Longitude 7° 12' 27" East.

James knew perfectly well where the Line of Partition had been drawn through the Mediterranean, but he called it up anyway, to be certain. Latitude 38° 0' 0" North in that part of the sea. He compared his figures to a map from his mini. There could be no doubt. *L'Oiseau blanc* had been sailing in InCo waters when it was attacked. And there was more.

In his mini, he had the alterations that had been made in the spybug deployment pattern the morning of the attack on the French yacht. In the deserted Security Corps offices in Quezon City he compared the figures with the default pattern of Mediterranean surveillance. The discrepancy left a broad and empty sea path running straight between the islands of Corsica and Sardinia and ending at the Bay of Naples, where the attacking boat originated. It wasn't a vessel carrying terrorists from the latent countries. It was Dirty Tricks Corps. It was, as it had been in Keelung, InCo attacking its own. There had been no need for murder, but something had gone wrong, something terrible, and they had tried to cover up the disaster. Colonel Corliss was right again. Everyone associated with the *L'Oiseau blanc* incident had disappeared.

Brain whirling, chest burning with fury, James returned to the video of Ebriel Serique. He ran it twice more to be sure. In the background, melting into the shadows of an oak tree, was the woman he had met in Taiwan, at the crash site of Ebriel's copter. It was the woman called Ty.

In the morning, James was waiting when Colonel Thurgren, his CO in Quezon City, arrived at the office.

Thurgren was a cheerful, easygoing sort, a plump man close to retirement, glad to have made full colonel, delighted to be finishing his career in the ease of a diplomatic post.

"Sir?" James said, stepping into his office. "Requesting a closed-door, sir."

Thurgren had just sat down, a fresh cup of coffee on his oak desk. Through his corner window, the brilliant Philippine sun blazed on the colorful city, and a man-made lagoon behind the sprawling City Hall shone vividly blue against the banks of morning glory that surrounded it. Thurgren waved a generous hand. "James, come in. Sit, sit. Sure, shut the door if you want."

James pulled the door closed behind him and sat in the chair opposite the desk. He hesitated, pinching the bridge of his nose. He had spent a poor night. His head ached and his eyes burned. "Sir," he began. He had lain awake planning how to say this, and now that the moment had arrived, the words seemed inadequate. "Sir. I want to lodge a protest."

Thurgren frowned. "About what?"

James took a deep breath. "Sir, there was an incident a long time ago. Two years. In the Mediterranean, very close to the Line of Partition."

Thurgren's eyes narrowed. He stiffened. "Major, you're treading on thin ice. We've been warned away from that incident. Terrorist activity, Red Omega—those are directly under the commander general's authority."

James sat very straight, his shoulders squared. "Sir, I'm aware of that. But the records have been altered. Civilians died. I have reason to believe the Corps did something illegal. And covered it up."

Thurgren put out his hand to turn off his panel before he spoke. "James. You don't want to do this. You'll screw your career right into the ground, and it won't change anything. That incident, whatever it was, is over and done with."

James thought of Ebriel's suffering, her planned revenge, her misery at her failure. The incident was not over with. Not so long as Ebriel still grieved.

"Look, James," Thurgren said. "You're an idealist, I see that. But this is the real world. Sometimes we have to compromise."

James looked away, out to the green hills edging the city. "Sir, where I grew up, the world was one big compromise.

I walked away from it, from my home, because I thought Security Corps had the right idea. Honor, loyalty, honesty. Chain of command. I left everything my father swore by, for the Corps."

Thurgren was silent for a long time. They sat in the wash of hot Philippine sunshine, listening to the murmur of voices in the outer office. "I can't stand with you on this, Major," the colonel finally said.

"I understand, sir."

Thurgren rubbed his eyes. "Okay, okay. You want me to pass your protest up the line?"

James didn't hesitate. "Yes, sir." He stood. "Thank you, sir."

"This is not good for your career."

"Sir. I have to do it."

Thurgren nodded, his eyes bleak. "Okay. Noted. Dismissed, Major."

"Yes, sir." James left the office and went down the line of desks to his own. He closed his door and stood by the window, ignoring the pointless stack of papers waiting on his desk.

The morning after James's call Ebriel stared out into the frozen courtyard of the Children's Home, trying to gather the patience to get her through the day. She had done a load of laundry that she would soon hang on the line beside the back steps, and she knew when she brought it in it would be frozen solid. Mounds of old, dirty snow clogged the sidewalks and streets and had to be swept from the play equipment whenever it was warm enough for the children to get outdoors for an hour. Winter lasted long and spring came late on the Roof of the World. Her skin, her hair, her lips felt as desiccated as an old woman's. She closed her eyes, imagining James in his shirtsleeves in Quezon City. Warm, so warm, and the delicious humidity beading everything with moisture.

It was silly, of course, to miss him. She had spent no more than twelve hours in his presence, but somehow over these last months, talking into the night while he fed pesos and centavos into the commercial panel, she felt as if they were attached, as if a great bond had grown between them. When they said good-bye, she felt the loss of his company as a pain in her midriff that was only assuaged by his next call.

She heard footsteps above her and opened her eyes. She had not yet filled the rice steamer, and she had to put the diapers into the big washer. She hurried to start her chores.

Nancy came downstairs a few moments later, and Ebriel saw that her eyes were heavy, her lips a little swollen. "Oh, Nancy," Ebriel cried softly. "*Mon amie!* You have been crying."

Nancy shrugged. "Not really," she said slowly. "I just didn't sleep well."

"It is Li Li. You are thinking of Li Li."

"Yes, Li Li, and the others. Bao and Chu Hua and the others, all the little damaged ones. Sometimes I wonder if we make any difference at all." She glanced at the empty rattan bassinet under the window, and her mouth trembled.

Ebriel laid down the scoop she was holding and went to put her arms around the older woman. Despite her denial, Nancy began to weep again. Ebriel led her to the table and seated her, then brought her a cup of tea. She rested a hand on her shoulder until Nancy quieted, looking up with wet eyelashes and a rueful smile. "Thank you," Nancy said. She wiped her eyes and sniffed. "My goodness. Sometimes you just need to cry it out, don't you?"

"*Mais oui,*" Ebriel said. "And of course you make a difference, Nancy. Where would these children be without you?" She stood up and went to fill the steamer. "Sit there, drink your tea. You are overtired. Yesterday was long and hard. Perhaps you should go back to bed."

Nancy considered this and then shook her head. "No, Ebriel, I couldn't sleep. But I will rest a little. And thank you for the tea."

Ebriel went back to her tasks. The children came down. Ting brought the baby from the nursery, and Ruan carried the ten-year-old boy in her strong arms, strapping him into his wheelchair, rolling it into place at the long table. Breakfast began in its usual noisy, orderly fashion. Nancy, with Li Li's empty bassinet in her arms, came to the stove. "Ebriel," she said quietly. "We don't know what tradition Li Li was born into. I think we will have a Christian funeral, but bury her beneath the stupa in the Buddhist cemetery. Will you play your flute?"

"*Mais oui,* Nancy, of course."

Nancy nodded and turned away to take the bassinet up to the storeroom. Ebriel was elbow-deep in soapy water when the bell at the front door sounded its tinny clang.

Ting was busy bundling children into coats and mufflers to go outside. Ruan had gone back upstairs with the infant. Nancy, from the first-floor landing, said, "Oh, Lord. What now?"

Ebriel dried her hands on the graying towel. "I will go, Nancy."

"Oh, I hope it's not another child. I don't see how I can deal with it just now!"

"Perhaps it is something else. I will see." Ebriel hurried down the hallway to the door with the towel still in her hands, her overlarge apron flapping around her.

Icy air swept into the hall as she pulled the door open, and the sun glared from the snowbanks lining the street, dazzling her. Squinting, shading her eyes, she said, *"Ni hao?"*

A youthful voice answered her. *"Ni hao."* The visitor said something else, but Ebriel couldn't understand the words.

When her eyes adjusted to the brightness, she saw a woman, a girl really, probably no older than twenty, bundled in one of the thick padded jackets worn by the mountain villagers. A hat of dark fur obscured her face, and beneath it her hair hung in a profusion of thin braids. She pulled off the hat and held it in her hands, looking up at Ebriel. Her eyes were narrow, the epicanthic fold long and heavy. She had flat cheekbones and very dark skin. She spoke again.

Ebriel stood aside, holding the door open. "Come in," she said. "My Mandarin is not good. I will get help."

She left the young woman standing in the hall and went in search of Nancy, who was just seeing the last of the children outdoors. "Nancy, I think you will need to come. It is not a child, in any case, but I could not understand what she wants."

Nancy followed her back to the front hall and spoke in

rapid Mandarin with the girl. A moment later, she was helping her off with her coat and her thick boots, leading her to the kitchen. Ebriel opened the door to shake snow off the boots, then hung the coat on a hook.

In the kitchen, she found the girl seated at one end of the table, her shoulders slumping, her eyes cast down. Nancy, at the stove, was filling the teakettle. "She's looking for her daughter," she said to Ebriel. "The baby should be almost two years old now." She glanced at the dejected young woman. "I've already told her the child isn't here. But I'm going to give her some tea, let her talk. Her name is Ming Xiu."

Ebriel took the kettle from Nancy. "Let me do this. Go and sit with her."

Nancy smiled at her wearily. "Thanks." She went to the table and pulled out a chair next to Ming Xiu. She said something in Mandarin, and the girl answered. Ebriel listened, trying to catch what words she could as she filled the kettle, set it to boil, and spooned tea into the teapot.

When the tea was ready, she laid out cups and spoons, and brought a little bowl of yak butter. She poured tea for Nancy and the visitor, and a cup for herself, and sat down with them.

The girl, Ming Xiu, fell silent. Nancy urged her to drink her tea, and she did, staring hungrily out the window at the children playing under the drooping boughs of the dragon spruce.

Nancy said in English, "She's from Gansu Province. Her family made her expose her newborn child. She left the baby on a rock beside the road, and then a few minutes later she changed her mind and went back for her." Nancy shook her head with weary resignation. "The baby was gone when she went back. She says she knew she had the right place, because the rock was warm where the child had been lying, but her baby had disappeared."

"*Mon Dieu,*" Ebriel exclaimed softly. "How terrible."

Nancy pushed the little dish of yak butter close to Ming Xiu, and the girl cast her a grateful look. "Yes, it is terrible," Nancy said. "In every way. That the mountain villagers are still exposing girl children, and that the child disappeared, and that this poor girl has been searching ever since. She never went home."

"But how does she live?" Ebriel asked. The girl's long, sad eyes swept over her, and then returned to the courtyard.

"I imagine she begs," Nancy said. "Works sometimes. She doesn't look as if she's been eating well."

It was hard to tell in the baggy and ragged clothes Ming Xiu wore, but she did look thin. Her wrists were bony, her neck hollow. Ebriel went to the counter, where the dishes still awaited her in the now-cooling wash water, and brought back a little left-over rice and milk from breakfast. She set it before Ming Xiu, smiling down at her. The girl smiled back, and said something Ebriel didn't catch.

"She thanked you," Nancy translated. "It's one of the mountain dialects. I can hardly understand her myself."

While Ebriel finished the dishes, Nancy sat on with Ming Xiu, talking, watching the children playing in the courtyard in the watery sunlight. The icicles were melting from the dragon spruce, and the mounds of dirty snow were shrinking, bit by bit. The high-ceilinged kitchen was bright with sunshine, promising the long-awaited spring. The house was quiet except for the faint drone of the fuel cell and the muted voices of the children outside. Ebriel savored the rare moment of peace.

The chiming of the panel from the storeroom broke the silence.

Nancy turned to meet Ebriel's eyes, her brows raised. "Are you expecting a call?"

Ebriel shook her head. "It is too early for Perk," she said. "And it is the middle of the night in Siwa."

Nancy rose. "Stay with Ming Xiu, will you? Don't let her leave until I speak with her again." She hurried out, and her footsteps pattered quickly up the stairs. Ebriel poured more tea. She had just returned the teapot to its holder when Nancy reappeared in the doorway.

"Ebriel. The call is for you."

Ebriel rose, glancing at the clock. It was only nine in the morning, and the same time in Quezon City. *"Zut,"* she whispered. "I hope nothing is wrong."

"It's your friend Ty."

Ebriel hastened up the stairs to the storeroom. The panel's

ready light blinked at her, and she said, "On," before she had even taken her seat in the rocking chair.

Ty's craggy features were tense, her eyes flashing as she looked out at her. "Hey, Eb," she said tersely. "Want to go on a mission?"

35

James arrived at the colonel's office to find his superior officer watching children sail paper boats on the lagoon below his window. Colonel Thurgren seemed diminished, somehow, his shoulders slumped, his hands hanging by his sides. James cleared his throat. "Sir? You wanted to see me?"

Thurgren turned to face him, his eyes worried in his round face. "Shut the door, please."

James pulled the door closed behind him and squared his shoulders. "Yes, sir."

Thurgren waved a hand wearily. "At ease, James," he said. "I just wanted to . . . listen, I just have to tell you . . ." He looked away again, out to the lagoon glittering dully in the sunshine.

"Sir?"

The colonel leaned one plump shoulder against the windowframe. "Damn it, James. You're a fine soldier. A fine officer." He paused. "You know I have a family. A daughter getting married in the fall. A son to get through college. Aging parents. I've put my whole future into the Corps."

"Yes, sir."

"You have a fine record, James. A hero's record. Promoted below the zone, good security clearance."

James kept his voice level. "Sir, has something happened?"

Thurgren stared blindly out the window. "It's this assignment you're going on, son."

The colonel hesitated so long, James thought he had changed his mind about speaking. He stood waiting, until at last Thurgren coughed, turned from the window, and settled with a little groan into the chair behind the desk. He reached out to his panel and hit the power with the flat of his hand. James sat down opposite him.

"I never said anything to you," Thurgren muttered.

"No, sir." James leaned forward, his elbows on his knees. An itch began at the base of his neck, just at the first vertebra.

"I don't like the looks of this, son."

"The assignment, sir?"

"Right. Look, I don't know anything, really. But I want you to watch your back, James."

James felt the prickle run up his neck and under his hair. He sat very still, his eyes fixed hard on the colonel. "Sir," he said, almost inaudibly.

"Ever hear of Dirty Tricks Corps?" the colonel asked.

"Yes, sir."

"This mission—leaving at night, no details, combat ready—sounds like Dirty Tricks to me. Rumors, you understand, that's all I've ever heard." Thurgren hesitated, one pudgy forefinger tracing the whorls of oak on his desk. "When I was a lieutenant, fifteen years ago, my CO got orders like these, all top secret, black ops stuff. He was a hell-raiser, always questioning orders, challenging policy." The colonel looked up at James from beneath his eyebrows. "Look, Security Corps is my life, my career, and I don't like saying any of this. My CO never came back, and there was a nasty story that he took a round in the back during the mission. Something out in Greece, right at the border—maybe over the border."

James's scalp prickled unbearably.

"This protest you filed, James—I'm not much of a believer in coincidence."

"No, sir. I'm not either."

"Damned odd, pulling a man off a desk and sending him on a night job."

"Yes, sir."

"You want to tell me more about it?"

James spoke in a carefully polite tone. "Sir, are you sure you want to know more?"

Thurgren coughed again. "No, you're right. I'd a hell of a lot rather not know."

James straightened and stood up. "Sir, this was very kind of you. I appreciate it."

"I hope you'll be back next week, James. Hope the mission is a success."

James nodded and saluted. "Do my best, sir. Thank you, sir."

Ethan and Semaya, with Yasmine between them, watched the projection of the globe turn slowly before them. A Mozart symphony was playing. Yasmine silenced it with a word. She said, "It's too late to call *Troll* back, Papa. It's just entering atmosphere."

They all understood that the spaceplane would not have enough fuel to return to the habitat. A full load of biomass and fully charged fuel cells were vital for every flight.

Semaya said, "I don't know what we're going to do. There's not enough fuel to get to Xiao Qaidam, either."

Ethan's fingers moved, and the voice synthesizer spoke for him. "Call—Vee."

Yasmine said, "I already did, Papa. She'll be here in a moment."

Ethan's ragged breathing grated in her ears. She glanced down at him and saw how gray he was, how pinched and blue his lips looked in the dim light.

Vee came through the slip and floated across to them. "Not good, Ethan," she said. They had known for several hours, from an informant in Geneva, that Security Corps was moving to capture one of the spaceplanes, was tracking its progress from the habitat. Vee said, "Siwa is our only choice. And Glass is going to come after it. I guess he ran out of patience."

Semaya said, "Could we ask Blackfield? Put the spaceplane down in neutral territory?"

"I looked at that," Vee said. "*Troll* doesn't have enough fuel."

"But," Semaya said, "we should warn Oceania. Reveal to them what Glass plans."

Ethan's synthesizer and Yasmine's light voice sounded at the same time. "No."

Semaya turned her head in surprise and had to catch herself before she floated away from them. "No? But why not? This is a violation of our neutrality!"

"But we must not let Oceania know of our operation, either," Yasmine said gently.

Ethan's mellifluous voice spoke, haltingly. "Chain—must be secret. Oceania has—its own—agenda."

Vee said, "We'll have to fight them, Ethan."

"Who do—we have?"

"Ty is at Qaidam with Kanika."

"Is that all?" Semaya asked with dismay. "Kanika is too young! Inexperienced!"

"I've already talked to Ty," Vee said. "Sorry, Semaya, there isn't anybody else. Nenet has been briefed."

Yasmine said, "There is someone else, Vee." Vee turned to her with raised eyebrows. Yasmine swallowed and said, "It's Ebriel. Ty can pick her up." She froze the spinning globe and pointed. "You see, with the copter it will be less than an hour out of their way."

"Order—it," Ethan said. "*Troll* will—be on the—ground soon. Glass—not far behind."

Semaya said, "Will Ebriel want to go?"

"Yes," Yasmine said, on her way to the panel. "She wants to go."

"How do you know that?" Vee asked, floating behind her.

"Ty has already asked her," Yasmine said. She spoke to the panel and then glanced back at Vee. The space window framed the old soldier's face with frosty stars.

Vee gave a sharp nod and said only, "Okay then. I'm getting back to Tacticals."

After Ty explained, Ebriel spoke with Perk.

"I am ready," she said without hesitation.

"Right. You three, Nenet, four of the Chain on *Troll,* you're all there is. Ty and Kanika are just firing up the bird now."

Adrenaline sang in Ebriel's muscles, fired her nerves. "I will watch for them."

"She'll have to put the copter down outside town. I told her to land to the east. There's an empty parking lot about a kilometer from you. Old grocery store. Can you get there?"

"*Mais oui.* I will be there."

"Her ETA is about thirty minutes. Go. But be careful, Ebriel. All of you. Take care."

"We will, Perk. *Au revoir.*"

He nodded, tugging on his ponytail. "Good luck."

Ebriel hurried downstairs to find Nancy standing in the front hall with their visitor. "Nancy," she said hurriedly. "I must go. I am needed by the Chain, something is happening."

Nancy blurted, "You're needed here, Ebriel!"

Ebriel had already turned toward her room. She stopped, torn by the pressure of passing time, by her duty to Nancy, to the children. "*Oui,* I understand, Nancy, but the Chain is at risk, the whole Chain. It is the spaceplane—*Troll*—and General Glass—" She realized as the words poured out of her that it was, again, George Glass who was her opponent, though doubtless he would not be present. A fierce exultation seized her. She was not sorry to have a chance to fight him, and a reason.

"*Troll?* What's happened?"

Ebriel told her what she knew. "I must hurry," she finished. She ran to her room, where she made a little bundle of clothes and picked up her old brocade bag. She hesitated, and then slipped her flute case into it. She knew that meant she did not expect to return, but there was no time to think it through. She shouldered the bag and picked up the bundle.

She found Ming Xiu and Nancy still by the front door. Ebriel shrugged into her coat and pulled a scarf around her neck. "I am sorry, Nancy. I know it will be a hardship for you."

Nancy took Ebriel's hand. "Ming Xiu is going to stay," she said. "For the moment." She smiled over her shoulder at the Chinese girl. "She will be a great help. I wish we had more time, time to say good-bye, to say thank you, Ebriel. But this is good, that Ming Xiu remains with us. She's a long way from Gansu Province. I don't think she's going to find her daughter, nor would she know her if she did find her. But she'll have a home here, and children to care for."

"Bon," Ebriel said hurriedly. She thrust her feet into her furred boots. "I will call you, Nancy, all right?"

"Ebriel—be careful!"

Ebriel felt the brilliance of her own smile. "Oh, yes. I will." She supposed she should feel regret, perhaps feel shame at her eagerness to leave, but she didn't. She only felt relief, and a burning desire for action, as she hurried out into the bright cold sunshine, tipping her head back to watch for the slender dragonfly shape of the copter.

36

Ebriel hurried through the streets of Xining, dodging icy puddles and gray mounds of crystallized snow. She heard the copter before she saw it, the whir of its blades singing through the clear sky, passing overhead just as she reached the edge of the city. She broke into an awkward run, her bag bouncing against her hip, her little bundle of belongings clutched to her chest. The sight of the bird filled her with joy at rejoining the Chain, going on a mission, being allowed to jump up into the copter and fly away, above the dreary Plateau, over the barley fields and the plodding herds of yak, through the mountain passes. She ran faster.

The copter lowered to hover over the abandoned store. Its tri-gear settled neatly onto the empty parking lot, its rotors slowing gradually. Panting, Ebriel ran across the cracked pavement and up to the bird just as the door retracted.

Ty grinned at her from the pilot's seat. "Hey, Eb. Ready for a fight?"

Kanika's eyes flashed dark fire. "Hello, Ebriel," she said, reaching down to give Ebriel a hand up. She took her bundle to stow it under one of the seats.

Breathless, Ebriel said, "*Merci*. Hello, Kanika. Hello, Ty."

She strapped herself in next to Ty as the bird lifted, tilted, accelerated toward the southwest. Ty spoke into her headset. "Starhold. We've got her." She listened to the flight monitor for a moment and said, "Okay." She pulled the headset off and turned her head to assess Ebriel.

"You're looking better than the last time I saw you," she said.

"I am more rested," Ebriel said.

"Yeah, well." Ty glanced ahead at the snowfields of the plateau, and then back at Ebriel. "I think it's more than that."

Ebriel lifted one shoulder. "*Mon amie.* When this is done, I will tell you all about it."

"Sure. Looking forward," Ty said dryly.

Ebriel looked back at Kanika. "You were at Xiao Qaidam," she said.

Kanika nodded. "We went to pick up some things from Perk," she said. "But now we get to do a mission instead."

"Ty, what do we know?" Ebriel asked. "Have they located the spaceplane?"

"If they haven't done it yet, they will soon, I'm afraid," Ty said. Her jaw tightened. "Damn that Glass, anyway. All we have is radio, because they shut down the microsats. No Newnet, no O-Net, no spybugs, but he doesn't care. It's all about power, with him. He just can't stand it that Papa doesn't fall under his control, like everything else in the world." She stretched her long arms over her head. "Still remember how to fly, Eb?"

"Oh, yes."

"Okay. Knock yourself out." Ty left her seat and went back to the galley for coffee. As she wriggled past Ebriel, she laid one hard hand on her shoulder. "Good to have you back."

Ebriel put her left hand on the collective, feeling it vibrate as the neural net adjusted the pitch. She watched the Tibetan Plateau flow past beneath them. It was glorious to be aloft, to be flying again! She only wished she had had a chance to say good-bye to James. With each kilometer they flew she drew farther and farther away from him. She felt a pang of longing to see his lean face, his clear dark eyes, to tell him . . . what? She couldn't tell him. She could never tell him.

The familiar dull pain grew in her midriff. She tried to breathe it away. She must concentrate on the difficult task ahead. This was no time for distractions.

There were two Security Corps copters, each with two pilots and six Corpsmen. Conversation was minimal, and James recognized no one. They were all in camouflage, weighted down with battle gear and night vision masks. The mission commander was Lieutenant Colonel Devlin, a thin man with flinty eyes. He eyed James without speaking for a moment. James stood with his hands crossed behind his back, waiting for his orders.

They were brief. "Major Bull, we're under the direct command of General Glass. This mission is need to know only. You'll have instructions when we reach our target."

James kept his expression blank. "Yes, sir."

It was a long, silent day of flying. The usual jokes and cameraderie were absent. No one mentioned their destination, but James kept an eye on the telemetry, and he knew when they passed over the Line of Partition in the South China Sea. Most of the men slept in their seats. James dropped his chin to his chest and folded his arms. He assessed his companions from beneath his lowered eyelids. He found them, to a man, as hard and dangerous as any he had ever encountered in the Corps. But it was Devlin, narrow-shouldered, shaven almost bald, with a voice like rocks grating together, who he watched most closely. Devlin spoke occasionally into his lipmike until they reached the mountainous region of Turkey. There he called radio silence. They flew on in a darkening sky.

James, too, was outfitted for combat, with a full block of caseless ammunition for his Glock and a mask hanging from his duty belt. He had hurried, in his billet, taking time to wrap a memory stick carefully in a tiny sheet of propylene. The memory stick held all the information he had collected, the O-Net video, the altered spybug routes, the default patterns. It was, in its way, as lethal a weapon as the little Glock at his hip. And it represented his final decision. He put it in an envelope and mailed it to Jimmy Walking Bull, Browning, Montana. Social Services would deliver it, in a week, perhaps two. His father would look at it, wonder, and set it aside to wait in plain sight in the old ranch house, more secure than any lockbox could make it.

He supposed that Ebriel, when he didn't make his customary call, would wonder, would perhaps miss him, or feel hurt. He was ready for whatever was to come. But he wished he could have seen her one more time. He wished he could have said good-bye.

Ty, Ebriel, and Kanika conversed casually, talking of trivial things, until they approached the African coastline. Then they fell silent, listening to the monitor's voice, and to Nenet's. *Troll* had landed at Siwa on schedule, with the flight crew and four of the Chain aboard. The long Egyptian evening faded slowly, the last of the day's light clinging to the rocks and the long, curling dunes as the copter flew over the old city. The ruins of Amoun and the blackened hulk of the bombed hotel lay in deep shadows.

"Good thing is, they're as blind as we are." Ty bared her teeth in a hawklike grin. "This'll be a good old-fashioned battle," she said. "We've never had it straight out like this—always been flank stuff, strike and run, just harrying them when we could. This will be a fight. Us and them." She sobered and looked out at the sand sea flowing beneath them. "Someone's bound to die tonight," she muttered, as if to herself.

Kanika's eyes flashed white. Ebriel's pulse beat hard in her throat.

Ty set the copter down beyond the old town, in the space between two olive groves. Ebriel had the shortband in her hand. "Nenet says she and the others are in the hangar. No sign of other aircraft yet."

"No, but they're coming."

"I know."

Ty squinted at her. "Yeah. You can feel it, can't you?"

"*Oui.*"

"Me, too." Ty strapped on her duty belt. "Eb, I brought you a belt. It's in my duffel, behind the seats. Kanika, are you ready?"

Kanika said, "Ready," but her voice shook. Ebriel cast her a sympathetic glance.

"If I were them, I'd try to pull off this little show in the dark," Ty said with deliberate casualness. "And they won't want to give us a chance to refuel *Troll* in the morning and lift her off again. That means they're coming tonight." She retracted the copter's door, and then said, over her shoulder, "Hope there aren't too many of 'em."

Ebriel found the duty belt and wound it around her. She had already changed into a utility suit and reveled in its familiar sleek flexibility, the strong, light boots on her feet. "Ready, Ty," she said.

And she was ready. But ready in a different way this time. When she and Ty had rescued the Russian children from their swamping boat, or when they had pulled Yasmine from her house, and especially when she herself had pursued George Glass through the streets of Keelung, she had been fired with the energy of a madwoman, the intensity that came from a total lack of fear. Now she felt the fear, but she held it closeted in a narrow space behind her active mind, real, but irrelevant. Now she had a goal that was bigger than herself.

She also cared a great deal about coming out of this battle alive. She believed that was an asset to the fight, a strength rather than a weakness. Her readiness was a cool thing, a controlled thing. It made her stronger.

The three of them jumped down from the copter, making sure all its lights were off. It would be invisible from the air, at least in darkness. With Ty leading, they wound their way through the olive grove, where the first creamy blossoms had just opened. Ebriel thought idly how strange it was that the olive blossoms, lovely as they were, had no fragrance, when the oil of the fruit had such a rich perfume. She smelled only soil and sand and clean desert air. There was no moon, but the stars gave a clear light, and their eyes adjusted quickly. They walked surely and swiftly toward the base, listening for the sounds of approaching aircraft.

Not until they reached the mud-brick ruins on the hill above the airfield did they use the shortband again. "Nenet," Ty said quietly. "We're here now. We'll stay up here, watch the sky, and let you know."

"Very well," Nenet said calmly.

"Everybody armed? What have you got?"

"Everyone has a pulse pistol. We have two Glocks. One rifle only."

"Right. Hang on, then. Soon as we see where they land, we'll have a plan."

"Very well."

Ty led the way to a spot at the base of a crumbling wall where they could sit, leaning their backs on the cool stone, watching the night sky. They sat still, conserving their energy. Kanika moved once or twice, restlessly, nervously, but Ty didn't reprimand her. Ebriel tilted her head back against the stone and stared up into the stars.

James would be sleeping now, or perhaps just rising. He would have tried to reach her last night. Would he be hurt that she didn't answer his call? In the months since he had been in Quezon City, they had talked every week. She hoped he would not misunderstand.

The night stretched on, hours of the deep, wide silence of the desert, disturbed only by the faint susurration of the desert breeze over the sand. Ebriel imagined she could hear the individual grains rolling along the shifting surface of the desert, colliding with each other, changing course, settling in new places. With a start, she realized she had dozed, her head falling back against the stone. She sat up straight and rubbed a kink out of her neck.

Ty, crosslegged beside her, turned her face to the north and held up a hand for silence.

Ebriel heard it, too, the slap-slap of the sculpted rotor blades, gradually and steadily increasing in volume. "How many?" she breathed.

"Two, I think." Ty got to her feet, stretching her calves, shaking the kinks out of her arms. "They'll be small, for speed and maneuverability, but they'll be full. Probably be twelve in all."

"We are outnumbered, then," Kanika said. Her voice broke.

Ebriel felt only relief that the waiting was over.

Ty spoke into the shortband. "Nenet? Hear 'em?" And when Nenet responded she said, "Okay. We're coming down."

"Can they hear the shortband?" Ebriel asked as they picked their way down the stony hill.

"Doubt it," Ty said. "They'd have to stumble on the frequency by accident."

The sound of the copters grew louder, and now they could see them, polycarb windows gleaming with starlight, hazard lights blinking dimly as they rose over the dunes and made a great circle over the deserted city, then swooped over the hill and down into the shallow valley that sheltered the airfield. Ebriel scanned the runways spreading out from the barracks, the dark shadows of abandoned machinery scattered here and there. At the end of the longest runway, closest to the hangar, the great hulk of *Troll* waited under a giant tarpaulin of coated fabric.

She felt as if the pounding of her own heart might be louder than the beat of the copter rotors. It was as if this were her first mission, because she was a new person, different from before. The copters were familiar-looking—well, of course, because the Chain's copters were all stolen from InCo Forces. They hovered above a dune west of the landing field and sank slowly behind, birds of prey settling to earth. Ebriel and Ty and Kanika reached the narrow alley between the barracks. Through the little window to her right, Ebriel saw the white gleam of kitchen appliances, the silver shine of a faucet in Nenet's common room.

Ty and Nenet were speaking in low voices over the shortband. "We can't let them get near it," Ty whispered. "If they get there first, we won't be able to stop them. Yeah, we'll make a triangle. When they move out, when they're, say, a hundred meters, you can fire. Stay in the cover of the hangar as long as you can." Nenet gave a short answer. Ty said, "Good luck."

Ebriel and Kanika watched Ty's hand, waiting for the signal.

"Remember," was Ty's last instruction. "Those Glocks cover a lot of distance. I wish we had more of them, but it's too late to worry about that now. They want the spaceplane, and they won't take a chance puncturing the hull with projectiles, so we'll keep her between us. We have the element of surprise, because they won't be expecting a fight. But remember, once they're clear of *Troll,* they won't be afraid to use their Glocks. We have to be ready, act fast. Clear?"

Together, Kanika and Ebriel breathed, "Yes." Kanika's arm trembled against Ebriel's.

Not until the InCo birds, flying in tandem, reached the great sand sea of the Western Desert did James know what the mission was. Devlin briefed them as the copters banked and began a long, slow descent over the desert, the rolling dunes mist-pale in the starlight. "The target's a spaceplane," the commander said. "It's on the ground at an abandoned Egyptian air base. Should be a piece of cake. Even if they know we're coming, they're not military. Any resistance will fold up like a newspaper in the rain. And don't fire anywhere near the target. The general has no use for a spaceplane with holes in it. Questions?"

There were none. "Okay. We're landing to the west. The target is on the eastern end of one of the runways, the longest. We'll deploy in twos, on the north and the south flank. If all goes well, we march in and surround the thing, take it over." There were nods, and the Corpsmen pulled on their night vision masks. "Bull," Devlin said. "You're with me."

"Sir." If James had any doubts before about the nature of the mission, they evaporated. There were only two spaceplanes in existence, and they both belonged to Ethan Fleck. This operation was a direct violation of InCo policy, and would be considered an act of war by Oceania, if it came to light. Perhaps it was true that Security Corps didn't expect a fight, but James understood there was to be at least one casualty. And he was it.

The InCo copters landed three hundred meters from *Troll's* position, in the lee of a long dune. The Chain couldn't see the Corpsmen until they swarmed silently over the mound of sand, faces masked, camouflaged figures indistinct in the starlight. Ty had been right, of course. The Chain was badly outnumbered. But they had a certain strength of their own, Ebriel assured herself. They had their sense of purpose. She sent a wordless prayer into the night.

Ty hissed, "Now!"

Later Ebriel remembered the battle as a blur, a swiftly moving stream of images and impressions and noises, the thud of bullets striking wood and concrete and flesh, the sibilant hum of pulse pistols, the muffled grunts of close fighting, the stifled cries of the wounded.

The attackers raced over the dune and fanned out, too many targets, too far apart. The Chain members in the hangar took two before the Corpsmen realized there would be resistance.

Ty and Kanika and Ebriel broke cover and raced toward the covered bulk of the spaceplane. In the dark, with their view blocked by *Troll's* blurred silhouette, they heard the plosive report of the Chain's single rifle, the smaller percussion of the Glocks.

Their responsibility was *Troll*. They reached the slight shelter afforded by a deep fold of the tarp where it swept back from the nose and up over the wing. They pressed their backs to the fuselage, weapons ready.

Kanika stood on Ebriel's left, breathing hard. To the right was Ty, her body hot, radiating energy. In the middle, Ebriel took deliberate breaths. She knew that the months away from the dojo had weakened her muscles, perhaps dulled her reactions. She must focus her mind, allow nothing to distract her. There was no time now to be afraid.

The sounds of fighting reached them from the far side of the spaceplane. Ebriel flexed her ankles, loosened her shoulders, concentrated. And so when he came, a short, heavily built figure slipping around the nose of the spaceplane, feeling his way, spotting the Chain and taking aim at the closest of them, she was ready. She felt as sharp as a knife blade, hard and flexible. All sound faded away. Nothing existed in her world but the enemy.

He was faceless behind his mask, anonymous, almost unreal. When his arm came up, Ebriel saw the small Glock glittering in his fist. He aimed it directly at the young, untried, and terrified Kanika.

The girl froze, mouth open, the whites of her eyes glistening in the starlight.

At the same moment, another Corpsman crept around the tail, stepping carefully over the tie-downs that secured the tarp. Ebriel had already turned to her left. She felt the heat of Ty's body against her back, the tensing of Ty's shoulder as she prepared to deal with the second commando. Ebriel leaped away from her position, shouting to distract the enemy's attention from Kanika, leveling her pistol, firing. There was a tight report as the Glock fired, a sound that pierced the ear. And it was all Ebriel knew of the battle for *Troll*.

Later, much later, she learned that Kanika, seeing Ebriel fall, broke out of her trance and fired her pulse pistol pointblank. Loyalty proved a powerful weapon.

The Corpsman slumped to the bitumen of the landing field, dead within seconds. Ebriel was more fortunate.

She had been in motion, midstep, whirling to fire. The commando's caseless bullet had caught her just below her collarbone, tearing through the soft flesh of her breast, banging along one rib at a forty-five degree angle. It glanced off the bone, fracturing it, shocking her arm to nervelessness. The projectile exited under her left armpit. The force of the shot drove her backward, and she struck the asphalt, hard. She lay still, her breath gone, gazing in amazement at the bright stars wheeling crazily above her.

37

James followed Devlin's narrow-shouldered figure to
the north, in the left flank of the formation. In his peripheral
vision, he saw the Corpsmen scattering neatly, ready to surround the spaceplane. James's scalp itched unbearably. He
kept his eyes on the man ahead of him and missed the first
clash with the defenders. The sound of weapons fire shocked
him, and instinctively, he crouched, still watching Devlin,
every nerve screaming alarm.

In his earplant, he heard curses, grunted commands. The
dull thud of flesh and bone colliding with the cracked pavement sickened him. He didn't dare take his eyes off Devlin.
Bent at the waist, he kept pace with him, staying slightly to
his right. Devlin broke into a run, and James followed, tensed
for the blow that could be a bullet.

A man raced from the protection of the hangar with a reckless courage that stirred his admiration. Surely these were
trained fighters here! This was not the easy mark the Corps
had expected. With the green-limned clarity of the night vision mask, James saw the defender dash to the inadequate
shelter of an abandoned tractor, firing a weapon, providing
cover for two more, who dove behind a bit of broken wall.
The voices in his ear were grim. Already two Corpsmen were

down, and they had scattered their forces. Like the defenders, they ducked behind whatever hardware they could find.

But James had to watch Devlin, to watch for the moment of betrayal. His breath came faster as the thin man veered to the left, leaving the rutted tarmac of the runway for the packed sand and dry grass beside it.

Devlin gave the hand signal for James to move ahead of him.

This was it, then. It had to be. There was no strategic reason to send James forward, out into the open of the landing strip. This was the moment Thurgren had warned him about.

There was no place for him to hide. Two Corpsmen, risking the fire of the defenders, were already halfway to the target, the shrouded bulk of the spaceplane at the end of the runway. Others were engaged to James's right. Even now one of them fell, grunting.

To James's left, his private enemy slowed, weapon at the ready, face angled to see that James obeyed his order.

James feinted, one quick, short step forward. Devlin's arm came up, following him, wasting no time. The little Glock was a shadow in his fist.

And then James hissed a warning. "Sir! Behind you!" He raised his own gun to train it on an imaginary target in the shadows of the north side of the landing strip. Devlin whirled to see what he was aiming at, diverting his weapon to defend himself. A fraction of a second later, he realized the misdirection, and with a snarl of fury, he swung his weapon back to its original target. But James was no longer there.

James felt the scrape of the tarmac on his shoulders as he dropped and rolled, and then the grit of sand against his cheek and in his hair. Devlin was already four strides ahead of him, whirling to find him, his mask glinting. Dawn had begun to lighten the eastern sky. Devlin dropped to the ground, too, unwilling to expose his back to the fight that now raged openly between him and the spaceplane.

The battle had grown noisy. Vaguely, James heard cries in other languages, shouts that rang out in the empty desert air. Spent rounds thwacked against the concrete of the airfield, and against flesh. The defenders were few, but they were determined, and the Corpsmen, for the moment, had lost their leader. James came to rest on his belly in the sand, facing Devlin. He steadied his Glock with his left hand under his right wrist, and they glared at each other.

Time suspended. The fighting went on, and the sky grew rosy. James recognized the moment, the pause before the drama, the anticipation and the dread, the blend of triumph and tragedy. Only this time, the prey in his sights was a man. A dishonorable man, perhaps, a deceitful man. But a human being.

Even as the perception was born, he understood that Devlin would feel no such compunction. The only constraint he would recognize was the barrel of James's weapon trained directly on him.

"Drop it, Bull," Devlin grated.

James didn't answer. He knew. He knew he was a better shot, faster, more focused. He knew when his prey was about to move. The stinging of his scalp subsided. He drew his bead, and watched Devlin's hand.

When Devlin's finger tightened on the trigger of the Glock, James had already fired.

James stripped off his mask and left it lying beside Devlin's still form. He crouched behind an abandoned oil drum and tried to discern his situation. The desert dawn came quickly, night shadows fading before the onslaught of a red, rising sun.

His earplant chattered. He thought quickly, then tongued his lipmike. "Devlin's out," he said flatly.

There was a pause, and then the second in command snapped, "Bull? Where are you?"

James didn't answer. He stayed where he was, keeping his head down behind the rusted drum. He had no way of knowing if the second in command had the same orders Devlin had. But his instincts told him that no one expected him to return from this mission.

"Bull?" The voice vibrated with anger, with enmity, the voice of someone he barely knew. He said nothing.

For James, the battle was over. The last shreds of his loyalty to Security Corps dissipated in the dry desert air, and he was left with no allegiance at all.

* * *

Within half an hour, the remnants of the attacking force, with three wounded, retreated to their copters on the far side of the sand dune and made their escape. Devlin's second in command, a sergeant major, walked out into the open with a white handkerchief in his hand. He laid his weapon on the ground, along with his night vision mask. The defenders held their fire as the sergeant major and another Corpsman retrieved their dead comrades from the tarmac. When the attackers retreated, they left the weapon and the mask behind.

James listened through his earplant, heard the curses of frustrated soldiers, the groans of the wounded, the muttered comments as they loaded into the copters. One, and only one, Corpsman asked about what happened to Bull, but the answer was unintelligible. No one came looking for him. He stayed where he was, hunkered behind a rusted oil drum on the south side of the airfield. The heat rose quickly as the defenders of the spaceplane collected their own casualties from the field of battle. He heard their muffled voices, a single cry of pain from one of their wounded, their shuffling footsteps as they carried whoever it was away.

At last silence fell over the airfield. The morning sun, in full spate, beat on James's back, and sweat rolled down his neck and his ribs. He cast around for a place to conceal himself. There was a second hangar, and he thought he caught a glimpse of the silver-blue of a copter there, something that startled him. How could there be a copter here, and whose was it? The barracks around him appeared to be abandoned. It was the distance between his current position and the buildings that concerned him first, and then the distance between this airfield, wherever it was, and anyplace safe he could go. If the defending fighters caught sight of him in his camouflage, they would surely assume the worst.

He squatted where he was for a long time, listening, watching, glad to be alive but at a loss for his next step. When he judged that no one was coming out of the barracks for the moment, he chose one of the empty buildings and made a run for it.

* * *

Inside Nenet's common room, Ty supervised a makeshift field hospital. Ebriel regained consciousness to find Nenet pressing bandages tightly over her left breast and under her arm, winding strips of gauze, strapping her arm down to hold the bandages in place. Ebriel had no feeling in the arm itself, but the pain in the wound made her grit her teeth. Nenet, pulling the elastic strapping tight, said, "I am sorry. We must staunch the bleeding first."

Ty pressed a narcotic ampoule to the inside of Ebriel's right elbow.

Ebriel sighed with relief. *"Merci,"* she said weakly. For a terrible moment she thought her breast was gone, but looking down, she saw the meager swell of it beneath the brown elastic. She sighed again and looked up at Ty's grim face. "Is it over?"

"Yeah," Ty answered. "But we lost Simon Blake."

"Oh, no. I am so sorry." Ebriel let her eyelids droop under the welcome relief the narcotic gave her. "Oh, Ty. And *Troll*?"

"Safe." Ty adjusted a pillow beneath Ebriel's neck. "You okay?"

"Oui. But what happened, Ty?"

"They weren't expecting a fight," Ty said in a flat tone. "They might still have beaten us, because there were a lot of 'em. But they didn't." She stood up. "Couple of 'em went down, and they bumped around for a bit before they regrouped, gave us an edge. But too late for Simon. He took a round right in the chest. He never had a chance."

"Will they come again?"

Ty shook her head. "I don't think so. They can't get away with this stuff. Everybody knows Ethan is neutral. Starhold will lodge a protest, and that'll make it public. Put a stop to it. Of course, nobody will own up to this. And we can't make too much of it, or we expose the Chain. Kind of a standoff."

Nenet came to bend over Ebriel and run careful fingers over the bandage. "It is a clean wound," she said. "She was lucky, though I expect the rib is fractured. But she cannot fly in the spaceplane, not with this."

"We'll figure something out," Ty said. Gently, she touched

Ebriel's hair with her big hand. "Rest now, partner. I'm taking burial detail."

And then Kanika was kneeling beside the pallet, her eyes wide, her full lips trembling "Ebriel! You saved my life, and I almost got you killed. I am so sorry!" Tears spilled over her dark cheeks.

"*Zut,*" Ebriel said with a breath of a laugh. "I am not killed, *chérie.* I am here, and so are you! Do not cry, now. You are needed. Go and help Nenet."

Kanika nodded, dashing away tears with her hands, and stood to go in search of Nenet.

Ebriel's eyelids drooped again, the narcotic making her drowsy. She looked down at her fingers, her hand bound tightly against her chest. They were nerveless, numb. She couldn't move them. She hoped she hadn't lost the use of her arm. How would she play her flute, with only one hand?

James rested his back against the fractured drywall of a gutted building. It looked to him as if it must once have been a barracks, small rooms opening off a long narrow hallway, the broken pipes and wiring that meant there had once been appliances. Beneath him, dust and plaster crunched when he moved. The broken windows let in the midday heat. His throat burned with thirst. He stripped to his undershirt, letting the air cool his bared arms and chest. He didn't take off his boots, worried that he might have to make a run for it at any moment.

He tipped his head back against the gritty wall and closed his eyes. In a jam now, Bull, he thought. Egypt! The thought made him chuckle. How the hell was he ever going to get out of Egypt? And who were these people who had surprised, and then fought off, a squad of Security Corpsmen? It was perfectly likely, he reflected, that having escaped an attempt on his life by Dirty Tricks Corps, he was now going to perish in the latent countries, from thirst, hunger, or one of the biochemical plagues InCo claimed were raging through the African continent. He thought of the cool Montana mountains, and a shiver of longing ran through him. He had never felt so displaced, not even when he first left Browning and rode alone to

Great Falls. He would have to wait, he supposed, until night. But what would he do then? Where could he go?

Uncomfortable as he was, the oppressive heat and the hours of sleeplessness began to catch up with him. He dozed, and woke with a start to find his mouth dry, his neck stiff. He heard voices, and footsteps on the gravel walks between the buildings.

Carefully, trying not to make noise on the gritty floor, he pushed away from the wall and crept to the window. With infinite care, he straightened, his hands on the windowsill, cautious of the shards of broken glass still in the sash. He rose just enough to peer out, but whoever it was had already gone past his hiding place, and was headed away from the barracks, up the hill to the ruins. He crouched down again, listening.

From a short distance, he heard the muted sounds of conversation and the dull clinking of metal and porcelain. Soon after, the smells of cooking wafted through the open window. James swallowed, tormented by hunger and thirst. But he waited.

An hour went by, and then another. James dozed, woke, dozed again. The heat became almost intolerable, but his thirst was worse. He told himself he need only wait until dark, and then he would make his way toward the old village he had seen as they flew over. He wouldn't be able to understand the language, or make himself understood, but he could at least find water. And then what? He had no idea.

The shadows were lengthening between the abandoned buildings when he heard the voices again, and the crunch of booted feet. He came to his knees and peered over the sill, trying to glimpse the owner of the boots.

He saw a tall figure with cropped blond hair and broad shoulders. He knew her! He had met this woman once, in a wooded park outside Keelung. He had seen her on that broadcast, lurking at the edge of Ariana Park. Damn! He cursed his slow mind, muzzy with heat and fatigue. What was her name? He couldn't think . . .

Ty! That was it. Ebriel had introduced her. "Ty!" he tried to call. His voice was hoarse, and it cracked into nothingness. He tried again. "Ty!" It was a bit stronger, but her lanky figure had already disappeared around the corner of the building.

He held his breath.

And then he heard a single step, a murmured command. She sidled to the corner and peered around it, her craggy features wary.

James put both his hands up into the empty window frame, palms out. "Ty," he said. He laughed with relief, with surprise. His voice cracked. "Ty, it's me. It's James, from Keelung. James Bull."

Yasmine, floating beside Papa's chair, gazed curiously at the man's face on the panel, briefly distracted from her worry over Ebriel. She had never seen an InCo soldier before. His uniform was strange, oddly patterned in what looked vaguely like green and brown leaves. The microsats were still down, but they could use a direct-feed from Siwa because their orbit was so close. The transmission was excellent, with almost no delay. She could clearly see his dark features, the arching nose, the tiny trefoil mark on his left cheekbone. Ty and Nenet Nasser flanked him, their silhouettes sharp against the white walls of the common room.

Ethan's synthesizer spoke. "This is—the man, Ty?"

Ty nodded. "He's the one who brought Ebriel out of Keelung," she said. She sounded tired and tense, and her features were drawn. "I met him at Ebriel's crash site."

The man spoke in a deep voice. "I'm James Bull, sir." He was almost as dark as Yasmine herself, with sharply planed cheekbones. His eyes were long and narrow, reddened now with fatigue. They had had a bad time, all of them. Yasmine had not yet taken in the immensity of the loss of Simon Blake. She wrapped her arms around herself.

"You're—Security Corps," Ethan said, and James Bull nodded. "Deserted?"

Yasmine saw the man wince at the word. She didn't know why.

"Sir," he began, and then stopped, lowering his eyes.

Ty leaned toward the camera. "Papa," she said. "His CO took a shot at him."

James Bull startled, and looked at her. "You saw that?"

"Yeah." Ty leaned back again. "You better explain to Dr. Fleck."

He turned his eyes back to the camera, and Yasmine saw the question in his eyes. How strange it must be to see the slack-faced man strapped into a floating chair, only his mouth and his eyes and the tips of his fingers mobile. She felt defensive for Papa, because of course James Bull could not know how great and kind and wise a man he was.

James Bull took a deep breath, and his jaw flexed. "Sir, the operation here was not sanctioned by InCo, or even Security Corps. It was black ops—sometimes referred to as Dirty Tricks Corps."

"I know about—Dirty Tricks Corps, Major," Ethan said.

"Yes, sir. I, uh, I didn't believe it existed until Keelung. And I didn't have the option of refusing this assignment. But I knew, or at least I was warned, that I wasn't supposed to come back from it."

"Someone in—Security Corps—wants you out?"

James nodded, his mouth a bitter line. "Dr. Fleck, sir, I took it on myself to do a little digging. The *L'Oiseau blanc* incident. I found the original spybug record. General Glass sent a team out from Greece to intercept the yacht, believing they were carrying medical contraband. Something went wrong, I couldn't find out what, but something went haywire—" Yasmine frowned over the unfamiliar term. "I can imagine someone tried to resist, pulled a gun. Everyone on the boat was killed, and a couple of Corpsmen, too. The team burned the yacht to hide their mistake. Glass covered the incident up." He shrugged. "That's what I found, sir. I lodged an official protest. I was warned against it, but . . ." He lifted one long-fingered hand, and let it drop. "But I had to."

"I thought it must be—something like that. So you—can't go back—to the Corps."

"No, sir." James closed his mouth, jaw muscles jumping, and waited for judgment.

"Ty?" Ethan said.

"It's fine, Papa," Ty said. "He can stay here, and we'll figure something out."

James glanced at her, then back at Ethan's image. He must have been full of questions, Yasmine thought, but he didn't ask them.

At last Ethan asked the question that had been tormenting Yasmine. "How is Ebriel?"

Ty said, "She'll be okay, thank God. It could have been nasty, but she took the slug at an angle. It missed the lung, and the clavicle. I think she broke a rib. She'll be laid up for a while."

"Keep us—informed," Ethan said, and ended the conversation.

He turned his chair and drifted slowly to the space window. Yasmine followed, relieved to hear that Ebriel would recover, puzzled over James Bull, who and what he was. "Papa?"

At first he seemed not to hear her. He slumped in his chair, his eyes on the stars. His fingers moved on the keyboard. "What a—terrible thing, Yasmine," he said. She wasn't sure which terrible thing he meant. "Those poor—innocent people. Ebriel's family. They were—victims of the quarantine—as much as the latent countries. Wasted—deaths. Meaningless."

He fell silent, and Yasmine only hovered beside him, her small hand on his shoulder. There was nothing she could say.

Ebriel dreamed. She was wandering through a needle-strewn forest, unfamiliar peaks towering above her head and a meadow of some thick, waist-high grass stretching out before her. She was trying to reach a little clear stream that ran over a rocky bed, but the grass was so dense, she could hardly push her feet through it. The blades tickled her bare arms, cool and scratchy and fragrant. She heard Ty's voice, saying her name, and she wondered what Ty was doing in the mountains of North America.

She started awake. Ty was bending over her. "Eb," she said again.

Ebriel blinked, coming out of her dream, realizing where she was. Nenet's kitchen. Siwa. The battle.

"Ebriel," Ty said. "There's someone here who wants to see you."

38

Ebriel took a sharp breath, and regretted it. Even through the pain medication, the breath hurt. But the stab of pain assured her she wasn't dreaming.

He looked just as she remembered. The tattoo crinkled slightly as he smiled down at her. His eyes were long and narrow. She lifted her good hand, her right hand, and touched his cheek with her fingers as if to be certain he was real. "James?" she whispered. *"C'est toi?"*

"Ebriel," he murmured. "Don't talk. Rest."

"But is it true? *C'est possible*—you are really here?"

He smoothed her hair back from her damp temples. His long fingers felt cool against her hot skin. "I'm really here," he said. "It's a long story. You rest, and I'll explain when you're feeling better."

She caught his hand with hers and tried to hold it, but her own fingers were weak, and they slipped free. "James, how— I—" Her eyelids drooped, and the room spun about her.

"Later," he said somberly. "Sleep now."

Hours later, when she woke, she raised her head to glance around, searching, sure she must have imagined it, dreamed it. But she hadn't. It was true. He was there. She saw his tall figure seated next to Ty, outlined by the light from the glowing panel. She laid her head back on the pallet, and slept again.

Troll left the next morning, with Kanika, Ty, and all her original crew and passengers except Simon Blake. They had laid Simon to rest under the ruins of Amoun, in the company of a hundred other unknown warriors. The two Chain members who had received light wounds were judged safe to fly.

Ebriel, shaky and weak, walked with cautious steps, leaning on James's arm, to the landing strip to watch the spaceplane depart. James still wore his camouflage trousers and the sleeveless brown undershirt of his uniform. Nenet could find no clothes to fit his long legs. He carried a stool for Ebriel and settled her on it. Nenet and Ty, following Dr. Nordstrom's instructions, had dressed her wound, put in a drain, rebandaged it and rebound her arm. She still had no feeling in her hand, but nothing could be done about testing for nerve damage. She was to rest for a week and then begin only gentle activities.

Troll lifted off with that deep roll of thunder that thrilled in the ears and shook the earth.

Ebriel glanced up and saw the blaze in James's eyes as he watched *Troll* depart. She remembered her own awe the first time she had seen it, and she wished now they were both aboard. But James didn't know yet what Starhold meant. It was up to her to explain. She hoped he would understand.

The pain medication made everything surreal. It was like dreaming to experience James's physical presence, to look up at his dark profile, to feel the solidity of his arm supporting her. After the months spent with women and children, his very maleness, his strong-fingered hands, his deep voice, the smell of his skin, surprised her. And reminded her.

In her brief, troubled sleep last night she had dreamed that she saw Paul, in a ridiculously small boat, drifting away from her on a dark ocean. Though she stood on the shore, calling after him, he didn't answer, nor did he look back. She woke to the fierce ache of her injury and a helpless guilt, because she was still alive when Paul was not.

The walk back to the common room was almost more than

Ebriel could manage. Her head swam, and her left breast felt as if it were on fire. James helped her to lie down, cushioned her head, brought her a glass of *khaloub*. With gentle fingers, he removed her bandages, cleaned the crusts of blood and serous fluid from her skin, careful not to disturb the drain. He applied new bandages, smoothing them carefully over her skin. He rebuttoned her shirt and then bound her arm once again.

"Merci," she whispered. "Are you a medic, too?"

"No," he said. He had a slow smile that just curled the corners of his long, thin-lipped mouth. She hadn't known that before. "I'm just a soldier."

Nenet frowned at the thinness of Ebriel's pallet. "I will make up a room for you," she said. "A better bed, someplace you won't be disturbed."

James straightened. "Let me do that, ma'am. Just show me where things are." Nenet nodded her thanks.

Ebriel let her eyes close. It was lovely to be taken care of, after so many months . . . She thought of Nancy Chao, laboring endlessly at the Children's Home. She must do something to help her . . . she must tell Perk . . . But she slept before she completed the thought.

After a week of bed rest, Ebriel felt strong enough to be up and around, to help Nenet a bit with cooking and to take short walks with James around the old airfield. James had been busy, working on a list of repairs he had persuaded Nenet to give him, going over the two copters stored in the hangars, sweeping and cleaning when those chores were completed, putting everything in military order. Eight days after *Troll* left, Nenet went off to the old town to buy oil, bread, and carob. The heat of the day had begun to lessen. Ebriel was sitting in a comfortable chair in Nenet's living quarters, scanning news on the panel. James pulled a chair up beside her.

"Anything interesting?"

She smiled at him over her shoulder. "It is mostly propaganda. Stories of how well InCo citizens are living."

"Not all of them," he said.

"No, I know this, James. Even in Paris, it was—somehow

shallow." She leaned back, wiggling her fingers under the elastic strapping. She was relieved to feel some sensation in them. "There has been nothing about *Troll,* or about Papa."

"Papa?"

"I mean, Ethan Fleck. The habitat."

James wasn't watching the panel, but Ebriel's face. "But you weren't on the habitat," he said slowly. "Were you? I mean, when we talked you were in China."

"Oui." She turned her body to face him.

His eyes were very clear, their irises a rich brown. "What's the connection, Ebriel?"

She laughed a little. "I hardly know how to tell you, James. But—I have been on the habitat. On Starhold."

He raised an eyebrow at the name.

She laughed. "It was to be Star Hotel One, did you know that? And now they—those who live there—they call it Starhold. It is very romantic, *vraiment!"*

"Ebriel," he said. "Will you explain it to me, now?"

She did, as best she could. She told him about Ethan Fleck, and Semaya, and the staff who maintained the habitat. Then she told him about the Chain, the dojo, Tacticals, the flight monitor. And last, choosing her words with care, she tried to explain about the children.

He didn't speak until she finished, giving her little shrug. "That is all, James."

He was silent for several moments. Newnet buzzed in the background, a blur of voices and images. At last he said, "It doesn't seem possible."

"No, so I thought myself."

And then he said, "But it's no wonder."

"What?"

"It's no wonder General Glass wanted the spaceplane. He thinks Fleck is connected to Red Omega. If he heard this—" James shook his head. "He wouldn't rest until he had it."

Ebriel said softly, "There is a connection, sometimes." She looked away, stared blindly out the window at the slanting shadows. "Oh, James—I hate him."

"I know."

"I know he is responsible for what happened to my family. I just cannot prove it."

"But I can, Ebriel. I can prove it."

She glanced up at him, startled. *"Quoi?"*

"After I met you, I did some digging around. It's why they were after me, why I wasn't supposed to come back from this mission. I found the altered spybug records, and I lodged a protest." His lips tightened. "Security Corps didn't like it."

"But—but, James, do you have them? The records?"

"Not here. But I know where they are."

Ebriel's eyes filled with tears as he told her that Glass had sent Dirty Tricks Corps after *L'Oiseau blanc,* convinced she was carrying illegal medicines. There were shots fired. Then, to hide their mistake, they destroyed the yacht.

"It was because your husband and his father were physicians. So many in Red Omega are. They take supplies out of the InCo hospitals, right out of the delivery vans and clinics. Glass was going to claim policy violation, I'm sure, make an example of them. But they found nothing on the yacht. Nothing."

Ebriel hung her head, letting her tears drop into her lap. "But how could they do it? A little girl—just a child—"

James shook his head. Shame made his voice harsh. "I'm sorry, Ebriel. I can't explain it. War, and soldiers, and orders—they are no excuse. Something went wrong, the way things sometimes go wrong in wars. Sometimes children die, too, the way yours did. No one can ever explain such things—and in this case, they didn't try to explain. They covered it up."

She pressed her hand to her mouth, covering a sob. He wanted to hold her, to draw her to him and comfort her. Her grief set her apart. He hadn't known her husband or her daughter. He couldn't share her suffering.

After a time, she lifted her head. Her eyelashes still sparkled with tears, and her lips trembled, but her voice was hard. "Can we use your evidence, James? Can we expose Glass?"

"Yes," he said. "I think we can. I think we must."

Yasmine floated beside Papa's chair and smiled at Ebriel's image. It was a relief to see her. Her left arm rested in a sling, but she looked well, her color good, her hair shining silver. "Hello, Yasmine." The dark man sat next to her, just at her shoulder. Yasmine saw that they were not touching, but that they were close, bound together by some ineffable tie. It was not a visible connection, but she felt it as a tangible thing. She hoped, for Ebriel's sake, that James Bull was as strong and honorable as he appeared to be.

Ethan touched his keyboard. "It's—good to see you—Ebriel."

Ebriel smiled. "Papa. I like your new voice."

Ethan's mouth stretched in his grimacing smile and collapsed immediately. Ebriel frowned, but the synthesizer spoke smoothly. "Thank you. I could—start a new—career, I think."

Ebriel explained what she and James wanted to do. "It would mean taking one of the copters," she said.

"I have the spybug deployment patterns," James said. "And I've figured our course. It's a long flight, but there's virtually no air traffic over Canada. We can do it, sir."

Yasmine glanced at Ethan and saw by the flicker of his eyes that he had the same question she did. "You mustn't be caught," she said.

It was James Bull who answered. "Right. The only InCo presence in Browning is a Social Services office. The town is isolated. I know a place in the mountains we can set down. And I instructed my father to release the memory stick to one of the underground nets if anything happened to me." He and Ebriel looked at each other and then back at the image from Starhold. "It's not perfect insurance, but it's better than nothing."

Ethan's fingers moved on the keyboard.

"The reward is—worth the risk," the rich voice said.

James Bull nodded. "I agree, sir. I think we can do it."

"I do, too" Ebriel said. "With your approval, Papa. And," she smiled, "Yasmine's."

"Be careful," Ethan's voice said.

"We will," Ebriel answered. "Wish us luck."

"Will you want the flight monitor?" Yasmine asked.

"No, ma'am," James Bull said. "Better chance of slipping through the spybug net if we keep radio silence."

"When you have the memory stick, you can transmit it to one of Papa's contacts, who runs an underground network out

of New Zealand. He will know what to do. We are sending his
address."

"Bon." Yasmine sent the routing symbols, and Ebriel nodded. "Yes, it is coming through now. Thank you, Yasmine.
Papa."

"Ebriel," the voice synthesizer said. Ebriel raised her eyebrows. "Your hand—is it better?"

She moved her fingertips in answer. "A little better. I have
feeling in my fingers, and in my palm. Dr. Nordstrom says
that's a good sign. My arm is still numb."

Ethan said only, "Your flute?"

"I have it with me. When I return, perhaps I will be able to
play for you."

"Good news. I will look—forward to that—very much."

After a quiet meal of vegetable soup and fresh flat
bread, James cleared away the dishes and Nenet went to her
bed early. Ebriel rested in the most comfortable chair, flexing
her fingers over and over. Sometimes the nerves tingled, as if
her arm had fallen asleep.

"Are you tired?" James asked, folding a towel and hanging
it over the edge of the sink.

"Not very," Ebriel said. "Shall we go out and walk?"

He gave her his hand, and she stood. Together they walked
out into the cool desert night.

Ebriel led James to the hill where she and Ty had sat and
talked, so long ago. She eased herself down on the same
hillock of sand and dry grass. James stretched out beside her,
leaning back on his elbows to look up into the clear night sky,
where the stars unfolded in eddies of crystal above their
heads. The habitat winked cheerfully from the western horizon, a star among stars. Ebriel felt, absurdly, happy.

She closed her eyes to feel the movement of the night
breeze on her cheeks, and when she opened them, he was
watching her.

"Comment?"

"I can't believe you're here," he said. "I wanted to see you
again, so much." He hesitated, and then he reached up, tentatively, stroking her cheek with his fingertips.

She pulled away from his hand, not meaning to, not able to help it. She looked out over the neutral waves of sand that swept away from Siwa, always changing, always the same. She remembered the way she used to be, in Paris, or on tour. She would toss her head at such a touch from a man, she would throw her hair back over her shoulder, say something quick and clever. This was different. *She* was different. She was not the same woman at all.

But she felt him next to her, his long body stretched out on the sand still warm from the sun, his shoulder not quite touching her arm. It would have been so easy to lie down next to him, to let the sand and the stars and the sweet night air overcome her. To allow him, James, to assuage the hunger of her body, the loneliness of her spirit.

But it was too soon. He had brought her a bitter courting gift, the means, at last, to avenge Paul and Renée. And until she had done it—until they had succeeded—she would deny herself, and him. She had no words to express this conviction, but when she glanced down, looked into his clear dark eyes, she saw that he understood, and she was infinitely grateful.

39

The long flight passed quietly. Nothing happened to disturb the peaceful flow of the hours. They watched the glittering ocean pass beneath them, first blue, then shading to green, and finally, in the far north, gray. James superimposed the spybug patterns from his mini onto the telemetry. He kept the Chain's zapper close at hand, delighted with the simple efficiency of it, but the spybug deployment was sparse, hardly more than a nod to monitoring the expanse of the Atlantic. He negotiated the gaps with ease, and they flew north to the unobserved coast of Newfoundland as if they had done it a hundred times. He flew until he was tired, and then Ebriel took over for a short while, one-handed. He didn't want to trust the autopilot until he was certain no stray spybugs might find them.

They slept when they were tired, chatted when they weren't. They took turns in the galley, eating InstaMeals in the cockpit, staying enough ahead of the sun to fly in daylight for sixteen hours, until they reached the rocky coast of northern Canada.

When James felt comfortable leaving the bird on autopilot, he helped Ebriel change her bandages. The wound was healing nicely, new pink flesh melding with her white skin. She seemed utterly unselfconscious about her exposed breast. Her skin was as smooth as satin under his fingertips, but he was careful not to allow his hands to linger. She was still a little stiff, and he thought she should leave the sling on for a few days yet.

"I am so tired of it, James," she complained. "And the bandages itch."

He buttoned her shirt for her and slipped the sling over her elbow. "A little longer," he said. "You don't want it to bleed again."

She made a face, and he chuckled as he returned to the cockpit.

He followed the great circle from St. John's to Edmonton, and then, with the rising sun glimmering on the mountain peaks, he turned south over the old park toward his home. They flew over the remnants of the glacial arêtes, the forested basins of the old shale mines. James pointed. "Look there," he said. "That was Glacier Park. No more beautiful place in the world. See that gleam in the west, up in the fork? That's one of the glaciers. There are more than fifty in these mountains."

He began their descent, and minutes later they landed in a grassy meadow three kilometers northeast of Browning. Stands of tamarac and pine surrounded them. A little stream ran between the trees and the open grass. He secured the fuel cell and the tri-gear, with Ebriel helping as best she could.

Before they walked out of the meadow, James paused. He unscrewed his earplant and lipmike. He weighed them in his hand, gazing out over the treetops to the valley below. Absently, he dropped them into his shirt pocket. He fingered the tiny, empty circles they left in his skin until he realized Ebriel was watching him. He dropped his hand.

"Are you all right, James?" Her eyes, in the gentle morning light, were luminous, flecked with gold. Her hair gleamed silver.

He smiled down at her. His lower lip felt light and empty without the lipmike. "I'm fine."

Ebriel struggled to hide her shock at the appearance of James's father. She forced a smile to her lips and put out her right hand. "*Bonjour.* I am so glad to meet you, *monsieur.*"

The hand that enveloped hers was dark, like James's, but wrinkled and thick-veined. The prominent cheekbones and arching nose that were so attractive on the son had grown mottled and distorted on the father. The years of alcohol and tobacco had weathered Gil Walking Bull as much as the sun and wind. He peered at her from faded eyes, and he smelled of age and smoke, but he spoke with courtesy. "Hello, ma'am. Glad to make your acquaintance. Please come in."

The ranch house was neither the polished home she had known in Paris nor the desperate, bare bones setting of Xining. They followed Gil down a short hall to a sunny kitchen with simple appliances, tidy shelves holding bags and canisters, some marked with the InCo globe, some not. Gil held a chair for her, a wooden one, clearly often repaired, but steady. A tablecloth with faded embroidery covered the table.

She watched the old man put coffee in a dented aluminum pot. It began a cheerful, musical perking, and a delicious smell of coffee filled the kitchen.

"Dad," James said. "I mailed something to myself here. Did it come?"

Gil eyed the empty circles in his son's earlobe and lower lip. He grinned, showing stained teeth. "Secrets, huh?" he rasped. "Goddam Security Corps can't be trusted?"

James looked pained, and Ebriel wanted to put out her hand to him. He said only, "Right, Dad. It was important. Is it here?"

Gil pushed himself up from the table and went to a sideboard, where a woven basket held an assortment of papers and envelopes. He dug down to the bottom and turned with a simple brown envelope in his hand. "Didn't even open it," he declared. "Saw the symbols for the neutral polities and knew it was from you."

James took the envelope in his hand. "Thanks, Dad. I didn't know where else to send it."

His father nodded his satisfaction. "This was the place, Jimmy. This was the right place."

Jimmy. Ebriel had never heard the diminutive. Jimmy. It charmed her. She hoped Gil would have pictures of James as a boy.

James took a knife from a drawer and slit the seal on the

envelope. He turned it over and shook out a little propylene packet. Ebriel could see the shape of the memory stick inside.

Hope surged in her. "Oh, James! Is that it?"

But when he lifted his eyes to hers, she saw how sad he was, how the disillusionment had hurt. "Oh," she said again, more softly. "I am sorry it turned out this way for you."

"Yes," he said. He laid the little packet on the tablecloth between them. "I didn't want to believe it," he said, speaking in an undertone, as if to himself.

"I know you did not." Now Ebriel did put out her hand to touch his. "*Pauvre* James."

"What is that?" Gil asked. "What's on that thing?"

James lifted it in his palm. "This," he said, "is evidence of a crime. And a direct violation of InCo policy. It could be the undoing of George Glass."

"Really?"

James laughed without humor. His mouth set in a bitter line. "Yeah, Dad. Really."

"Then what about the Corps? Your career?"

James began to unwrap the little sheet of plastic from the memory stick. "That was already over," he said.

Over the next days, through Gil's panel in the ranch house, the three of them watched the shock wave roll over the infrastructure of the International Cooperative Alliance. It began in the underground nets. Ethan's contact in New Zealand did a thorough job of disseminating James's information. O-Net picked it up, revelling in the sensationalism of it, playing the unedited spybug video over and over, until finally, when General Glass could no longer dam the flood, it surged through Newnet. The video was analyzed and dissected and discussed from morning till night. One of the Corpsmen involved in the incident came forward, and then another. Frank Dimarco's face, his insistent voice, was on every screen, every network. It seemed he refused no request for an interview, a comment, an appearance. After the first couple of days, even Newnet broadcasted his voluble attacks, giving voice to the opposition for the first time in years. It was as sure a sign of Glass's waning power as any other.

Ebriel hid her eyes as a Corpsman told the awful tale, Luc Serique pulling a weapon to protect his family, an unidentified soldier firing on him, too soon, with disastrous consequences. Tragedy piled upon tragedy. Not only were the yacht passengers lost in the melee, but two Corpsmen died as well, and their bewildered families protested while the ubiquitous cameras panned the falsified death reports.

Gil Walking Bull shook his grizzled head over the story. He could hardly be persuaded away from the panel even for meals. He watched the dominoes fall, swearing at the panel, shaking his fist. Otis Blackhand showed up on the third day, giving a victory yell from the front yard before he was even out of his truck.

Within a week, Premier Takanagi demanded Glass's resignation, scrambling to protect InCo's image, to placate Oceania, to shore up the damaged bulwark that had been Security Corps. Even the French *Présidente* made a speech, demanding reparation, demanding explanations. And Ebriel saw Michau, her old agent, being interviewed, saying into the camera, "Where is she? What have they done with her?"

After the prolonged struggles of the past years, it seemed to Ebriel that it all ended with incredible simplicity. Takanagi awarded General Dimarco's persistence, appointing him head of Security Corps. The new commander general immediately called a conference of the heads of all the InCo polities to discuss the quarantine. His opposition to the Line of Partition was well known. It was, at the very least, a beginning.

"You could go home," James said to Ebriel. "To Paris."

The two of them stood on the hillside above their landing site. The copter still waited, tied down and secure in its bed of thick grass. Ebriel sighed. It was like her dream, the peaks in the distance frosted with the last of the winter snow, a meadow of waist-high grass stretching at her feet. Canary grass, James called it. They had brought a picnic, a canvas bag of sandwiches and fruit waiting for them on a rock beside the slender stream at their feet, a thick wool blanket, ragged at the edges, spread over the needle-strewn ground.

"I will at least send a message to my parents," she answered.

She flexed her left arm, free now of its sling, her wound healed and leaving only a vague stiffness in the shoulder. "And Michau. To tell them I am all right."

She sat crosslegged on the blanket and took the canvas bag into her lap. Gil had lent them a thermos, and she unscrewed the top and poured cups of iced tea. James squatted opposite her, watching, his elbows on his knees. They both wore denims and flannel shirts, old and soft, unearthed from back closets of the ranch house. Ebriel found them delightful, original fabrics redolent of age and history and an unfamiliar culture. She wore one of James's belts around her waist to hold up the trousers. The shirt fell halfway down her thighs.

She felt James's eyes on her. She dragged one finger through the thick spill of pine and spruce needles surrounding their island of blanket. Her finger came away blackened with pitch, and she scrubbed at it with the frayed edge of wool.

"I do not see how I can go home," she said. "Paris is no longer home to me." Her fingers strayed to her scarred wrist. "InCo is no longer home to me, no matter who leads it. I am so changed, James." She looked up. "And you? You have given up Security Corps?"

"I suppose." He put out his hand, the palm up, the long fingers waiting. She didn't hold back this time, but put her hand in his. "We're both lost, aren't we?" he said. His fingers were warm and strong, his voice husky. "Guess we'd better stick together."

Ebriel's breath came quickly. Her lips felt dry, and she touched them with her tongue. She turned her hand in his to entwine their fingers. His dark eyes burned into hers, and a surge of repressed longing flooded her heart, inundated her body. She pushed the canvas bag aside, untangled her legs, rose to her knees.

James knelt, too. With only a little shift, a little kneeling step, their bodies came together. He held her carefully, as if she were made of porcelain, but she put her arms around his waist, squeezing herself close to him, savoring the heady perfumes of clean old cloth, of soap, of pine, of earth, of flesh. For a long moment she pressed her cheek against his chest, her eyes tightly closed. She took one deep breath, and then she lifted her face.

His lips were smooth and firm, tasting of tea and salt. He gathered her more closely in his arms, and pressed his mouth against hers with a controlled intensity that set her body afire. It was so new, and so long-awaited. Her head swam with it. Her body trembled with hunger. Everything fell away as the two of them came together, and for a time, a brief, precious, intoxicating time, the world held only James and Ebriel, Ebriel and James, two souls become one.

For weeks they lived in a blissful recess. Ebriel sent a carefully worded message to her father, and to Michau, assuring them of her safety, promising that she would speak to them directly in time. She sent a message to Yasmine as well, saying that she would be away for an undetermined time, and would be in touch. After that, she and James didn't speak of Starhold, or Security Corps, or the Chain, or indeed anything to do with the outside world. It was an unspoken agreement that they lived in a sort of pocket of time, a shining moment in which nothing could touch them, in which they avoided anything that might cause discord. They stopped watching Newnet, though Gil triumphantly reported every new development. They ate enormous meals, and they fished in the Two Medicine River. They walked for hours in the mountains, and made love under the trees, beside the river, their bodies dappled with summer sunshine, the sounds of rushing water drowning the sounds of their laughter and their joy. Ebriel pushed aside all rational thought, all constraints.

They fell into a comfortable pattern of life, Ebriel and James and Gil. In the afternoons, Ebriel would begin meal preparations while Gil and James worked around the ranch, repairing the old barn, spading the front yard to seed it with grass.

In the evenings, while Gil sat in the living room watching whatever program Newnet broadcast, or more often one of the underground nets, Ebriel and James sat on the slanting front porch, and Ebriel played her flute. She played Mozart, and Vivaldi, and Ravel, and Debussy, hearing the orchestration in her mind sometimes, but other times just enjoying the slender monodic sound under the wide night sky. Once, when she had played for an hour or more, she realized that Gil had come outside. He sat in the shadows at the far end of the porch, smoking his handrolled cigarettes, gazing out into the darkness. He didn't say anything, but every time she brought out her flute after that, he was there, listening.

The spring passed, and the short, hot summer. James grew restless as most of his projects around the old place neared completion. As much as he would have liked to avoid the news that Gil followed so avidly, he could hardly help hearing the voices of Newnet and the undergrounds coming from the panel in the living room. The world was changing beyond Browning, and he, James, was not a part of it.

Once James and Ebriel hitched a ride in Otis's little truck to the cemetery at the edge of town. They walked among the mounds, mostly untended, with scraggly dried-up flowers or cracked plastic bouquets stuck in rusting holders. They found James's mother's grave with its modest headstone and stood looking down at it.

Maria Walking Bull. James couldn't recall her face, though he remembered that she was soft to the touch, her dark skin cushiony, her long black hair always tied back in a single thick braid. She had been proud of being almost one hundred percent Blackfoot. His father, in his worst moments, had taunted her with the diluting drop of white blood in her veins. In his best moments, Gil had been proud that Maria was a true daughter of the Nation. And now there was only this bit of carved cement, worn and pitted, to remember her by. Well, and he himself. James. He was her only legacy.

He glanced down and saw Ebriel's eyes swimming with tears. "Ebriel! What is it?"

"I am sorry, James. I am being selfish. But I have no grave, nothing to remember them by. Paul, and my Renée. Even their ashes are gone. It is as if they never existed."

He caught her hand and pulled her to him. "No, Ebriel," he whispered into her hair. "It will never be like that. They are part of you, and I care about them because of that—because I care about you. I promise you."

Her tears dampened his shirt, but she tightened her arms

around him. *"Merci beaucoup, chéri,"* she said. "You are kind."

The new boards in the barn walls shone yellow in the sun, contrasting with the old, weathered ones. James thought of staining them, or painting the whole thing, but decided that soon enough the new boards would look just like the old ones in any case. And at the moment, there was no livestock to put in the barn. He stored a few of Gil's bits of discarded appliances in what had once been a tack room, and he saw that the stanchions and the loose box were in good repair. Everything was in perfect order. He had to face his next decision.

The face of Security Corps had changed dramatically with the departure of George Glass. Newnet reported that the general had taken early retirement and gone into seclusion at his family home. Dimarco announced that no charges would be pressed against his predecessor, but every policy would undergo review. He promised that all corruption would be rooted from Security Corps. James, wary but curious, contacted Chang from the single public panel in Browning. He didn't tell Ebriel he was going to do it. He didn't want to upset her, and he knew that it would.

Chang wasn't in his quarters the first time he called, but James tried again after buying a few groceries, and this time his old buddy answered. Chang's eyes widened when he saw James on the screen. "James!" he choked. "Good god, man, I thought you were dead!"

I keep hearing that, James thought wryly. But he only smiled, and said, "Hi, Michael. Is that the official word, that I'm dead?"

"More like unofficial." Chang shook his head in wonderment. "Damn it, James, why didn't you let me know? Everybody in the unit's been mourning you! No news, this vague idea that you'd been transferred to . . ." He hesitated and then shook his head again. "Better not say it. Anyway, supposedly it doesn't exist under Dimarco. But rumor had it you'd gotten sideways with our former general and disappeared. Permanently."

"Pretty close," James said. "It didn't turn out to be permanent."

"But what happened? Where did you end up, after Quezon City?"

"Listen, Michael, I'll tell you all about it sometime, but maybe this isn't the best—I mean, I'm on a public panel."

He saw Chang's eyes drop to the routing symbols, then up to his. "Montana?"

"Yes. Michael, could you keep this between us, for the time being? I need to know where I stand. Before I make a decision."

"Are you coming back, then?" Chang asked. "Now that things have changed?"

"I'm trying to figure that out. Think you could nose around for me, maybe do a search and see what my status is?"

"Yeah, James, I could do that. I mean, you're a pilot. The Corps needs pilots. And needs experience."

"The question will be whether they want the kind of experience I've had. It may be I'm more of an embarrassment than an asset."

"Yeah. Could be. Listen, call me again tomorrow. I'll see what I can figure out."

"Thanks." James signed off and sat staring at the blank panel, wondering. It hardly seemed possible he could actually go back, resume his course. Did he want to? And would Ebriel go with him?

Gil had made it clear he was welcome in Browning. "Nation could use some young blood," he said with feigned casualness.

James had answered, "Thanks, Dad. I wish I could." He let it go at that. It wouldn't help Gil to hear that James saw no hope for the Nation, no future in resurrecting a culture that had been dying even before the Crash.

On a day when the tamarac needles already glowed with the early colors of fall, and the hot, dry days of late summer— Indian summer—dried the grasses, James went out to walk alone in the hills. The blackberry bushes bore tiny, sweet fruit protected by sharp thorns, and the creeks ran low. James found the place where he and Ebriel had had their first picnic. Where they had first made love. He squatted in the shade, looking out over the grassy meadow, and tried to think.

If the Blackfoot Nation was not the future, then what was? Starhold? James saw no point in it, the Chain hiding in space, playing at rebellion. It seemed to him, somehow, untidy. Random. Without order.

He remembered the strength of his early patriotism, the devotion he had felt to InCo Forces, to the Corps. He thought of the principles he had memorized, honor, loyalty, unity. Even if he now doubted the quarantine, the Line of Partition, even the leadership of InCo, the principles were still worthy. General Glass had proved himself unworthy. Would Dimarco be better? Or would the institution of Security Corps itself be stronger than the sum of its parts, rise above the flaws of leadership and politics and prove an honorable instrument of change?

James sighed and stood up, stretching. It seemed there was no single answer. Maybe that, by itself, was the lesson.

He was suddenly eager to get back to Ebriel, to hold her in his arms, to put away all thoughts that threatened their peace.

Their respite ended with the arrival of a message for Ebriel on Gil's panel. It was voice-only, and not attributed, but she recognized Yasmine's light voice.

"Ebriel," she said without preamble. "Papa has very little time left. He would like to see you. Can you come?" She paused and then finished with, "Perk is expecting your call. I'm sending the routing symbols, in case you have forgotten them."

The line of symbols was there, at the bottom of the screen. Ebriel hadn't forgotten, but still she wrote them down, and holding the paper in her hand, she went in search of James.

He was ripping rotted boards out of an old corral fence. A pile of newly sawed lumber lay in the September sunshine, smelling richly of pine. He was shirtless, his lean muscles gleaming with sweat. When he saw her face, he put down the crowbar and pulled a bandana out of his pocket to mop his face. "What's happened?" he asked.

"It's Papa," she said bleakly. She held up the paper. "He wants me to come to Starhold."

She saw how still he went, his eyes fixed on her face, his hand with the red bandana arrested halfway to his hip pocket.

She felt it, too, the end of their idyll, and she didn't think she could bear it. "James," she said. "The spaceplanes do not fly often. I will be there for some time, weeks at least. Come with me."

She saw how his eyes shifted away from hers, how he took extra time to tuck the handkerchief into his pocket. Her heart sank. "I don't think I can," he said.

"But—" She felt her cheeks flame. "But—why not, James? Why?"

He glanced across at Gil, who was pulling nails with a hammer. "Ebriel, let's go inside. Let's talk."

He guided her with his hand on her shoulder. His somber expression, as he led the way around the side of the house and in through the kitchen door, made her heart quail.

She sat at the kitchen table, watching his efficient movements as he reached into the refrigerator, brought out the pitcher of iced tea, and poured two glasses. She crumpled the bit of paper in her fingers.

He set the glasses on the table and then turned one of the wooden chairs so he could straddle it, wrapping his long arms around the back. He looked into her eyes with an intensity that made her pulse race.

"Tell me, James," she said. She leaned forward, put her hand on his arm. "Quickly."

He covered her hand with his. "Ebriel," he said slowly. "I love you. I think you know."

She waited, her mouth dry, her heart pounding.

"What you're doing, what *they're* doing—the Flecks, the Chain—I just—I can't—" He broke off and looked away, out to the sunburnt fields beyond the window. Ebriel had hung new white curtains from the old-fashioned curtain rod. "I want you, Ebriel. I want to marry you, to have you with me always. I want you to stay with me."

"Stay with you where, James? Here, in Browning?"

For a long, painful minute, he didn't speak. Ebriel's heart began to ache with the new pain that she could feel was coming, could sense in her bones and her blood.

"I'm not good with words," James said in a low tone.

"Non."

"I went into the service to get away from home," he began,

and then faltered. She lifted her hand from his arm and let it drop to the tablecloth. "I stayed because I cared about the work," he said awkwardly. "About helping to establish a safer world."

Ebriel did not, would not, argue with him. He had helped her in her battle, had stood with her, had saved her. She wanted to cry out that the world was no safer, that his "service" was a sham, a pretense. But she understood, deep in her soul, that he would never agree. She felt him slipping away from her, their shining, precious moment dissolving in the on-rush of time.

"Ebriel, stay with me."

"But, James—what would I do, if I stayed?"

He turned to her, his eyes hooded, as full of pain as she was sure her own must be. "Wouldn't it be enough," he asked, "just to be with me?"

"Oh, James—" Her voice broke. How could she explain? Papa, and the Chain, had given her a new life. "Would it be enough for you, just to be with me?"

He dropped his gaze.

"You see, James?"

"If you go," he said softly, "I'm afraid you'll never come back."

She twisted her fingers together. "I do not understand why you cannot come with me," she said. "Just come, and see it. You have not seen, you do not know—"

He put up one hand, touched her lips with his fingers. "Ebriel. I want to go back to the Corps. Be a part of things."

"But that is behind you! You are free now!"

"So are you," he said.

She tried to be still, tried to let it be, but it was too hard. She jumped up and bent over him, her arms around his neck, her mouth against his ear. "Please," she whispered through trembling lips. "*Mon chéri,* come with me!"

His arms came up to hold her, to draw her close. He pressed his face to her breast. "I wish I could," he murmured, his words muffled against her flannel shirt. "It wouldn't be right. It wouldn't be honest."

They stayed where they were for a long moment, holding each other. When they finally drew apart, Ebriel fell back into her chair, and sat slump-shouldered. "Because you do not believe in it," she said at last. "In what they—we—are doing."

"No," he said. "I don't. It's the wrong way."

"Is there a right way?"

"You and I did something right, something big. We can do more."

"I could never be part of Security Corps."

"General Glass was your enemy. Not Security Corps. Not InCo."

"They need me, James. Papa, and Yasmine. The Chain."

"I need you, too." He put his hand out to stroke her cheek. She lifted one shoulder and he gave her a rueful smile. "I love you, Ebriel."

It would have been enough for the old Ebriel, the Ebriel of Paris and La Villette. But the new Ebriel, the Ebriel of the Chain, could no longer close her eyes to things she didn't want to see. Through an aching throat she whispered, "*Je t'aime aussi,* James. *Je t'aime aussi.*"

40

Ebriel flew to Xiao Qaidam with only the flight monitor for company. She promised to get word to James the moment she arrived safely. She made a great northern loop, straight up through Alberta, turning west over the Yukon, avoiding the Todokai polities, where throngs of spybugs haunted the Line of Partition. She welcomed the mild turbulence she encountered over the Aleutian Islands and the storm system above the Sea of Okhotsk that drove her even farther north. Dealing with the weather distracted her from the ache in her midriff.

She and James had clung together the night before, murmuring words of love and passion, saying nothing of the future, making no promises, and asking no questions. In the morning, Gil pressed a packet of sandwiches and dried fruit into her hands as he said a taciturn good-bye. James gave the bird a thorough going-over and stood alone in the meadow as she hovered, lifted, then banked to the north. He raised one arm in farewell.

She waved back, whispering, *"Au revoir, mon chéri."*

Perk welcomed her, gave her dinner, and routed a call for her through Oceania to Browning. She and James spoke briefly, unhappily aware of Perk listening in the kitchen at

Xiao Qaidam, and Gil in the living room of the ranch house. *Unicorn* arrived early the next day.

Ebriel watched the lights of the habitat come into view, the graceful arc of its silhouette, the butterfly wings of its rectennae glistening with reflected sunlight. She wished with all her heart James were beside her, to see the wonder of it, to appreciate its beauty, to understand the immensity of Ethan's accomplishment.

Ty was waiting in the loading bay. "Hey, Eb," her old partner said. "Good trip?"

"It was all right," Ebriel said. "I thought Yasmine would be here."

"She's in the aerie," Ty said. "You okay to go straight up there?"

"Oui," Ebriel said. She lifted her brocade bag to her shoulder. "What is happening, Ty?"

"It's Papa," Ty said heavily. She waited as two or three people passed them. "Come on, I'll tell you in the tube."

They passed through the slip. Ty shot upward, but Ebriel lagged behind. The months of her absence, it seemed, had spoiled her coordination in microgravity. With difficulty, her bag dangling from one hand, she floated after Ty, twice bumping against the side of the tube. She felt awkward and foolish, as if she were a beginner again. She steadied herself with one of the staples by the slip on the aerie level. Ty grasped the same one, and the two of them hung suspended, facing each other.

Ty's freckled face was grim. "Papa's leaving," she said. "But we're not telling everyone. Not until it's all over. He wants it that way."

"Pardon?" Ebriel exclaimed. "Over? What does that mean? And where is he going?"

"Well, that's the thing," Ty said. "Ethan doesn't want to die here, on the habitat. He wants to be—" She stretched out her long arm in a vague gesture, pointing outside the habitat, at the stars, at space, at the universe. "He wants to be out there."

Ebriel breathed, *"Mon Dieu.* He is dying then. The doctor is certain?"

Ty nodded. "It's been coming. We could see it. The sclerosis has reached his lungs, and he can't bear for it to—" Her eyes reddened. "He can't bear for it to reach his brain."

"Oh, Ty. This is a terrible thing. A tragedy." Ebriel glanced through the cylinder of the slip as if she could see right into the aerie. "And Yasmine? Is she all right?"

"Funny thing about that," Ty said. She managed a shadow of her usual grin. "Yasmine understands better than anyone, it seems. Yasmine is managing everything, the aerie, the monitors, even Semaya. And this, Papa's—I don't know what to call it. His departure."

"But, Ty, you have not said—where is he going?"

"He's going into space, Eb. He had a pod built. He says—" Ty's voice broke. For a moment she hung in the tube, her head down, and Ebriel saw her knuckles whiten on the staple. She put her slender fingers over Ty's long ones and waited, pressing her friend's hand. At last, in a tight voice, Ty whispered, "He says he wants to be alone. And that he would have been buried there in any case."

For long moments Ebriel grappled with the idea, struggling to comprehend the cold reality, the utter loneliness, of such a death.

She couldn't do it. "I should see Papa now."

"Yeah. He's waiting for you."

Ty led the way through the slip and into the dim hemisphere of the aerie.

Yasmine, speaking with one of the air-quality technicians over an internal circuit, looked up to see Ebriel and Ty come through the slip. A surge of pleasure at the sight of Ebriel washed over her, and relief as well. Ebriel was the answer to Ethan's last wish.

She looked lovely. Her hair had grown longer, curling ashen strands floating around her chin and her face, until she tucked them behind her ears. Her hazel eyes were clear. Her skin had a glow that only good food and enough sleep could give it. And she had gained weight, so that her bosom curved, and her hips, which had been so narrow, rounded under the denims she wore. When she smiled at Yasmine, a deep dimple appeared in her cheek.

Yasmine ended her instructions to the technician and

floated swiftly to Ebriel. "Welcome home," she said.

"Hello, Yasmine," Ebriel said, offering her hand. *"Chérie."*

Yasmine touched Ebriel's hand with hers, just for a moment, before she withdrew it. "I am glad you came," she said. "Papa wanted so much to have you here."

The null-grav chair floated, empty, at one side of the aerie. "Where is he?"

Yasmine folded her arms around herself. It was good to see Ebriel well and strong. Perhaps she could borrow some of that strength. She was weary of pretending, pretending to herself as much as to others. Minute to minute, she kept it up, speaking calmly, with authority, pressing down her sadness, her doubts, sometimes her panic. At her worst, she allowed herself to wonder if everyone else was pretending, too, the Chain, the starchildren, Semaya, Dr. Nordstrom. And if so, what would keep everything from falling to pieces? But all of this she would have to consider at another time. There was too much to be done.

"Papa is in Dr. Nordstrom's clinic," she told Ebriel. "She is giving him oxygen."

"How is Semaya?"

"Semaya is with the children. Or in the kitchens. She works all the time."

"Ah," Ebriel said, nodding, floating awkwardly away with the movement. "Shall I go to the clinic, then, Yasmine?"

"Yes," Yasmine said. "I will go with you. Just wait a moment, while I call for Semaya to come here and watch over things while I'm gone." She propelled herself to a mike and spoke her request. She looked over her shoulder at Ebriel. "You look so well."

"I am, Yasmine."

"And your friend? The major?"

"He is also well."

Yasmine steadied her own mask of calm. "What are you going to do, Ebriel? Are you coming back to us?"

"I think so, Yasmine. I think I must."

Ebriel had forgotten how bright the clinic was, its vividly painted walls with their posters in a multitude of languages. Emily Nordstrom greeted her and led her into one of the exam rooms. Ethan lay on a bed with the head raised, the security rails up, padded straps securing his chest and legs. He had an oxygen tube taped to his sunken cheek and running into his nose and an IV drip fastened to the inside of one elbow. A keyboard of some kind rested under his hands. He looked horrible to Ebriel, half dead already, his chest barely moving, the hiss of oxygen loud in the silence. She went to his bedside and put her hand on the rail.

Yasmine went to the other side and touched Ethan's skeletal hand with hers. "Papa?" she said. "Are you awake? Look who has come, Papa. Here is Ebriel."

Ethan's eyelids struggled to lift. Ebriel watched them, holding her breath, shocked at how challenging such a small act had become. His brown eyes were no longer bright. The pupils wavered left and right, endeavoring to focus. His forefingers moved on the keyboard, and the mellifluous voice spoke haltingly. "Hello—Ebriel. It's—good—to . . ." His fingers stopped. Ebriel looked to Yasmine for help. Yasmine shook her head, still covering Ethan's fingers with her small brown ones.

Ebriel ventured, *"Bonjour,* Papa."

"You—look . . . wonderful."

His eyes had barely opened.

Yasmine said, "Papa, can you see Ebriel?"

One of his fingers moved. A programmed chuckle sounded. "Not—too—but—"

Yasmine squeezed his fingers. "Yes, Papa, you're right. Ebriel looks wonderful."

Ebriel put her fingers against her lips, steadying them. Yasmine went on, "She has gained weight, Papa. Her dimple is back, and her hair is longer."

Ebriel let her fingers stray to her right cheek. James, too, had noticed the reappearance of her dimple. She dropped her hand. "Papa," she said. *"Je suis désolée*—I am very sorry to find you so ill."

The chuckle came again. And then, with agonizing pauses, "Thank—I've—time. To. See. What . . ."

Yasmine spoke for him. Ebriel had the sense she had been doing it for some time. "Papa has said he wants to see what lies beyond. And he wants to see the stars, really see them."

One of Ethan's wasted fingers moved. "Moon."

"Yes," Yasmine said. "You will go past the moon. It's been programmed."

Dr. Nordstrom leaned against the wall, her arms folded.

With a sense of unreality, Ebriel said, "You wanted to see me, Papa?"

"Yes." There was a pause, while Ethan's eyelids fluttered, and the sound of his struggling lungs seemed loud in Ebriel's ears. "To—hear . . ."

"You play," Yasmine finished for him. "Not a recording, but the real Ebriel Serique."

Ebriel murmured, "Of course I will play for you, Papa. I wish I could do more."

"You've—already . . ." There was a pause as Ethan breathed, his eyelids closed. No one moved. The tension was unbearable as they waited for his chest to rise and fall. Dr. Nordstrom straightened, watching. At last his fingers moved again, and the voice said, "Yasmine. Gift."

Ebriel looked up into Yasmine's eyes, their irises richly dark against the whites. Yasmine's voice was steady. "Do you have your flute, Ebriel?"

For answer, Ebriel pulled the leather case out of her shoulder bag.

"Papa wants everyone to hear," Yasmine said. "Especially the children." She stepped to a wall panel and gave a command.

Ebriel opened her case and began to assemble the black and silver cylinders. She said, "The sound may not be very good over the internal speakers."

The chuckle came again from the synthesizer. One finger moved. "A—start."

And so Ebriel Serique, for the first time in three years, gave a concert. There was no conductor, and no orchestra, and no stage lights. She wore a pair of denim trousers and a shirt far too large for her. She played Mozart, and Bach, and Debussy, and Ravel, bits and pieces she could remember. She thought of the slanting porch of the ranch house in Browning, of James's long legs stretched out beside hers, of Gil smoking under the eaves.

In the classrooms, the children came out from under the

study hoods. In the dojo, the training stopped, and everyone sat crosslegged, listening. In Tacticals, in the gardens, in the kitchens, people turned off their equipment to follow the slender sound. Ebriel heard from them later, heard where they had been, how they had felt, what they had thought as they heard her play.

In the aerie, Semaya listened.

Yasmine listened and watched Ebriel with shining eyes.

Ethan Fleck lay still. One forefinger lifted, poised, and when Ebriel at last ceased playing, it touched the keyboard. The synthesizer said, *"Magnifique."*

41

Ethan's pod, a cylinder two and a half meters long, less than a meter wide, rested on supports in the loading bay among the metal skeletons of the lifts and pallets and dollies. He lay in it, his eyelids closed, his chest barely moving. Cushions elevated his head and shoulders, and the synthesizer keyboard rested under his fingers. His legs fitted neatly inside the pod. The coffin, Ebriel thought bleakly. The pod was his coffin. It would rest in a mausoleum of stars.

The monitors and mikes and panels of the aerie could not be left unattended, even for such a momentous occasion as this one. With Semaya on duty, Yasmine descended to the loading bay to say her farewell. Ebriel saw that she had prepared herself well. She wore white cottons, with a scarlet sash, and she had dyed her palms and her soles scarlet. She didn't weep. Her features barely moved as she bent over Ethan's inert form, murmuring in Hindi, words Ebriel couldn't understand. His eyelids fluttered up, and then down again.

She caressed his cheek with her red palm. "Papa," she said. "Are you comfortable?"

His fingers moved, and the synthesizer spoke. "Yes. Reports . . . Yasmine."

"I will. You will look out at the stars and hear my voice in your ear."

"Yes. Go. Now. Send. Semaya."

"Yes, Papa." Yasmine touched his ear with her thin brown fingers, checking that the earplant was secure. She said, "I will talk to you later, Papa."

"I'll—be—" The pause was long, his finger trembling. "Listening."

A little circle of people stood in the loading bay. Ebriel, Ty, three of the Chain, Emily Nordstrom, and Vee Eyckart watched Yasmine back away from the pod and turn to leave. As she stepped over the the sill of the airseal, she stumbled. Ebriel took a step forward, to help her, but the girl was already in the slip. Her scarlet sash trailed behind her as she floated upward. Ebriel saw that Yasmine, always so deft in microgravity, bumped against the sides of the tube, twice, three times, on her ascent.

Moments later Semaya arrived in the loading bay. She had something in her hand. She bent over the pod to tuck it inside Ethan's shirt.

The synthesizer spoke. "What . . ."

"Just sending something with you, Ethan," she said. She straightened and turned empty eyes to the doctor. "Is it time, Emily?"

"I think it is, Semaya."

Dr. Nordstrom stepped up to the pod. "Are you ready, Ethan?"

The synthesizer gave its rich chuckle. "For—days," it said. Ethan's eyelids didn't move. "Take—the—synthesizer."

"But, Ethan—we won't be able to talk to you then. To hear you."

"Said—all—I—have—to—say." The fragmented sentence took many seconds to complete. "Semaya." Semaya stood beside the pod as if turned to stone. "I—love—you—always."

Semaya, the statue, couldn't answer.

Dr. Nordstrom slid the keyboard out from under Ethan's slack fingers. She looked up at Semaya. "Say good-bye, my friend."

For long seconds, it seemed Semaya would not even be

able to do that. Then she bent over Ethan and pressed her lips to his slack mouth.

She straightened and stepped back. She watched the doctor bend over Ethan, checking his oxygen tubes, feeling his pulse, stroking his forehead once. "Ready?" the doctor asked.

For answer, Ethan's eyelids rose and fell once.

Dr. Nordstrom nodded to Vee. Vee touched the button on one end of the cylindrical pod, and the translucent top, the same fused silica of the space windows, slid slowly and surely closed.

The Chain members stood in a tight knot, shoulders and elbows touching. They watched together, breathing together, not speaking, as the small airlock opened enough for the pod to pass through. The flexible airseals dragged at it as Vee pushed it on rollers. It took perhaps thirty seconds to pass all the way through. Vee had a remote in her hand, and when the pod was free of the airlock, she fired the little jets that would send it away from the habitat. Moments later, she fired them again, checking for attitude and trajectory. And then, "It's away," she said somberly.

Semaya gasped once, a hoarse and painful sound. Emily Nordstrom immediately circled her with her arms, and Semaya collapsed against her shoulder, great racking sobs shaking her thin frame. The doctor glanced up at the Chain.

"Ebriel," she said quietly. "Could you help me get Semaya to the clinic?"

The Chain members gathered in the gardens much later that night, when the children were safely abed in the crèche and most of the Starhold inhabitants were in their cubbies. Ty and Pilar had plotted the course of Ethan's pod, and they thought they could just see the twin sparks of its tiny jets. It hadn't carried much fuel, and the jets would burn out quickly. They stood together, all of them, peering past the curve of the Earth at the two pinpricks of light. Momentum would carry the pod on, out past the moon, as Yasmine had promised. It would fly into the orbits of the planets, and perhaps, with the passing of years, and if nothing happened to it, even farther. But they wouldn't know.

"No one put a tracker on it?" Astrid asked.

"Vee said not," Pilar answered. "She said Papa wanted it that way."

"And he made Dr. Nordstrom take out the synthesizer," Ty said. "I don't understand that. We won't know—I mean, when he can't talk to us anymore, we would at least know, wouldn't we? I don't get it."

"I think I do," Ebriel said. The others, Pilar and Astrid and Johna and the others, turned to her, their faces intent. She felt her cheeks warm. "Oh, perhaps I do not. I only . . ."

"Tell us, Eb," Ty said.

Shyly, Ebriel said, "I think that Papa may have—might have felt if we did not know for certain—know the moment of his passing—it would be as if he were still with us. Always with us."

"Kinda hard on Semaya, though," Ty said. Pilar and Astrid nodded.

Johna, whose partner Simon Blake had been killed in the battle for *Troll,* said, "It's hard enough when you do know, when you're right there. I think this was cruel of Papa."

"Me, too," Ty said. "Funny thing, from a man who was never cruel in his life."

"Maybe," Ebriel offered, "at the very end, he did one thing, just for himself."

No one had an answer for that.

After a time, while they all watched the distant pair of lights twinkle above the dark horizon of the Earth, Ty said, "How long will his oxygen last?"

Ebriel had helped Dr. Nordstrom put Semaya to bed, had held Semaya's hand while the doctor pressed an ampoule of sedative to the inside of her arm. Once Semaya was asleep, the doctor and Ebriel had gone out of the clinic to stand in the curving gallery. Ebriel had asked about the oxygen.

"Dr. Nordstrom said about three days. But she said his lungs would not last that long. He was close to the end, and he knew it. And Semaya knew it."

"But the waiting . . ." Astrid said, her voice trailing off.

"I cannot imagine what Semaya must be feeling," Pilar said in her gentle voice.

Ebriel understood all too well. She remembered, with

painful clarity, the unbearable tension. She pitied Semaya. And she pitied the Ebriel of three years before, suffering in the Paris apartment, awaiting the terrible news that some part of her already knew was coming.

Now, in the fragrant garden of Starhold, she gazed out at the great globe beyond the space window. That other Ebriel, that tragic and helpless woman, was gone. And the new Ebriel was torn in two. What was she to do now? The dark ocean below gave her no answers. James was somewhere on the other side of the globe, in sunshine, out of her reach.

Chang said to James, over the public panel, "You're MIA." He grinned. "You look pretty good for being presumed dead."

"Did the report say where?"

Chang held up a memory stick. "I have it here, buddy. I can transmit it to you right now. It wasn't hard to find, though. Right there in the personnel files. It was still pending because no one knew where to send the notification. No family of record."

"Right. Yes, Michael, transmit it, will you?"

"Sure." Chang tapped a few keys, and James watched him insert the memory stick beneath the screen. Lights flashed as the data was recorded on the blank one James had brought with him. It took only a few seconds. "That's your whole file," Chang said. "Boot camp to officer training school to missing in action. Now what, James?"

James extracted the memory stick and put it in his shirt pocket. "I don't know yet," he said. "But thanks for doing this, Michael. Nobody can trace it, can they?"

"Nope." Chang sat back and folded his arms, squinting slightly into the camera. "Things are changing in the Corps, James," he said.

"Enough for an MIA to resurface without too many questions?"

Chang shrugged and laughed. "There'd be questions, for sure. But I guess we could come up with answers." He leaned forward again. "What are the answers, James? Where've you been? What happened?"

"They sent me over the Line," James said shortly. "There was a whole squad, and I think they lost a couple of other guys. I don't think they're going to want that to come out."

"That was General Glass, though," Chang said with confidence. "Dimarco's a different story. And he's having a heyday collecting evidence against the old administration."

"I doubt it will be that simple," James answered. "Listen, just keep it all under your hat, okay? I'll let you know what I decide."

"Sure, James. But even if you decide to stay gone, call and fill me in, okay?" He hesitated, shrugged. "Listen, buddy. We all felt bad. We really did."

James smiled at his old friend, touched and surprised. "Thanks, Michael. Give me some time to think things over. I'll get back to you."

Time passed slowly after the launching of Ethan's little vessel. Semaya remained in her room and spoke to no one but Dr. Nordstrom. Life went on, although it seemed to Ebriel that even the children were quieter than usual, as if they sensed a change. Ebriel kept busy in the crèche or in the kitchens, trying not to think of the hours passing, and what they meant. The rest of the Chain appeared to be doing the same thing, tiring themselves in the dojo, helping in the classrooms, finding work in the gardens or under the study hoods. At dinner one evening, Ebriel realized she had not seen Yasmine since that day in the loading bay. Reluctantly, she thought back over the last days, counting on her fingers. She saw Ty watching her, nodding.

"Yeah," Ty said. "Four days. He's gone by now."

"I have not seen Yasmine."

Ty shook her head. "No one has. She's been staying up there, all alone. The cooks take up her meals, but she won't let anyone come through the slip. She closed the exit."

Ebriel waited until the children were in bed and everyone else was settled for the evening. The tube was empty as she floated up to the aerie.

Yasmine had indeed closed the exit from the slip, sliding the door out of its slot in the side of the cylinder, latching it from the inside. Ebriel heard a murmur beyond the closed door. She knocked lightly and listened for a response.

"Yes?" It was Yasmine's voice.

"Yasmine?" Ebriel called. "It is I. Ebriel. Will you open the slip, please?"

Ebriel waited, clinging to the edge of the slip. Beyond the closed door she heard the murmuring resume, stop, then begin again. "Yasmine!" she called, more urgently. "Please let me in, Yasmine!"

Moments later, the latch released and the door slid back. Yasmine was there, still in the same white cottons and scarlet sash she had worn in the loading bay. Her hair, escaping its pins, hung in untidy, oily strands. Her face was slightly grimy, as if she had rubbed dirty hands across it. The staining in her palms had started to fade. As Ebriel sidled through the slip and into the aerie, she sniffed. Yasmine needed to bathe.

The holographic projection of the planet was on. Ebriel glimpsed the expanse of the Pacific Ocean, blue and green, with great rolling fields of gray cloud. A Newnet broadcast glimmered from one of the panels, and two others were also on, other networks, different scenes. Ethan's empty chair floated to one side. Yasmine glided back to the projection.

Ebriel followed her. "Are you all right, Yasmine? I have not seen you since . . ."

Yasmine glanced up at her briefly, and then away. Her dark eyes gleamed with reflected blue and green from the revolving globe. "Look, Papa," she said. "Ebriel is here with us."

"Comment?" Ebriel asked uneasily. "Yasmine?"

Yasmine looked up again, her expression bland. "I am transmitting to Papa," she said.

Ebriel clung to a wall staple. She couldn't think of a response. Yasmine hovered before the image of the planet, moving her fingers now and then to steady her position. The ends of the long sash fluttered around her. She wore a headset, the input mike curling under her small chin.

"The sun is shining on Xiao Qaidam," Yasmine said, as if she were speaking to someone right beside her. "I'm sure Perk has the doors open to let in the fresh air." She looked over her shoulder at the Newnet broadcast. "Newnet says that Commander General Dimarco has taken up his offices in

Geneva. Premier Takanagi is on his way to meet with him."
She laughed. "You'll like this, Papa! The premier is calling
the abuses of General Glass an outrage. He has launched a review of all Security Corps actions."

Ebriel whispered, "Yasmine? Do you really think—are
you sure he can hear you?"

Yasmine glanced at her. "Of course," she said calmly. "I
put in the receiver myself." She looked back at the globe.
"There's a dust storm in eastern Brazil, Papa." She spoke con-
versationally. Ebriel noticed how clear Yasmine's English had
become, how unaccented, while her own never seemed to improve. "But it should blow itself out. I don't think it will cause
too many problems." She nodded, as if she had heard Ethan
speak. "Yes, I will send word to Manaus to remind the people
to cover the fuel cells. I'm doing that now."

Ebriel didn't know what to do. Should she call the doctor?
Should she leave Yasmine alone? "Yasmine—" she began,
and then broke off.

"Yes, Ebriel?"

"Yasmine—*ma chérie*—will you not come down and have
something to eat?"

Yasmine gave a slight shake of her head, compensating with
one hand. "No, thank you," she said. "I can't leave the aerie."
She looked to her right, to one of the panels. "Oh, look, Papa.
They've already cut the spybug deployment in half. O-Net has
the numbers. Takanagi must have sent them to Blackfield as a
goodwill gesture. Not even Geneva has released them yet. I'll
follow this, see if the numbers are real. But a good sign, don't
you think?"

She propelled herself to another panel, still talking in that
casual way. There was nothing in her manner to indicate that
she knew her audience was already thousands of kilometers
away. That he was no longer able to hear her, or to hear anything. That he no longer breathed.

Ebriel, anxiety making her stomach quiver, turned and
went back through the slip.

When she reached the clinic she found Semaya with
Dr. Nordstrom. They looked up at her entrance, and Semaya

put something into her pocket. Semaya looked almost like her old self, possessed and calm. Only her puffy eyelids showed that she had been grieving.

When Ebriel explained about Yasmine, the doctor raised her eyebrows at Semaya. Semaya sighed, and said, "Yes, you're right, Emily. I'll have to tell her."

"I do not know if she will believe you," Ebriel said.

Semaya reached back into her pocket and took out a mini. She held it up for Ebriel to see. Ebriel lifted one shoulder. "I do not understand."

Dr. Nordstrom said, "Semaya put a heart monitor in the pod. She attached it directly to Ethan's chest, right at the end."

Semaya said in a steady voice, "My husband died two days ago. I knew the moment his heart stopped beating."

Ebriel put out her hand and touched the older woman's shoulder. "Oh, Semaya. I am so sorry. I, too, lost my husband. You have my sympathy."

Semaya stood up. "Thank you," she said with dignity. "You have mine as well, Ebriel." She nodded to the doctor. "I'll go up to Yasmine, Emily. I'll show her the time and the date, and I think she'll believe me. I should have gone before this."

"Do you want me to go with you?" Dr. Nordstrom said.

"No. It's better if we're alone."

"Let's go to dinner," the doctor said to Ebriel. "We'll check on them later."

Ebriel looked down at her meal, the green soybean casserole, a handful of tiny carrots picked from the gardens. Despite the sadness of the last days, she was hungry. She couldn't seem to get enough to eat. She supposed she had grown used to big meals during her time in Browning. She had been fantasizing, before dinner, about the venison roast she and James had cooked the night before she left. The thought of its rich juices, the remembered smell of roasting meat and potatoes glazed with real butter, made her stomach contract with fierce appetite. She took another mouthful of casserole and wondered why it couldn't satisfy her.

Dr. Nordstrom, sitting across from her, frowned. "Are you feeling well?"

"Oui," Ebriel said hastily. She laughed a little. "It is so silly," she exclaimed. "I cannot seem to get enough to eat. I suppose I will now become very fat!"

The doctor looked closely at her, but she didn't answer.

Ebriel pushed her empty plate away. "I will go to Yasmine now," she said. She swung her legs around to rise from the long bench, but she stopped. A child stood beside her knees, holding something up in one chubby hand.

It was Xiao Sying, a toddler now, full-cheeked, merry-eyed, everyone's pet.

Ebriel crouched beside her. *"Ni hao,* Xiao Sying," she said. "What do you have for me?"

The little girl pressed a crumbling fragment of cookie, damp with saliva, into Ebriel's hand, babbling an incomprehensible mixture of Mandarin and English. Ebriel took it, caressing the child's cheek with her other hand. *"Xie xie,"* she said softly. "Thank you."

She straightened and watched the child gambol away to distribute the rest of her moist offering to other lucky recipients.

"Dr. Nordstrom," she said. "Where is Xiao Sying from? I have forgotten."

"Gansu Province," the doctor said. "Why?"

Ebriel felt a strange quiver in her abdomen, a vaguely familiar queasiness, not an illness, but—what was that? She had felt it before, surely? She touched her stomach with her hand, then dropped it. "Oh—I do not know. There was something—I cannot think what it was." She would return to it later, try to remember.

She said, "I will go up to Yasmine now."

"Do you want me to come with you?"

"No, I can manage, Dr. Nordstrom."

"Fine. Let me know how it goes." The doctor waved a casual hand, but Ebriel felt her eyes follow her as she made her way through the crowded dining hall to the gallery. She sidled through the slip and into the tube.

She found Semaya Fleck clinging to a staple beside the space window. Yasmine, her sash and her undone hair floating behind her, sobbed in the older woman's arms. Semaya, remote and unapproachable Semaya, held the girl, patted her back, murmured soothing words. Ebriel stayed where she was, watching the two of them outlined by the star field, engrossed in their own process of grieving and comforting, sharing their loss. Empathetic tears came to Ebriel's eyes, tears for Yasmine, for Ethan, for Semaya. Some were for herself. There had been no comfort for her except the passage of time, and the passing away of her madness. And then, of course, James. But she feared he was lost to her.

Carefully, making no sound, Ebriel backed out through the slip. She was glad of Yasmine's tears, healthy, normal girl's tears. And she was glad Semaya was there, had come out of her brittle shell to comfort Yasmine.

Ebriel glided down the tube, still awkward in the microgravity, to report to Dr. Nordstrom.

42

"I am so much out of condition," Ebriel complained, leaving the dojo with Ty. She wiped perspiration from her face and neck with a towel and tugged her wet cottons away from her hot skin. "I am a beginner again."

Ty followed her into the slip. "Yeah," Ty said. She sailed ahead of Ebriel and spoke over her shoulder. "Seems like it was mostly the sit-ups that bothered you."

"Those I could not do at all," Ebriel said. "My muscles are all gone."

"You'll get 'em back. But you're gonna be sore."

"Mais oui!"

They showered side by side. Ty scrubbed herself quickly. Ebriel turned under the mist jets, trying to capture the meager flow with her washcloth before it could reach the recycler. "I miss real showers," she said. "Water running all down your back, in your hair. And I miss the food! It seems I am always hungry."

"Life in space," Ty grinned. She turned off the jets and toweled her broad, freckled back. "I guess now you could go back to Paris. Real showers. Better food."

Ebriel shook her head. "No," she assured her. "I will not do that. But I would like to see my parents. My mother is still in a sanitarium. I spoke to my father—he is lonely."

"And what about James?" Ty asked. They moved into the narrow locker room, squeezing past three others who had come to shower. "Don't you want to see James?" She dried her hair and dropped her towel into the laundry chute.

Ebriel turned over the fresh cottons in her hands. "I think we cannot always have what we want, Ty."

Ty's eyes narrowed. "You want to talk, partner?"

Ebriel sighed. "There is little to say, Ty. James is—*zut*," she laughed a little, sadly. "He is James! He likes things to be very neat, very ordered, whereas I—I am one of the Chain."

"For real this time, huh?"

Ebriel pulled her shirt over her head. *"Oui, mon amie,"* she said. "For real. I want to be a true *maquisarde*—a member of the resistance. I want to fulfill Papa's wish, that I teach music to the children. I feel I must do this."

"And what does James want, Eb?"

Ebriel leaned against the bank of lockers. "He wants something very different. And it seems we cannot have both."

That night Yasmine came to the dining hall for a meal and had slept in her cubby, in gravity, bowing to the doctor's orders. The next morning Ebriel found her poised before a monitor in the aerie. She had stopped transmitting to Ethan. A yellow sash brightened her dark blue cottons, and she had gathered her freshly washed hair into a tidy knot. She kept the hemisphere dim, as Ethan had, and the stars glittered through the space window.

She looked up when Ebriel came in. "I would like to send you on a mission," she began.

"D'accord," Ebriel said swiftly, smiling. "I would like to go on a mission."

"I'm sorry, Ebriel, I didn't finish," Yasmine said. She turned from the monitor. "I have just received other orders. Someone else will have to go with Ty."

Ebriel's smile faded. "But—why is that? Do they still not trust me? Did Vee say—"

"It was not Vee," Yasmine said. "It was Dr. Nordstrom."

"Comment?"

Yasmine said delicately, "She has asked to see you. I think she wants to give you a test."

Ebriel opened her mouth, and then closed it. She felt a rush of sensation in her body, a thrill of awareness in her abdomen. Of course. Of course. She should have known.

Yasmine's dark eyes glistened with flecks of colored light reflected from the banks of equipment. "I don't know why she thinks this," she said. "Perhaps it is an intuition?"

Ebriel stared at her for one long, breathless moment. Her heartbeat thudded in her ears. She drew a deep, sudden breath and pressed her hand to her stomach. "Yes," she whispered. "Intuition. A feeling."

The world turned over. Ebriel's blundering fingers searched for a staple, and her vision dimmed. She might have muttered, *"enceinte,"* or she might not, she wasn't sure. She felt Yasmine's cool small hand under her arm, her fingers on her cheek.

"Ebriel? Ebriel? Shall I call the doctor?"

"Non," Ebriel managed to whisper. And then, with a breathy gasp, *"Non.* Oh, Yasmine! *Mon Dieu!* What am I to do?"

Ebriel sat in Dr. Nordstrom's small office, the panel ready before her, but she didn't give the command. She gazed at a poster on the opposite wall, little children playing on a beach. None of them looked like Renée. She twisted her trembling fingers in her lap. She had to call him. But what would she say? And what would James think of this?

The panel chimed. Someone, no doubt Yasmine, had already placed her call. She looked into the small screen. He was there, his narrow eyes searching for her. The room rocked around her, and she gripped the edge of the desk with both hands to steady herself.

"Ebriel!" he said. "Is everything all right? Did you see him?"

"Oh!" She had forgotten all about Ethan, and why she had come to Starhold. She put up her hand. "Wait, James. Please wait a moment. I must think how to say this."

He frowned. "What's happened?"

"I must explain to you," she began. "I did not think this could happen—I was so thin, and the doctor had said—and I never intended—"

"Ebriel, why are you crying?"

"Crying? Why, James, I am not—" Except she was. She put her hands to her cheeks and found them wet. "Oh, James. I cannot—I simply cannot do this! I cannot bear it."

He leaned forward, closer to the camera. "Tell me what's happened."

She wiped her eyes with trembling hands. "James, I am—*enceinte*—do you understand? I am pregnant!"

Even through the small panel, she could see how his dark eyes lighted, how his lips curved in his slow smile. "But—Ebriel, are you sure? That's wonderful—"

She interrupted, not wanting to hear him say it. "*Non!* No, James, I cannot do this! How could I risk it again? Suppose something were to happen, another tragedy—James, I am too much afraid!" More tears fell. She tasted their salt on her lips. They burned on her cheeks. She covered her face with her hands and sobbed.

Through her weeping she became aware, bit by bit, that he was talking to her, calling out to her over the great distance that separated them. "Ebriel. Ebriel, listen to me. Don't cry. There's no need to cry. Talk to me."

Gradually her tears subsided, and she mopped at her eyes with the sleeve of her cottons. She took a shuddering breath, and then another. *"Je regrette,"* she whispered. "I am sorry. It is too much, after everything."

He shook his head, his eyes steady. "No. It's not too much. This is the best news I've ever heard. The best thing that could happen."

"Is it? Are you glad?"

"Glad! Of course I'm glad. And you should be, too."

"No, James, you do not understand. I am afraid—"

"I know." He smiled at her, and even over the thousands of kilometers between them, and the fractional delay, his strength reached out to her, calmed her. "I know, Ebriel," he repeated. "But life is scary. And this is what it's all about! Whatever's coming, you and I will face it together."

Ebriel, shakily, tried to return his smile. *"Oui,"* she breathed. "I suppose so."

"Yes," he repeated. "Everything is different now. A baby!" She saw pride, and a deep happiness shining in his eyes. "A baby changes everything."

A little, hesitant bubble of joy began in Ebriel's body. She watched his smile widen, and the bubble grew to bursting, spreading through her body, shimmering to the ends of her fingertips. "Yes, everything. James, I need you to be here. I will be so much stronger if we are together. Oh, please, James. Come to Starhold!"

Ebriel occupied herself as best she could, doing modified workouts in the dojo, keeping Yasmine company, helping in the kitchen and in the storeroom. The mission team had to complete their task first and then drop down into Montana to pick up James, to transport him to Xiao Qaidam, and *Unicorn.* It was to take four days.

Ebriel thought she would burst with impatience. She haunted the aerie, pestering Yasmine or Semaya with questions about what was happening, where they were, when they would arrive. She spoke to Perk, and she called Nenet. She decided to speak to Nancy Chao as well, to share her news, and it was then that she remembered what it was about the toddler Xiao Sying, the youngest inhabitant of Starhold, that had been niggling at her mind.

She interrupted Nancy in the middle of a sentence. "Nancy," she blurted. "Is Ming Xiu still with you?"

Nancy raised her eyebrows at the abrupt change of subject. "Yes, for the moment, at least. She's getting restless, talking about leaving again." She shook her head. "It's sad. I don't think she has a prayer of finding her baby."

"Where did Ming Xiu come from?" Ebriel pressed.

Nancy thought for a moment. "Just now, I can't remember. A mountain village, I know that, some tiny place—I'm not sure she ever said the name. But it was in Gansu Province, I remember that."

"Yes," Ebriel said eagerly. "Yes, that is what I remember. Nancy—I think her child could be here. On Starhold."

The conversation caught Semaya's attention. She propelled herself to Ebriel's side and clung to a staple. "Gansu Province," she said. "You're thinking of Xiao Sying."

"*Oui.*" Ebriel nodded toward Nancy Chao. "There is a young woman in Xining, at the Children's Home. Looking for her lost child." Ebriel smiled at Nancy, and at Semaya, wanting to include the whole world in her own happiness. "Would it not be wonderful, if we have Ming Xiu's daughter?"

The day came at last. Ebriel stood in the loading bay with Dr. Nordstrom, Semaya, Vee, and a handful of the older children who had come to help offload cargo.

Two women in utility suits came first, carrying a canister of zeolite between them. After them, one of the Chain escorted the Chinese girl, Ming Xiu, who looked around with wide, frightened eyes. Ebriel stepped forward to greet her in her poor Mandarin. Ming Xiu stared at her without recognition.

"Never mind," Ebriel said with a little shrug. She patted the girl's shoulder. "I know how confusing it is. Soon you will feel right at home."

She turned back to watch for him.

He had to duck as he stepped through the airseal. His tall figure, in a simple white shirt and denims, dominated the loading bay. His eyes flicked over the equipment, the Chain members, the children, and his lips tightened.

Ebriel moved forward, where he could see her, and held out her hands. "James," she called. He turned at the sound of her voice. "Welcome to Starhold."

He crossed to her. He clasped her hands and bent to kiss her cheek, and then his eyes swept the loading bay again. "All this," he said. "All this was here all along."

Semaya came forward, and Dr. Nordstrom, and there was a little rush of introductions and greetings. Ebriel led James into the gallery. Glancing up, she saw the muscles jump in his jaw as he looked around at the kaleidoscope of colors, the classrooms, the dining hall, but she didn't know why. There was no time to ask. She had promised Yasmine she would bring him directly to her.

He managed the slip better than she had her first time,

stepping out into microgravity with no more than a slight hesitation. She guided him up the tube, and they went through the slip into the aerie. James blinked at the dimness and looked around at the ranks of panels and monitors with his brows raised. "This is the control center," Ebriel said. "And this is Yasmine."

Yasmine looked up, the whites of her eyes vivid in the half-light. Ethan's chair was gone.

Yasmine floated to them, stopping with the precision of a dancer just before James, regarding him solemnly "It's good to meet you, James Bull."

James, one hand on a staple, nodded to Yasmine. "Hello." He didn't put out his hand. Ebriel had explained about Yasmine.

"Ebriel has been so eager to see you," Yasmine said.

He gave the girl his slow smile. "I'm glad of that."

A monitor chimed, and Yasmine glided to it. James stared after her. "What is that?" he asked Ebriel. "A spybug video?"

"Yes."

His eyes were bleak when he looked down at her. Something had taken away his joy at her news. She tugged at his hand. "Come with me, James. We will go to my cubby."

In the cramped cubby, she sat on the cot and pulled him down to sit beside her. She kept his hand in both of hers, stroking his long dark fingers. "James. Tell me what is bothering you."

He gestured with his free hand, indicating the whole of the habitat. "This is magnificent. It's unbelievable." His voice was hard.

"Why should that make you angry?"

"Ebriel, the world needs this technology. InCo has nothing to compare with it."

"But InCo knows about it. They knew that Ethan lived here, in space."

"Yes, but they think—certainly Security Corps thought— that it was rudimentary, only the shell of the old star hotel, for a sick and eccentric man." He shook his head again. "It's a shock."

"Are you sorry you came, then?"

He put his hand under her chin and turned her face up to

him. "You can't think that." He kissed her forehead. "You can't possibly think that." He kissed her mouth, and then he smiled at her, a smile tinged with regret "Ebriel," he said. "What are we going to do?"

James wondered if his world would ever seem in order again. Since Ebriel's call four days before he had gone through every stage of elation, eagerness, confusion, and now, faced with the reality of Starhold, resentment, even indignation. Ethan Fleck, the creator of these wonders, was no longer there to be challenged. But it was true, as he had said when he first heard Ebriel's news, that everything was changed.

Ebriel and he sat with Ty on one of the cast-foam benches before the space window. Vines crawled over the back of the bench and up the curving walls. Hydroponic flats stretched behind them, and aeroponic racks rose to the ceiling, everything dotted with fruits and vegetables ripe for picking.

Ty saw him taking it all in. "Impressive, isn't it, Major?"

"Please," he said, "call me James. I don't know whether I'm an officer anymore."

"Possible, though?" she said in her laconic fashion.

He looked down at Ebriel's strained face. He moved so his shoulder touched hers, and she glanced up, her eyes dark with emotion. "Yes," he said. "I'd like to go back to the service."

He felt Ebriel tense beside him.

"I don't think you like Starhold much," Ty said bluntly.

"I like it too much," he answered. "Do you know how much this—" he waved a hand at the abundance around them. "All this knowledge—how much it would help down there?" He made a gesture toward the space window.

"You mean, help InCo."

He shook his head. "Not just InCo, of course. I can't help wondering why Dr. Fleck didn't share more of what he knew, what he had."

"He was a good man, James," Ebriel said softly.

Ty nodded. "And he tried. He and Semaya tried. InCo wouldn't let them carry on their inoculation and education programs in the latent countries. They stopped them from shipping fuel cells over the Line. They tried to close down Fleckcell plants in the neutral polities."

"But—" James searched for a way to explain himself. "Things are tough on both sides. In my own hometown, people don't live much better than in the latent countries."

"James," Ebriel said. "Children are dying of hunger. Of disease."

"And of ignorance," Ty said. Her tone was flat. "How does that help InCo?"

"But the plagues," James said. He wished he were better at words. "And the wars—how do we control those things, protect our own people? Our—" involuntarily he glanced down at Ebriel's abdomen, just beginning to curve. "Our own children," he finished.

"I wish there was a simple answer," Ty said.

"Me, too," he said. "Or even a best answer."

"Yeah." Ty fingered a vine that fell over her shoulder and eyed Ebriel and James. "So," she said. "Speaking of answers. What are you gonna do, the two of you?"

There was a little pause. Ebriel looked up at James, and he took her hand. "This is a hard question," she said. "I want my child to know all the things Starhold can teach. James wants his child born in his home, in Montana. To know its grandfather, and its roots."

"Sounds like a problem," Ty said.

James glanced once again at the vista beyond the space window. "We're going to compromise," he said. "We'll have to."

Ebriel leaned against him. He put his arm around her shoulders. "*Oui*," she said softly. "We will compromise."

"And what does that mean?" Ty persisted.

Ebriel laughed. "This is what Yasmine asked. First she defined the word—something in Latin that meant a mutual promise, she said. Then she asked how we would compromise."

"And you said—"

James answered, "We're going to do both things. Give our child—we hope—the best of both worlds."

A small group gathered in the loading bay to see Ebriel and James off, the doctor, Ty, Vee Eyckart, Pilar and

Astrid, Kanika. The spaceplane crew was already on board. Ebriel wore cottons and sandals, and the breeze from the air-lock blew silver fronds of her hair across her face. She pushed them away and looked around at the faces of her friends. "I will miss you all," she said, but she was smiling. She was content. She took a step closer to James, to feel the warmth of his long body.

Kanika ran forward to embrace her. "Good-bye! I can hardly believe you're going!"

Ebriel hugged the dark-skinned girl. "You will be going soon yourself." Kanika laughed, and stepped back. She was due to be resettled in Sierra Leone before the year was out. In all likelihood they would never see each other again, but it was the practice of the starchildren, and of the Chain, to be cheerful about such partings.

Pilar and Astrid also embraced Ebriel. The doctor shook her hand and said, "The protein will be good for you," as if continuing a conversation begun somewhere else. "Walk every day."

"Oui," Ebriel said. "I will do everything you have told me."

Ty stepped forward and gave Ebriel a quick, hard hug. "Hey, partner," she growled. "Good luck. Don't forget to call me."

"I will not forget. I will let you know the moment the baby comes."

The captain of the spaceplane put her head out and said, "Time, people."

James picked up his duffel and Ebriel's battered shoulder bag.

At the last moment, Yasmine appeared, coming into the loading bay with hesitant steps. She wore her scarlet tunic. The white sash fluttered behind her as she crossed to Ebriel.

James said, "Ebriel, they're waiting for us."

"Oui," she said. "In a moment." She put out a hand to Yasmine.

The girl touched her hand and then took a quick step forward to put her cheek to Ebriel's, a feathery touch on the left and then right, and left again. She whispered, *"Au revoir,"* then turned to flee the loading bay, not waiting to see them go into the airlock.

Ebriel waved once more at the Chain as she stepped over the airseal. James took a last look across the bay. "Ty," he said. "Keep up the good work."

Ty saluted.

James waited in the shade of the stand of tamaracs, listening for the sound of the copter, impatiently scanning the sky. He shaded his eyes to watch the horizon.

On the slope below the meadow, blue spears of lupine showed above the long grass. The red and yellow bells of wild columbine nodded in the breeze, and the air sparkled with the ephemeral magic of a Montana spring. James felt it in himself, a sparkle of anticipation, of promise. He pulled off his flight cap and folded it into his pocket. He had only just arrived from Colorado Springs.

At last he heard the familiar sound of the rotors. The silvery-blue craft rose over the ridge to the north, gleaming in the sunshine, and whirred down into the valley. It hovered over the meadow, its downwash blowing a flattened circle in the grass. The tri-gear settled to the ground, and the grass sprang up around it as the rotors slowed and stopped. James strode forward.

The door in the side of the copter slid open, and she was there, jumping nimbly down, slender in her gray jumpsuit, silver curls shining. She waved to him and turned back to reach inside the copter.

He heard the little piping voice before he saw her. "Papa! Papa!" He quickened his step.

A moment later, he had them both in his arms, hugging them, pulling Ebriel off her feet. She laughed and turned her face up for his kiss. He took his daughter from Ebriel's arms and nuzzled her soft cheek. She babbled at him, a two-year-old's mix of English, French, and nonsense.

"English, Marie-Renée," Ebriel admonished their daughter. "Speak English with Papa."

"Fly, Papa! Mimi fly!"

James tousled the little girl's dark hair. "Oh, yes, Mimi, Papa knows. Mimi flies! Next time Mimi flies with Papa, okay?"

"You should call her by her proper name," Ebriel said. "She thinks her real name is Mimi. Everyone on Starhold calls her that."

James lifted the little girl to his shoulders. "My dad does, too," he said. "Don't worry about it. When she's older, she can use the whole thing."

Marie-Renée tugged on her father's hair, pointing at the yellow and black butterflies rising from the meadow, squealing with delight at the birds that swooped above her head. Ebriel shouldered their duffel bag and took a deep draught of the sweet mountain air.

"Mimi's grown," James said. "She changes so fast."

"I know," Ebriel said. "Wait till you hear how much she is talking. She never stops!"

"Maybe you can stay longer this time, Ebriel."

She squeezed his hand. "I hope so. But it is hard on them if I am gone too long. Could you not get more leave?"

"I've used it all," he said. "But let's not worry about that now. It's just so good to have you here. You, too, Mimi!" he added, turning his head to kiss the dimpled knee of his daughter.

She threw both her chubby arms around his head, and kicked her heels. "Go, Papa! Go!"

"Okay, sweetheart, I'm going." They started off across the meadow.

"Is there news?" Ebriel asked, tucking her free hand under his arm.

"You probably know Takanagi's up for reelection," he said. She nodded. "He's got a very liberal opponent, and there's a chance the Line could come down if the opposition gets in. But we'll have to see. The best thing about Dimarco is that he keeps the Corps out of it."

"I hope it happens," she said fervently. "And soon."

"And I have your instruments," he said, watching her face to see her dimple with pleasure.

She did. "Oh, James! Really?"

"Yes. Dad helped a lot," he said. "We've rounded up three more flutes, a clarinet, and a whole lot of recorders in different sizes. I don't know what the quality is, but they're all in a box at the ranch house."

She squeezed his arm. "How wonderful of you. And of Gil."

"He liked doing it. He's missed Mimi," James said as they passed through the stand of tamarac and started down the hill. "He talks about her all the time. He's missed you, too."

Ebriel leaned against him as they walked, pressing her cheek to his shoulder. "And you, chéri? Have you not missed me?"

He laughed down at her. "Foolish Frenchwoman," he said. "You'll just have to find out."

Please visit Louise Marley's web site at
www.louisemarley.com

Louise can be reached by e-mail at
LMarley@aol.com

A novel from the author of *The Glass Harmonica*

LOUISE MARLEY

THE TERRORISTS OF IRUSTAN

A talented doctor defies the rule
of men—and changes the lives of every
woman on the planet.

"A DARK, RICHLY IMAGINED TALE...A THOUGHTFUL
MEDITATION UPON THE DANGERS OF FANATICISM
AND THE STRENGTH OF THE HUMAN SPIRIT."
—SHARON SHINN

"RICH WITH ALIEN ATMOSPHERICS."
—PUBLISHERS WEEKLY

0-441-00743-0

Available wherever books are sold or
to order call 1-800-788-6262

A256

SHARON SHINN

NATIONAL BESTSELLING AUTHOR OF THE ARCHANGEL TRILOGY

A NOVEL OF SAMARIA

ANGEL-SEEKER

Ace
0-441-01134-9